VALKYRIE LOST

SHANNON PEMRICK

Valkyrie Lost
Valkyries Rising | Book One

Copyright © 2025 Shannon Pemrick
www.shannonpemrick.com

Cover Design by Covers by Combs
Editing by Sandra Nguyen
Character illusations by Tomy Fanggidae, Alifka Hammam, Tommy Suhartono
Chapter art by BRoseDesignz

First Edition © 2023

Print paperback ISBN 978-1-950128-40-2
Print hardcover ISBN 978-1-950128-41-9

BOOKS BY SHANNON PENRICK

VALKYRIES RISING

Valkyrie Lost
Valkyrie Unknown
Valkyrie Destined
Valkyrie Renewed
Valkyrie Restored
Valkyrie Confused
Valkyrie Condemned
Valkyrie Freed
Valkyrie Shattered
Valkyrie Transformed

LOOKING FOR GROUP

Spellbinding His Ranger
Protecting His Priestess
Summoning Their Elementalist
Binding Their Elementalist

EXPERIMENTAL HEART

Destiny
Pieces
Secrets
Exposed
Surrendered
Reborn

ORACLE'S PATH

Prophecy of Convergence
Prophecy of Unbroken Oaths

See all books and learn more at
www.shannonpenrick.com

For everyone who would lay the bodies of their enemies
at the feet of those they love.

CONTENT WARNING

VALKRIE LOST contains mentions, discussions, and depictions of content some readers may find distressing. Reader discretion is advised. Please review the listed topics below and proceed with caution if needed. Your mental health is important.

Abduction & hostage situation

Ableism/ableist language

Addiction & alcoholism

Arranged marriage

Assault

Discussions of death & the afterlife

Familial, parental, & spousal death

Graphic (consensual) sexual content including: degradation & praise, light bondage, impact play, oral, rough sex

Loss of Limb

Magical limb regrowth

Mental illness

Miscarriage, infertility & pregnancy complications

Misogyny/misandry

Non-monogamous relationship discussions & thoughts

Nudity

Profanity

Resurrection & reincarnation

Slavery & indentured servitude

Violence, gore & death

AUTHOR'S NOTE

VALKYRIE LOST is a Norse-inspired, alternate history fantasy romance featuring a slow-build polyamorous relationship set during the Viking Age. Later chapters, however, extend into the modern era, as well as the rest of the series books.

While I drew on extensively researched history and Norse mythology, incorporating a great deal of what I've learned throughout this story, I've also created many events and situations through the lens of fantasy. As such, I don't promise entirely accurate depictions of either the time period or myth.

ONE

ASTRID

To have völva magic is a blessing. It is a power passed down from mother to daughter. It is the ultimate gift that brings honor and glory to one's family.

I released a frustrated breath and opened my eyes. Nothing. There was no magic slumbering beneath my skin. It had been like this for all eighteen winters of my life. Searching for it was pointless.

"Keep trying, Astrid," Father said.

My eyes flicked to him. Father, a sturdy, scarred man with well-kept fair hair and a bushy beard, and my younger brother, Leif, a sturdy young man like Father, with long, braided fair-colored hair shaved on either side of his head, and some scruff around his chin, worked at the table. Soft, crisp scraping and slicing sounds accompanied their motions as they shaped legs for a new table the jarl commissioned.

"This is pointless," I said. "It's not there."

"It is. You just have to find it."

Frustration burned in my chest. He didn't understand. If I was meant to inherit our family magic, it would have manifested long ago. I *am a disgrace to this family.…*

His gentle blue eyes shifted to me. "Your mother and I both have faith in you."

Leif looked up from his work and smiled at me. "You can find it, Astrid. If anyone can, it's you."

I slumped in my chair and stared at the crackling hearth in the center of the house. Why was I the only one willing to see reality? *Cursed…*

"Try again," Father said. His tone was gentle and understanding, but still firm and unyielding. He wasn't going to allow me to give up.

Sucking in a deep breath, I straightened and closed my eyes to try one more time. If I found nothing, then I'd stop these pointless attempts. I'd accept I had no magic and get my family to accept I would not bring them the same honor had I been blessed.

Focusing inward, I tried to find the dormant feeling Mother always described of her magic. Something chaotic and powerful, yet familiar. Not that I understood what that meant. Still, I tried.

Deeper I searched.

Searching.

Searching.

The longer I searched, the more my frustration and desperation began to rise and mix. I wanted to be a völva like my mother. Like her mother and her mother's mother. I wanted to be special. I wanted to be someone worthy, instead of a cursed disgrace. *Please, weavers of fate, bless me with the magic that will bring my family the ultimate glory and honor.*

Something stirred in my chest. Something warm like fire. Something deep and powerful. Something… ancient?

A loud, frantic knock came at the door. My eyes snapped open and the sensation within me vanished.

The knocking came again, along with a voice. "Bjǫrn, open up. It's urgent."

That sounds like Sigurd.

Father's gentle air faded and a harder, more serious one manifested. Nothing dangerous, yet. He abandoned his work and hurried to the door. Leif stood and brushed wood shavings from his clothes. He didn't follow Father, but he did reach for a dagger, just in case.

A strange sensation twisted down my spine in my belly. Something didn't feel right.

Father opened the door. "What is it?"

The door blocked my view, but when the person on the other side spoke again, I knew it was Sigurd. "It's Arne. He's calling everyone to the mead hall courtyard."

"Did he say why?" Father asked, an anxious hitch to his voice. "Is it about the war party?"

Jarl Rune had taken most of our best warriors earlier today to fight in a battle that'd come too close to Runavík. I wasn't sure what the altercation was about, but the jarl seemed furious. Whatever the reason, it was big enough he ordered Mother to go with them. If they needed völva magic, then it was a serious situation.

But not all of our warriors had gone, like Father. Rune had kept many behind to protect Runavík, should our enemies somehow make it to our doors. Everyone in the town could fight. Even I knew how to pick up a sword or an axe. But I wasn't a seasoned warrior like Father.

The twisting in my stomach worsened and I nervously played with a lock of my fiery hair. *Has something gone wrong? Or is it something else?*

"I'm not sure," Sigurd admitted. "He just said it was urgent and everyone was to gather. He also stressed that you and your family had to be present, no exceptions. He seemed… off. I don't know how else to describe his behavior. Whatever is going on, it must be big."

Father agreed and called us to follow. I worriedly chewed my lip as I complied. I couldn't shake the feeling that something was very wrong. *Gods, protect us.*

TWO

TÝR

The stench of iron and smoke lingered in the air. My feet sunk into the churned earth, the soil mixed with blood, ash, and bodily innards. The stillness of the twisted landscape, filled with broken shields, lost and shattered weapons, and lifeless bodies of fallen warriors, pressed against my senses.

A mournful wind wove through the former battlefield, carrying with it the muted cries of active fighting in the distance. Several ravens hopped around the fallen, croaking and crying now and then, breaking the silence, and feasting on what they could before the survivors came back to reclaim their fallen—if they were reclaimed at all.

Voices whispered in my ear—Berserkers chanting vows and battle cries in my name, warriors praying for strength to spill the blood of their enemies. Some I acknowledged, pushing a touch of power toward my followers. And some I didn't. I had my reasons for both, but they weren't easily put into words.

My body hummed with power, strengthened by their worship and their craving for battle.

And yet, my feet carried me away from it, toward the prayer of a far more quiet voice—a woman. I strained my senses to block out everything but her.

Her voice, while quaking in fear, held impressive strength. She pleaded for justice, not strength. A wrong had been committed against her family. *I may be a god of war, but I am also a god of order and justice.* And I felt the conviction in her prayer. This was not a feeling that could be faked. She truly believed an injustice was being committed, and it called to me.

I didn't regularly interact with mortals beyond the times I engaged in their wars or needed a woman to warm my bed. Their lives were so fleeting, it didn't make much sense to me. But today would be different.

I will see to justice this day.

I'd teleport to her location if I could, but my ability wasn't so precise. I could arrive at a battle in a blink, but to choose any location I desired, like the goddess Freyja or her twin Freyr, that was beyond my capabilities.

This battle had brought me close to this woman's prayer, and now I strode through the forest with purpose. The pungent scent of the pines smothered the smells of battle, and soon I found myself facing the wooden palisade of a town settled on the river.

A few loose chickens clucked and scratched at the ground, and two dogs crossed my path, but they were the only life to greet me. The town was of a decent size compared to others I'd graced, which made the lifelessness of this area unusual. If I didn't know for sure that a prayer came from here, I'd assume this place was abandoned. *Am I too late?*

No, I could still hear her, though she wasn't praying anymore. I'd tapped into her presence enough to know she was screaming profanities at someone. She certainly knew which words to use, emasculating whomever was the focus of her wrath. It made me smirk. This woman sounded feisty.

My walk into town, through timber homes and fence-lined streets, brought me to the center, where I found the people I sought. They clustered around a commotion in front of the mead hall—some cheering, while others cried out in protest. The injustice in the air was palpable. It drew me closer.

Gravel crunched under my feet, alerting those in the back of the crowd of my approach. Eyes wide, these mortals were quick to clear a path, bowing and reveling at my feet. With their worship and our physical presence in their lives, it wasn't often that the mortal nord-menn didn't recognize us immediately.

I didn't pass them a single glance, my attention focused on the central commotion.

Three figures, two men and a woman, were held captive by several other townsfolk, though they struggled against their captors, not willing to submit. The older of the two men, maybe in his mid to late-thirties, had a sturdy frame, well-kept fair hair, and rather nice clothing adorned his body. Scars littered his light skin. *A man who has seen battle.*

His vibrant blue eyes bore into one man of dark hair who loomed over him.

The younger man, I guessed him to be fifteen or sixteen winters, had a similar build and long, braided fair hair shaved on either side of his head. There were enough similarities between the two, I suspected he was the other man's son. And the woman…

I stilled, unable to pull my gaze away from the fierce beauty before me. Skin as pale as the moon, with freckles splattering her like stars in the sky, and hair vibrant like wildfire. She had an elegant contour to her face with a tapered jawline and high cheekbones.

Piercing green eyes, framed by thick lashes, blazed as hot as Sól's wrath, and her full lips that may be temptingly soft when forming a smile, were curled in a deadly snarl. A long scar cut across her face from her eyebrow, over her petite nose, and down her opposite cheek, adding to her stunning, ferocious visage.

She had to be about a few winters older than the other young man, seventeen or eighteen was my guess. While lacking identical features of the two men, she was no doubt the older man's daughter.

Their captors froze, as did the older man. However, his two children hadn't noticed my presence, and instead, took advantage of their cap-tor's distracted states and fought back harder.

The woman slammed her head into the chin of her captor. He

yelped and released her, stumbling back. Blood trailed down his lip. Her brother broke free of his captor's grip and drew a short blade he hadn't been relieved of, and smashed the hilt into the man's face.

Instead of going further and drawing more blood, he snagged his sister by the arm and yanked her behind him, shielding her. "Astrid, stay with me."

Her name hummed in my veins. A divine beauty she was.

Astrid gave her brother a withering glare, but without a weapon of her own, she understood her brother was better equipped to defend them. If I weren't there to distract everyone, that is.

And that's when they also noticed me.

The son's eyes popped wide, and his mouth hung open as he gawked witlessly.

Astrid gasped. "Týr…"

The way she looked at me—the way her piercing eyes snared me—it stirred some feelings of familiarity, yet I'd never met a woman like her in my life. I would know if I'd laid eyes on such perfection before.

"Have you come to witness justice, mighty Týr?" the dark-haired man standing over the father asked. It was then I noticed the axe in his hand.

"This is not justice," the captive man snarled. "You've gone mad, Arne."

Arne lifted the man's chin with his axe. "You conspired against Jarl Rune, Bjǫrn. Planned to lure him to battle and assassinate him, acting as though they were our enemies."

Though Arne spoke these words, I tasted no certain truth of justice in them.

"You lie," Astrid shouted. Her brother still shielded her, though it was clear her fury called her to attack in defense of her father. She may be small, but she was fearless. "You cowardly mare, you spew nothing but horse shit from your mouth."

My lips twitched, and it took all my willpower not to laugh.

"You and your family are all accused of treason," Arne continued, ignoring Astrid's outburst.

All of them? That explained Astrid's prayer. Though it intrigued me, she never specified herself. Her cry for justice had no traces of selfish-ness and had only been for those she loved.

Arne raised his axe into the air and Bjǫrn fought against those who held him. Astrid lunged toward her father and her brother held her back, though his eyes gave away his rage and desire to also save their father, if it weren't for the other men standing in their way.

"With Jarl Rune off destroying our enemies, I will exact justice," Arne said. "We can only pray your völva wife does not manage to enact your plans, and he returns to us safely."

A witch for a wife? That was certainly rare, if true. I'd heard of many claims of sorcery and witchcraft by mortals in my time, but most were false. Magic had been more prevalent once upon a time, but for some reason unknown to us gods, it had become far more rare outside the gods and certain types of immortals.

I shook those thoughts from my mind. This wasn't the time for musing. "Wait."

Arne halted and regarded me with both curiosity and reverence. "Do you wish to exact justice yourself, Týr? I willingly offer you my axe."

I studied him for another moment, making sure I was seeing this situation correctly. "You seem to misunderstand why I am here. I have not come to enact your so-called justice. I am responding to the prayer of a woman whose family was under the threat of injustice."

Astrid sucked in a quiet breath, and her brother's attention snapped to her.

"You prayed to him?" he hissed.

"How was I supposed to know he'd answer with a personal visit?" Astrid snapped back in an equally hard but hushed tone.

This time, I did allow my amusement to show through a chuckle.

Arne hesitated. "Are you also accusing me of lying?"

I waited a moment before responding. "I cannot detect lies. I can taste injustice. And this proceeding is heavy with it. Does your jarl know what you are doing? Or are you exacting this execution without his knowledge? I wonder, if he does not know, what your true motives are."

"As would I," a deep masculine voice said behind me.

Arne sucked in a sharp breath, piquing my interest. I turned. A tall broad-shouldered man with fair hair and skin approached. Blood splattered his bare skin, which would have appeared strange were it not for the prominent and intricate tattoo of a bear paw on his chest. *Berserker.*

A petite woman with flaming hair kept stride with him. The dark makeup around her blazing green eyes enhanced the threatening aura about her. She was dressed for battle, though instead of a typical shield maiden's weaponry of a sword or axe and a shield, she carried a staff and shield. *This must be the witch Arne mentioned.*

Warriors followed this pair—weary from battle, but ready for another fight, as evidenced by the energy humming off of them.

"Jarl Rune," Arne said. "I—"

"You will unhand my husband at once," the woman snapped. "Or I'll see to it your names are cursed in every hall from here to Valhǫll."

The two men holding Bjǫrn hesitated for only a moment before releasing him, fearing her more than Arne's wrath. Fake magic user or not, vǫlvur and the supposed power they held were feared by most nordmenn.

Bjǫrn rose to his feet and rolled his shoulders as if he'd only been minorly inconvenienced this whole time.

"Explain yourself, Arne," the jarl demanded, his green eyes unwavering and intense.

Arne hesitated for only a moment, the witch's gaze boring into him, and he again explained his supposed findings of treason. This time, he offered up evidence, from allegations of supposed times Bjǫrn met with others to plan, to early attempts of poisoning and more subtle ways to assassinate the jarl. But even I found each accusation weak.

The witch's lips curled into a snarl. If I had questioned her relation to Astrid, it would have evaporated then. Their shared expression of fury before an insult was like staring into a mirror.

The jarl held up his hand to silence whatever retort she planned to spit out. "Stay your tongue, Randi."

The witch gave him a side-eye glare, but listened to her jarl.

"Bjǫrn, how do you plead on these accusations?" Rune asked.

"Innocent," Bjǫrn said without hesitation. "As does my family. We are wholly loyal to you, Rune. Never once have I had thoughts to conspire against or held conversation, even in jest, of such treason with my family or anyone else."

My body hummed with the energy from his conviction. The scales of justice leaned, and I knew whose favor it was in.

"Nor would I ever believe you ever could, my friend," the jarl said, his voice warm with affection. It was clear friend was no mere friendly title, and the two held each other in high regard outside of the jarl's status. "However, I must wait for Týr's judgment, as he has offered his services for such a matter."

All eyes fell on me, but the weight of Astrid's felt heavier than any other. Her soul-piercing eyes stared through the armor I wore, as if peering at my core where I held my most closely guarded secrets.

"These accusations are unjust." My voice echoed through the waiting crowd. "And the means by which they were accused are suspect and cowardly."

Murmurs rose through the crowd. A smug smile graced Randi's lips; Astrid's relieved breath enveloped all my senses. I strove to make the right calls—not based on my own personal feelings, but on how the scale tipped. If the scale hadn't tipped in her favor, I wouldn't have hesitated to state as much in my verdict. But hearing how my decision had impacted her positively, a sensation I didn't have the words for sparked through my body.

Arne gaped, and then his face reddened with newfound fury. He turned on Bjǫrn. "You bewitched the gods with foul magic!"

My brow rose. Even if that was possible, this man couldn't honestly believe his own words. He had to be desperate, for whatever reason he had for this whole farce.

"Arne, be reasonable," Bjǫrn said. "We have known each other since we were boys. I can be willing to overlook this slight to me and my family, and only require minor compensation, if you would—"

The crazed man wouldn't hear it. "You will suffer for your transgressions at the end of my blade!"

"Father, stop this madness!" a warrior who had returned from the battle shouted. He was around Astrid's age, by the looks of it.

Still, the pleas fell on deaf ears. Arne brandished his axe at an unarmed Bjǫrn. My own axe appeared in my hand out of nothing, but before I could flex a muscle to strike, Astrid shrieked.

Things happened around me so quickly that if I weren't a god, I'd have missed most of it.

Randi flung up her arms, and the unmistakable taste of magic coated my tongue as it wrapped around me in a protective shield. Then, a concussive force blasted through the town. Anything not protected by the witch's magic—fences, buckets, loose boards meant for building—was sent scattering.

Arne was cast through the air as though struck by the force of Mjölnir itself, and crashed to the ground with a sickening *thud*. His body rolled with the momentum and then stilled.

I snapped my gaze to where that blast had originated from. Astrid stood rigid, her breath coming out in heavy gasps. Then she listed to one side, her eyes glassy.

Her brother reacted with lightning reflexes and caught her before she fell. "Astrid…"

"I'm fine, Leif," she mumbled. "I'm fine."

She clearly was not.

Nor was I.

Not only was Randi a true witch, but Astrid, the woman who called me here, was too.

I took a moment to glance at Bjǫrn and then Randi. Both radiated pride in their daughter.

Rune grunted. "Seems Astrid has come into her magic, just as you predicted, Randi."

The witch clacked her tongue. "Have my predictions been wrong yet?"

The jarl's lips spread into a thin line. "No. That would make three since last winter."

"The fourth will happen soon." Randi's eyes flicked to me for the briefest of moments, before focusing back on her children.

What was that look for?

"Leif, take Astrid home," Randi ordered. "She used all her magic in one release. She needs to recuperate."

Her son nodded and repositioned his grip on Astrid, but she fought him. "Astrid, please don't be stubborn."

She shook her head. "I'm not leaving until this is over."

"It is over. You killed him," Leif said.

He was right. It would have been impossible for Arne to have lived through that. And yet something felt off.

Astrid lifted a shaking hand and pointed to where Arne had landed. All eyes turned, and gasps rippled through the townsfolk. Arne's body jerked and writhed—it looked like it was trying to get up, but struggled.

I squinted to make sure I was seeing this correctly. Black tendrils leaked from his dead eyes and gaping mouth. A dark aura seeped out of the twitching body.

Gasps and murmurs rippled through the gathered crowd. Bjǫrn reached for a weapon, and I held up my hand. "No one go near this. He's no longer a man."

I'd seen this before, but only on the battlefield. Some sort of dark spirit, maybe a malevolent fae, I wasn't sure, had possessed a mortal. It fed off their negative emotions and desires, burrowing deep within the body until the person was merely a husk of their former self. Desperate, dying men were easy targets.

How it had found Arne, I couldn't begin to fathom. If he'd seen battle in the last few weeks, which wasn't uncommon these days, it could have found him there. Or the being had happened upon this unlucky soul around the town.

Either way, it was clear Arne wasn't actually alive when he set about this crazed course against Bjǫrn and his family. As if an illusion was broken, where skin had been on his arms and face, rot now set in. Bones were exposed in some areas, and the smell of decay was unmistakable. I doubted he'd been alive for several days.

I needed to put this thing down, before it sought out a new host. With so many mortals around it, and all the intense emotions flying, it'd easily find one. And if it latched, there was nothing more to do than to put them out of their misery before the creature took over.

I strode up to the twitching monstrosity. Normally I'd be more cautious, as the creature heightened the reflexes of the human. But it was clear its struggle was due to all the broken bones caused by Astrid's attack.

Brandishing my axe, I swung when I came in range, aiming for the base of the creature's neck. My blade sank into its flesh and a sickening *crunch* came when the axe cracked its spine. The creature twitched more, its head jerking to the side to stare up at me with unnerving dead eyes. I lifted the blade out of its body, the metal slick and dripping with discolored blood. I then slammed my axe down on it again, this time severing the head from the body.

The head rolled, and the body thrashed unnaturally, spraying blood everywhere before going still. The dark aura and tendrils faded, and soon, Arne looked like a normal but decayed man again.

I turned away from the gory mess pooling at my feet, only to be slammed with regret at the sight of Arne's son staring in horror. I'd just butchered what he thought was his father. By this point of the host consumption, mortals would be able to see it, but that wouldn't make things better for the son. This was still his father.

I wouldn't apologize for my brutality. I'd acted in order to protect these mortals. Had I not, this whole town would have fallen victim eventually. But I did allow an apologetic gaze to land on Arne's son, so he knew I never meant to make things worse for him. "Build him a funeral pyre. It's the least he deserves after that spirit violated him."

The son numbly nodded, and several others offered their assistance.

Randi rushed over to her husband and fussed, now appearing as a loving wife, rather than the scary witch from before. Though, I did note there was still a chilling air about her. She fussed so much that Bjǫrn laughed and reassured her he was fine.

He looked my way and held my gaze when I approached. "You have my eternal gratitude, Týr. I and my family owe you a great debt. I will ensure a proper sacrifice be made in your honor as thanks. If you desire more, request anything of us, and you will have it, no questions."

The man's offer barely registered in my mind, as I was distracted with Leif escorting Astrid away. Another man around her age, having features similar to the jarl, was assisting.

Astrid glanced back and a small smile spread across her lips. The fury in her eyes now replaced with vibrant joy, captivating me a moment longer before she turned away once again.

I didn't want her to focus elsewhere. I wanted to gaze at this beauty a moment longer, and hear her voice one last time.

I wanted her favor—her worship—more than any other mortal, and I couldn't understand why. I hadn't even spoken with the woman. *Why does this mortal intrigue me so much?*

I wasn't starved for attention. I could visit any mortal dwelling and pick from any of the women there. They'd all offer their beds and company to me, and yet those thoughts hadn't crossed my mind with Astrid.

Well, now they did. Thoughts of how long I'd be searching her skin to find every last spot speckling it, and indulging in her taste and sounds, now flitted through my mind. But that hadn't been my initial thoughts about her. Why was she so different? Why did a mortal woman—one whose life was so fleeting, it'd be snuffed out in a blink for a god like myself—captivate me? Why was I allowing her to be taken away when I had no answers?

"Anything at all," her father repeated next to me, "and it's yours."

I looked at him, and the man stared at me with more intensity than I had anticipated. It carried a feeling of knowing, as if he already assumed what I'd demand of him and his family in payment.

"I will keep your offer in mind."

The wooden door clacked behind me. I adjusted my basket and set a hurried pace out of town. I prayed my journey would be quiet and uneventful. The last thing I needed was another visit from—

"Heill, Astrid," someone called.

I refused to visibly cringe at the one voice I didn't want to hear. Turning, I painted on a polite smile for the dark-haired man approaching me. "Erik, good morning."

He smiled, seemingly oblivious to my forced friendliness, and stopped nearly on my toes. He stood a head or two taller than me, but I wasn't easily intimidated. How I'd acted toward his father several weeks ago was quite clear on that matter. "Good morning. Where are you off to?"

I didn't want to tell him, but most of my attempts to be rid of him in a gentle way hadn't worked so far. "To find some herbs. We're low, with me learning so much from my mother, and our garden doesn't have enough to continue our supply."

Erik nodded. "I'm sure you're learning a lot. Must be difficult

balancing so much around the house while also learning magic and herbal remedies."

I nodded, but refused to admit how difficult it was. Growing up and watching Mother do all kinds of things with her magic, I thought it was easy to do, and couldn't wait to come into my power. Now I was seeing just how wrong I'd been.

Not that I minded—the challenge was fun, and I desperately wanted to control magic. I'd be so much more useful to my family if I could.

An awkward silence settled in.

"Do you… want any help with your search?" Erik finally said, though his words were neither smooth nor confident.

I shook my head. "There is no need. I know the exact spots I need to get to and how much to pick. It's a quick and simple task for one person."

"Are you sure?" he pressed. "It wouldn't be any trouble for me."

I sighed out loud. I did not wish to deal with this today. "I have no need for your help nor do I seek to share my life and bed with you."

Erik gave a weak smile and an uncomfortable laugh. "I must be mistaken that I heard you refuse me."

I adjusted my basket. "Maybe you have some wool in your ears. That's all right, I'll speak a little louder. My father has refused you twice. I hold no interest of marriage with you, so I will not ask him to change his mind."

"Astrid, please hear me out," Erik said, trying to stay calm by the way his face twitched. "I know what my father did was horrible—and he paid for that, even if it wasn't his fault he was possessed."

"This has nothing to do with your father." Truly, it didn't. I didn't hold Erik accountable for his father's actions. "I'm merely not interested. I respect your courage in asking, but I will not change my mind. It is best you accept this and move on."

Erik scowled. "Why not?"

"She doesn't have to provide you with an explanation," a new, deep, and familiar voice said.

I turned toward the road in the direction I had been heading; a small gasp escaped me. The man approaching us was scarred and broad-shoulder with an impressive musculature any mortal man would covet, and mortal woman would desire.

He had a strong and angular face with high cheekbones and a prominent jawline, adding to his rugged and masculine appearance. His nose was well-proportioned for his face as well.

The nicest clothes I'd ever seen on anyone, covered his sun-darkened skin and accentuated every part of his frame perfectly.

He was tall—taller than any other man I'd met, and I only came up to about the middle of his chest. Like many men, he wore a full, well-groomed beard and his well-kept, if slightly wind-swept, long dark chestnut hair grew past his shoulders.

Thick, dark eyebrows added to the intense and brooding, if slightly intimidating and unapproachable, expression resting on his face. But it was his striking blue eyes that captured my full attention. "Týr."

Why was he here? I still couldn't understand why he'd shown up several weeks ago when I prayed. When I woke the next morning after my magic-drained sleep, I'd actually wondered if I'd dreamt it all.

"I believe I heard her tell you to leave," Týr said to Erik. "It would be wise to listen to her."

Erik scowled, and for a moment I thought he'd argue with the god or try to request I change my mind again, but instead he spun on his heels and stomped away. *Hopefully that will be the last time I have to deal with that.*

If my father refused his third offer, he was required to move on, though I wasn't convinced he'd let go immediately.

"Are you all right?" Týr asked. His voice rumbled deep in my chest. It was nice, nicer than any other man I'd heard speak.

I blinked, banishing the strange thoughts from my mind. "Um, yes, thank you. What brings you here? Overseeing a battle, or just passing through?"

I didn't exactly know the proper way to speak to a god. Did any mortal? Maybe Mother. She'd had the pleasure of being in their presence in the past.

"Neither, actually," he said. "I wanted to make sure you and your family were well after that ordeal."

My head tilted as I tried to process. Was he concerned about us? Or was this part of his duties since he oversaw judgment? "We're fine. Well, better than fine. We always had good standing here in Runavík, as well as with the jarl, but it's even better now."

"That's good to hear." He smiled. It was a pleasant smile that broke up the stoic look he had, making him seem gentle and kind, even with the scars. It also sent a warm tingle down my spine.

He then reached for my basket. "Let me help you with that."

I opened my mouth to protest, but he took the container and tucked it under his arm.

"Where are we off to?"

I blinked before I found my words. "You don't need to help me. I'm sure you have far more important things to do with—"

He smiled again, and this time, my reaction manifested as warmth on my cheeks. "I would like nothing more than to spend time with you on a nice day like today."

My heated cheeks burned hotter. Why would he want that? I wasn't anything special. There were plenty of other, more worthy women to take up his time. But I didn't voice any of that. My father had told us all, if Týr returned, to not refuse any of his requests. We were indebted to him. "If you'd like."

I led the way into the forest where I'd find my first patch of plants to pick. The walk was silent between us, only the sounds of the forest to keep us company alongside our thoughts. There were many things I wanted to inquire with him about, but I struggled to speak. The questions were probably rude, and it was best not to offend him.

"Why did you answer my prayer?" There went my mouth, without my permission.

He didn't answer right away, and regret clamped in my chest. *I shouldn't have said anything.* "I don't know."

I glanced up at him to find the man in deep thought.

"I've been thinking about it since that day and still cannot come up with a definitive answer—just that your voice spoke the loudest to me over all the other prayers."

I found that hard to believe. Warriors prayed to Týr. And with so many battles out there, there had to be far more worthy prayers to answer than mine, a helpless woman who needed a god to save her family from a crazed, possessed man. "Is that why you're really here today, even with the number of weeks that have passed since we last saw each other?"

His gaze went thoughtful. "Has it been that long?"

That didn't surprise me. Gods were eternal; their perception of time was nothing like us mortals.

Týr shook his head. "To answer your question, yes, that is the deeper reason behind my visit." He turned those brilliant eyes on me. "I want to learn more about the mysterious woman with hair the color of blood, who prays louder than any warrior and harnesses magic."

I blinked, unable to understand why he'd want to know me. "You can ask me anything and I will do my best to answer. It's only fair after I made my inquiries."

"Mortals having the ability to harness magic is rare," he said. "How is it that you and your mother can?"

I shrugged and stopped in front of the patch of ferns and moss I'd been looking for. "I don't know how to answer that, and I don't think my mother can, either. It is just something the women from her family can do."

His brow rose. "All of them?"

I nodded and bent down to pick some ferns and moss. "She says it's all the same magic, but each person harnesses it in a different way. She told me my grandmother was a healer, but couldn't ever use magic offensively. Mother, on the other hand, can't heal. Both of them receive cryptic visions of the future, though my grandmother's mother did not."

"And what about you?"

I shrugged. "I don't know yet. That day was the first time I used magic. So my training has only just begun. As for the visions, only time will tell. That is a manifesting power none of us have control over."

Týr made a thoughtful sound. "That's right—Rune seemed surprised you used magic. Why is that?"

My lips twisted, and my picking paused. "Because I should have had my magic some time ago."

Týr crouched to be on eye level with me. "What do you mean?"

"For most of us, our power manifests by the time we've seen seven winters."

His eyes widened. "That early?"

I nodded. "And at eighteen winters, it was assumed by everyone but my mother I was never going to inherit that ability. I would be the first in a long time." *Adding to my cursed nature…*

"It's amazing to hear one mortal has the ability to harness magic, let alone an entire family line." His wonder faded to curiosity. "What's wrong?"

I mentally cursed. I should have been more careful hiding my emotions. "Nothing you need to worry about."

His brows knitted together, but I tucked away the last fern into the basket and stood, dusting my knees. "We can move onto the next patch."

It was better to move away from that topic. No need to dump my problems on a god. He couldn't help me, nor would it be right to request him to try.

Týr followed me. His intense gaze made my pulse quicken, and I had to fight my body's urge to flee from it. Not out of fear, though. His attention sent a wave of heat through me, and I wasn't sure what to make of that feeling.

"Why are you wearing trousers?" he finally inquired. "I don't often see Norse women wearing them outside of battle."

I blinked up at him. That was why he stared? "Convenience. Dress skirts hinder my movements when I'm out in the forest. Is that a problem?"

Some found it strange, so I wouldn't be surprised if he said yes. Mother had designed this style of dress for me with an open skirt when I'd complained once how difficult it was to forage with typical dresses.

Even with the trousers, she'd made sure the rest of the dress hugged my figure just right, so the overall outfit would remain feminine enough to prevent too much harassment from others about "appropriate" attire.

Though, just being my mother's daughter keeps most from saying anything, in fear of her wrath. One day I'd be as feared and respected as her.

Týr seemed momentarily taken aback by my question. "No, of course not." His striking gaze flicked up and down my body in a way that sent heat coursing through me. "In fact, I think it's quite fitting. You have nice legs."

I bit my lip and turned my gaze away, my face growing hot. It wasn't the most poetic compliment, but it was still one. *And to receive such from a god…*

Silence fell over us once more. I wanted to ask questions, ones that steered away from me, but I bit them all back. They were questions to know him better, beyond his god status. But what right did I have to inquire? After his own curiosity about me faded, he'd be gone, and I'd fade into a vague memory of his.

"Why aren't you married?"

I tilted my head, surprised by such a question. "Say again?"

"Erik was seeking your hand. By your age, I would have expected you to be married by now. Or are you a widow?"

The purpose behind this question eluded me. Why would he care if I was married? "No, I'm not exactly a widow…"

His brow rose, and he tilted his head as if to urge me to continue.

I chewed my lip and looked down at the ground. I had wanted to avoid this, but since he asked such a direct question, it wasn't something I could avoid now.

"If you spoke to anyone in town, they'd tell you I'm cursed." I gestured to my face and a long scar on the underside of my right arm. "When I was younger, I obtained these scars from an accident. It's made me… less desirable to many men who have looked at me. However, there have been a few willing to overlook it, and I've been betrothed three times. But each time, before the marriage ceremony was held, they died. No one has wanted to risk marrying me for some time."

Silence. Deafening silence.

My gut twisted. I didn't want to look up at him. I'd see either disgust or pity, and I didn't want to deal with either.

"But Erik does?"

I jerked my head up. Instead of disgust or pity, I only saw contemplation. I didn't understand this new reaction. "It's a bit more complicated. Because of your help, our family is seen more favorably. Others are now more willing to try to gain my father's approval, thinking maybe the curse is lifted."

I played with a loose thread on the sleeve of my dress. "Erik, though, is trying to mend what his father broke—or what he thinks his father broke. My father doesn't fault Erik, but for some reason won't agree to marry me to him. Erik has made two attempts and my father has turned him away each time. He's been trying to convince me to change my father's mind, but"—I shrugged—"He's a fine enough man, but I can't find interest in him as a husband. So if my father has no intent to arrange a marriage with Erik, I won't push for something I'm not excited for."

Týr mumbled something to himself. It sounded like a negative reaction to the idea of an arranged marriage. I would agree with him, but that's how it was. I would be lucky if my father picked a man for me whom I liked, or even be allowed to pick a man myself, but, given my lack of reciprocating prospects, I'd since let that ridiculous, improbable dream go.

I smiled. "This has worked in Leif's favor however. He was in negotiations with Jarl Rune for his daughter Frida's hand. After you stepped in, the jarl accepted without any further negotiations."

"That makes you happy," Týr observed.

"My brother is completely smitten with Frida. And she cares for him back. I know they'll be happy." Even if me finding what they had was slim, I could be happy for them.

"You will have that," Týr said.

I wished I could agree with him. But between my curse and Father rejecting marriage proposals, I was sure I'd become a lonely völva.

We continued on to the four other locations I needed to pick from. Conversation was strained, as I tried to feel out what was and wasn't fine to discuss. Týr inquired about my family, including our relations with Rune and why he'd chosen my mother to go to battle instead of my father, which was an interesting discussion, since I didn't know much on the politics about those decisions, more just what my parents spoke about to each other and I'd overheard.

Týr was kind through all this, never pushing when I wasn't comfortable answering a question, nor cruel when I admitted I didn't know. It was a stark contrast to what I expected from a god of war. And the warmth I felt being around him, was… familiar. It reminded me of the strong feelings I had with one of my betrothed, but it wasn't quite the same. *I don't understand what it is about this interaction that is even causing this feeling.*

When I had collected everything I needed, we headed back to Runavík. But when we came to the outskirts, Týr stopped and gazed out into the horizon. "I must go."

I painted on a smile, ignoring the prickling disappointment in my chest. My small moment where I was someone special enough to walk beside a god had ended. It was inevitable that reality would return. "I wish you luck with whatever it is you need to do. And thank you for horning me with you time to spend it with me picking herbs."

He smiled. "I should be the one thanking you. And I would like to do it again sometime."

Surprise rippled through me. *He doesn't mean that. He's just saying it to be polite.* "Our home is always open to you, Týr."

The god nodded and walked off toward the woods, disappearing before my very eyes. Had I not been familiar with magic, I might have been startled.

I shook this moment from my mind and set a path for home. *It was fun while it lasted.*

TYR

Water lapped at the shore. I stared out over the river, my mind restless. Blood clung to my armor, clothes, and skin, and although my wounds had healed, my body ached.

Steel clashed and warriors cried. The coppery scent of blood clung to the air.

I blinked slowly. The events of the battle lingered in my mind, tangling with my other thoughts. Loss of mortal life on both sides. Gods and immortals joining and switching sides.

Thunder cracked. A blinding light stole my vision. Jolting, excruciating pain raced through my arm and into my body.

I wince when my arm ached—a reminder of Thor turning on me. I couldn't fathom what had gotten into him, the asshole. But he'd turned on the wrong gods. Both Fenrir, the wolf-god of war, and Baldr, a war god of courage, were nearby to back me up. I could always rely on them in battle.

We'd won in the end, but at what cost?

Grass shifted behind me and a waft of herbs assaulted my nose before a familiar voice spoke. "Týr?"

I turned to see Astrid standing a few paces off. I smiled, unwilling to fight off the warmth that came with her appearance—a ray of sunshine in the darkness that surrounded me. "Astrid."

Her gaze slid over me, and I found myself doing the same, but for a very different reason than I guessed her to be. This dress she wore, perfect for these warmer days of Sólmánuður, hugged her body like it was part of her. It was nicer than what I'd expect her to wear out. And she even wore more makeup than usual. *She's done up her hair, too.*

My body hummed, cock straining against my now too-tight trousers, craving a reward after a hard-earned fight.

I could request her. I could have anything from her family as debt, including her if I so pleased. But I wouldn't ask that. I couldn't—she was mortal. To become attached to someone who would be gone in a few decades, if not sooner… I shook the thoughts from my mind. I needed to be careful around this woman, or I'd make a mistake I'd soon regret.

"You're covered in blood," she said. "Are you hurt?"

Her concern was touching. I shook my head. "Not anymore."

She stepped closer. "But you were."

"I am a god, Astrid. We heal rather quickly."

Her concern didn't evaporate. She closed the distance between us and knelt. "Do you hurt anywhere?"

My brow lifted, my interest piqued. "Are you offering to heal me?"

A mischievous smile slipped up her face. "Perhaps I can. You've been gone for some time."

It'd been a good month or so since I'd last seen her. She could have learned something new with her magic in that time.

I'd wanted to come back, make good on what I told her, but hesitated. I knew becoming attached to this woman would be unwise. I still didn't understand why she, of all out there, tempted me to be that idiotic.

"What have you learned since I've been gone?"

Her smile remained. "Do you have any bruising?"

I did. Wounds healed fairly quickly in most cases, but the body felt the aches and pain a little longer. It sometimes resulted in lingering bruises.

I offered her my arm not injured by Thor. A nasty purple bruise took up most of my bicep. "I think I have one or two you can show off your magic on."

She chuckled, her eyes sparkling. *Creation, this woman…*

Astrid set her basket to the side, the container full of herbs. She took my arm into her small, delicate hands, the contact sending a surprising jolt of warmth through me. She paused for a moment, as if she had felt it too, then concentrated, golden light springing out of her fingertips. She traced a light path of connected runes with her finger, the magic following her motions while threads also branched out.

Warmth lingered in the areas she touched, and the aching I'd felt disappeared. *She's healing me.*

"Why are you here?" I asked. Was it risky to speak to her while she did this?

"I live here?"

I half-laughed. I deserved that answer.

"Better question is, why are you here?" she asked.

I made a thoughtful sound. That was a good question. I hadn't thought of this place when I left the battlefield. I merely wandered, as I typically did. I wasn't always up for rowdy celebrations after a good battle, especially not when Fenrir and Baldr were involved. As much as I enjoyed celebratory drinking and sex, there were times I wanted to be alone with my thoughts.

"This place is quiet. It allows me to think." I glanced down at her. "And it rewarded me with some beautiful company."

I couldn't believe it when she told me that face scar of hers made her less desirable. She was a stunning woman, especially with that fierce mark.

Astrid's eyes flicked up to meet mine, then she quickly refocused on her work. Her cheeks tinted a shade of pink. "You flatter me. Though, I can't help but think you've sustained some damage to your mind, as you've mistaken me for someone else."

"I disagree."

Her cheeks flushed darker. I smirked. Why did I enjoy that so much? Was it because this side of her, the side I experienced while walking through the forest, was so different from the ferocious woman the day of the trial? I liked this tender side just as much.

Astrid pulled away, taking the warmth with her, much to my disappointment. "How does that feel?"

I blinked and looked down at my arm. The bruise was gone. I flexed and tested with a false punch. No pain. No tension at all. "Wow, I don't think I've felt this good in a long time."

She beamed at the praise. "You mean it?"

I nodded, still gazing at her work. "So, you're a healer?"

She swayed her head back and forth, that mischievous grin back. "I can heal and I can use the same magic as my mother."

My head snapped up. "Really?"

She nodded. "Mother is so proud. She says I'll be the strongest völva the family has ever had."

"And your father?" I remembered them both being proud of her the day her magic manifested.

"He says I am the pride of the family."

I caught the mix of emotions cross her face. Was there something bothering her?

Before I could inquire, she gestured to my body. "Do you have any more injuries? I can't do a lot, as I'm still building up my power, but I think I can handle one more."

I motioned to my other arm. I was tempted to see how she'd react to having to heal areas under my tunic, but refrained. The people here didn't have as much issue with nudity as other civilizations out there, but I had the inkling she might struggle a little. It wasn't like I was the typical mortal man.

Astrid slid behind me, sending my senses on alert. I was always careful of my blind spots in the event of a surprise attack. But I then relaxed when she appeared on my other side. She took my arm in her hands. "My father said you were in the battle. He said your presence raised our men's morale."

I hadn't realized her people were fighting in that battle.

She traced along the dark zig-zag marks and discolored skin that had been left from Thor's lightning. "He said Baldr and Fenrir were also there, and you were fighting Thor."

"That's all true." There was no point lying to her.

Astrid began her healing. "Why were you fighting him?"

"He attacked me for some reason. We're still not sure why."

"Did you do something to make him angry?"

"It's possible I angered Odinn, so he sent Thor after me." I wouldn't be surprised if that was the case.

"Why would you make Odinn mad?"

I shrugged. "Because I don't follow him without question, and I do not care about a prophecy that foretells Fenrir will kill him. In fact, I question a lot of what Odinn does, and embrace my friendship with Fenrir. And Odinn doesn't like any of it."

She smiled a little. "That sounds like something you'd do."

I was quite surprised by her response. "Not going to chastise me?"

Astrid pulled away, her healing complete. "No. You know what you're doing when it comes to your actions with the other gods." Her gaze flicked up to me. "But do be careful who you anger. You don't know if the next time, their wrath might result in you losing your hand."

I ran my hand over the newly healed arm. Not a mark remained to show for Thor's attempt on my life. I couldn't help but marvel at her ability. If more caught wind of this, she would be sought after by so many kings. The thought left a sour taste in my mouth. "Thank you for the healing. I'll have to come by more often to have you improve the rest of me."

She smiled, though it didn't reach far up her beautiful face. Somehow, I got the feeling she didn't believe me. I couldn't blame her. I hadn't had that great of a track record for returning in a timely fashion after making such claims. They probably hurt her, sounding more like lies offered as a pretty gift.

I told myself to stay away and let her live out her life, but staying away didn't feel right, either. I needed to make a choice either way, because this indecision was hurting a woman who didn't deserve that treatment.

Astrid grabbed her herb basket and rose to her feet. "The whole town is celebrating the return of our warriors and those who died with honor. You are welcome to join."

That might explain her attire.

She looked toward Runavík. "I doubt it'll be of the same splendor as a celebration the gods may hold, or one we would hold after the harvest, but we do our best. And I think the warriors would be thrilled to share drinks with a god they fought alongside."

I had wanted to avoid celebrating, but as I gazed up at her, that choice didn't sound appealing anymore. "Will you be there?"

She seemed taken aback by my question. "Uh, yes, I planned to attend."

I stood, dismissing what armor I wore to the pocket space war gods could access. As a god, I required little in the way of armor, and what I did have was more for show. Though, as a result, my attire underneath hadn't been spared from the blood of my enemies.

It would have to do in this situation, as I had no way of acquiring anything else quickly. I doubted Astrid's family could provide me with even a loaner tunic. I was quite a bit taller than most of the nordmenn. I even towered over Astrid, and she was rather average in height for a woman.

I offered my arm to her after taking her basket. "Then I'll be happy to attend."

Astrid hesitated for a moment, as if surprised by my offer, and then smiled and wrapped her arms around mine, pressing her figure against me. Her warmth seeped into my skin and traveled through me. *What would it be like to have her pressed against me, under me, writhing in pleasure until she screamed my name?*

This was idiotic. I was playing a dangerous game for a woman I barely knew. But I wanted to know her. I wanted to unravel the mystery of this woman who wrapped you in kindness and protected you with burning ferocity. I wanted to understand what she truly could mean to me, even if that risked more to me than to her.

We walked through town, stopping at her home so she could leave her herb basket and I could freshen up, before heading to the mead hall. I heard the celebration before I could see it. All of Runavík was here. They were already feasting and drinking. A minstrel sang, and I was fairly sure a flyting was in progress.

The jarl and his wife, along with many other nobles, were seated at one end of the building, the jarl himself up on a raised dais. I took in the seating arrangements, noting the seating was set up like most other towns and villages in this region, with the nobles and warriors closest to the jarl and the poor and children farthest away.

A huge fire roared in a central hearth, meat roasting over it.

Cheers arose when my presence was noticed, and I was ushered away from Astrid to join some warriors in a retelling of my battle with Thor, as well as anyone else who wanted to hear. An exaggerated tale was told, but that was to be expected. Even the gods did it.

Of course, I wasn't as present, trying to find Astrid. I'd come here because of her. I didn't want to go through these festivities if she was off somewhere else.

Bjǫrn slapped a hand on my shoulder and bent close to my ear. "Looking for someone?"

I hadn't been all that subtle in my search. Nor did I feel the need to lie. "Yes."

He smirked and then Astrid's voice came from my other side. "More mead, Týr?"

I turned to find her standing beside me, a decorative pitcher in hand. Where had she disappeared to all this time, only to reappear when I desperately wanted her near?

Bjǫrn chuckled and patted my shoulder before leaving. I ignored his behavior, fully focused on Astrid, and held up my drinking horn. "Yes."

She eagerly poured the honey wine and then set the pitcher down on the table, not offering to serve anyone else.

I gestured to the open seat beside me. "Sit with me."

I didn't know if she had planned to or not, but I wanted to make sure she did. She wasn't leaving my side until this was over with.

Astrid smiled and took the seat before grabbing the drinking horn on her hip to fill up. I was tempted to take that away from her and offer to share mine, but I didn't have the right yet to share a drinking horn with her.

She didn't pick up the pitcher again, though. Instead, Astrid reached for a different one on the table.

I gestured to the pitcher she'd brought. "This one is closer."

She vehemently shook her head. "No, that one is just for you."

It was then I realized just how ornate the pitcher for me was. I wasn't having it. She would share with me. I lifted the pitcher and tried to offer her a pour.

Astrid gasped and pulled her horn away. "I can't."

I snatched her wrist and gently pulled her back, pouring the drink. "It would honor me if you'd share this mead with me."

I didn't care what these mortals around me thought. And I knew they were watching. Even the jarl seemed to have an interest in our interactions from where he sat in the hall. Bjǫrn was with him, Randi sitting on his lap and sharing a drink with him.

A raucous cheer erupted, and it was clear a winner of the flyting had been declared.

"Astrid, where is your brother?" her father called out. "I want to see him wipe the smirk off Canute's face with his poetry."

Astrid, mid-sip of her mead, shrugged at her father. He rolled his eyes and shook his head. Randi whispered something in his ear and he laughed.

I bent closer to Astrid and kept my voice low. "Where is he?"

"Truly, I don't know. However, if I had to guess, he's serenading Frida with his poetry in celebration of his return from the battle."

I grunted. I could completely understand their desire to do so.

"They're always sneaking off to make love. Mother and I are convinced she'll be pregnant before they're married at this rate. I'm betting by the harvest. She thinks within the next month."

This time I laughed, throwing my head back in the process. Astrid drank some more, pleased with herself.

"I will have to let Freyja and Freyr know of your bet. They might be interested in playing along with a blessing or two toward one of your wagers."

Astrid laughed. I liked the sound, like a joyous songbird. But the way her face lit up, and her eyes squinted, it was adorable. And the pink in her cheeks, influenced by all the alcohol, only added to her allure.

I raised my drinking horn and offered a battle tale of my own—one of Fenrir and me, exaggerated for the entertainment, but I was in a much better mood to integrate in these festivities with Astrid here.

<h1 style="text-align:center">FIVE</h1>

<h2 style="text-align:center">ASTRID</h2>

Mother checked another jar, shook her head, and set it back on the shelf. I made a mental note to look for that herb as well. We were running low after treating all our warriors yesterday. We were going out fishing soon, so it would be smart to look for replacement herbs while we were out. With so many raids from rival kings, our king and Jarl Rune had agreed that this summer we wouldn't send our men out on as many raids. It was better to weaken our enemies this way, while keeping us strong.

Or, that's what I'd overheard Mother and Father talking about. While women weren't usually involved in politics, because of my mother's status as a völva, and our family's favor with Rune, he made exceptions with her. When I was farther along in my training, I suspect this responsibility would be extended to me.

Father finished sanding his current project, an intricately carved table leg, and inspected his creation. Leif looked up from his own project to watch the master scrutinize for any imperfections. When Father was satisfied, he quietly left his spot and pressed a finger to his lips when he spotted Leif and me watching him.

Father snuck up behind Mother, who didn't appear to notice that he'd moved from his spot, and reached around her, messing with the shelves. Mother let out a scoffing laugh and slapped his hand away playfully. He grinned and continued until the two were laughing in each other's arms. Leif and I joined in. Something twinged in my chest, but I ignored it.

Our laughter died when someone rapped on the door. I was closest to the door, so I opened it to greet our visitors. I smiled at the man on the other side. "Heill, Rune."

He smiled. "Good health to you, Astrid. Is your father home?"

I nodded and then noticed his son Bjarke and daughter Frida with him. "Father, Rune is here."

I backed away from the door to allow them in and glanced at my brother. "And Frida is also here, Leif."

In a flash, he was on his feet and dusting off his clothes. *He's not eager to see her at all.*

Our guests entered the house, and Frida rushed over to Leif. He pulled her into a loving embrace. That feeling from before returned, and I shoved it away again. I knew what it was, but it didn't matter. Father had rejected three more proposals recently. I didn't understand.

Yes, I didn't have much interest in any of the men who were willing to brave my curse, but at this rate, I'd have taken them if they treated me well enough. After having no prospects since I made it to my fifteenth winter, I would have thought my father would want to make sure I was married before my nineteenth winter.

Of course, after spending time with Týr, I doubted any mortal man could quite compare. I shook the thoughts from my mind. *A god such as him will never favor in me in that way.* He could have anyone, and I wasn't the most beautiful woman in Runavík, let alone amongst nordmenn.

And it was clear he was only trying to be kind whenever he promised to return. It was nice seeing him last night, and fun pretending I mattered to him during the celebration, but I knew I wouldn't see him for some time, if ever again. *He has better things to do than waste his time with a mortal woman who will quickly turn into a passing memory.*

"Astrid," Mother said. "Why don't you head out and get done what we planned. We'll be entertaining our guests for a while."

I nodded, though I wasn't sure why she was sending me away. I would have thought she'd want me to help. However, when I reached for my bound baskets and fishing spear, I felt Rune's intense gaze on me. He'd been watching me more since my magic manifested, and I realized he and Bjarke had come around a lot more since. *Are they the reason why Mother wants me to leave?*

"Where are you going?" Rune inquired.

I smiled pleasantly. "To the stream. There are some herbs that grow there and I'll catch some fish while I'm out."

His brow furrowed. "Alone?"

My gaze flicked to Mother since she was supposed to go with me. She nodded her consent to handle this. "Mother was going to accompany me, but I'm capable of handling it alone."

"It could be dangerous." Rune looked to Bjarke. "Go with her."

Mother's eyes narrowed, and I knew something wasn't right. "I don't need to trouble him. I have magic to keep me safe." I reached for an axe. "And I know how to wield this."

The jarl's eyes leveled on me. There was always strength in his stare, but this felt stronger than usual, as if he were trying to intimidate me into complying. Thing was, I wasn't easily intimidated.

"Astrid," Father said in a calm tone. "Head into town with Bjarke."

I resisted the urge to argue and nodded. I wouldn't disrespect him in front of the jarl. I still attached the axe to my hip in open defiance.

Bjarke took my baskets from me and we left. He let out a deep sigh when the door clacked shut. "Sorry."

My brow rose. "For?"

"My father isn't taking no for an answer. I think he believes you'll plead with your father to change his mind if we spend time together."

My eyes bugged out, and my mouth hung open. "He wants to marry us?"

Bjarke laughed. "Your father never mentioned it?"

I shook my head. "I know there have been several proposals, but he never told me who." My brows pinched together. "What happened with Ingrid? I thought you were going to approach her father."

Bjarke was a fine man. Well-muscled, well-kept, and a fun personality, along with being the jarl's son and heir to take over Runavík when his father died, I'd likely be happy with him. But he loved someone else. She was beautiful and talented, and would make for a good alliance between their families.

Bjarke made a displeased face. "I was… until my father told me no when your magic manifested."

I frowned, and my shoulders drooped. "I'm sorry. I don't mean to cause you trouble."

He waved me off. "As long as your father continues to refuse and you don't insist he change his mind, I'll be able to speak to Ingrid's father soon enough."

"You'd make a fine husband—for someone with the patience of Thor himself."

Bjarke barked out a hearty laugh. "Me? If we were to wed, I'd be driven to madness within a moon from all the bickering and nagging."

I laughed along with him. Bjarke had been a good friend since we were children. I could never see him as more, even if it were crazy of me to not want to become the wife of a future jarl. And as his friend, I couldn't take away his chance to be happy. Most didn't get what my parents had—a choice.

Is that what Father is trying to give me?

We entered town, and near the center, I stopped. "You can go find Ingrid if you'd like. I don't need someone to go with me."

"My father wants me to accompany you. I'm not willing to suffer his wrath."

I smirked. "Yes, well, my father said I only had to take you into town."

Bjarke blinked and then laughed. "I should have realized that's what he meant. But still, Ilka was in town, and she'd tell my father if she found out."

I made a face. I didn't like Ilka. She was beautiful, but that's about it. Because their family had a number of thralls, she hardly ever had to lift a finger, so she spent her time using her status as the jarl's daughter to push her weight around.

"Speaking of…" Bjarke muttered.

I turned my attention in the direction he looked to find a shapely, fair-skinned woman with even fairer long hair. With her was another woman with sun-darkened skin and chestnut hair. A collar hung around her neck and she carried a basket full of items.

There was also a man standing next to Ilka. My gut clenched when I realized it was Týr. Why was he here? He never came by so soon after a previous visit. And why was he with Ilka?

He provided her with his intense, undivided attention while she spoke to him. Ilka leaned close, her posture alluring, and it was clear by her facial expressions that she was being flirtatious.

My fists clenched, and I pressed my lips together, struggling to shove back the burning sensation building in my chest. I turned away from this. "Let's get moving. I have a lot to do."

I didn't have a right to be jealous. He could request any woman to entertain him, and Ilka was a beauty. Possibly the most beautiful in Runavík. She would be perfect for a god like Týr.

"Are you sure?" Bjarke asked. "Týr is there. Don't you want to speak with him?"

"He's busy." My response came out too clipped.

"Who is busy?" a familiar, deep voice said close to my ear.

I shrieked and jumped back, whirling around. Bjarke and Týr barked out laughs. I pressed my hand to my chest, my heart threatening to beat out of my ribcage.

"I think we're lucky she didn't use her magic," Bjarke said through laughs.

My cheeks burned hot. "I have control over it now, thank you."

Týr grinned and took my fishing spear. "Just in case, I'll hold onto this."

My nose scrunched. "You're not taking my axe."

His eyes drifted down my body, sending a flash of warmth through me, before settling on my tool and then flicking back up to my face. "I would never touch a woman's assets without her permission."

A smile curled up half my face.

Bjarke chuckled and handed me my baskets. "I see you're in capable hands now, so I'll be off to find Ingrid."

I glanced his sister's way, where she still stood, fuming. "Not afraid your sister will say something to your father?"

He grunted and gestured to Týr. "If my father thinks I'm brazen enough to compete with him, he's clearly taken too many blows to the head."

I blinked. *Compete with?* I shook it off. "Have fun with Ingrid."

He smirked. "Oh, I will."

A devious idea came to me. "If your father needs convincing, a child in her arms is no greater argument."

He belted out a boisterous laugh and walked off. "I like the way you think, Astrid."

Týr took my baskets to tuck under his arm. "I'm curious what that was all about."

I tried to take back my baskets. "Why are you taking those?"

"I'm going with you, wherever you're headed."

I pursed my lips. "Why? You were spending time with Ilka."

His brow rose. "Spending time with? No. Being talked to while I was trying to find you, yes."

My gaze slipped back over to her. She still stood there, glaring. "She would make good company."

He smiled. "Why would I have a candle when I can have the sun?"

Heat returned to my face, hotter this time. "You flatter me. I wouldn't mind the company while I collect herbs and fish."

"I'll fish, you collect."

I rolled my eyes. "I'm not going to make you do my chores."

"You're not. I'm choosing to." He smirked. "As much as I enjoy watching you work, I'm not going to sit on my ass while you do everything."

I thought about this compromise. Watching him fish would be quite the pleasing sight. "Fine. But I at least need my herb basket back."

He held the baskets out of my reach and headed for the edge of the town. "No, I'll carry both."

"Týr," I warned. "Give me my basket."

He smirked and then took off down the road. I gasped and chased after him, calling his name several times. Townsfolk were quick to move out of our path, most cackling at our antics rather than showing anger. Then again, with a god involved, who would be dumb enough to get angry?

I finally gained some ground on him once we left Runavík, and I managed to latch onto the bound baskets. "Ha, got it!"

Though his grip made it impossible to take them from him.

Týr slowed his pace until he came to a halt and he tugged the baskets, but I refused to let go. "Astrid."

"Give it back, Týr."

He lifted it higher, and I refused to let go. My feet rose off the ground, and still my grip didn't fail me. Neither did the leather strap holding them together. Týr's eyebrow lifted with surprise and interest. "You've got one hel of a grip."

I smirked. "I've been told I know how to hold on tight."

Týr stared at me for a long moment, and I swore I saw him swallow hard. He then set me back down on the ground, though didn't relinquish either basket. "Did that man you were with tell you that?"

I grunted. "No, Bjarke and I have never enjoyed each other."

He made a thoughtful sound and then tugged me closer. A quiet gasp escaped my lips. Týr pulled me against his hard chest and wrapped his muscular arm around me. The embrace blanketed me in warm protection and his strong masculine scent.

I liked it. *I shouldn't.* I knew I shouldn't if I didn't want to be hurt, but I couldn't help it. I was willing to pretend to be special enough for this god. I'd allow this man to be my downfall, if it meant I could have something I'd never have with another man.

"I'll let you have the herb basket, if you answer my questions," Týr said.

"All right." I'd answer questions even if I wasn't getting anything out of it. This was a bonus.

"What were you two talking about when he said he wouldn't compete with me?"

"Ah…" My face flushed hot. "Well… Bjarke is Jarl Rune's eldest son. And our jarl is trying to convince my father to marry us to add another strong marriage between our families."

Týr remained quiet. A stoic expression blanketed his face, making it hard to read why.

"Do you wish to marry him?" he finally asked.

I shook my head. "No, which is why I'm not trying to change my father's mind. And why I told Bjarke to just impregnate Ingrid. He loves her, and they should have the chance to be happy."

Týr's expression finally turned to a curious one I could read. "You would pass up the chance to marry the jarl's son so he can be happy?"

I nodded.

He smiled and tugged the leather strap holding the baskets together. The leather released its hold, allowing me to take my herb basket on top. Týr then tucked a strand of my red hair behind my ear. His calloused skin brushed against my cheek, but it wasn't uncomfortable. The action was tender and sweet.

My heart beat faster in my chest. Right now would be the time a mortal man would recite me poetry. But I knew a god wouldn't recite me poetry.

Predictably, the next thing out of his mouth confirmed that. "Who was the woman who wouldn't leave me alone?"

I continued toward the forest. "Ilka. She's Jarl Rune's eldest daughter."

He followed. "Why did she give you those dark looks?"

"Because she doesn't like any of the women in Runavík. She finds them competition in her pursuit of a new husband. And she didn't like that someone *inferior* to her could steal your attention from her."

His brows knitted together. "She was trying to keep my attention?"

My head tipped back as I laughed. "Oh, what I wouldn't do to hear you say that to her face."

Týr grinned. "If it'll get you to laugh like that again, I'll announce it to the whole town."

And I laughed some more. Public humiliation could do that woman some good.

We arrived at the first area for me to pick supplies. This one wasn't on the list for immediate replenishing, but I knew it'd be needed soon.

"Who was the woman with Ilka?" Týr asked.

I shrugged. "I don't know the names of the jarl's thralls."

He knelt beside me. "Does your family have thralls?"

I dug at the roots of one plant. "We used to have two. One man was indebted to my father and worked his freedom back. The other died of illness."

"I see."

When I was done picking, we moved on and he continued with his questions. "Is Leif your only sibling? I've only heard you talk about him, but wasn't sure."

I frowned, my chest constricting. "We had a younger sister, but sickness took her three winters ago."

"Forgive me for bringing up such a sharp loss. I didn't mean to cause you grief in my attempts to know you." He sounded sincere, and I appreciated it. People died of sickness all the time, but it still hurt when it was someone you loved. And I knew that all too well, even beyond my sister.

We came to the next herb I needed.

"What do your father and brother do for a living?" Týr inquired. "You seem well off, and don't have a large farm."

"My father is a carpenter and is part of Jarl Rune's main raid band. Leif is still learning from Father, but is almost at the point my father would feel comfortable with him taking over if something were to happen to him."

"Sounds like your father knows quite a lot."

I nodded. "He's the best in Runavík, and even better than many others in surrounding towns and villages nearby. It's one of the reasons he has such good standing with the jarl. Only the best for him will do."

"How long have the men of your family been doing this craft?"

I paused to think. "My father didn't start out a carpenter. His family are farmers. They're well known for the exceptional horses they breed. My father married up with my mother, and learned her family craft. I think the men have been carpenters for several generations. I never met them, so I don't know for sure."

"I would like to see your father's work."

I smiled and stood. "I think he'd like that."

Týr's gaze drifted down my body again, sending heat pulsing through me and down between my thighs. "Would you like that?"

I opened my mouth to speak, to find it dry. I swallowed and tried again, only for a gasp to escape instead. Týr whirled around, seeing my wide eyes, and took a defensive stance in front of me.

I peeked around him to stare at the large black wolf walking around a crop of trees. It was the size of a horse, or maybe even a little larger. *Is that—*

Týr relaxed. "Fenrir."

The wolf-god padded closer before shifting into a man. A man with a well-built frame, an intricate wolf tattoo on his shoulder and arm, along with a few other runic tattoos on his light skin, and dark-golden hair in long braids. A man who was naked.

Fenrir chuckled. "So, this is where you're hiding. I've been looking all over for you."

He leaned, noticing me, and grinned. "Ah. It all makes sense now."

I looked up at Týr and then back at this new god to grace my life. "You're really Fenrir?"

He smirked. It was a look I was sure convinced women to throw themselves at him. Maybe even some men, too. But I liked Týr's smile more. "I am, and you are the woman Týr is so fond of."

Fond of? Was Týr fond of me, or was this god just embellishing his words?

Fenrir came closer, his eyes never leaving me. It was intimidating in a way I wasn't used to. Like I was staring down a predator on the prowl. And yet, I wasn't afraid of him.

"Fen," Týr warned in a low voice.

He chuckled. "What? If you're not going to make a move, maybe I will. She seems to have a good backbone."

My gaze flicked to Týr, who suddenly looked displeased, and a bit irritated, and then back to Fenrir. I unabashedly took him in. He was impressive, that was for sure. *Are all god men this impossibly tall?*

"Do you prefer a few rounds of fetch to warm up?"

Was that rude? Yes.

Did I care? Not really.

It was funny to me. And either being around Týr emboldened me, or becoming a völva like my mother gave me the confidence to be around such powerful beings.

Fenrir's mouth curled into a predatory grin and he continued to stalk closer, his blue eyes gleaming. "I'm a big fan of a good chase."

"It's a good thing I'm quite good at disarming a beast with belly rubs."

He towered over me now, and yet, even with the small shiver of fear racing down my spine, I wasn't backing down.

Then Fenrir broke out in raucous laughter. He patted my shoulder and turned toward Týr. "Yes, I do like this one. She's a good pick for you."

"What do you want, Fen?" Týr said through gritted teeth. My eyebrow quirked. *Why is he so tense?*

That wolfish grin returned on Fenrir's face. "Someone is a little territorial, for a man who hasn't claimed her yet."

Claimed me? He couldn't be implying—

"What do you want?" Týr repeated.

Fenrir shrugged. "Your help with something, but you're busy, so I'll seek you out again later. It's not life or death."

Fenrir punched Týr in the arm and walked off. His body morphed back into a wolf again, and just before he disappeared into the darkness of the trees, he glanced back, and I heard his voice around me and also in my head.

"It was pleasant to meet the woman who can bring the mighty Týr to his knees. I look forward to seeing you again, Astrid."

I shivered. That was a new and unusual sensation. His voice also didn't sound right. Clearly wolf, which distorted the words.

"Damned mutt," Týr muttered.

I smiled. "I like him."

Týr blinked slowly and then laughed. "You are unlike any woman I've had the pleasure of knowing."

I smiled, accepting the compliment. I scooped to grab my basket, but Týr snatched it with lightning-fast reflexes.

I huffed. "Týr, you said I could have it back."

He grinned. "And I allowed you to carry the basket. Now I'm taking it again."

I rolled my eyes. "I swear, you're more stubborn than a bear in winter."

Despite my teasing, a part of me couldn't help but like it about him. It was a challenge but not an obnoxious one.

We moved onto two more locations for me to gather at before making it to the stream. There were a few things I needed to gather, but found myself distracted.

Týr tied his hair up to keep it out of the way, and then grasped the bottom hem of his tunic to pull it over his head. I did not look away, too interested in seeing a piece of the man that lay beneath.

I was rewarded with a spectacular view of his muscular back and broad shoulders, littered with scars. He also had a tattoo of Yggdrasill on his back, along with the protection and strength runic tattoos banding his arms and neck. *How does a being who can heal so fast obtain this many scars?*

"I can feel your eyes on me, Astrid," Týr said, not looking back at me as he waded into the knee-deep water.

I bit my lower lip, still ogling his planes of hard muscle. "And?"

He glanced back over his shoulder, the spear poised to strike with tight, corded muscles rippling up his arm. The visual before me sent my heart skittering and heat pooling in my belly. "Are you comparing me to another god you recently saw?"

"I can't see enough of you to properly compare," I said.

He glanced down at himself and then focused on the water. "Maybe I should have removed my trousers."

The heat building in my body flooded through me like a wave of molten liquid. I was no stranger to a man's body, but Fenrir's body had not been anything of the likes I'd ever seen before, and I didn't take a lot of time to appreciate all his assets. However, if Týr did the same—the heat inside me intensified.

I didn't think I could trust myself if he decided to do that. I'd either be unable to keep my eyes on him, or I'd make a bigger fool of myself by attempting to touch him—if being exposed to such a sight didn't send me to a blissful early death.

I picked a few riverside herbs, and Týr speared several fish. He walked back to shore with them in hand, and the frontal view of him... *Freyja, help me.*

I stared at the sight before me, my breasts heaving a little. Each hypnotic, flexing muscle looked carved into his body with the most artful skill Creation could offer. The dusting of hair across his chest trailed down in a line that disappeared beneath his trousers, tempting me.

The strong ache to reach out and trace each scar and dip and peak of his sculpted physique nearly overcame me. What would it be like to touch such perfection? What would it feel like to be under him, right here and now? To have him inside me and making me writhe in pleasure?

"Is this enough for you?" Týr asked.

"No," I said too quickly and with too much heaviness in my voice. I swallowed and gave myself a mental slap. "No, I need a few more fish."

Týr wore a wicked grin, his eyes sharp and almost dancing with amusement, but didn't make a comment about my pathetic state. He stored the fish in their designated basket and reentered the stream.

When Týr was about to strike the last fish I needed, something rustled in the woods behind me. The hairs on the back of my neck stood on end and every instinct I had screamed to run.

I whirled around to find an enormous bear lumbering out of the woods toward me. It sniffed the air and then huffed and snarled before picking up its pace. I shrieked and flung my hands up. Magic welled up inside me, tingling along my limbs, and exploded out, pushing the bear back.

Water splashed behind me and Týr launched out of the water, dropping the spear with skewered fish and summoning an axe out of nothing. He slammed into the bear with his full weight, and before I knew it, the bear crashed to the ground, unmoving.

With heavy breaths, Týr turned back to me. Blood splattered his skin, but he otherwise seemed unharmed. "Are you all right, Astrid?"

I nodded, my heart slowly returning to normal. "I'm fine. You're the one who got within range of that beast. Are you harmed?"

"No, I am fine." He looked down at the dead animal. "Do you think your father will be pleased with this?"

I blinked. "You can't possibly be planning to carry that back."

He grinned. "Don't underestimate what I'm capable of."

A thrilling chill ran down my spine.

To distract myself, I collected the fish and made sure I had everything. "All right, I'm ready to head back into town."

I could go out tomorrow for the missing herbs. I didn't want to continue today if it meant Týr had to carry around a bear.

Týr, for all the tall, muscled god he was, hauled the bear over his shoulder after he'd cleaned himself of the blood and threw his tunic back on. "Lead the way."

I gawked for a moment, struggling to believe what I was witnessing. Then I shook it off before I thought too much into how strong this man really was.

When we arrived back in town, the townsfolk were all too willing to move out of our way. Many of the men nodded approvingly at Týr's kill.

We arrived home a short while later, Týr never breaking a sweat. Outside the front door, the thrall woman I'd seen with Ilka stood, head bowed. She looked up at our approach and rushed down to intercept.

"You shouldn't go in," she said in a hushed tone. "Master Rune is angry."

"Let me guess, Ilka told him about what she saw in town?" I said.

The woman nodded. "He's not pleased Bjarke left you to go off somewhere."

I suspected that would happen. But I knew just how to handle the situation Ilka was attempting to make worse on purpose. And Týr's presence would only help me. "I can handle it."

The thrall opened her mouth to speak, but I silenced her with my hand. She bowed her head and stepped out of our way.

Just before I reached the front door, it flew open and Ilka exited my family home. When she spotted me, she gave me a smug smile. I ignored her, gaining an indignant huff, though based on the following offended sound and her storming off, Týr had as well.

I slowly approached the now-open door, straining to listen. Rune was ranting.

"They parted ways!" he shouted. "Parted ways when they reached the mead hall. They were supposed to go out together, not separate because—"

"Because Týr showed up," Father said. "Your son is smart, Rune. He won't push a matter that he won't win."

The jarl snarled. Actually snarled. I wasn't surprised, though. Rune was a Berserker—warriors capable of transforming into bipedal wolves or bears, with enhanced strength and other senses. They were known for making more animalistic sounds when they were worked up. It was how you knew a man was a Berserker, unless you saw his identifying tattoo.

Rune and Bjarke, as well as the other Berserkers in Runavík, had theirs on their chest. It was usually hidden by their tunics, except for a small portion that always peeked out around the collar. I'd never seen a Berserker take their animal form, however.

Rune continued to rant. "And we had an agreement, Bjǫrn. You and Randi help me obtain the jarl position and I make sure your family has high favor and be just as well-off. Then we'd marry our eldest daughter and son each to solidify our alliance and ensure we had a strong bloodline to carry our families' respective gifts."

Father sighed, as if they were rehashing a conversation, yet again. "I've honored half of it with Leif and Frida's marriage, even though Frida isn't your eldest daughter because Leif took to her over Ilka. But as I've told you, things have changed with Astrid. I cannot agree to marry her to your son until I have confirmation."

My brow lifted. *Confirmation about what?*

"And if he never does?"

"He will," Mother said. "I've seen it."

"Stay out of this, Randi," Rune snapped. "Your predictions can be wrong."

"And you only began pushing this marriage issue when Astrid's magic finally manifested." Mother's tone had a dark edge to it. "You were content to allow your eldest son to pursue another alliance until that moment. What does that say about your desire to uphold our previous agreement?"

"Watch your tongue, Völva, or I'll rip it out of your mouth personally."

My hands balled into fists, and my lip curled. A muscle in my neck twitched in rhythm with the rising pulse pounding in my ears. *How dare he talk to my mother that way.*

Wood scraped on wood. "I will tell you this once, Rune, out of respect for our friendship. If you ever speak to my wife like that again, I will turn you into a bleating mare."

I choked on a laugh, my anger cooling. *Father certainly has a set of balls.*

As entertaining as some of this was, I needed to give my parents a break from the jarl's anger.

"Father? Mother?" I called out, approaching the door. "I'm back."

I poked my head inside to find Father and Rune standing toe-to-toe in a glaring contest. Mother sat at the table watching with a bored expression, and Leif was nowhere to be seen. *Probably off with his betrothed.*

"Did you get everything?" Father asked me, without looking away from the jarl.

"No, not everything, but I do have something extra," I said. "Plus, we have a guest."

Mother's attention snapped up, and Father finally looked away from Rune. Rune also turned at the same time to see me leading Týr into the house. He had to duck low due to his height, and the bear only made it a little more complicated.

Mother gasped, and Father's brows shot up. "Týr, I do hope our daughter didn't cause you any trouble."

Týr smiled. "She never does. Only keeps my life interesting."

Father nodded approvingly. "Randi, I think bear would be better for tonight's meal than fish."

"I agree, my love. Týr, you'll be staying of course, yes?"

He smiled at Mother. "I would be happy to."

"Rune, will you be joining us as well?" I inquired, only out of politeness. I knew by the frustrated look on his face what his answer would be.

He shook his head. "No, I must be returning home. However, Astrid, I have a question for you."

"Rune…" Father warned.

"Yes, what is it you wish to ask?" I could handle this scrutiny.

"Was my daughter correct in telling me you and my son parted ways in town?"

I blinked, putting on my best innocent act. "Yes, that's right. Father said I only had to go into town with him."

I could see Father trying to bite back a proud smile in front of our jarl.

"But you didn't insist he join you with your tasks outside the town, as I had requested?" Rune pushed.

Before I could speak, Týr did. "You have an intelligent son, Rune. Not every man is wise enough to see what's already decided."

I swallowed and squeezed my legs together at the possessive tone to his words.

Rune sucked in a tight breath and then nodded. "I should be leaving. Have a good day, all of you."

He left without even a glance back and slammed the door behind him. There was silence in the house for a moment, and then Father laughed. He came up and kissed me on the forehead.

He then turned to Týr. "Thank you for keeping my daughter safe beyond the town borders."

"You do not need to thank me," Týr said. "I do it of my own free will."

Father smiled and then looked down at the bear. "Why don't we take care of this so my wife and daughter can create a delicious meal for us?"

Týr nodded. "After, I would like to see some of the work you do. Astrid speaks highly of your craft."

Father's eyes flicked to me; I smiled in return.

The two men left, Týr lifting the bear with his godly strength, leaving Mother and me to store my herbs and fish and prepare for the meal.

Mother patted my hand and gave me a knowing smile. I cocked my head, but she didn't elaborate. *What was that look for?*

SIX

TÝR

Squirrels chattered in the trees above, and a twig snapped under my boot. The crisp air carried the scent of the forest, and the promise of colder days and nights to come. A raven called overhead. I strained my senses to find the bird and then moved on. It wasn't one of Odinn's ravens. I didn't need to deal with his spies right now.

The trees thinned, and soon I walked the familiar road leading to Astrid. My pace increased, that deep part of me desperate to see her. It'd been some time since I could visit. I had been doing well, coming by daily or every few days, but I hadn't seen her in a month. I hoped she wouldn't be too mad. She never seemed to show any anger or disappointment, but Astrid was also good at masking how she felt.

Getting her to talk about anything that bothered her was difficult. It was like she didn't want to burden me with anything, or that she thought her problems didn't matter to me.

Frustration burned in my chest. I didn't want her thinking that. She mattered. As much as I knew this mortal shouldn't, and that I should have left her to live her short life with other mortals, I couldn't let her go. She mattered to me. Her smile, her laugh, her brazen personality mixed with a gentle kindness not even a god like me deserved.

I glanced down at the variety of violet-colored flowers I carried for her. I hoped this would be enough. I couldn't romance her with poetry like she deserved. The last time I attempted to create a poem, Freyja fell over laughing at me. Literally fell over. I couldn't embarrass Astrid like that.

I caught sight of her, and my heart skipped. Those gorgeous flaming locks drifted in the breeze, as if calling me to tangle my fingers in them. They draped along her slender neck, taunting me to wrap a hand around her and pull her close. I'd be able to tip her head up and lean into those tempting lips of hers.

I closed my eyes and sucked in a deep breath. I was hard as a damned rock.

Fenrir's taunting words echoed in my mind. He thought I moved too slow, that I should take and claim her as mine. But he didn't understand. She was a woman worth taking one's time with—to woo and romance her until our souls mingled and bound, and all we could see and want was each other.

My feet halted when I realized she wasn't alone. A man with braided golden hair and a short, groomed beard spoke with her. His posture was animated, and as I strained to listen, I wished I hadn't. He recited poetry. A good poem at that.

Astrid smiled at him, but I couldn't tell if she was being polite or sincerely enjoying it.

When the man finished, he gazed at her expectantly. Astrid's smile shifted a little, something subtle, but one I could read as her being polite.

"That was lovely," she managed.

The man let out a long breath. "But…"

Astrid grimaced. "Some advice? If you're going to recite poetry to every unmarried maiden in Runavík, maybe try to use a different poem each time?"

I made a face. That was a desperate man.

Astrid's attention on the man waned just enough for her to notice me. She jerked her attention in my direction and a big, beaming smile overtook her. "Týr!"

She rushed over to me, without even a second glance at the man. He frowned, but otherwise didn't try to pursue. At least he was smart enough to know a desperate man like him could never compete.

Astrid wrapped her arms around mine and pressed her full body against me, gazing up with those soul-snaring eyes. *Creation…* My cock strained against my trousers even harder.

"I'm so happy to see you," she said. "I was beginning to wonder if the call of battle had carried you off for good."

I smiled. "There is no battle call strong enough to keep me away. Though I am sorry it's been so long. It was never my intention."

She shook her head. "No apology needed. I'm sure you had more important things to do."

I frowned. I did not like how she saw that. I presented the flowers to her. "It was only important because it meant you were safe."

Astrid's eyes widened, and the most adorable gasp came from her lips. "Týr… these are… I've never seen such lovely flowers."

She took the bundle and smelled them. "And they're in such perfect bloom. Where did you find these?"

I smirked. "I know someone."

A perk of being a god. Knowing a god or immortal with flora affinities wasn't that difficult. And it made my life that much easier when it came to wooing Astrid.

"Thank you. You've brightened my day more than the sun could with your thoughtfulness." A fresh sparkle illuminated her eyes. "Oh, you'll never guess what happened!"

I tilted my head. This had to be good.

She grinned. "I won the bet."

It took me only a moment to realize what she meant. Today was the day before the harvest, making it the last day of the season. And that could only mean Frida had made an announcement recently. I threw my head back with a laugh. "Freyja will be pleased her blessing was stronger. And just in time for the wedding, yes?"

Astrid nodded. "This Frigg's Day."

She looked down and her cheeks tinted pink. "Will you be there?"

"If you're inviting me."

She looked up and smiled. "Yes, I am."

I brushed a stray strand of hair out of her face. "I promise I will be there."

"I am pleased to hear this," a masculine voice said.

We looked up to see her father and mother approaching. Both smiled, and this time, her mother spoke. "We are always grateful for your presence and blessings, Týr."

"I hope you don't mind, but I will be taking Astrid with me today."

Astrid stared up at me. "You want to take me somewhere?"

Bjǫrn grinned. "You are welcome to take her anywhere for as long as you wish. Though I believe her brother would like it if she were there for the wedding."

I chuckled. "I'll do my best to make sure she's back in time for that."

Today's plans wouldn't keep her longer than today, but it was a tempting idea to take her back to my home on the island, and never let her leave. Of course, I wouldn't do that without consulting her first.

Randi walked up to her daughter and took the flowers. "I'll take care of these for you, Sunshine."

Astrid thanked her, and I led her away from town.

"Týr, where are we going?" Astrid inquired.

"Fenrir, Baldr, and I plan to engage in some sparring. Freyja will be there to supervise, as we can sometimes get out of hand."

She cocked her head. "Why do you want me to be there for that?"

I smiled. "Because I want you there, and I thought it might be a good opportunity for you to practice your magic."

Her face reddened. "Oh, I practice with Mother. You don't need to—"

I pressed my thumb to her lip, and the feeling of her soft flesh on mine sent a spark of need flooding through me. "I will make sure you're the most powerful völva Midgard has ever seen. Freyja even wants to teach you something."

The color in her face deepened, and her gaze fell to the ground. "All this attention… you make it hard not to feel like the most special woman in Midgard."

I grinned. That was the idea.

A wolf howled in the distance, and a moment later Fenrir barreled out of the woods. Behind him, Baldr, a lean yet sturdy and muscled man with pale skin that had been tattooed with runic arm and chest bands, barreled after him, his braided golden hair flagging behind him. Before I had the chance to warn her, Astrid gasped and her hands flew up. Fenrir found himself pushed back several paces. Baldr was far back enough to stop in time before the blast touched him.

The attack was nothing like she'd done with the bear, but not too bad of an attempt against a god.

Fenrir stood there, head cocked, as if confused. I laughed. "Serves you right, Fen."

His words projected into our minds. *"What did I do?"*

Astrid huffed. "Don't startle me like that."

The wolf-god snorted and Baldr laughed. The two walked up to us, at a much-less-rushed pace.

I gestured to the new god to come into Astrid's life. "Astrid, this—"

"Baldr." She nodded. "Mother made sure we could recognize any of the gods, should we be graced with their presence."

Baldr grinned, his pale eyes sparkling, and spoke with a deep voice. "It's nice to meet Týr's weakness finally."

Astrid laughed, releasing the tension in her shoulders from meeting yet another god, and I glared at him. It wasn't like he was entirely wrong. This woman would be the death of me at this rate. But he didn't have to say it out loud.

"Has Freyja set up our sparring location?" I asked.

Fenrir nodded. *"We wouldn't be here if it wasn't ready."*

I held my hand out to Astrid. "This means I can teleport us there."

She tilted her head. "How does that work for you?"

"Unlike Freyja and her brother, I can't teleport us anywhere I wish. I have to go somewhere with a battle aura. However, with Freyja, she can create us a special sparring area that gives off that aura. Since it takes a while to prepare, it's easier for her to do that and for me to bring us to her."

"Wow…" she said, her voice filled with awe. "I'd love to be able to do that. Not even Mother can."

I smiled. "Maybe Freyja will teach you."

Astrid smiled back, but I could see she doubted the possibility. I suspected she was experiencing some struggle around having so much contact with us gods. It wasn't uncommon for us to be in the presence of mortals, but her type of inclusion was fairly unique. And it's how I wanted it. If she was going to be mine, she would live what mortal life she had like no other mortal could dream of.

Astrid took my hand, and I pulled her into me. The way her body molded into mine, it was difficult to not think about changing plans and send Fenrir and Baldr away so I could undress her right here.

Fenrir sauntered up to me and inhaled deeply. He chuckled. *"Want us to leave? Or maybe you're good to put on a show. Perhaps an interactive one for me and Baldr?"*

Baldr laughed and slapped his hand on my shoulder. I jammed my elbow into Fenrir's side, at the same time using the contact to transport us to the battle aura I sensed that was distinctly Freyja's magic.

In a blink, we were no longer at the forest edge, but in a clearing far from Astrid's home. Freyja, a woman with pale hair knotted past her shoulders, lounged near the far edge of the clearing. She had a strong, honed body, showing the warrior she was, even in this relaxed state, which also maintained a strong feminine allure. With her were two cats.

She smiled. "I thought I'd die of boredom waiting for all of you. Heill, Astrid. I'm glad you could join us."

Astrid stared at the woman, clearly awestruck. The reaction surprised me, given she hadn't had it with Fenrir or Baldr.

Baldr nudged Astrid with his elbow, spurring her to speak out a hasty hello.

Freyja's blue eyes sparkled, and she patted the ground next to her. "Come, sit with me. I don't bite." She winked. "Too hard, at least."

Astrid laughed, the tension rolling off her. As much as I didn't want to, I released her from my grip and the brave woman who had my soul sauntered over to the goddess.

I went to stretching to loosen myself up, while listening in on Freyja giving Astrid fair warning how brutal Fenrir, Baldr, and I could be.

"I can't repair missing limbs, so they better not expect that miracle," Astrid muttered while affectionately petting one of the cats.

Freyja laughed. "Hear that, you three? She's got conditions."

"Finicky little she-wolf," Fenrir said.

Astrid stuck her tongue out at him in response. Freyja laughed more. Creation, I loved this brazen side of her. Once comfortable, she fit right in amongst gods.

Fenrir stretched his large body once and then positioned himself some paces away for us to square off. Baldr stood off to the side. We tried for one-on-one fights, but as war gods, we tended to get excited and jumped in, creating a free-for-all.

"Stakes this time?" I prompted Fenrir, still not done with my stretching. I knew better to warm up for these.

Fenrir's eyes flicked to Astrid. *"Her."*

I sneered, and Astrid scoffed. "Like hel I am."

His wolf lips pulled into a toothy grin. *"Yes, I will take her, attitude and all."*

I brandished my axe and shield. He would not win this if he wanted to wager *my* Astrid. Fenrir bared his teeth and his hackles rose.

"They're not wagering me," Astrid said, clearly offended by this.

Freyja tried to ease her. "Don't think too much on it. These wagers are fun motivators for them. Týr will ensure he won't lose if you're the wager. Though, even if he did, you'd be in good hands with Fen. He wouldn't do anything you wouldn't want."

Astrid gave an indignant snort.

"Why don't we discuss what magic you know," Freyja said. "Then we'll see what I can teach you."

I tuned the two women out to focus on Fenrir. The wolf licked his chops and paced back and forth, growling hungrily for blood. I followed his movements, patient and waiting. Fenrir always struck first; it was only a matter of time.

A shift of my weight triggered him to lunge. I slammed my shield into his muzzle and swung my axe, landing a blow. Fenrir ripped the shield from my grip and tossed it aside, then came at me again. I ducked and threw my shoulder into him, but he was ready for that. His teeth clamped down on my shoulder and I gritted my teeth, refusing to cry out in pain. I sliced my blade into his shoulder again and he yipped, releasing me in the process.

Fenrir snapped his teeth. I jumped back, but not fast enough to prevent him from ripping my axe from my grip and casting it aside. Now I was without my shield and weapon.

A low chuckle came from Fenrir, and he lunged before I could summon my sword laying in wait to be used. But mid-movement, he shifted back into a man and threw a punch. I blocked it, the impact jarring and sending painful shockwaves through me. I swung a punch of my own and he also blocked.

We were only moments into this when Baldr barreled into Fenrir. He wasn't on my side, though. With Fenrir on the ground, he pivoted and came at me with wild, unpredictable attacks. I threw in a punch when I could, though I knew it'd do very little, given Baldr couldn't feel pain. He was a difficult opponent to fight. But that added to the thrill.

Back and forth, the three of us exchanged blow after blow. None of us was willing to dodge or evade, only feeling the rage of battle humming in our veins the longer we duked it out. This was what we lived for. This was part of what made each of us a god of war.

I sucked in a tight breath and froze when a blade suddenly appeared at my throat. Fenrir and Baldr also found themselves in similar positions. The three of us stared at each other, breaths coming hard, and I realized what kind of mess we'd made of each other.

My body ached, and blood smeared my skin and stained my clothes. Cuts and gashes knitted back together with our quickened god healing. These blades made sense. Freyja wouldn't be stupid enough to jump between us. As a goddess of war, she'd likely be dragged into our fight. So, she separated us this way.

However, there was something different about these blades. They weren't Freyja's typical ones. And when I tasted the magic around us, I realized it wasn't her doing at all. *Astrid.*

My gaze flicked to the two women. They both stood now, and Astrid held a hand out. But her gaze… *Creation, that look.* I'd never seen such a deadly expression on her face, and hel did it make me want to throw her under me.

The weapons flickered and then vanished. Astrid released a tense breath, showing how difficult that had been for her. Freyja murmured praises.

"Does she give you that look all the time?" Baldr asked, his voice strained. "Because, hel, I don't think I could resist her if she did."

I suppressed a groan. "No. This is new."

Astrid's expression changed to one of confusion, and Freyja laughed. "There's enough sexual heat in the air to forge a sword."

Astrid made a face. "You can't possibly be aroused by weapons poised at your throats."

"There were a lot of factors here that already got our blood hot before you and that dangerously alluring look of yours stoked the flames," Fenrir said.

Her confusion returned. "What look?" She then shook her head. "Never mind. All three of you, come here so I can heal you."

"We're gods, we don't need healing," Fenrir said.

"Trust me, Fen, you'll want this," I said, not hesitating to jog over to Astrid, even with my body protesting.

She sat on the ground, and one of Freyja's cats hopped into her lap to curl up. They seemed to like her. *I'll get her a cat of her own.* They made good gifts, right?

Astrid glanced up from the cat when both felines hissed at Fenrir's approach. They didn't like wolves or hounds of any kind. "And, Fluffy, put on some trousers. I don't want your small berries in my face."

Baldr and I threw our heads back in laughter. Fenrir scoffed, "Small? You clearly haven't gotten a good look."

Freyja grinned and created an illusion of a bush of mistletoe with some of the smallest berries I'd ever seen in front of his cock. Fenrir glowered at her. I laughed harder. Even Astrid joined in. He stalked off to a pile of clothes, throwing on trousers, and only those. That seemed to be enough for Astrid, as she didn't say anything more about his appearance.

Astrid chose me for her first healing session. While she worked, her golden light searching for the worst, slower-to-heal damage and Fenrir and Baldr watched on, enthralled by her ability, she asked Freyja questions. "Freyja, I always wondered, how can you be a goddess of sex and fertility and war? They seem too opposite to work."

Freyja hummed. "They're not all that different, really. Love, childbirth, family, they're all their own kinds of battle filled with passion."

Astrid made a thoughtful noise and then focused on a particularly stubborn damaged bone. Seemed someone had struck me better than I thought.

"How do gods obtain scars when you heal so fast?" Astrid asked.

"Some weapons and magic can cause us to heal slower, resulting in the same improper healing you mortals experience," I said.

She nodded slowly. "Is this how war gods pass the time, beat each senseless if you don't have others to fight?"

"We eat and drink and fuck, too," Fenrir said.

Freyja, Baldr, and I laughed. Astrid shook her head while chuckling.

After some more healing, she let out a long breath, and gave me the all-clear. Like the last time she healed me, I felt better than before we'd even arrived here. Her abilities were amazing for a mortal. And once Fenrir got his chance to feel this wondrous power of hers, he wouldn't shut up about it.

Much to my irritation, Astrid ate up the praise. It didn't bother me that it boosted her confidence. No, it just showed me how quiet I'd been about it around her. Fenrir wasn't serious about taking her from me. He was only trying to get under my skin. But hel if he didn't also show me how much I was failing her. *If only I didn't struggle with the right words when she looks at me.*

"What are the two of you going to offer as stakes for your second round of punch-each-other-into-unconsciousness?" Astrid asked. "Freyja said you make multiple bets."

Fenrir's brow rose. "There was no winner, so you're still the prize."

Astrid snorted. "There was a winner. Me."

My eyebrow spiked, and Fenrir laughed. "You?"

"I stopped all three of you, so I won."

This time I laughed, while Fenrir stared at her, dumbfounded.

"You can't win yourself," Fenrir argued.

Astrid's sly grin rivaled that of Loki's. "Can and did."

Fenrir shot a look at me while I continued to laugh. Baldr joined in. "She's perfect for you."

Astrid's cheeks turned pink, though she didn't voice any agreement or rejection. I'd noticed this several times when the teasing came up. She either grew quiet, or deflected. I knew my intentions were still muddy, and I was working on that, but most women in her position would be more excited to hear the implications.

Is she not interested? She'd been quite vocal about the men she didn't want, so if she wasn't interested, wouldn't she have told me? Or was my status as a god preventing her from being honest? *Or maybe the debt?*

Ice prickled my veins. Astrid always seemed so genuine in her reactions around me. I hadn't thought she might feel obligated to agree to anything I requested of her.

"You're all set," Astrid said, her voice strained. It was clear healing took a lot out of her, by the way her shoulders and eyes drooped.

Fenrir flexed. "I've never seen anyone with healing capabilities like you. I can't remember the last time I felt this good. It's a shame you're mortal."

I ground my teeth. *Why did he have to bring that up?*

Astrid shrugged. "Fairness isn't in the woven threads of the Norns."

Fenrir, Baldr, and Freyja gazed at her with concealed sympathy. We gods accepted that mortals died. Gods could die as well, but old age was never a factor for us. But hearing a mortal just accept her reality, like Astrid did, somehow made that fact harder to tolerate in this instance.

"I can only hope, if I have a daughter of my own, she'll also be blessed with this much power," she said.

I swallowed. *Children.* I could see it in my mind's eye; her heavy with child—*my* child. I'd be happy to give her as many as she desired if that's what she wanted.

"Baldr, it's your turn," Astrid said.

His mouth twisted. "It's not necessary for—"

Astrid's eyes narrowed, and she pointed to the now-free spot in front of her. "Now."

His eyebrows rose high toward his forehead, and I choked on a laugh. My Astrid was getting quite comfortable around us.

Baldr let out a long breath and complied. Astrid took his arm and inspected him for damage.

"They say you feel nothing. Is it only pain you're spared, or does all sensation escape you?"

He grinned. "I'm enjoying the warmth of your hands."

"So only pain." She checked his upper arm. "Explains all this damage. You don't allow your body heal because you don't know you're injured."

I pursed my lips. That was a fascinating assessment from her.

"How does this magic work?" Baldr inquired. "Do you just sense internal injuries?"

Astrid shook her head. "No, I'm using magic to feel under your skin. It catches on damage, like water finding cracks in a bowl. I do have to be careful, of course, because like water, if I use too much magic in my search, I could make that damage worse."

Fenrir leaned forward. "How do you know when to heal?"

"That's a judgment call. If something doesn't feel right—like this, here"—Astrid ran her thumb along the back of Baldr's arm—"then I'll focus my magic into healing."

"How do you heal?" Baldr asked.

She squinted. "Um… that's harder to explain."

Made sense. I didn't have a robust knowledge of magic beyond being able to summon and dismiss my weapons and armor, which Freyja insisted was different. From what I'd learned by being around those who could use it, it came so naturally to them, it was more instinctual. That's what made it difficult for magic practice to be passed on, and why I found Astrid's maternal line of völvur even more fascinating.

"How does that feel?" Astrid asked Baldr.

He rotated and flexed his arm, his eyes wide. "I can move it better. I didn't feel anything you did, but it's clearly better than before."

Astrid smiled wide; her pride was well-earned. That was an important breakthrough for her. It added a layer of complexity to her healing. *Next she'll be healing cripples.*

Astrid continued, finding Baldr really did have a rather messed-up body, even with god healing. She wasn't able to get to it all, as the healing taxed her too much, but she was adamant she wanted to do another session with him later if she was up for it, or some other day. Baldr agreed, and I had no issues with him coming around her more.

"I want to try something," Freyja said. "Magic might be rare in mortals, but I've met my fair share of gifted individuals. Even still, I never thought a mortal would be able to do this, but given the promising power you have, Astrid, I want to see if it's possible for you to learn teleportation."

Astrid's eyes grew wide. "You really want to teach me that?"

"I do."

I expected Astrid to explode from the beaming excitement on her face, but she managed to stay controlled. "I would be honored if you taught me that magic."

The flapping of wings caught our attention, and we looked up. A woman with golden hair and black feathered wings garbed in armor swooped down and landed gracefully.

Her vibrant blue eyes swept over us. "I apologize for being late. I was held up."

Fenrir grinned. "You mean tied up by your precious Berserker."

She didn't refute the accusation.

I noticed her gaze flicked to Astrid a few times, who gazed at her with awe. "Kirby, meet Astrid. Astrid, this is Kirby, she's—"

"A Valkyrie," Astrid finished. "Your wings are beautiful beyond words."

Kirby smiled. "I thought I'd like you. Though, why you'd waste your time with an oaf like Týr is beyond me."

I punched her in the arm; she laughed while wincing. Kirby and I got along well. And of all those I knew, Kirby understood my position with Astrid the best. She'd taken a Berserker lover, Starkad, who had yet to develop his immortal soul, risking an early death.

"I'm about to see if Astrid can learn teleporting with her magic,"

Freyja said. "Then we'll get back to watching these three pummel each other to a pulp."

"A völva with that kind of potential?" Kirby smirked. "I'm glad I showed up in time."

Pink tinged Astrid's cheeks. "Don't get too excited; we're not sure I can do it. All völvur have different abilities in their magic. I can heal and cast other spells, but my mother can't heal. However, she has visions, and so far, all of them have come true, even if they seem strange and farfetched."

"I never doubt Freyja, so if she thinks you can, then you can. But I am curious about these unusual visions your mother sees. Has she told you some?"

Astrid nodded. "One of the oddest ones was that she saw mortal women in strange clothing becoming Valkyries."

We all stared at her. *That's not possible, is it?* Regardless of the stories the mortals made up, a majority of us gods didn't know where we came from—we just were. And the Valkyries were of Odinn's creation, but none could recall how it happened, and he had never made any after the initial group.

Astrid shrugged. "Like I said, the visions are unusual and sound impossible."

Kirby made a thoughtful noise, and Freyja decided to steer the conversation over to Astrid's training.

I took a comfortable seat on the ground to watch. I'd never seen Freyja teach anyone anything, so I was interested in how this would go. Plus, watching Astrid do anything was an added bonus.

One of Freyja's cats, Bygul, rubbed against me, and I allowed her to hop up in my lap. I preferred dogs, but cats weren't too bad.

Fenrir attempted to convince Trjegul to tolerate him, but his attempts only made it look like he was harassing the feline. The whole ordeal provided me with a great deal of entertainment, especially when the shifter god started pouting.

Freyja instructed Astrid that they'd work on having her go to the other side of the clearing. It wasn't too far, but a good enough distance to train for. I listened as she explained the basics of teleportation, and how Astrid had to visualize where she was going, either based on a place or a person she knew. Astrid followed along like the perfect mentee, her entire focus on what the goddess said.

"Ready to try?" Freyja asked when she finished explaining.

Astrid sucked in a deep breath and nodded. She closed her eyes and her brow furrowed in deep concentration. Several long moments passed before her physical being blurred and then solidified.

My back straightened. *That was a sign that it's possible, right?*

Astrid cracked open an eye and then let out a sigh, her shoulders slumping. "Didn't work."

Freyja clacked her tongue. "Actually, it did. Your form blurred, with a partial teleport that ultimately failed. Try again."

Astrid's lips twisted. Then she tried again. And then again. And again.

Each time, her form blurred more and more, until…

I jumped to my feet when Astrid disappeared, startling Bygul, and frantically looked around for her. "Where is she?"

All four of us gazed around the clearing, but Astrid was nowhere to be found.

"Oh no," Freyja mumbled.

Freyja could sense the location of any immortal, as could I to a certain extent. However, Astrid was mortal, and that meant none of us knew where she was.

"Týr?" Astrid's voice called from the distance of the surrounding forest.

"Astrid!" I shouted.

"Oh good, I'm still in the same forest. Um, give me a moment and I'll try to get back to all of you."

"Walk to us. Don't try the magic again," I said. "We can't track you down if you go too far."

I didn't receive a response, and that kicked up my pulse. *She wouldn't be rash enough to try again, right?* "Astrid? Astrid!"

A shrieking gasp behind me was the only response I received. I whirled around and stared at Astrid, scrabbling for purchase on a high-up tree bough she now hung from.

Fenrir fell to the ground, laughing. Baldr, while bent over, at least managed to stay on his feet.

"Quiet, mutt," Astrid muttered. She finally got her leg over the tree branch and laid on it, clutching the limb for dear life.

Kirby ran her fingers through her hair. "Well, that settles it, I think."

Freyja's eyes sparkled, as if she found nothing concerning in this situation. "I knew she could do it."

"Not very well," I said, jogging over to the tree.

"She merely needs practice."

I wasn't sure I was keen on this idea anymore. If her magic would send her to random places before she got a handle on the ability, how were we supposed to make sure she didn't get lost in the process?

"So, I did all right?" Astrid asked.

"I think that went a hel of a lot better than expected for a first attempt," Kirby said. "You could have gone across Midgard with that lack of control, and none of us would have been able to find you."

Kirby voicing that reality made my gut churn. I would not lose her to this magic.

When I reached the tree, I held out my arms for her to jump into, but Astrid looked at me like I was insane. She was fairly high up there, so I didn't blame her.

I frowned when Kirby flew to rescue her. Yes, it was the most logical thing to do, but I wanted to be the one to help her. Astrid made a dramatic joke about being saved, making Kirby laugh.

"I think I should wait a little longer before trying again," Astrid said when her feet were back on solid ground. "That took a lot out of me."

Freyja nodded. "I'll look for an enchanted item to help us keep track of you in the future when we practice."

Astrid smiled, though I still was uneasy about all this. However, I didn't have a right to say no. This was Astrid's life and her magic. And if she wanted to learn this, I couldn't stop her.

Astrid settled down in the grass with the other women, and Fenrir, Baldr, and I went back to sparring. It would keep my mind off my worry, at least for the time being.

Some time into our session, Kirby joined in, adding another exciting element to the fight. We called it quits around the time the sun hung low in the sky. Astrid treated us to another healing session, as well as to Freyja and Kirby, to soothe and mend some of their older injuries.

They were so pleased with the results, it was clear that Astrid may not have a traditional mortal's living experience much longer. I no longer cared if she lived like a mortal anymore, so long as no one thought they could take her from me.

We all parted ways, Freyja offering to transport Astrid and me to the edge of Runavík, as I couldn't sense out any battles nearby.

I walked Astrid home from our transport drop-off, enjoying this quiet moment with her. She hung off my arm, her beaming smile contagious.

"Did you enjoy yourself?" I asked when we arrived at her front door.

She nodded. "I'm still not sure why you're going through all this trouble for me, but I do appreciate it."

I stared at her. "Why wouldn't I do this for you?"

Astrid stared back, as if my confusion created an endless loop between us. "Because I'm mortal? You'll blink and I'll be long gone—a memory, at best, in the vast sea of experiences you'll have for eternity."

It felt like Odinn himself reached inside my chest and squeezed my heart. She may not have believed she deserved all this special treatment, but I didn't agree. I'd lay the bodies of her enemies at her feet if she desired it.

That revelation struck me. I couldn't recall a time I'd ever felt this deeply for someone. And yet, those thoughts were so clear and strong that I couldn't deny them even if I wanted to. It would hurt to lose her to her mortality, but I'd rather spend the next few decades with her than go through eternity without ever crossing paths. I needed her to see she was more than just a passing memory.

I blinked. "You're still here."

Astrid's lip twitched. Then she laughed. "That's not what I meant, and you know it."

I reached out and cupped her chin, cutting off her laughter as I forced her to hold my gaze. "I return here for a reason, and it's not because of some outstanding debt or because this place is quiet. She's standing right in front of me. Yes, you're mortal, Astrid, but you'll never *just* be a memory, no matter how far into eternity I go."

Her cheeks turned a bright shade of crimson, and her gaze fell away. My eyes flicked to her mouth when her bottom lip caught in her teeth. I could easily fix that for her. It'd be so easy to just… lean in and—

I paused mid-lean when a chill ran up my spine. My head snapped up, and I gazed out into the distance. Something was wrong. *But what?*

"Týr?" Astrid said.

"I… have to go." I hated having to say those words. I didn't want to leave, but I couldn't ignore this, either. There was unrest again with Odinn and some other gods. I felt the tension. It called like battle, and I needed to be there to either diffuse or fight.

She nodded, her face relaxed. "I understand."

Did she? Of course she did. She put such little importance on her role in my life, she'd always see things I needed to take care of as more important. She wouldn't fuss, and would let me go.

I didn't want her to think this way. I wanted her to see how important she was. I'd have to make it up to her as many times as I needed until she understood.

Astrid cocked her head just as I turned. "Wait."

I paused and when she beckoned me closer with a finger, I complied. She had an unusually serious look about her, piquing my interest. She continued to beckon me until I felt her hot breath on my skin, sending a prickle of want through me.

Her soft lips pressed against my temple, and before I could react to the sudden, intimate contact, the warm sensation of her healing spread through my face.

Astrid pulled away. "I missed a spot. That should help you see the situation better."

I could, but not because that magically fixed my sight. My body hummed as I stared at her, taking in who she was. The strong, alluring temptress of a mortal who'd beguiled and ensnared me, and I was all too all right with that.

I wanted to kiss her until her lips were swollen from my possession.

I wanted to pin her to the wall and have her feel what she did to me by just existing.

My cock strained against my trousers, but like a bucket of cold water, the incessant warning grew louder in my senses.

I'd have to indulge in her later, and settled for taking her hand in mine. "I'll be back as soon as I can."

I kissed her knuckles before vanishing from her sight.

I tugged my boot ties to ensure they were tight and then fussed with my hair. It wasn't cooperating today, no matter what I did with it. I turned around when someone knocked on the door frame and smiled at Father.

"Are you ready?" he asked, walking in.

"I think so?" I honestly couldn't be certain. This was the first time I'd been invited to train with the warriors, but Rune specifically requested Mother and I attend today. "I'm still unsure why we're doing this today and not after the wedding tomorrow. Shouldn't we be finalizing so everything is perfect?"

Father and Rune's decision to have Leif and Frida's wedding so soon came as a surprise. I'd never seen a wedding planned in less than a year.

He chuckled and placed his hands on my shoulders, gently squeezing. "You worry too much, Astrid. Everything is taken care of."

"But how? How was this pulled together so quickly?"

Father glanced over his shoulder and then dipped his voice as if he were afraid someone would overhear. "Don't tell your brother, but Rune and I had been discussing his and Frida's betrothal the moment he showed interest in her after our failed push toward Ilka. Not that I blame your brother for the woman he chose. She's a better fit for him, just like your mother had warned me."

I pursed my lips. That made far more sense. "So, you were actually planning this wedding for a few years."

He nodded. "Yes. We had everything prepared for a wedding to happen this year. Rune only rejected Leif's first betrothal proposal to see how serious Leif was. He had every intention of approving your brother."

So the approval had nothing to do with Týr saving our family. I smiled. That made me feel better, about a lot of things. I wanted my brother to be happy, and knowing my parents wanted this as much as him, I knew he'd have that.

Father shifted uncomfortably. "I should warn you, Rune is still insisting I discuss your marriage prospect with Bjarke. I believe he plans to push the issue again today by pairing you two together for training."

I gazed at him, contemplating whether I should bring this up. "Father, forgive me for knowing, but I'm aware of the alliance you brokered with Rune. I don't know the details on how that came about, but I do know you promised both your first-born daughter and first-born son in marriage to his two first borns."

Father's eyebrow spiked. "How did you learn about that?"

I smiled sheepishly. "I overheard your argument that day Týr took Bjarke's place on my foraging trip."

Instead of anger, he belted out a hearty laugh. "I suppose I shouldn't be surprised. But yes, I did make some agreements many years ago with Rune as an effort to cement our family's position and wealth when he aimed for control over Runavík. Your brother's marriage was part of that. Why do you bring it up?"

I puffed out a breath. "Why have you gone back on that with me?"

He gazed at me for a long moment, his eyes searching for… something. "Because after seeing you grow into the woman you are, I realized that marriage was not going to be a good fit. Bjarke would make a fine husband for you, I have no doubts, but you… you and him would not be a strong match for a lasting marriage."

While what he said made sense, it felt as though he wasn't telling me his whole reason. "If you had this agreement with Rune, why did you allow me to be betrothed several times before?"

Rune had been our jarl since before I was born. I grew up on the stories of how he'd taken control of the town and made us prosperous.

Father nodded. "Yes, you're correct; I did approve of your other betrothals. The reason was because Rune decided he was not interested in pursuing the marriage alliance for you. He still intended to keep the agreement with your brother, when he came of age, but that was it."

I frowned. I knew where this was going. "My lack of magic meant Rune hadn't seen me worthy of Bjarke. The moment it manifested was when he pushed the issue again, isn't it?"

Father scowled. "Yes, which is also why I have denied him."

I blinked slowly.

"I will not allow him to disrespect you like that. Your worth is greater than your völva magic. And if he cannot see it, then he is not worthy of a past promised alliance."

My smile wobbled, emotions tightening my throat. "Thank you, Father. I'm trying my best to do you proud."

He leaned in and kissed my forehead. "Since you first drew breath, you have been the light of my days and the strength of my heart. You have made me the proudest father, and that pride has grown with every step you've taken. There is no greater honor than to call you my daughter. That is why only the best will do for you. I do not care about alliance tradition. Your mother and I broke that ourselves, and I will uphold that path. Your happiness comes first."

Father patted my shoulder. "Now, let's get moving. Your mother should be done with Leif by now, and we don't want to be too late."

I nodded and we walked out of my and Leif's shared room. "Is there anything I should expect?"

This would be my first time training with the warriors. Hel, it would be my first time seeing a Berserker in their bestial shape. There was a Runavík law that prevented Berserker warriors from taking their beast form within the town. It had been like that for generations, to supposedly protect us.

Father made a thoughtful sound. "Seeing a Berserker for the first time in their beast form might be frightening."

I shrugged. "They can't be any scarier than Fenrir, and I can handle him."

Father shot me a perplexed look. "When you returned from your excursion with Týr, you only mentioned that Freyja taught you magic. What was Fenrir's involvement in that?"

Oh, right, I had left out that part. I'd been so tired that day, and then there were the wedding plans to focus on. "Týr, Baldr, and Fen were sparring while Freyja trained me in some magic. The three gods fell too far into the throws of battle, so Freyja showed me magic that would stop them from a distance."

Father took great interest in this. "How did you do?"

I shrugged. "Well, I think. They stopped immediately, like they were supposed to."

"And was Fenrir as terrifying as they say?"

I thought for a moment. I had expected to fear Fenrir. All the stories told of how frightening the wolf-god was. But I never felt fear. Yes, seeing him run at us at a full gallop had startled me into using defensive magic, but his presence didn't frighten me, no matter the shape he took. "I believe others would have found him frightening, even though he wasn't as monstrously large as he's said to be in battle. But, as odd as it might sound, I never felt in danger in his presence. He's comfortable and fun to be around. I don't find him frightening."

Father stared at me for a moment and then belted out a hearty laugh. "You remind me every day how much like your mother you are."

"Except scary," I said.

He smirked. "Trust me, Astrid, that is not a fault of yours. No one is as frightening as your mother."

I grinned. Father was drawn to Mother's danger. He told us the stories of how he fell in love with her more times than I could count. I never grew tired of hearing it—hearing his passion for her.

"I'm frightening, am I?" Mother said. She stood behind Leif, braiding his hair. Like me, she was wearing trousers and a padded tunic. She also had an added layer of specially made maille hauberk.

I was shocked when she brought me the clothes to wear. People took such issue with my gathering dress, I didn't expect it to be okay to dress this way for fighting. But Mother did have a good point, a dress was wholly impractical for battle.

Father left my side and swept Mother into his arms. He pressed his forehead against hers. "You are a force greater than the fiercest storm and sharper than the finest blade. No warrior nor god would dare cross you, yet the Norns saw fit to bless me with you as my wife. I am the luckiest man alive to stand beside the most terrifying, magnificent woman I have ever known. There is no greater honor."

She hummed appreciatively and kissed him.

I smiled, fighting back the twisting emotions inside me. Their love was only something I could dream of having. *My chance died many winters ago...*

A loud knock on the door saved me from my spiraling thoughts. I opened it to find Bjarke on the other side. Unlike Father and Leif, who donned maille hauberks, Bjarke only wore a simple tunic and trousers.

I knew I didn't have anything as sturdy as the rest of my family because Mother claimed standard metal armor interfered with our magic. We needed specially crafted armor made of elven silver, and acquiring it was difficult. I'd be lucky to have my own hauberk before Leif's child was born.

Yet, I did not expect for Bjarke to appear so casual, especially not for one of his position. Was this normal for Berserkers? I supposed I'd find out soon enough.

"Heill, Bjarke," I greeted.

He grinned. "Morning. I was tasked to fetch you. Are you ready?"

I glanced at my family, who were gathering a few last minute things. "I believe so."

"Excellent. I want to see what your magic can do. Father hasn't stopped talking about how you were trained by Freyja recently. Is that true?"

I rolled my eyes. "Mother should have kept her mouth shut about that."

The moment I mentioned to her that Freyja had taught me magic, she gushed to everyone who would listen how special I was.

"I will not," she said as she came up behind me. "It's an honor for a völva to be trained by Freyja. I remember when she blessed me with her experience."

Bjarke took a startled step back. "You as well, Randi?"

Mother smirked. "Oh yes. I was about Astrid's age."

I blinked slowly. I knew Mother had come in contact with the gods before, a long time ago, but she never specified who. And Freyja had never mentioned she'd met and trained Mother. I'd have to ask about that more in private.

A wide grin appeared on Bjarke's face. "Now I must see what you've learned, Astrid."

I shook my head. "Don't get excited. I promise you, it's nothing special yet."

His doubt was plain as day on his face. "We'll see about that. Let's catch up with the others before we annoy my father."

Mother ushered me out the door. "He knows better than to rush völvur. But if not, I'll be sure to remind him."

"I would like to request that it be extra painful," Bjarke said. "He's been grouchier than normal lately and it's got us all on edge."

"I will keep that in mind." The wicked smile on her lips sent a chill down my spine. It even gave Bjarke pause, as if he momentarily regretted making his request.

Everyone but me knew where we were going. Out of town was all I understood, but not far since we were going by foot. The sounds of the forest died off the closer we came to the gathering. I didn't know what to expect, but such a large gathering wasn't it.

My eyes darted around at all the warriors. Most were men, but there were women here, too. *I'm going to have to embarrass myself in front of everyone here?* I liked this whole situation less and less. And as conversations died and eyes turned our way, that feeling grew.

Rune approached, a scowl on his face. He, like Bjarke, was wearing simple clothes, not real armor. There had to be some significance to that choice I wasn't aware of yet.

He opened his mouth to speak, but Mother said something first. "You tell us we're late and you'll be a mare by the end of this training."

he grunted, his lips quirking. "I see you're in a good mood as always, Randi."

"As much as you are." The warning in her tone sent a shiver down my spine. It, however, made Rune grin.

His reaction to her behavior confused me. The last time I overheard her bite back at him, he'd threatened her and Father had stepped in. Maybe I didn't understand the dynamic between the three of them. There was a lot of history that they never talked about.

Rune turned his attention to me. "Are you ready, Astrid? We're interested to see what you've learned recently."

I pursed my lips. "I feel as though you all expect I learned years' worth of training in a single day. It is clear no one here understands how difficult it is to harness magic, even with a goddess' guiding hand."

Rune grinned. "We'll temper our expectations. At the very least you'll be able to show us what you're able to heal when we're—"

I held up a hand to silence him. "I won't heal reckless wounds."

Warriors murmured amongst themselves. Rune's face twitched as he tried to remain pleasant with me, while he was clearly annoyed with my interruption. "What do you mean by that? You are our völva. Your duty is—"

"To use my magic to aid our people, yes," I said. "However, I will not allow anyone to take advantage of my magic."

"You can't deny our warriors healing."

"I never said I would. I will, however, refuse to heal those who are needlessly reckless, assuming I will heal their injuries. You can go home to your wives and families and explain how you have the wits of a sheep."

"You don't decide that." There was a dark edge to his voice that teetered on that growl I'd heard him use on Mother.

The thing was, he didn't frighten me. Maybe it was my time spent with the gods that emboldened me. Maybe it's because Fenrir truly was the most terrifying being I'd crossed paths with, and I didn't find him scary in the least. Maybe I never gave myself enough credit for how little anyone would intimidate me.

I offered him a sickly-sweet smile. "Actually, I do. I'm a völva, as you so kindly pointed out, Rune. That means I decide how my magic is used."

His jaw and shoulders tightened and his eyes narrowed. It added to his intimidating presence that tested my stubbornness and grit. Even a few warriors shifted uncomfortably.

Then, Rune grinned and relaxed, the intimidation and danger vanishing. "You do well taking after your mother. Good. We need our völvur with strong wills."

Mother grunted. "As if you thought she'd be intimidated by you, Rune."

"Wait until she sees us Berserkers," someone shouted out from somewhere in the gathered warriors. Many, those who I also guessed were Berserkers, chuckled.

I crossed my arms. "You won't scare me."

Bjarke mirrored my stance. "You may have a strong will, Astrid, but not even you will be immune to our terrifying presence."

"I spent an entire day with Fenrir—none of you will frighten me," I said.

No one spoke. There were silent exchanges made, as if everyone was gauging who believed me.

Bjarke grabbed the edges of his tunic. "Well, then let's test your bravery."

Father pulled me back a few paces, muttering something about it not being safe to be around transforming Berserkers. Bjarke removed his tunic, showing off his well-toned and muscled upper physique, and the prominent tattoo of a bear paw on his chest. I may not be interested in pursuing him as a husband, but I appreciated a handsome man when I saw one.

Bjarke took in a slow breath and as he breathed out, his head twitched. He twitched again, this time his shoulders joining in. His face contorted and brown hair began to grow all over his body. His form twisted and grew in a hulking way.

I watched, awed by such a slow transformation. Fenrir's was much quicker. Were all Berserkers this slow to shapeshift, or was he doing it for my benefit? Everyone seemed convinced I'd be terrified seeing the Berserkers for the first time.

A low, huffing growl came from Bjarke as his transformation completed. Gone was the man I arrived here with, and in his place was a massive bipedal bear. Not entirely a bear, though. There was a humanness to his shape that separated him from an actual bear on its back legs.

I could see why he needed to remove his tunic. It would have been in tatters by the end of the transformation. Though, I was surprised his trousers held up. *For the best. I'm sure none of them want to be running into battle with their manhood flopping about.* I'd seen enough drunken, naked men running about in my life, and watched Fenrir fight naked, to know how silly they looked, rather than intimidating.

I took a step forward. Bjarke chuffed just like a bear. His nose twitched and sniffed the air, and his small, round ears swiveled in my direction as he watched me. His focus and presence alerted my senses to a dangerous predator in my midst. And yet, like with Fenrir, I was not afraid.

Bjarke's massive head swung side to side as I closed the distance, and then he roared at me.

I stopped, blinking bemusedly at him. "Was that supposed to make you frightening?"

Laughter boomed through the gathering, my words cutting the tension in the air like the sharpest blade.

Bjarke blinked and shook his head. *"You are a rare spark."*

Like I'd heard with Fenrir in his wolf form, the sounds out of Bjarke's mouth were more harsh growls and grunts than actual words, but what penetrated my mind was a slightly clearer formation of words.

I motioned for him to bend closer. I wanted a better look at him. He was of an unusually tall stature as a man, towing over me on a regular day. Transformed, he was even larger.

Bjarke crouched, the motion strangely human, messing with my mind. At least Fenrir looked and moved like a true wolf. I reached out to touch Bjarke and he didn't stop me.

My fingers sunk into the plush, soft fur on the top of his head. *Wow.* It was just like touching a real bear. I touched his ears, unable to resist.

Bjarke jerked away. *"Astrid."*

I laughed at the warning growl in his voice. "Can't blame me for trying."

He grunted. I resumed my exploration, touching his shoulders and trailing my hand down his massive arms. Bjarke offered his enormous paw, pads and claws facing up. His claws were a sharp weapon. I could see how easily they'd tear through flesh and bone.

I stepped back when I was satisfied. "Not frightening in the least."

Bjarke grunted, though I wasn't sure if the sound was one of disappointment or something else. Hopefully the more I was around Berserkers, the easier it'd be to decipher such sounds.

Rune's eyes narrowed, as if my claim was offensive. Then, faster than I could fully process, his tunic tore and his body transformed. He took his bear shape faster than Bjarke, at the speed I had originally expected. My pulse raced as Rune roared.

Magic built in me and in my fright, it shot out, slamming into Rune like an invisible barrier and throwing him back. Warriors scrambled out of the way. Rune landed hard on the ground with a pained grunt. I breathed hard, my heart pounding in my ears.

Mother and Father burst into a fit of laughter, Father patting my shoulder.

"Serves you right, Rune," Father said.

The jarl grunted and slowly pushed himself off the ground. *"I needed to be sure she had survival instincts. She was too calm."*

Mother sniffed. "Of course she was. She's my daughter."

Bjarke grunted. *"Leif almost soiled his trousers his first time."*

Leif punched the Berserker in the arm. "I did not."

I laughed. I had a feeling I was part of a select few who didn't have a healthy fear of Berserkers. Honestly I should—I should have feared Fenrir more than I did, too, but for some reason I didn't. And as more of the warriors transformed, many bears but some—warriors who were of leaner builds—became wolves, that fear should have really shown itself as I became surrounded by man-beasts. Yet, this was the safest I'd felt in a long time.

Bjarke nudged me. *"We've shown you our tricks. Now, show us yours. What did Freyja teach you?"*

I shook my head. "It's nothing special. She taught me how to make my magic take physical shape."

And to teleport, but I wasn't going to reveal that to anyone yet. I'd promised Freyja I would only practice that with her until I could control it better. She was working on finding an enchanted artifact that would help them find me should we have a repeat what happened last time, or worse.

Even though I'd said the manifesting spell was nothing special, the murmurs of excitement from the warriors said I was the only one who thought that way. And so I was going to have to perform a new spell in front of everyone. *Freyja, please let this go right.*

Taking a deep breath, I concentrated on my hand to manifest a dagger. It was the easiest for me right now. I had tried larger weapons in my alone time, but that hadn't gone so well.

Golden light formed in my hand and a shape took form. It solidified into a near-perfect weapon. More murmuring erupted through the gathered warriors. They were far more excited about this than I expected.

Father held out his hand and I handed over the weapon, curious as to whether this would hold. I'd yet to let anyone touch them. Most of the time I had them hover in the air.

The dagger remained stable through the transfer and I noticed a sensation shift in me with my magic. Father manipulated the weapon in his hand and sliced the blade through the air. Someone procured a shield for him to stab over and over. He even tested it on the boss of the shield. The weapon didn't so much as chip.

When Father was satisfied, he turned his attention to me. "I don't want to hear you downplay your magic ever again."

I huffed. "It's a magical weapon. It's not that special."

"This weapon holds up better than anything we've brought here today," Father corrected. "One of these in the hands of a warrior would be—"

I released my hold on the magic and the weapon dispersed in a shimmer of gold. "A risk. I need my full concentration to maintain the magic. Even the slightest slip and the warrior will go from the most powerful, to the most vulnerable."

"The more you practice the magic, the easier that should become,"

Mother said, not helping my case. Yes, I wanted them to see me as more than just a healer, but I also didn't want them thinking they could rely on me to replace their weapons.

"How many of those can you make?" Leif asked.

I pursed my lips. "I've been successful at maintaining three for extended periods of time. Brief periods, I can do five. All small weapons, too. Larger ones, I'm still trying to figure out."

"You will use this time to practice, then," Rune commanded. *"Bjarke, you'll train with her."*

Just as Father warned. I couldn't say I was surprised, either. The more useful a völva I was, the more desirable a match I'd become despite the other areas I lacked in before. And that made those men an unworthy match. I was more than my völva magic.

"Leif, you'll train with them," Father said. "We don't need you getting too hurt before your wedding. Frida is forgiving, but not that forgiving."

Chuckles rumbled through the warriors. My brother rolled his eyes but didn't argue. I also didn't miss the side-eye Rune gave Father. But he was at least smart enough not to make a scene in front of everyone.

Warriors grouped up. When Mother loudly announced Rune would practice with her, everyone caught his wince and uneasy agreement. Bjarke chuckled as he encouraged me to follow him away from the gathered warriors.

"Bjarke, what's it like being a bear?" I asked.

He made a rumbling sound that I guessed was him thinking. *"It's hard for me to describe as it feels natural to me. It's a more primal side to me, but it also doesn't feel wholly different than being a man."*

I pursed my lips. That response wasn't any more helpful than when I asked Fenrir questions about him being a wolf. "When did Odinn make you a Berserker?"

He shook his head. *"He didn't. I was born this way."*

My brow furrowed. "I don't understand. The stories say Berserkers are men Odinn blessed with an animal spirit that would transform them in battle."

He nodded. *"Yes, that is how the first Berserkers and some lucky warriors after were made. However, the sons they had, and in rare occasions even their daughters, were born with their own beast inside them."*

I pressed my lips together. "Then… how have I not known that? We've known each other since we were children."

"For other's safety, we Berserkers are kept separate from everyone else until we're able to control ourselves. It can take a few winters. We met a few days after I was deemed safe to be around."

I nodded slowly. That made sense. "How do you know a child is born a Berserker?"

He gave a toothy grin, which was a strange thing to look at. *"It's quite obvious when your baby comes out looking half-beast."*

I blinked, my eyes wide. That… was not what I expected him to say. "Well, I suppose that's quite the sight, I'm sure."

"As strange as it might sound, they're actually rather cute," he said. *"I'm sure, with your healing abilities, you'll be asked to oversee some Berserker births in due time."*

I made a thoughtful sound. I did want to see that. "Is there a difference between made and born Berserkers?"

"Father says it is easier for us to coexist with our beasts. Our beast is comfortable in our bodies because it was born in it. As a result, our beast understands us better and it's easier for us to understand our beast. Those who are made lose control more often because they're having to fight their beast regularly."

"Do you lose control?" It was important to know what I was possibly dealing with during this training.

He nodded. *"I can. My control is good for my age, so you don't have anything to worry about."*

"If you lost control, what would we have to do?"

"Beat him into submission," Leif said, as if that was the easiest task ever. "The beast has to be tamed back to allow the man to wrestle control again."

I pursed my lips. That seemed excessive. There had to be another way.

A hand clamped down on my shoulder and I jumped out of my skin. I might have even shrieked. Bjarke and Leif laughed, as did Father.

I pressed my hand to my chest. "Don't do that. I thought you went with the other warriors."

Father grinned. "No, I will be overseeing your training while your mother teaches Rune a lesson."

My eyes flicked to where Mother was summoning tendrils of dark magic to fight with. "I'm a little disappointed I won't be able to watch that."

"There will be other times," Father promised. "The two of them pair up like this all the time."

I nodded slowly. It was clear I didn't know depth of the relationship between my parents and Rune.

Bjarke found a good spot away from the growing chaos of the other warriors. The shouts, roars, and cheers were overwhelmingly distracting, even this far away.

Father nodded his approval. "This will do nicely. Since this will be Astrid's first time in this environment, I want to ease her in before we push her as hard as any other warrior. And to do that effectively, I want to start off by understanding what happens when Astrid tries to make a weapon larger than a dagger."

I pressed my lips together and nodded. This wasn't the time to try and argue about my abilities. That's what training was about. I could do a lot on my own or with Mother or Freyja, but this style of training offered me something those other trainings couldn't.

Focusing on what a sword should look like, I drew my magic out. In front of me, a golden flame-like formation manifested in the shape of a sword.

Father's brow rose with interest and he took a good look at the magical weapon. He reached for it and his fingers passed right through. He shuddered and took several steps back. "Interesting. There is no heat but it felt dangerous. With some more focus, that could be deadlier than a real weapon."

Bjarke tapped his shoulder with a massive claw. *"Let's try."*

I hesitated. "Are you sure?"

Father chuckled. "The larger reason you were paired with him is because of how hearty Berserkers are. They have self-healing capabilities."

My back straightened. "Like the gods do? I was able to watch how quickly they heal. It was quite fascinating."

Bjarke shook his head. *"If I were a made Berserker, I would heal similarly to immortals and gods. Odinn's blessing is stronger in them. We born Berserkers heal slower and sometimes not as well. They heal in minutes, even a deadly wound, whereas we would need a day or two to heal from something like that."*

I tapped my lips. *Interesting.* I knew so little about Berserkers, yet it was clear a good number of warriors in the town had these bestial souls. I was eager to learn more from these experiences.

Angling the magical weapon toward him, I made sure he was ready before spearing his shoulder. The magic pierced his body like he was made of water, sticking out the other side of him. Bjarke thrashed his head and grunted, his lips pulling back in a snarl. Not as much of a pain response from him as a real weapon might have caused, but as he scrabbled at the weapon protruding from his shoulder, I watched him fail to remove it.

I also noticed something interesting about his movements. "Can you not move your arm?"

He shook his head and grunted in frustration. *"No."*

Leif glanced at me with an impressed expression. "Unexpected but impressive result, Sister."

Father nodded. "I agree. That may have more potential than fully-formed weapons."

I tapped a finger against my lips. "I should focus on these. They're not as draining on my magic, so I should be able to produce more while getting used to so many distractions around me. I can work on solidifying them later once I find my next limit."

"Then that will be your task while I train these two." Father placed his hand affectionately against my cheek and smiled. "I expect to see you pushing yourself while we do the same."

I grinned. "I hope you don't expect me to heal your old bones when the big bear knocks you around too often."

He laughed. "These old bones are far more experienced than this child bear."

Bjarke chuffed out a half-growling sound and squared his shoulders. He wouldn't take Father's challenge lying down.

I took several steps back and focused on my task, while the men began theirs.

EIGHT

BALDR

Gravel and loose forest debris crunched under my feet. A raven called in the distance. I set a leisurely, unhurried pace down the well-used road through the forest, enjoying the solitude after so much rowdiness the last few days. I thrived in battle and enjoyed the energy and activities of the celebrations after, but sometimes, I just needed calm and quiet. Or, as quiet as a god could have with prayers whispering over our senses.

I didn't have a destination in mind. I wasn't even sure how long I'd been wandering. My feet carried me and I allowed it. If my father or anyone else needed me, they could come find me.

I came to a stop when a hen chicken casually walked out of the brush onto the road. She pecked at the ground without a care. I watched the peculiar sight. What was a chicken doing out here? Was there a settlement nearby?

Listening, I heard the rush of flowing water in the distance. Then came the sounds of a town. *I wonder where I am.* Deciding it would be best if the hen wasn't left to its own devices, I scooped her up. She clucked and let out a disgruntled sound, but didn't try to fight my gentle hold. Not that she could harm me.

Cradling her in my arm, I moved through the forest until it thinned into a riverside clearing. A wooden palisade protected this side of the town, though as I approached, magic whispered over my skin. *A ward.*

Normally those couldn't be felt, but this one was done this way intentionally. The völva protecting this place wanted the warning to be known.

It also felt… familiar.

An old dog lay at the entrance of the palisade. He lifted his head and wagged his tail. I took the time to stop and give him some attention. It'd be a crime to walk by and ignore him.

When I was ready to continue on, I found I'd caught the attention of curious eyes from the townsfolk. No doubt I looked rather strange: a giant of a man petting a dog while holding a chicken.

Two young women approached. One woman, who seemed around Astrid's age, stood tall and exuded an air of confidence. Her long golden hair cascaded down her back. Her sharp keens eyes tracked my movements. The other woman, I guessed a few winters younger, had a gentler presence. Her long golden hair flowed in soft, loose waves down her back, a few strands framing her soft face.

Both women dressed in fine clothes and adorned themselves with quality shawls and jewelry.

With them, several people followed at a reserved pace. Most of them carried something. They wore basic tunics and had short cropped hair, regardless of their sex. Every one of them had collars around their necks. Thralls.

"Heill, Baldr, son of Odinn," the older woman said. "I am Ilka and this is my sister Frida. On behalf of our father, Jarl Rune, it is a pleasure to have you in Runavík."

Runavík? I'd made my way to Astrid's town. While a surprise, it was a pleasant one. I'd wanted to see her again after Týr introduced us the other day.

I smiled at them both. "Thank you. I found this hen wandering the woods on my way here. I thought maybe her owner would want her back."

Frida smiled. "That was kind of you. We'll ensure she's returned to her proper owner."

She gestured to one of the thralls with free hands to take the bird from me and instructed them to find the proper owner.

Ilka approached. "Is there anything in particular we can help you with, Baldr? Or are you passing through?"

Her words were throaty and her posture was alluring. This woman was quite the beauty.

"Could you point me in the direction of Völva Astrid?" If I was here, I didn't want to leave without seeing her. I wanted to know more about her. She was such a fascinating woman. I understood why Týr was so taken with her.

Ilka's nose scrunched, and her allure turned sour. "What do you want with her?"

The corners of my lips turned down. I didn't like the underlying tone of animosity in her voice.

Frida rolled her eyes at her sister. "It doesn't matter. Baldr, I'll be happy to show you where she's training with the warriors."

I liked this woman. She seemed genuinely kind. "I don't need to trouble you. Directions will be fine."

She shook her head. "I was going to stop by with some food for them just now, so it's no trouble at all."

How convenient my timing was. Or was Creation trying to tell me something?

"You don't have time for something as ridiculous as that," Ilka admonished. "We have preparations to finalize. Send the thralls out to feed them."

"Feeding our warriors is a great honor, Ilka. They keep us safe and ensure we have many riches when they return from their explorations. But if you're so worried about preparations, you can handle them while I step away."

Her sister's scowl was ugly. It fractured her beauty and showed a more real appearance of her.

"I would appreciate that, thank you, Frida Runesdóttir," I said, hoping to diffuse any fight about to transpire between the two women.

Frida shot her sister a warning glare and then encouraged me to follow her. I swore I heard Ilka growl.

"Please don't pay me sister's behavior any mind," Frida said when we'd left earshot. "She's as temperamental as my father, and the stress of my wedding has made things worse."

I smiled. "I will not hold her behavior against you. When do you wed?"

"Tomorrow."

Ah, that explained much. "Does she take issue with Astrid? She didn't even try to hide her distaste to my desire to see her."

Frida blew out a tired breath. "Unfortunately, yes. Because my sister seeks a new husband, she has a foul attitude toward all the unmarried women in Runavík, but she has a particular distaste for Astrid."

"Why is that?" I couldn't see why anyone would hate Astrid.

Her lips twisted. "She's jealous. Any woman who holds a man's attention better than her earns her scorn, but with Astrid's more recent magical developments, and now the attention of gods along with eligible men, it's made Ilka act worse toward her. She has an inflated sense of self and can't accept that she is not the most desirable eligible woman in town."

"Fixing her attitude would greatly improve her standing, I would think."

Frida laughed. "I should not find that truth amusing, or speak so ill of my sister, but I also cannot be dishonest about the very truths about her."

I smiled down at her. "It takes more courage to be honest and feel the wrath of those who do not appreciate such an approach than it is to lie and be falsely loved by all."

She nodded slowly. "Yes, that's very true."

"Do you like Astrid?" I was curious what a kinder person like Frida thought of the woman with hair like fire, a tongue and wit sharper than the dagger Loki used to cut Sif's hair, and a personality that made you feel as though the sun was gently caressing you with warmth.

"I love her." Her beaming smile couldn't be faked. "She's so kind and intelligent, as well as resourceful. Her fierceness, in the way she protects those she is loyal to, is admirable. I am so honored to be marrying into her family."

My interest grew. "You're marrying her brother?"

Her eyes lit up. "I've never known such warmth in my heart. To know that I will share my life, my hearth, and my heart with such a man as Leif… the Norns themselves had to have selected our match. I cannot wait to stand by his side, to face whatever comes our way."

The way she exuded joy, I had no doubts he made her one of the happiest women alive. That was good. I could tell she was a woman who deserved to be treated like the most valuable treasure a man could ever possess.

Frida gestured ahead of us. "There they are."

I blinked and took in my surroundings. We'd apparently left the town without me realizing and were in a forest clearing. There were many gathered here, all spread out, but they appeared to be mostly conversing. There was a faint sense of battle here whispering across my senses now that I wasn't distracted. *They must have stopped for a rest recently.*

I took in the unusually large number of Berserkers in the area. I wasn't aware this town had so many. To my knowledge, there were few places in these parts where Berserkers congregated in high numbers. They were on the rare side, given how my father rarely bestowed that honor to a warrior these days—*I can't remember the last time he deemed a man worthy*—and how often they died in battle.

These Berserkers had to be born ones, yet they all couldn't have been born here, right? They must have migrated this way. But if that was true, why? Was it related to how this town had two völvur with a long ancestral bloodline of women possessing magic?

My gaze slipped to a small woman with red hair and dark makeup. I blinked. *Randi?* Could it be her? It'd been so long. But if that was the case, then…

Frida waved to someone, drawing my attention. A young man with fair, braided hair bolted from a cluster of mostly sitting people and rushed right for her. I couldn't stop my smile when he reached her and hauled her into his arms as she giggled. These two were so madly in love, Freyja or Freyr could have blessed this match themselves.

He froze when he finally noticed me. I chuckled when Frida shut his unhinged jaw.

"It's good to meet you, Leif," I said. "Your sister speaks highly of you."

He hadn't come up much in conversation, but Astrid had nothing but good things to say about her brother. It was nice hearing the two were close. I knew all too well how difficult some family could be. Getting along with at least one sibling was a blessing.

"What's wrong, Leif?" a familiar low feminine voice called out. "Berserker got your tongue?"

I snickered as he snapped out of his daze and shot a glare over his shoulder. Astrid sat on the ground in front of a wolf Berserker, her golden magic crawling along one of his legs. She was dressed for battle, in a way. Not in something I'd recommend a völva to wear, but maybe there was a reason for it. She'd made attempts to tame back her hair, but it was as resistant to be controlled as her.

Sitting with her was a large young man around her age who shared similarities with Frida, as well as an older man whom I could tell was related to Leif. *I know him as well.*

My feet carried me toward Astrid without me having to think. It was like some pull to be near her. I felt it when I first laid eyes on her. It intensified every moment I was with her that day. The more I glimpsed who she was, the more I needed to see and learn.

Astrid glanced up from her work. Those stunning eyes of hers snagged my undivided attention. And the way she smiled, it was like being greeted by the sun itself. My pulse skipped for the briefest moment. *If only Týr hadn't laid claim to her before I could...*

"I hope you didn't come out all this way to see me," she said.

"I'm sorry to disappoint you, but"—I grinned—"I did."

She laughed. That whimsical and warm sound was an addictive fiery caress along my senses, drawing me in, burning and leaving me wanting more.

I sat next to her, watching her work. The man didn't appear injured on the outside, but his leg did look as though it bent incorrectly. I was also aware of how much pain the Berserker was working hard to hide.

Frida whispered to Leif, asking what was going on, and I listened in on the answer: Astrid was attempting to heal an old injury. Apparently she was putting the knowledge she obtained with us gods to good use, though everyone around her was a bit skeptical from what I could tell. They were in for quite the surprise.

"This will be the most painful part," Astrid warned the Berserker.

"There's more?" he gritted out through clenched teeth.

She tried not to smile. "The last."

"Fine, get it over with."

Her brow lifted and she stared at him instead of advancing her healing as promised. The two stared at each other.

Eventually the Berserker huffed. *"Please."*

With a triumphant smile, she focused on her healing. I didn't hide my amusement. That might have been a first for me to witness. Berserkers were notoriously stubborn.

Astrid inhaled a slow, deep breath and then her magic intensified. The Berserker bared his teeth as he clenched his jaw. Unable to fight it anymore, his head tipped back and he howled in pain. His head snapped back down and his snarl sent alarm through me. My war instincts engaged, and I moved to jump to Astrid's defense.

Her healing magic died and she punched the wolf Berserker in the nose. "Enough of that."

I blinked.

So did the Berserker.

So did everyone around us.

There hadn't been any weight behind the punch, but it'd certainly done its job in stopping the man-wolf.

"You don't get to snarl and snap your teeth at me when I'm doing you a favor and healing this messed-up leg of yours," she continued to scold. "I expect better out of you."

The Berserker's ears flattened and he ducked his head. He also let out a pitiful whine that made me think of a kicked dog. He looked like one. *"Sorry, Astrid."*

I blinked more. Who was this woman who held miracle magic in her hands and didn't fear Berserkers?

There were few out there who truly didn't experience fear. Most who didn't were arrogant and it always caught up to them quickly. But Astrid wasn't that type of person, and yet I wondered how she didn't radiate the slightest bit of fear around Fenrir. Even gods feared him.

Yes, he'd startled her the other day, causing her to use her magic, but that was the only time. No matter what my friend did, she found him amusing more than anything.

And here she was, scolding a Berserker as if that were normal and safe to do. *Is it because she lives with them that she lost her fear?*

I had so many questions about this woman that I wanted answers for when others would tell me it was pointless. I didn't care she was mortal any more than Týr did. Freyja and Fenrir also liked her. She strangely fit with us where others couldn't possibly.

"You're all done," Astrid said. "Don't put too much stress on the leg for a while, understood? I will not heal you for recklessness."

The Berserker nodded and rose. He was hesitant on the leg at first, but then soon found out she really had repaired the damage. From his excitement, I suspected the injury had been a rather old one.

Those gathered marveled and talked amongst themselves about Astrid's ability. I seemed to be the only one not surprised. Well—me, the man pulling Astrid into a proud fatherly hug, and the other witch who was now approaching.

While a frightening aura surrounded her, she had a gentle smile for Astrid. "Well done, Sunshine, well done."

Sunshine. That was the perfect name for her.

Astrid smiled at the völva's praise. "Thank you. I had good practice before making this attempt."

"Oh?"

I raised my hand. "On me. My lack of ability to feel pain makes me the perfect test subject."

Astrid's lips pulled into an amused smile "That's why he's here. He's looking for more healing."

Well, I wasn't going to say no to that, but it wasn't the only reason. "I'm also here to see you. I haven't reduced your importance to just your magic."

The doubtful expression she gave was irritating. I couldn't be the first to say that to her, right? From the way a few flinched at my statement, maybe I was one of the few. Did these mortals only see her worth for her magic? How could they not see more that she offered? I certainly needed to know more about Astrid—not the völva, but the woman.

I turned to the scary völva. "It's good to see you again, Randi. Your beauty remains as untamed and wild as a storm."

She smiled. "It's been a while, Baldr. You seem to be doing well. And you've now become acquainted with my daughter."

Things made a lot more sense to me now. I didn't know Randi well, as I'd only met her a handful of times many winters ago, but she'd been an accomplished völva then. And terrifying. This explained a few things about Astrid.

Astrid glanced between us. "You two have met?"

Randi smiled. "Your father and I met him when we were about your age."

Her father nodded to confirm her statement. "It really has been that long. It's good to see you again, Baldr."

Astrid's eyebrows rose high on her forehead. Then she turned her attention to me. "You didn't mention that the other day."

"You didn't mention you were their daughter."

She pursed her lips. "I suppose this is a draw."

I grinned. "We can have a re-match anytime."

When she laughed, my pulse jumped. Her whole face lit up, like the first ray of dawn breaking, and the way her eyes squinted... For a moment, Midgard fell away, and all I saw was her.

A large bear Berserker made his way over, Frida and Leif walking with him. As he did, he shifted out of his beast shape, his stride not breaking. He was a massive man, typical of bear Berserkers, but not so much for the average man in these parts. He and the young man sitting next to Astrid shared many features, and Frida also shared similarities. I guessed this to be Jarl Rune.

He dipped his head in greeting to me. "Heill, Baldr. We're honored to have you here. Will you be staying, or stealing Astrid from us as Týr does?"

I chuckled. To abscond with her was a tempting thought. If Týr wasn't my friend, I likely would. "I intend to stay here."

"Good. You'll eat with us, then." His tone was more of a command than an offer. He was lucky I was in such an agreeable mood.

The meal was simple but hearty, perfect for warriors needing to build their strength. Conversation was good. Many here were tense and struggled to converse with me at first—a common reaction to us gods when we integrated with mortals for brief moments.

But eventually the tension eased. Astrid and her family made that easier. They were comfortable immediately and all conversation came effortlessly with them, especially Astrid.

Her mind was a fascinating labyrinth as complex as Yggrasill's roots. She spoke with wisdom beyond her years, and held a playful spark that challenged me in the best ways. I lost myself many times chasing her cleverness that she wielded like a finely honed sword.

And then there was everything else about her. She was like a flame forged from the sun itself, fierce yet warm. I could bask in her radiance forever. *Sól has nothing on this woman.*

Only, Týr was being territorial with Astrid for some reason. He'd never been this way before with a woman, so it was difficult to understand. And frustrating. The more I got to know this woman, the more I desired from her.

But, I could settle for friendship… hopefully. If that's what Astrid wanted of course. *It would be nice if she wanted more.* She could have us both, I didn't mind.

Though, I couldn't say if that would be something she'd want, or even feel she'd be allowed to have. Such allowances of women differed between the nordmann communities. *I don't understand why mortals limit themselves so much.*

The warriors broke out into training groups when the meal finished, and Frida left with her thralls to resume her wedding preparations. Astrid remained where she was with me.

"Still recovering?" I asked. It'd come up between her and Randi that she'd nearly wiped herself out in all the practice she'd done before I arrived.

She nodded. "Only a little longer. Then I should be able to heal you."

"There's no rush. And if you don't feel you'll regain enough by the time the day is done, so be it."

"Well, if I believe it'll take that long to recover, I'll let you know so you don't feel compelled to stay longer than you wish."

My brow knitted. "I'm not compelled to be anywhere. It's a choice I willingly make."

She gazed up at me with an odd look. "If not for healing, what truly brings you here?"

"A chicken."

Her eyebrow spiked. "A chicken."

I allowed a moment of silence to pass between us before cracking a grin. She laughed. Then she smacked my arm.

"Tell me the truth."

"I am. I was taking a walk of solitude to sort out my thoughts when a hen in the forest needed my help getting home. That home happened to be Runavík, and that's when I decided to come and visit you."

"Why?"

My brow furrowed. "Why? Because I enjoy spending time with you without conditions. Is that so strange?"

Her mouth pressed into a thin line. "Well, maybe. I'm struggling to understand why gods would bother when we mortals don't live all that long. And I would assume you'd find a man to have far more agreeable qualities for friendship."

I wasn't surprised by her thought process. I'd watched mortals and their rules long enough to see the rarity it was for the sexes to mix if it was not for sex, marriage, or some sort of deal. "Does friendship need to have such limiting conditions?"

She blinked slowly. Unspoken thoughts reflected in her captivating eyes as she processed my question and I wondered what in her life she was using to help her understand the meaning of my words. "No, I suppose it doesn't."

"Right, so I am here because I wish to know you more as my friend."

Astrid's lips pulled into a soft smile. My gaze flicked to her mouth briefly before I caught myself and refocused, only to be snared by her piercing eyes. There was something about her eyes—something familiar—that made it difficult to look away.

They hooked me, then peered deep into my soul, past every defense I could muster, and saw my darkest secrets and weakest parts of me that I dared not show anyone. Or maybe I'd merely spilled the truth, compelled to answer anything she asked of me because how could I deny her anything?

"I would like that."

Good. Because I wasn't sure I could stay away from her. I needed to understand this compulsion to be so close to her. And maybe, if Creation had my favor, I could convince Týr to allow me in. *What does sunshine taste like?*

I leaned back on my hands and took in a deep breath, acting as though I were getting comfortable and not trying to fix my straying thoughts. Astrid centered her attention on where her mother sparred with Rune, now back in his bear shape. He was formidable, but Randi was even more so.

She hadn't changed much. Her magic was fearsome as was her personality. And Bjǫrn, as gentle as he seemed, had turned into a fierce fighter, even for these trainings. I saw pieces of them both in Astrid. She was gentle, much like her father, but that only lured you into falsely believing she was no threat.

My mind wandered back to the other day, when she had held that magical weapon to my throat. The look she had… I still saw it in my mind's eye. Such a deadly and alluring expression that got my blood hot and cock rising against my wishes. That look she inherited from her mother.

I shifted my attention back to Astrid. I took in her features, from her beautiful cheekbones to her many freckles painted perfectly on her soft pale skin, to the perfect size of her nose, and even that stunning scar of hers that told me so much about who she was, and yet inspired more questions and desire to know more.

Her armor did little to hide her physique. Her legs were shapely and strong and her alluring body was lean and proportional. My fingers itched to run along her womanly curves that weren't overly accentuated, but still tantalizing and tempting. *Creation, help me.* I desperately wanted to know what it would be like to fall under her spell and be consumed by her.

My attention caught on a golden tendril of magic wrapped around her finger that lazily swished back and forth. It seemed she'd regained a little bit of her magic already.

Astrid focused on the tendril, and it took me a moment to realize she was trying to mimic her mother. She wasn't succeeding, from the looks of it.

Magic didn't confound me like other gods. Father used it to some extent, and Mother, she loved showing me all the tricks she knew, all the way to her last days. Thus, I understood how a user needed to learn their magic by trial and error most of the time.

There was no one way magic manifested, and it could also change over a person's life. That made Astrid's late manifestation both fascinating and strange. It usually came to a practitioner early, ensuring they used their most formidable years becoming so intimately acquainted with their magic, it was second nature for them to exist with it.

"Don't forget to breathe," I said.

Astrid puffed out a breath. "Freyja reminded me of that, too."

I snickered. "What exactly are you trying to do? I may not be gifted with magic, but I know enough that maybe I can help you."

She gestured to Randi, who was slashing Rune with her tendrils. "That. I can turn my magic into different shapes, so using it like that in its natural form shouldn't be so hard. But it just has a mind of its own."

I thought of how I'd seen her use her magic thus far. "You use it like that to heal, though."

She nodded. "Yes, but I'm not controlling that. They act on their own accord, wrapping around people where I am healing them."

"Hmm…" That didn't sound right. Magic didn't have a mind of its own. It couldn't act independently from its caster. She had to be misunderstanding how her magic wanted to be used if it worked so easily while she was healing.

My thoughts paused on that last part. She excelled at healing in ways many of us gods had never seen. But it appeared offensive uses of her magic didn't come as easily. *Maybe...*

I held up my arm. "Try to use me as a target."

Astrid blinked. "Huh?"

"When you heal, you have a target. Your mother has a current target. When you try on your own to mimic, you fail because you have no target. Maybe that's the piece you're missing."

She thought about that a moment and nodded. "It's worth a try."

Astrid repositioned herself to face me and she focused on my arm. For a long moment, nothing happened to the wisp of magic. It continued to sway like a blade of grass in the wind. Then it stilled.

Remembering to take steady breaths, Astrid focused harder. The tendril lashed out, growing and wrapping around my arm. It pulled taught, fighting against my rigid strength. I didn't feel the pain it tried to inflict, only the warmth of her magic wrapping around my skin, like a sun ray caressing me. And yet, I could see its attempt to bind as my skin discolored under the strain of her magic.

I tried to fight the magic with my strength. Astrid's face grew tighter and more determined in her concentration. To my surprise, she held against me well. I maintained quite a bit of movement, but not nearly as much as I expected.

Then the magic broke.

Astrid released a harsh breath, her shoulders relaxing. The magic dissipated into shimmers of refracting light before disappearing.

"Well done, Sunshine. Well done." As the name rolled off my tongue, a warm sensation washed through me. *Yes, that is the perfect name for her.*

Astrid blinked for a moment, as if surprised, and then smiled. Her cheeks tinted a light shade of pink. "Thank you. That wasn't as easy as I hoped, but it wasn't the most difficult thing I've tried. And thank you for the suggestion. I'm understanding how my magic works much better now."

I smiled. That was good. Any way I could help her, I was happy to do so.

"Are you ready for your healing?" she asked. "I'd like to focus on your back. I noticed some issues that I'm more confident tackling today."

I'd been hit in the back enough times to know she was likely correct and had no reason to ask her to focus on another part of me. She instructed me to face away from her and how to sit that would be best for her. I followed every instruction, from how to breathe to not moving as much as possible, to even ignoring the growing interest of the mortals around us. Whatever she wanted, I gave.

Her soft hands ran along my shoulders and down my spine. Her touch left prickles of longing trailing after her—the desire for her to touch me more. Elsewhere. Lower. Her fingers curling around my hard cock and—

I mentally chastised myself again and tried to think of anything but her hands on my body.

It wasn't working.

When she finally settled on the middle of my spine, her magic radiated out, washing over me with warmth. That was all I felt as she worked, her movements precise and calculated.

"This might sound strange," she warned just before the loud *crack* came from my back.

My spine straightened. Another crack and then a *pop*. I blinked. That sounded… unsettling. *What is she doing to me?*

Astrid tapped my hip. "Twist toward this side of you without lifting your legs."

I complied.

"Now the other way."

I twisted the opposite direction and my back popped on its own. Astrid hummed thoughtfully, instructing me to sit straight again and checked me with her magic. There seemed to be something more she was trying to figure out.

A large presence grew behind me, but I couldn't turn to see who approached. It felt familiar, and many of the mortals became tense and whispered to each other.

"Fluffy, if you interrupt this healing session, you'll be eating those tiny berries of yours," Astrid mumbled, her hands continuing to work along my back without pause. I chuckled at her threat, but it earned me a reprimanding tap on the back of the head due to my body shaking.

Fenrir gave a wolf-grunt then heavily plopped down behind us. *"Bossy today."*

I tried to glance back at him, but, again, Astrid tapped the back of my head and reprimanded me. Fenrir chuckled, then yipped when her magic flashed in my peripheral and smacked him.

"Both of you need to behave." She tapped my spine between my shoulders. "Bend forward as far as you can."

I did, folding over rather well. I tried to maintain flexibility, along with all my strength. Astrid ran her fingers down the ridge of my spine. The touch was tantalizing and distracting.

One of her hands stopped in the middle of my back, while the other continued to migrate down until she reached the lowest part of my back where it met my hips.

She pushed her fingers hard into me several times. I felt the pressure, but nothing else. It was an odd experience, though. No one had ever touched me like this.

"Found it," she mumbled. "Sit up straight again and prepare for… something. I don't know what."

That was fair. This was certainly new for me, too.

Her magic flared and then the loudest pop so far sounded from my body. Air flooded into my lungs as my back straightened more than I ever remembered it being before. A weight lifted off me that I never realized had plagued me. I felt… better. I had no words to describe this feeling.

The warmth of her magic dissipated and her hands lifted off my skin, leaving me cold. "How's that?"

I looked over my shoulder. "I've never felt this amazing. I don't know what's more magical, your abilities or you."

She responded with a beaming smile and pink tinted cheeks. It was short-lived when Fenrir laid his head on her. She squeaked as his weight overwhelmed her small body and crushed her into the ground.

"Get off me, you oversized fluff ball," she complained, pushing against his massive head. Her legs kicked helplessly as she failed to move him.

My head flew back in a burst of laughter. There was no fear in her, only annoyance, even as he pretended to get mouthy with those terrifying teeth of his as if he were going to eat her.

It didn't matter that those wolf teeth could snap out at any moment and break her. It didn't matter that Fenrir could crush her with his size if he truly wanted to. She didn't believe he'd harm her, and she was right.

Fenrir could be terrifying. He could kill as efficiently and brutally as any other war god. But that wasn't all he was. He was protective and could be gentle if he wanted. He wouldn't hurt Astrid.

Yet there was so much distrust toward Fenrir. My father didn't trust him because of some claimed prophecy predicted by one of the dragon fate sisters—what the nordmenn called the Norns. Those predictions caused most of the issue amongst the gods. Fenrir's own father, Loki, didn't help matters with his poor reputation. All of Loki's children felt the sting, whether they deserved it or not.

Not that I thought Loki deserved all the hate he received. Sure, he was an ass at times—a lot of times—but there were far worse gods who didn't get the same bad reputation as him.

That mistrust didn't extend to Astrid. So far removed from the turmoil of the gods, she saw him in ways he deserved.

And as Fenrir finally let her up and Astrid playfully flicked his ear, like the two were siblings of sorts, I couldn't help but smile as I saw yet again how oddly perfect this little mortal fit. We had only just met her, yet, it was like she had been part of our lives for so much longer. *Why would Creation create such a perfect woman, only to make her mortal?*

"What brings you here?" Astrid asked Fenrir.

"I was bored, and I overheard a bird reporting Baldr was sneaking over to see you, so I thought I would, too."

I rolled my eyes. "I don't sneak, and neither can you."

I wasn't surprised Father sent one of the ravens to check on me, even in secret. He did that a lot, and not to just me. For some reason Father felt the need to check up on all the gods, as if it were his business to know every detail of our lives.

Astrid opened her mouth to say something, when shouting and a bear roaring cut her off. Tension spiked up my spine, the sensation of conflict slamming into me.

We whirled our attention to where warriors backed away, weapons ready but unsure. The wolf Berserkers fanned out, using themselves as body shields for the human warriors. The bears clustered around one that raged out control. *This isn't good.*

A raging bear wasn't easy to subdue. Someone was going to get hurt. Astrid gasped. "Bjarke!"

She was on her feet and sprinting before I could think to stop her. *What is she doing?* My pulse spiked higher as she rushed toward the conflict.

Fenrir and I were on our feet in a blink, yet we remained planted. Why wasn't I moving? She needed to be protected. She needed to be stopped before she got too close. Not even Randi was running in. She was shouting at her daughter to stop.

Magic flared around Astrid. It formed into a flaming shape of a weapon and launched toward Bjarke. The raging Berserker swiped at the magic, missing, and exposing his arm. The magic pierced his shoulder. It didn't draw blood, but it stuck into him nonetheless.

The Berserker's arm went limp.

I blinked slowly. What was this magic?

"Bjarke, stop," Astrid ordered. Her voice was harder than I ever thought possible from her. That look—that intense, deadly look—had returned.

I sensed her fear, felt it as much as the other warriors here. But her determination was pushing harder. I wrapped my power around it, pushing down her fear. I shouldn't. I should step in, put my body between her and this beast. But that wouldn't be right. She could handle herself. That was why she ran in. *She knows what she's doing.*

Bjarke roared and lashed out with his other paw. He hit another Berserker, who raged back and shoved him. This wasn't good. Using Berserkers to subdue another was never ideal. It could trigger a chain reaction of rage, especially for bears. It was one reason bear Berserkers were more likely to be solitary.

Astrid summoned more magic and lanced it toward Bjarke. He

ducked and charged. She gasped and dove away. She clumsily hit the ground and rolled, but didn't stop. Her hands slammed down on the ground and a pulse of magic flared. I felt it from over here. It was so strong. *She has all that inside her? How much more magic has she yet to tap into?*

Golden tendrils of magic shot out of the ground. They wrapped around the Berserker, much like how she'd practiced with me earlier. The tendrils bound and constricted until Bjarke was immobilized. He thrashed and roared against the magical restraints.

Astrid's face creased with concentration. "Bjarke, snap out of it!"

That wouldn't work. Only brute force snapped a Berserker out of their rage.

My heart leapt into my throat. Astrid launched toward Bjarke. *What the hel is she doing?* He was restrained. She didn't need to get close. Now the others could beat the bear into submitting.

I took a step forward. This was going too far. She couldn't get that close. Fenrir stopped me. *"Wait."*

I glanced at him, wide-eyed. "We have to—"

"Wait."

My attention snapped back to Astrid. She closed in on the restrained Berserker, her magic pulling him closer and closer to the ground, onto his knees. She reached out and her hands clamped around his snout.

"I said stop!"

Bjarke froze.

Everyone froze.

Only Astrid's exhausted panting and the Berserkers' heavy breathing could be heard in the clearing.

My heart pounded hard in my chest. She'd done it. She'd subdued him without the typical means. *Who is this woman? What is she?*

Something pressed against the back of my mind. A vague memory. A red-haired Valkyrie with silver and gold fire wings, subduing a raging Berserker so similarly to this. No, not fire wings. Valkyries didn't have wings like that. It had definitely been just silver and gold feathers.

Why did this moment make me think of that memory? Who was

that Valkyrie anyway? I couldn't recall any of my father's Valkyries sharing that appearance, and I knew all the Valkyries. *Don't I?*

"Bjarke, come out of that form," Astrid ordered, her voice strong and commanding in the silence. "Your bear needs rest."

His ears swiveled toward her and a low growl rumbled from him. She jerked his head down in reprimand. "Rest."

The bear huffed and slowly released the man. Astrid let out a small breath and lowered herself to her knees.

Bjarke chuckled, quiet at first, that grew louder. Astrid joined him in his laughter, the tension of the situation releasing.

"Crazy völva. What is wrong with you?" Bjarke said between breaths.

Astrid shook her head. "I don't know."

This only made them laugh harder. Others joined in. Even Fenrir was chuckling. I was still trying to process what I'd witnessed.

Astrid released her magical hold on Bjarke and she checked him for any injury she may have caused. She'd barely gotten done with her check before he pulled her into a headlock and lifted them both to his feet. His massive size lifted her right off her feet. She complained and flailed, which only intensified the mirth, even in me.

"Bjarke, let me go," she demanded.

He grinned and released her. She stumbled and glared up at him before punching him in the arm. He pretended she wounded him, listing to one side, then grabbed her around the waist and hauled her on his shoulder.

She squeaked, but didn't complain, instead looking around on her perch. "Wow, you can see a lot from up here."

Bjarke barked out a laugh and said something I missed. I was distracted by the way Rune looked Bjǫrn's way, and Bjǫrn's glare in response.

It appeared she had a unique relationship with Bjarke that caused some tension between their fathers. They were about the same age, it seemed; Astrid might have been slightly older, but Týr said she was not promised to any man. So if that was the case, why the tension? I was clearly missing something about this relationship that caused the strain.

"As you can see, this is a good place for Berserkers," a familiar female voice said.

Eyes turned where Freyja, Týr, and a burly woman with dark brown hair stood. Astrid immediately waved at them. Freyja waved back and Týr's stoic expression cracked immediately.

Before Astrid, I couldn't remember a time he looked this happy. He always seemed a little… lost. A lot of the older gods did, like they were missing something. It was like Astrid was the piece he was missing. *Another reason to respect my friend's desire to have her, even if the temptation is strong.*

Why it was so strong was a mystery to me. But as I watched the way she smiled and sat so comfortably amongst gods and Berserkers, I knew this woman wasn't someone I could walk away from.

"Jarl Rune, a word with you," Týr said.

Rune approached, as did a few others. They didn't follow as closely, their attention on people behind the newcomer and two gods whom I didn't notice before. There were quite a few, and from the looks of it, they carried everything they owned.

Rune conversed with the burly woman, who had a strong air about her that made me think of bear Berserkers. Was she one? Female Berserkers were rare, as their bodies couldn't typically handle the beast within, but they did exist.

Bjarke delivered Astrid to Fenrir and me and then went to join his father. Being a jarl's son, it was important for him to be involved in whatever was going on.

Astrid looked to us for answers. "Do you know what's happening?"

I shook my head. "No idea."

"The woman smells like a Berserker," Fenrir confirmed. *"Many that have arrived are Berserkers."*

More Berserkers?

Randi approached and wrapped her arms around her daughter. "They may be looking for a new place to live. That's how we've obtained so many over the years."

That explained quite a bit about this place and its Berserker population. "This group is quite sizable."

"Yes, that part is strange."

Fenrir lifted his head. *"We may get some answers."*

I looked up. Kirby, her dark wings flared wide, descended from the sky. She landed lightly beside me. She noticed the newcomers and nodded, seemingly to herself. "They made it. That's good."

"What's going on?" I asked.

"Nothing good. All war gods are being called back by Odinn to discuss the situation." She grinned at Astrid. "But first, is it true you subdued a raging Berserker with your bare hands?"

Astrid blinked. "Uh, yes, but no? I used magic for most of it. How did you hear that?"

Kirby gestured to the trees where a large raven perched. "Muninn communicated to Huginn, who announced it to Odinn while I was receiving orders."

Astrid's mouth parted in a bit of awe. "He's beautiful."

Even from here, I could see his prideful puff-up of feathers and he croaked back softly. Father didn't like it when the ravens engaged with mortals, so he wouldn't, which was a shame. I was sure she'd like both Huginn and Muninn.

Bjǫrn came up behind Astrid and Randi, and placed his hands on each of their shoulders. "I think it best to introduce ourselves now and find out more of what's going on.

"Oh, their town was invaded," Kirby said. "There weren't enough people at the settlement to defend it, and the help we sent arrived too late."

We all looked at her, shocked.

Fenrir growled. *"Who?"*

Kirby shrugged. "We don't know, however some reported the presence of a powerful god. It's believed he's after land, though we're not sure why. We didn't exactly claim the best lands this far north in Midgard. Either way, Odinn is furious someone would have the audacity to try and take what isn't theirs. He won't let it stand."

Randi advanced toward the refugees. "No, we will not."

Astrid and Bjǫrn followed her, the rest of us immortals following.

Freyja squinted at Astrid when we were close enough. "Why are you not wearing appropriate armor?"

"I don't have anything else yet." That explained a bit.

"I will remedy that immediately."

"You don't have to bother yourself with such a task, Freyja," Randi said. "I can manage."

"No, I can source something quicker and of the best quality, like I did for you. She'll have it in two days."

Randi smiled. "Very well."

"Hilda, please meet Runavík's völvur, Randi and her daughter Astrid," Freyja introduced the new woman before Rune could.

The woman bowed her head respectfully to Astrid and Randi. "Good health to you, völvur of Runavík. I look forward to getting to know you and seeing what magic you hold."

"Well met, Berserker Hilda," Randi said. "It will be good to have another strong woman to handle the Berserkers when they get out of hand."

Hilda barked out a laugh. "I may defer to Astrid here. She seems to have quite the effective strategy."

Astrid grinned. "I won't mind the extra help. And speaking of which, do any of you need any healing?"

Hilda turned to an elderly man standing with the other refugees. From the formation, he was in charge of them while Hilda was with us.

The man shook his head. "The Berserkers have healed by now, and the rest of us got out before we could be harmed."

"If you realize that's not the case, tell me immediately," Astrid said. "I will not allow pride to be the cause of death when I could have easily prevented it."

"Astrid is the best healer in the region," Freyja praised. "There isn't much she can't do at this point."

Rune grunted his agreement.

Astrid rolled her eyes. "I'm the only healing völva in the region."

"And you're still the best."

"Her merits as a völva can be discussed later," Rune interjected, a serious, hard edge to his voice. "We must discuss this attack and work on finding places for everyone to stay until we stake out land. And collect resources so everyone will survive the coming winter."

"Leave the attack to us," Týr said. "If a god is truly involved, we cannot tolerate them thinking they can take our land or kill our people."

"We will fight with you," Hilda said, a growl entering her words. "They will pay for what they have done. We will avenge those who fell protecting us as we were ordered to escape."

Her pain and fury contorted the expression on her face. I couldn't imagine what she and the others had gone through, but it clearly hadn't broken them.

"We will also offer our aid," Rune said. "You need only call on us."

The gathered warriors murmured determined agreements. I grinned. There was no shortage of courage and willingness to fight here.

"And I will send word to King Geir about this," Rune continued. "He needs to be aware of what is happening in our lands. No doubt he will also send word for warriors as well."

"Leave the message to me," Kirby said. "I'll be faster, and it will provide me direct knowledge of the number of warriors who will be willing to fight. Odinn will want to know that."

"We should head back so we can discuss and plan with the others," Týr said. His eyes flicked to Astrid, lingering on her a moment before he refocused.

I understood. It was frustrating this had come up. The thought to take her with us did cross my mind, but that would not go over well with Father.

"We'll be in touch," Freyja said.

Fenrir moved behind Astrid and dipped his head down. His teeth snagged the back of her padded tunic. He lifted her off the ground as if he were scuffing the tiny woman. *I have our völva, we can leave.*

Astrid flailed and kicked her legs helplessly. "Fen, you over-sized fluff ball, put me down!"

I couldn't not laugh. It was such a ridiculous sight, between their antics and the shock and near horror of our audience, who couldn't believe she'd said those words to a god.

Fenrir continued to refuse to release her, and Týr came to her rescue. He grabbed a hold of her, careful and mindful of her fragile mortal body, and yanked. Fabric tore.

Astrid came free and squeaked as Týr pulled her into him, leaving Fenrir with a mouth full of her padded tunic. Týr held Astrid against him a little longer than necessary as he glared at Fenrir before allowing her to step away.

Her cheeks were flushed and she fussed with her armor. A sizable tear ruined it in the back. She scrunched her nose and pulled the tunic off, leaving her with her thinner tunic underneath that showed off her womanly curves far better.

Týr and I barked out a laugh when she balled up the cloth armor and tossed it at Fenrir, hitting him square in the muzzle.

Freyja placed her hand on my back. Her eyes sparkled with mirth, but she did better remaining serious. "It's time we left instead of harassing our young völva here."

"No fun," Fenrir grumped.

"And, Astrid, try to behave and not get into trouble while we're gone," Freyja teased.

Leif grunted. "That's a tall ask for someone so tiny."

Astrid's eyes narrowed. The last thing I saw, before Freyja teleported us away, was the amusing sight of Astrid chasing down her brother and threatening him with bodily harm.

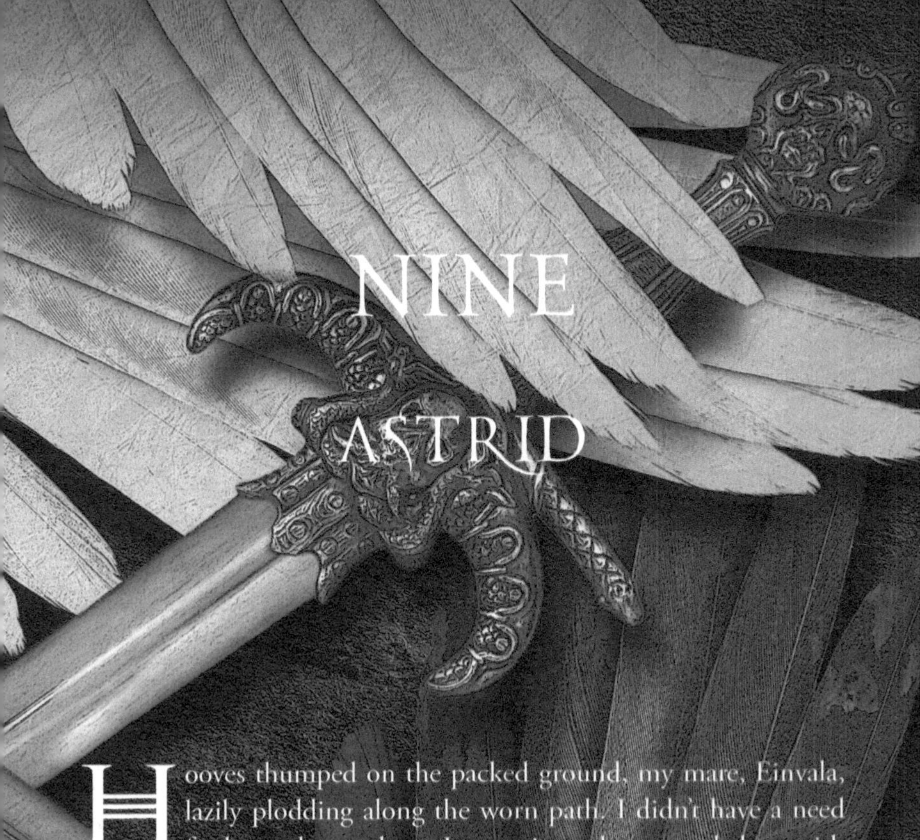

NINE

ASTRID

Hooves thumped on the packed ground, my mare, Einvala, lazily plodding along the worn path. I didn't have a need for her to hurry along. It was nice to be out and alone with my thoughts, especially after all the training I'd had to squeeze in the last few weeks, on top of the week of festivities with Leif and Frida's wedding. Everything had gone to plan and it had been a fantastic celebration. Even Freyja, Fenrir, Baldr, and Týr had each made an appearance.

I knew Týr had planned to, after we had invited him, but with the looming danger that brought Hilda and the survivors of her town with her, the gods had been busy uncovering the source of the threat. I wouldn't have been surprised if none of them had been able to find the time for some insignificant mortal wedding.

Their blessing and priority toward the wedding had been much appreciated, and certainly elevated Leif's marriage even higher in the eyes of the community. *At least one of us has that...*

I sucked in a tight breath and banished the negative thoughts. I'd been fighting them far too much the last few days. There was no point in thinking them. *I must accept my fate in life.* I was not destined to have a family of my own.

I would train in my magic and be as strong as I could. I would be a völva worthy of stories told for generations, just like my mother. And when Leif had a daughter who also inherited the family magic, I would be there to teach her.

Of course, accepting my fate was easier said than done when I reacted the way I did to Týr's presence—and now Baldr's. It wasn't the same as with Týr, but there was this sensation I got when he came by to just spend time with me.

His outwardly expressed desire to be my friend, despite me being mortal, was confusing in many ways. And then during the wedding celebrations, he insisted on spending as much time with me as Týr did.

I feared these feelings would continue to grow as intense as my reactions to Týr. I couldn't get my heart to understand how foolish it was to yearn for gods. *What could they possibly see in me?*

The towering trees of the forest opened to a clearing. I pulled on Einvala's reins, bringing us to a halt. An expansive meadow spanned around the travel road, snow-capped mountains rising high on the horizon. The once-green grass was now a ray of gold and amber. The last flowers still clinging to life were dotted about, adding a dash of color against the sunny hues.

Babbling streams and pools of shallow water filled the open landscape. A few lone trees stood, their yellow and orange leaves rustling in the crisp air.

A raven called from somewhere back in the forest I left, and Einvala's movements startled a frog. Small birds called and sang. Flying bugs hovered and darted around the water.

We wandered from the road. The soft ground beneath Einvala squelched under her hooves. I scanned the meadow, searching for berry clusters. This was likely to be my last chance to forage before the snow came, and I wanted berries to go along with all the mushrooms, nuts, and herbs I'd already found.

A large cluster of amber in one of the last scrapes of green of the meadow caught my eye. I smiled and hopped off Einvala, the soft ground sinking under me. Removing a basket from the saddle, I moved quickly, abandoning Einvala to graze.

The juicy, succulent berry clusters awaited me, and I was quick to pick them, popping a few in my mouth every now and then. Honey-like sweetness splashed over my tongue, followed by a tart *zing*. The tartness faded quickly, leaving behind a subtle, sweet flavor. I hummed with delight.

I had to be careful not to eat too many. My family wouldn't be happy if they didn't get any of these. And I wanted to make some jams. I'd been craving it all year.

A shadow flashed overhead. Einvala chuffed and stomped her foot. I glanced up, finding her watching the sky. Her ears flicked back and forth, nervous but not quite ready to bolt. I didn't expect her to, which was why I always chose her. For as young as she was, she was one of our bravest, most stubborn mares.

I turned my attention skyward. Kirby, her magnificent black wings spread, descended toward me. I smiled. "Well, this is certainly a surprise."

Kirby smiled back and landed next to me. "I agree. What are you doing so far from Runavík?"

I gestured to the berry plants. "Getting in what last harvest I can."

Her eyes lit up and she practically pounced on the berries, making me laugh.

Crouching beside her, I resumed my picking. "What brings you out here?"

"Scouting," she said through a mouthful of fruit.

My brow rose and picking paused. "Scouting?"

She nodded and swallowed her treat. "Odinn sends us Valkyries and his ravens out to keep an eye on our lands. With the current threat, he's suspicious of spies."

Tightness formed in my stomach. "Should I not be out here?"

She shook her head. "Don't worry. We haven't found anything, so I'm certain you're fine. Though it's not exactly safe to be out by yourself, even if you have magic."

My magic ability protest died on my tongue. "Well, I have Einvala, so if something does happen, I can get away quickly."

Kirby glanced over to my mare. "She's beautiful. Where did you get her?"

I smiled widely. "I bred her."

Her eyebrows rose high on her forehead. "Really?"

I called Einvala over. She resisted a moment, wanting to nibble more on the grass, but gave in when I called her a second time. I affectionately touched her soft muzzle and scratched her dun neck when she lowered her head to nose the grass. "My father's family has been raising prized horses for generations. My uncle inherited the farm, but he allows us to pick breeding combinations and permits us to hold our own herds on the family land. Einvala is the product of the first breeding I was allowed."

My hand traveled over her shoulder to her round belly. "And she's carrying her first foal, that I also bred. My uncle so far is pleased with her and our hope is that this baby turns out just as good, as well as a second breeding with her mother to the same stallion."

Kirby rubbed Einvala's neck. "I can see why. She seems to be well tempered."

My mare lifted her head and sniffed Kirby's hair. Kirby laughed when the horse lipped one of her tight braids in an attempt to grab one, and she pushed Einvala away. "If my Berserker can't pull this out, neither can you, so don't try it."

Her Berserker? Was that a personal claim or her meaning she was paired up with one for war? "Is that why you're wearing it that way?"

"It's tight and good in a skirmish, keeping my hair out of the way and difficult to grab." Kirby grinned. "But it's a little frustrating for a partner when you're playing with his sword in a tussle in the sheets. And trust me, he's been stubborn enough to try a number of times."

My head tipped back as I laughed. So, this was a deeper relationship she had with him. That was interesting.

"I'll show you how to do it," she offered.

"Do what, play with a sword?" I grinned. "I already know how and I'm quite skilled at it."

She laughed. "No, your hair. Though if you want some pointers with a sword, I can offer a few. I know I don't look it, but I've been around a while and have plenty of experience."

Immortality was such a strange concept for a mortal like myself to understand. She looked maybe slightly older than me, yet like she said, her years far exceeded my comprehension. What was it like to live so long? How did such a life impact the way they saw Midgard and us mortals?

"Tell me about this Berserker of yours," I said as Kirby helped me untwist my current braids. I wanted to hear how an immortal like her saw mortals like us if she were willing to have such a relationship with one of us.

My heart did a little hopeful pitter-patter and I squashed it. There was no guarantee I'd be offered the same.

The smile that appeared on Kirby's face was so soft and filled with infatuation, it was adorable. "Many think me foolish for loving a mortal man, but they don't know him as I do. He is everything I have ever dared asked Creation for. He's as fierce as the wild wolf within him, yet gentle enough to cradle my heart as though it were a fragile ember. His strength is unmatched, and his loyalty unwavering. His wildness is intoxicating in ways I can't resist. When he's near, the weight of my burdens fade like mist under the morning sun. In his arms, I find a peace I never thought possible to find. With him, I am home."

The way she spoke of him filled my chest with warmth. That type of affection couldn't be faked. What she had with him was as real as any mortal had with another. "I don't think you're foolish at all. The heart's desire is not something any of us can control, mortality status be damned. Loving a mortal is no more foolish than a mortal loving another mortal."

I gazed out at the sprawling wet meadow. "An immortal is guaranteed to outlive us, but we even outlive other mortals. We die of age, war, and sickness. No matter how hard we love and how much we fight for it, one of us will always outlive the other in some way."

Memories bloomed in the back of my mind—ones I'd long since buried to protect myself from the pain. Dark, captivating eyes—exotic features—a gentle voice that spoke endless poems and confessions. "The pain is excruciating. You may even believe it impossible to live with that loss. But you do. You manage to keep going. Eventually the wound scars, and it may even fade with enough time, but it doesn't ever disappear. They leave a permanent mark on your soul that you carry with you until you take your last breath."

I let out a shuddering breath and pushed the pain and memories away, turning to Kirby with a smile. "As horrifying as that all might sound, especially for someone who lives for as long as you do, finding a love like that is worth every moment you have them in your life. It's worth dying for. But even more, it's worth living for."

Kirby stared at me. Her eyes had the unspoken question I knew she wanted to ask: *Who did you love so deeply and lose far too soon?*

And yet, instead of prying, she smiled and nodded. "I knew you'd understand. Maybe one of these days you two will be able to meet. I think you'd like him."

"I'd like that." Was it too dangerous for me to hope that if Kirby could love a mortal, I could possibly have the same? Even if I believed it wasn't wrong for her to love him, it was also hard for me to see what gods and immortals might see in us. But maybe if I saw them together, I could gain some insight. And maybe it'd help me finally figure out whether these feelings inside me were truly foolish and misplaced, or worth having and waiting for reciprocation to be offered.

Kirby braided my hair while we chatted about anything that came to mind. She was quite knowledgeable on war tactics, and it was fascinating listening to her enthuse about that.

We also talked about things we enjoyed doing, things we didn't like, and anything else that came to mind. Nothing was off limits for either of us, though we both knew it was a bit soon to ask anything too personal yet. I felt the growing friendship between us and I liked it. I liked that despite her being a Valkyrie, she wasn't much different from me.

When Kirby finished with my hair, I tried to use my magic to see it better, but that failed, so I had to look at myself in a pool of water. I'd never had it braided like this, but I liked it.

Kirby helped me pick more berries. We took every good one we could find from this cluster and then she flew around looking for another patch. I admired her gracefulness in flight and the beauty of her wings. I wanted to touch them, but I figured that'd be rude.

We didn't stop picking until my basket was full. *Everyone will be so happy to have all this.*

"I should get back to scouting," Kirby said. She sounded anything but happy to do so.

I understood. I was enjoying this time with her too much. But I also didn't want to get her into trouble. "I hope everything goes well. I should also get home before I lose all the sunlight to guide me home. I can only do so much with my magic right now."

We said our goodbyes and I rode Einvala down the road toward home at a quick pace. There wasn't a need for me to rush, but a growing sense of warning niggled the back of my head. I didn't doubt Kirby's scouting mission was the reason for it, but I wouldn't dismiss my paranoia. It really was unsafe for me to be this far from home alone.

Einvala's ears swiveled in a direction I didn't like. *What did she hear?* Glancing around, I saw nothing, but the forest hid much in the shadows. I wasn't going to chance it. I spurred her into a faster pace.

My mare's pace picked up to a canter, her hooves thumping harder on the ground. A raven in the woods let out short, shrill calls, the sound spiking my senses. *Is that an alert?* Sometimes we knew when bears and other dangerous beasts were lurking in the woods close to home when the ravens got riled up.

A shrill voice spiked along my senses, startling me for a moment, but only a moment. *"Run, Völva!"*

My heels dug into Einvala's sides. She reacted immediately, bolting into a gallop. Movement in the forest flashed. Something whistled past me. An arrow sunk into a tree with a *thunk*. In front of my path, two men jumped out from behind trees on opposite sides of the road. *That won't stop me.*

I summoned my magic. Golden tendrils shot out, grabbing the men, just as I'd been practicing. My magic tossed them aside with ease, and I hardly heard their shouts and cries as I pushed Einvala on.

We just needed to get a little closer to town. Even though Mother had erected a magic barrier around Runavík, Rune wanted to be extra cautious, especially when it came to beyond the town proper. So he had set up sentry points guarded by our best warriors. It also put Hilda and the newcomers at ease.

When I'd left earlier, the sentries had been concerned about me going off beyond them alone, but I'd wanted my space. *I should have listened.*

A raven shrieked in alarm nearby. I swore I saw it flying frantically in the trees, even diving down, as if attacking something.

Instinct flared and my magic shot out behind me, forming into a golden barrier. Two balls with rope attaching them smashed into my shield and crashed into the ground. *What do they want with me?*

It didn't make sense for them to keep trying to attack if I wasn't a specific target. But why would anyone want to attack me? What could I have done?

More men rushed out of the forest and I fended them off the same way as the first two men. Projectiles flew, and they weren't just aimed for me, but my horse. My magic lashed and blocked. I wouldn't allow them to harm her any more than me.

My heart pounded in my ears. Fewer and fewer attackers came, and for a moment I thought I might have outrun them. Then a large man in unusual clothes stepped out onto the road. A weapon was strapped to his hip, yet it wasn't drawn.

My senses kicked up, like a sensation of power leaking from him clashing against my active magic. Something was dangerous about this man.

"Danger!" came the shrieking voice. *"Get away!"*

I veered Einvala around him, using my magic to grab and throw him. He may be large, but my magic was strong.

Only it didn't work.

The man grinned and his gloved hand shot out. The moment it made contact with my magic, the golden energy burst into shimmers of light. *What the hel?*

I tried to force my mare into escaping with a wider berth between me and this dangerous man, but he was fast—faster than an ordinary man could possibly hope to be. His hand grabbed a hold of my cloak, and before I could rip off the clasp, he yanked me off my mount.

I crashed painfully to the ground, tumbling on the hard packed road. Einvala kept running. I tried to catch my footing and jump to my feet, when pain slammed into the back of my head and everything went dark.

"Astrid!"

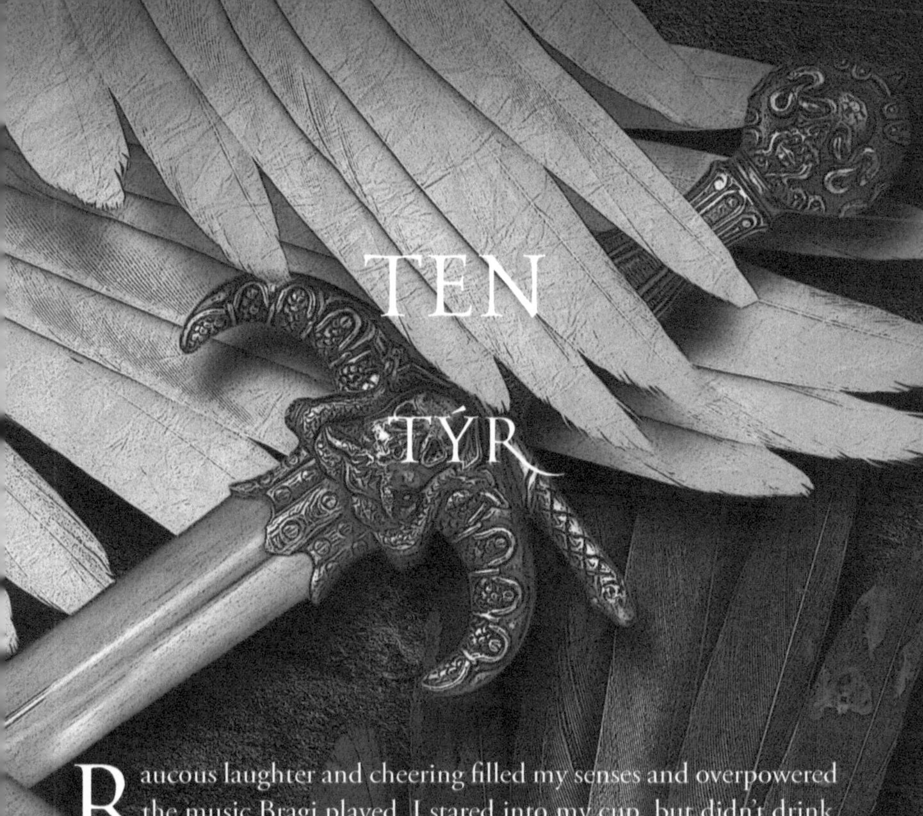

TEN

TÝR

Raucous laughter and cheering filled my senses and overpowered the music Bragi played. I stared into my cup, but didn't drink the frothy ale inside. I should be celebrating after that well-fought battle. We won. We rid ourselves of the invaders who'd had the audacity to steal Hilda's home.

There wasn't anything left of the place, and she and the survivors chose to settle in Runavík permanently, but at least we could send the enemy running. Those few who survived to retreat, that is.

We didn't know their identities. Odinn didn't think it was needed to look into them or their motives any further. But I didn't agree. I couldn't quite shake there was some hidden importance there. We're missing something. My instincts screamed this wasn't the time to celebrate, and those were never wrong.

A warm, soft hand slid along the back of my neck and over my shoulder. A tiny body pressed against me, followed by a rich and velvety voice. "Týr, you're being so boring."

I glanced up from my drink to look at Sól. Her wild mane of flame-red hair framed her warm speckled face, and her amber eyes danced with amusement.

Sól held up her cup, the golden drink inside sloshing out with her movements. "Drink and celebrate with us! You war gods won. You shouldn't be sitting here moping as if it wasn't enough glory for you."

"I'm not upset with the results," I mumbled before taking a swig of my ale, not tasting it.

"No?" She made a thoughtful sound in her throat and grinned. "Or perhaps your mind is somewhere else? Wishing you could celebrate with that special völva I'm hearing so much about?"

Astrid hadn't been on my mind given my focus, but now that Sól brought her up… *I would much prefer to be celebrating with her.* Unfortunately, Odinn had ordered the celebration to be held in his hall. That meant no mortals were allowed and we gods weren't permitted to skip.

Sól leaned into me more. "Well, since you can't go and see her, I could be her stand-in if you'd like."

I took another drink and gently brushed her hand off me. "Thank you for the offer, Sól, but no."

My mind wasn't in the right place to be entertained. Not even if Astrid were here. I couldn't shake this feeling.

Sól chuckled. "This mortal really has captured you. I think I want to meet her one of these days. Baldr, what about you? You've been unusually quiet as well for all this."

I glanced my friend's way. He sat at the same table, but wasn't doing much more than sitting there. He wasn't even nursing a drink. His eyes faintly glowed with power, the lingering effect of prayers he'd received.

Baldr's brow rose as if he hadn't quite caught what she said. "What?"

Sól tipped her head. "Don't tell me you're also so smitten with the mortal."

"Who?"

"Astrid," I said. He was unusually unaware of conversation around him. Was he, too, feeling the same as me?

"Oh, she's a lovely woman. But my thoughts have been elsewhere."

Sól's eyes narrowed at us both, her carefree demeanor turning more serious. "What is it?"

"Something isn't right," Fenrir said as he sat heavily next to me. He gulped down some of his drink. "All of us war gods are feeling it; Freyja confirmed it. Even Thor begrudgingly admitted something felt off."

Máni, Sól's twin, came up behind her. He pushed his pale, silvery hair over his shoulder and bent low. "You didn't hear this from me, but Odinn sent many Valkyries out for some scouting."

My back straightened. That was strange. Odinn had claimed certainty of our victory. He was a paranoid bastard, but to send Valkyries to scout when his raven spies were more than sufficient, and so soon after a battle… Did he know something he wasn't willing to reveal? *Why?*

A shrill cry cut through the jubilant atmosphere. Huginn appeared out of nothing and frantically flew around the hall. *"They took her! They took her!"*

Tension coiled in my neck. The warning sensation I sensed pulled harder.

Odinn rose from his throne and called to Huginn. "Son, calm yourself. Tell us what it is you saw."

Huginn landed on Odinn's shoulder. *"They took the red-haired völva. Muninn saw it! Muninn saw it!"*

The table bench I'd previously sat on tipped over and crashed to the ground as Fenrir and I both jumped to our feet.

Baldr had also reacted. "Huginn, do you mean Astrid?"

Say no. Say no.

The raven bobbed his head. *"They took her. The enemy took her!"*

Fuck!

"They lured us with a decoy, then?" Odinn said. He was far too calm. He could be indifferent to Astrid's existence, but he should be at least concerned our enemy not only deceived us, but abducted a völva. They were too rare to dismiss them as expendable.

Discomfort crawled through me at the thought of anyone thinking of her as anything close to expendable. She wasn't.

"Then what are we waiting for?" Fenrir said. "We need to find her."

"And how do you propose that?" Thor asked, his tone bored. He smoothed his red beard and didn't bother adjusting his lounging position in his chair near his father. "Do you know who took this völva? And why should we rush to find this woman? She's just—"

Fenrir snarled at the same time Odinn held up a hand to silence his son. "We mustn't act as though the völva's life is expendable. They are too rare. Especially ones as powerful as she, and with strong bloodlines. Yet, we cannot act until we know where she's been taken. Muninn is working on that. We will need to wait."

"Waiting is too dangerous, Father," Baldr argued. "If we can learn where they took her from, we can begin a preliminary search from there."

"My thoughts exactly." Freyja placed a hand on Fenrir's and my shoulder. "And I know where we can begin our search."

Without questioning her, I reached for Baldr. It didn't matter how she knew where to look. We'd find Astrid, and we'd make those who took her pay.

Baldr clamped his hand around my wrist, and in a blink the four of us found ourselves in Runavík.

There was already a commotion of people running around. And among them was Randi, standing with a saddled horse. Bjǫrn was checking the horse out. On its saddle it had several baskets that looked far too familiar.

Randi looked at us, her eyes filled with both terror and fury. And the words I hoped she wouldn't say uttered from her lips and sent cold dread into the pit of my soul. "Where is my daughter?"

"So, she was taken without your knowledge, then?" Freyja said, her voice neutral so as not to set off the völva.

Bjǫrn stopped his inspection of the horse. "She went out earlier today to forage. Her horse just returned, riderless."

Baldr and I swore. Runavík was supposed to be safe. That was why we'd brought Hilda and the rest here. It'd been far from their home. *Who is behind all this? And why would they take Astrid?*

Fenrir approached the horse. She shifted her weight, and eyed him with pinned ears and the wary look of prey in the presence of a predator, as many animals did, yet she didn't rear or attempt to bolt.

Fenrir leaned in close to the horse and inhaled deep. "I don't smell any others on this mare. Only Astrid. You said the horse was running?"

Bjǫrn nodded. "She bolted past the sentries before they even realized she was riderless."

Fenrir's eyes narrowed and he inhaled again. "Then Astrid was knocked off her horse. I smell her magic, so she was attacked while riding."

He continued to sniff then paused around the baskets. His brow furrowed and he smelled again.

"What is it?" I asked, taking a step forward. This was testing my patience and nerves. Astrid was in trouble and I needed to get to her.

"I smell... Kirby."

Freyja, Baldr, and I exchanged equally confused looks. What was Kirby's scent doing on Astrid's gathering baskets?

Fenrir sniffed again. "Definitely Kirby. It's strong, meaning she was with Astrid for a while."

"Maybe they crossed paths during her scouting," Baldr said.

That could explain a few things. "But if Kirby was with Astrid, how was she taken?"

"How do you know she was taken?" Randi asked. Her magic flared in dark sparks, barely contained by her raging emotions.

Before any of us could explain, Freyja spotted a fast-moving object in the sky. It was a black-winged Valkyrie. *Kirby.* We'd finally get our answers.

When she landed, the state she was in was shocking. Blood trickled down the side of her face, and even more coated her armor. "Please tell me I'm wrong and Astrid made it home."

"No," I said. "What the hel happened?"

She detailed how she and Astrid had met up by chance in the wet meadow and spent a good amount of time together. When they'd parted ways, Kirby had noticed something in the forest near the wetlands and went to check it out. Muninn had barely managed to warn her when she was ambushed.

Kirby had managed to dispatch her attackers, but when she'd gone to search for Astrid, she'd only found the evidence of a second ambush.

"I don't know if they were after me or Astrid," Kirby said. "I can't think of a reason why they would go after her, but they waited until we separated. They knew we would."

"Which means it's likely they were watching her before you showed up," I said.

Kirby nodded. "That was my fear."

"Whoever they are, they'll pay for taking my daughter," Randi snarled with intensity that sent a shiver of cold running through even me. "Show us where the attack happened."

"I should be able to pick up a scent from there," Fenrir said.

"If Muninn followed Astrid and is close enough to—" Baldr's words cut off and his back straightened. His eyes went momentarily unfocused, as they did for many of us gods as we answered prayers.

At the same time, a voice whispered across my mind—a prayer that wrapped around my soul. A prayer for strength and courage, and justice, and a fiery passion to destroy the enemies in front of her for their audacity. And with the plea for help came a warning—a promise of a trap laid for us should we come to her aid.

All four of us uttered the same name. "Astrid."

ELEVEN

A thick, heavy fog enveloped my mind. Fragments of light and sound seeped through, though I couldn't make sense of it all. A dull, persistent throb in the back of my skull radiated in waves, making it hard to think. *What happened to me?*

I tried to open my eyes, but my eyelids were impossibly heavy. They wanted me to sleep. Sleep sounded so nice. Maybe this pain would ebb if I slept a little longer.

"Astrid," a voice said. It was distant and seemed familiar in some way, but I couldn't be sure. Nor could I tell if it came from my ears or my head. *"Astrid."*

There seemed to be urgency in the voice, a reminder of something I forgot, like why I was like this. *I was riding my horse, right? What happened?*

Memories cut through the haze and pain. It shot urgency through my mind. I'd been trying to escape the ambush. I'd been knocked off Einvala.

I tried to open my eyes again, pushing through the fog. With effort, I finally managed to crack them open. A sliver of light assaulted my eyes, blinding me. I squeezed them shut again, but that was enough to awaken my senses. Slow at first, but steady.

Something rough was wrapped around me, holding me tight against whatever hard object pressed into my back. My limbs felt stiff and unmoving. *Am I bound?*

Voices cleared in the haze of sound. They were close, right near me. But I didn't understand them. I tried to focus harder, but my mind tried to slip back into the fog where it was easier to exist.

"Astrid!" the voice screamed, piercing my mind with shocking intensity. It cut the fog like a sword, slicing it away permanently.

I wanted to respond to it, but dryness coated my throat. I swallowed, though it did little to help.

I forced my eyes open again, blinking slowly. The light's harshness dulled to something softer, and warm. Some sort of fire crackled. Shapes and colors formed in my blurry vision and slowly solidified—a ceiling and walls, knocked over chairs and discarded household objects, as if whoever lived here left in a hurry—or it was looted after they left.

Moving shapes turned into people, and the rest of my memory flooded back. These were the men who attacked me. They wore clothes I wasn't familiar with, and some didn't look prepared for the cold day. Their features were not like those up here. *Who are these people?*

There were maybe five of them in this room. It wouldn't be too difficult to take them, if I could concentrate on my magic. But I also didn't know how many more were beyond these walls. I could hear the evidence of them out there.

I tried to move, only to be stuck. Rough rope tied me to a chair. Someone spoke. I lifted my head and found one of the men had moved closer. He spoke again. I squinted at him, unable to understand his words. This seemed to displease him from the face he made and he extended a hand toward me. I reached for my magic; I didn't want him to touch me. But my magic didn't activate.

I tried again, and still it lay dormant. My heartbeat picked up and my already-dry throat felt as though it were closing. *What did they do to me? Where is my magic?*

The man grabbed my face. His grip wasn't painful, but I would not allow him to touch me. I jerked against his hold, breaking free, and snapped my teeth down on his hand. He yelped and jumped back. He said a few other things as he held his hand and inspected it while some of the other men laughed.

I narrowed my eyes and tried to speak, but it came out as barely a croak. I swallowed, trying to bring moisture back into my throat.

One of the men said something and left the building. I shifted my focus between all these strangers. What did they want with me? Why had they gone to such lengths to capture me? How did they even know of me?

I wasn't an imbecile. With magic being as rare as it was, these men wouldn't casually carry ways to bind my magic unless they knew their target possessed it. But I wasn't well known outside of Runavík besides with our gods. Not with how recently my magic manifested.

And then there was that man… He was able to dispel my magic from touch alone. *Who was he?*

Someone entered the building. Large and imposing, he had to duck through the doorway. My hands curled against the rough grain of my seat. Like many of these men, he had exotic features with skin that looked as though Sól had caressed it herself, and dark brown curly hair.

When he leveled dark eyes on me, I knew without a doubt, this was the man who had knocked me off my horse. There was a dangerous energy about him, and his presence reminded me of when I was around my gods.

He spoke to me, his voice rumbling deep in my chest, but I didn't understand him any better than the other men here.

"I don't understand you," I said, hoping maybe that'd help them realize the issue.

The man regarded me a moment before approaching. It took all my control to not shrink away. I wouldn't show weakness. I had to be brave and hope for a chance to escape, or that I'd be rescued. *Hopefully before it's too late.*

He lifted his thumb to his mouth and bit down hard, drawing blood. Then he reached for me. I tried to lean away from him, but I didn't have anywhere to go.

His finger slid over my forehead, smearing his blood over my skin. "Now, you will understand."

I blinked slowly, processing the odd way his words sounded right and wrong. "How did you do that?"

He smiled. It was pleasant, though unsettlingly so in this situation. "I am a titan. I can do much, as can you for a mortal woman."

"How do you know about me?"

"I know much. Just as I know you can help us."

I narrowed my eyes at the man. "You attacked me."

"A misunderstanding," he tried to assure with that easy smile that was hardly believable. There was something about him that felt oddly familiar. Especially that smile. It made him seem less trustworthy than any other person here. "We merely need your help."

"Keep him distracted," came that voice in my head again. *"Help will arrive."*

"You want a random woman's help?" As if I'd believe that.

"Ah, but you're not random, now are you?" A wickedness slipped into his gaze. It was gone in a flash, but the warning signs were there and sent my nerves on full alert.

"I'm not clear on what you're trying to imply," I said.

He tipped his head as he gazed at me. "You look just like her."

This man wasn't making any sense. "What are you talking about? What do you want with me? Who are you?"

"Kronos." He said it in a way as if I should know the name. "No? Not even a single inkling?"

"I don't know what you're going on about."

He hummed thoughtfully. "No, I suppose you wouldn't. It would be impossible for you to be her. But I can see why he'd keep you close. Just in case."

Kronos stepped closer, his posture becoming more imposing but not aggressive—yet. "Tell me, woman, where does Odinn hide these days?"

I blinked dumbly. "Odinn? I don't know. I've never met him."

His pleasant mask slipped a little more. "I know that you know, woman. All you have to do is tell me where I can find him, and we'll let you go. It'll be as if you never met us."

I grunted. Like I'd believe that. Once they got what they wanted from me, I'd be dead. Not that I could tell them. Nor could I understand what this… titan wanted with a god like Odinn.

Kronos' pleasant mask shattered. In a flash his hand was around my throat, his fingers so long, they gripped my face. My breath caught and my body went rigid. "I will not ask you again, woman. We have seen you with Odinn's winged slaves and the other pathetic excuses called gods under his thumb. You are clearly a pet of theirs. You know what I need, and you will tell me."

My jaw set. I would not say a word. I wouldn't make up lies to save my skin. And even if I did know, I wouldn't tell this enemy anything. I'd rather die.

He jerked my head to the side. "Tell me, else you will end up like them."

I was forced to look at something behind me. My gut churned at the sight of the lifeless, bloody body of a woman, a weapon within her reach, as if she'd dropped it before she herself fell. Behind her, in spaces where they'd tried to hide, two small children lay in an unmoving heap.

My pulse thrummed harder and harder until it was beating in my ears. A tingling sensation fell over my extremities. My nose flared, air rushing through my lungs. *How dare they!*

Baldr, I ask of your unending pool of courage. Fenrir, I beg of your untamed fury and strength. Freyja, fuel my heart's passion. Týr, I ask of your guiding hand for swift justice. I beg for what I need to destroy the enemy before me.

I jerked in Kronos' grasp and latched onto his hand with my teeth, biting down hard. Energy surged in me. The metallic taste of blood filled my mouth as my teeth sank into his hard skin.

Kronos roared and jerked his hand back. Blood oozed out of the teeth marks I left. He raised his hand and swung it at me. The back of his hand landed with a sharp *crack.*

Pain exploded across my cheek, my head snapping to the side. My vision flashed, blackness taking over for a moment, and my ears rang with a high-pitched whine.

As my senses returned, I turned back to look at him. My skin burned, the sting spreading across my cheekbones and jaw, and built in a dull lingering ache beneath the surface. But the pain didn't burn as hot as my fury. It paled in compassion for my desire to shred him limb from limb.

I bared my bloody teeth at him and snarled out insult after insult. I struggled against my bindings, their strong hold only fueling my rage.

Please, if you can hear my pleas… if you have thoughts to aid me… be careful. They wait for you to come. They expect you to save me. This is what they want.

Kronos' laughter cut through my rage and prayer. He looked at his hand again, the wound I'd managed to inflict on him already healed. *Is a titan a type of god?*

He grinned at me. "Feisty. I see why they keep you around."

For the second time in this encounter, his hand flashed out and wrapped around my throat and jaw. The pain from his slap flared. I had to ignore it. I wouldn't show weakness.

He leaned in close, his hot breath puffing against my skin. A bitter, earthy yet smoky scent wafted off him and invaded my nose. "Odinn will pay for what he did to me—for his betrayal. Those who support him will perish. But you…" The grin that split his face made my stomach churn. "If you survive, I might just turn you into a pet of my own."

His mouth opened wider and I lurched as his slimy tongue slid up my cheek. I twisted just enough in his tight grip and once again bit him. This time his disgusting tongue was my victim.

He howled in pain and recoiled. I lunged against my bindings. The back of the chair lifted and my forehead smashed into his nose. Pain exploded in my skull, and his nose gave way with a crunch.

The force of the blow traveled down through my neck and shoulders in an intense shockwave. My vision flashed white. The sensation of wet, warm blood splattered against my forehead and trickled down my face.

My chair slammed back down on the ground. I didn't move for a long minute. My brain felt as though it was rattling around in my skull, and more pain throbbed along my forehead where I could feel blood oozing from a split in my skin, mixing with his.

Kronos staggered back a few steps, holding his face and groaning in pain as blood poured through his fingers. *Weak.* A titan was weaker than a god, I decided. No god would be so affected by a mere mortal like me. Not without my magic to aid me.

The barking laugh that rolled through him sent a wave of unease through me. His intense eyes focused on me, and the malevolent grin of his made my stomach churn. "Yes, you're going to be fun to break. You—"

A raven landed on the windowsill of the open window near me. It tilted its head, one beady eye focusing on me with eerie intelligence. The raven opened its beak and let out a grating cry, the sound echoing through the building.

At the same time, a voice, the one I'd heard before, entered my mind. *"They come, Völva Astrid. Prepare."*

I blinked slowly. A raven was speaking to me. A bird spoke in my head like Fenrir. *Is it a bird shifter?* I'd never met one, but I'd heard about them. *Unless...*

A wolf howled in the distance. A sound that sent both relief and a surge of vindication. I grinned at Kronos. "You made the mistake of taking the wrong völva. You'll now pay for your transgressions."

That malevolent smile returned on Kronos' face and he turned away from me. "I will crush the force Odinn has sent. And then you, pet, will watch as I destroy everything he dared try to build after what he did to me.

He barked orders to men in the room. "Watch her. They will send another to free her."

Kronos disappeared outside. The men in the room turned into a defensive formation with weapons and shields drawn.

The raven in the window cried again then hopped into the building. He moved around as if scavenging and had little fear of people. These fools treated him as an annoyance and wild bird, rather than the threat he truly was, losing interest in him, thinking a bigger threat was about to come.

Maybe it would. Or maybe I'd be that threat.

The raven continued to hop around the house, picking up small objects then putting them down for another, as if he were selecting the right prize. One of the men kicked something at him to try and scare him off. It only rewarded the man with a startled squawk and a hiss.

I wriggled in my chair in an attempt to draw attention away from the raven. It earned me a few disdainful looks, but did have the desired effect. They had no idea the raven was making his way over to me.

He disappeared behind my chair and a moment later I felt his tiny determined tugs as he tried to help me with my bindings. I continued with my occasional struggle to hide his attempts, but it was turning out to be a fruitless effort. Whoever tied me up knew what he was doing.

My captors stilled, as did the raven and I. An eerie quiet had fallen outside. Tension coiled in my gut.

The raven slipped under my chair and leaned against my legs. He crooned softly, then cackled. *"They come."*

Then, in the distance, I heard a deep thunderous rumble. It was faint at first, then grew louder. My heart skipped. I knew that sound. I'd heard it enough times during training. *They're here.*

A cacophony of sounds exploded in my ear. War cries and bestial roars. The clashing of steel and the sounds of the fallen. Battle raged outside.

The heavy sound of charging footfalls drew closer and closer to my prison. The walls of the building trembled in its wake. My captors tightened their formation, tension radiating off them. One even visibly trembled. I grinned at their backs. They would pay for what they'd done.

Suddenly, an enormous body appeared in the window the raven had entered through. The wall exploded inward, splinters and debris flying in all directions. My heart leapt into my throat, stealing all of my breath, as the opposite wall with the outside door also splintered and broke with the same force.

Cries of terror, the crunching of bone, and the splattering of blood fill the chaos of the small home as Baldr and Týr quickly tore through my mortal captors.

The noises inside the house suddenly stopped. Amidst the destruction, Baldr and Týr stood over what remained of my captors, their chests heaving, and their bodies visibly shaking.

They turned intense gazes onto me. My heart stuttered. Desire pooled between my legs. Their intensity sent a thrill down my spine.

They destroyed these mortals so easily and barely batted an eye. It should frighten me they could do the same to me. *How easy would it be for them to wrap their strong hands around my throat—* Need pulsed inappropriately stronger.

Yet, I knew they'd never harm me. I never felt safer with them. And the denied desire I had was ignited to a blazing inferno.

I craved their touch. I'd give my body and soul to these gods even for a night as thanks for coming to my rescue, while hoping—craving—one of them would ask me to stay until my last days.

"Are you hurt?" Baldr asked.

The intensity in his voice made me pause for a moment. "I've been better, but I could be worse."

The raven hopped out from under my chair and croaked. Baldr blinked at him. "Muninn, were you helping her?"

My lips parted. This was Muninn? One of Odinn's favorite ravens?

Baldr smiled. "I see. Thank you."

Had Muninn spoken only to him? Was that a special ability of his because he was one of Odinn's birds?

Muninn hopped up onto a tipped over table, what was left of it at least, and croaked at me. *"Be safe."*

He then flew out the giant hole in the wall.

Týr approached me and touched my shoulder. Then he ran his large fingers up my neck and along my cheek where the pain still throbbed. His eyes darkened when I winced. "Who touched you?"

Was that a growl? Did men growl?

Baldr bent closer to peer at me. He scowled. "Your skin is bruising. They'll pay for this."

Yes, those were definitely growls. And it did all kinds of things to fuzz my mind with more inappropriate thoughts that sent heat pooling in my belly.

I tugged at my restraints, the material biting into my skin and jerking my mind back to important pressing matters. "I hurt him back, trust me."

"Him?" Týr snarled. "Tell me, who is the man I'll break?"

I continued to fight my bindings and my relentless desire the more these men talked. "Someone by the name of Kronos who claims he is a titan or something of that sort. I struggled to understand some of his words. He is not from here."

Baldr snapped my bindings with ease, and my magic rushed back into my awareness. "I don't recognize the name or this term 'titan.' What does he want with you?"

I took a breath, relishing the feeling of my magic. I never wanted to experience that empty sensation ever again. I then explained to them what this being was after and how he had tried to use me as bait. The more information I gave, the angrier Baldr and Týr became.

My mother burst into the building just as I was about to detail my hostage treatment. She ran to me, straight through where Týr stood, forcing him to step aside. Her dark magic filled her eyes with inky blackness, and blood coated her armor.

"Astrid." She fussed, checking me over. "You're bleeding."

"It's not all mine," I said. "I bit Kronos and slammed my head against his nose."

Baldr blinked. "Why did you bite him?"

I scowled. "He tried to touch me with his mouth, telling me I'd become his pet if I survived this."

Both gods growled this time. Týr spun on his heels. "Stay here."

Even though my pulse jumped at his command, I wouldn't be told what to do. I opened my mouth to protest, but Baldr cut me off. "We will handle this so-called titan. He will pay for touching you."

Mother hummed thoughtfully when they left. She didn't verbalize what was on her mind though. "You should heal yourself, Sunshine. You'll need to be at your best when we defy the orders of those protective gods."

I grinned and spent a moment fixing myself up. The sounds of battle continued to rage outside, calling to us to help. Black feathered wings sprang into our path when Mother tried to lead me outside.

"Kirby?" I questioned.

"You two need to wait in here where it's safe," she said. "Freyja is already calling back all mortal warriors. The confrontation between the gods and this titan is too much for them to be involved in."

"We aren't typical warriors," Mother said. "Our magic works against immortals and gods."

Kirby nodded. "Yes, but… there is something not right about this Kronos. I can't place it, but it's safest if you don't engage for now."

She glanced over her shoulder at me. "I'd rather you both not suffer any more for matters that involve the gods."

I placed my hand on the back of her armor between where her wings were accommodated. "Don't blame yourself, Kirby."

"I knew there was potential danger. I should have stayed with you until you made it home safe."

I shook my head. "There was no way to know they had been watching me. They hid themselves too well. If anything, our time spent together was their downfall. They would have grabbed me sooner had you not been around."

"Muninn may not have witnessed them take you, either," she mumbled.

That explained why the raven was involved in all this.

"And you're here now. You arrived just when I needed it. And I'm more than grateful you all care enough to do that."

"We'll always protect you, Astrid." Her gaze was intense and unwavering. I believed her.

I didn't know how I'd earned the favor of these gods and immortals, but I had nonetheless, and I needed to get used to that.

Kirby stood as a sentry for a long while. Warriors from home joined us slowly, the intense sounds of battle between gods and a titan raging in the distance. It rattled the walls and quaked the ground.

I tended to the wounded. I reprimanded a number of the Berserkers for some of the heavier wounds they sustained. Kirby also showed us that Valkyries had their own form of healing ability, which helped me.

Throughout this, I couldn't shake the feeling something was off about the gathering. The longer it took the gods to return, the more that sensation grew.

Then, everything went silent. No one scarcely breathed as we waited to know who won the victory.

From the shadows of the forest, the gods emerged, no titan to be found. Fenrir had a limp to his walk, and the others looked rough, but their god-healing was already taking effect. Only Baldr was able to stroll up to us with ease, thanks to his ability to feel no pain.

"He got away," Fenrir snarled.

"He won't win," Týr said. "Now that we know of his plans, he no longer has the benefit of surprise. He foolishly believed Odinn would come instead of us, and underestimated our power."

Baldr turned to Kriby. "Muninn is following him. We should know soon where he's hiding, and other tricks he might have."

She nodded. "Odinn will be pleased with that."

"Astrid, what's wrong?" Freyja asked.

I continued to look around, that feeling now a strong, tight pit in my stomach. "Where is Father?"

Mother whirled around, looking through the warriors. "Rune and Bjarke aren't here either."

"Hilda is missing, too," someone said.

My feet were already in motion. I rushed past the gods, ignoring their calls. I didn't know where I was going, just following my instincts past broken houses and unmoving bodies.

I stopped in the forest, my breath heaving. My magic pulsed beneath my skin. The sound of pained groaning had me whirling. "Sigurd!"

The pale man with long dark hair had propped himself up against a tree. He held a hand against his abdomen, blood running in rivulets between his fingers.

He weakly smiled at me when I rushed to his side. "You found me."

"Hold tight." My golden magic latched onto his wounds and knitted his skin back together.

Sigurd breathed heavily. "I was trying to find help. That god targeted us. He wiped so many of us out in one attack. But he left the rest of us injured, clinging to life."

I nodded and focused. "I'll get to the others, too."

When I'd healed him enough to not be at risk of dying or infection, he convinced me to stop. I didn't protest. I needed to heal who I could. I told him where to find the town and he pointed me in the direction of the warriors. I took off without hesitating. *I knew something was wrong.*

Not long after, I found another wounded man, one of the refugees. He was in worse shape, but I had to try.

Black wings curled around me. I looked up at Kirby. She had a sorrowful look on her and she shook her head. My magic died and she reached out, placing a hand on his chest that I hadn't realized was no longer moving. "I'll make sure he makes it safely."

What did that feel like, touching their souls and carrying their weight to Valhǫll? What was it like to be a Valkyrie? This wasn't the place to ask, but I was so curious about her and her sisters.

"Astrid!" someone shouted.

That's Father. I bolted to my feet and looked around. I found him some ways off, flagging me down. Three bears were with him, and two weren't standing.

Kirby wrapped her arms around my waist and lifted me off the ground with her. I didn't startle, nor did I fight her. She flew faster than I could run. The experience might have even been fun, had it not been for the circumstances.

Kirby landed in front of Father. He stepped aside, revealing a gruesome sight of Bjarke and Rune trying to prevent the jarl's insides from spilling out, and Hilda holding her severed arm to the removal spot, possibly hoping her Berserker healing would reattach it.

I swallowed back the bile rising in my throat and jumped into action. My magic spilled from my fingers and I split my attention between both Berserkers, attempting to heal them at the same time. Kirby offered her assistance with Rune. My healing actually worked for Hilda, much to my relief, and soon enough the two were in a condition to rely on their Berserker healing.

Bjarke didn't need any, and Father managed to come out rather unscathed, thanks to Hilda and Rune jumping in front of the killing attack. I was sure to thank them both profusely.

More Valkyries arrived, descending from the sky in breathtaking fashion. They walked the battlefields and woods. Kirby moved to follow their lead, drawn to her task of ferrying souls. My feet moved with her.

I wasn't sure why, but making this walk with her felt right. Maybe it was because I felt responsible. Maybe it was that strange feeling that still tugged at me.

I watched the way Kirby would look at someone and took only a moment to either stop to take their soul or move on. I didn't ask her what her thoughts were in these split-moment decisions, or if it was merely instinct. This was what a Valkyrie did, plain and simple.

In my following, I found people to heal. Kirby would stop for me, and help if I needed it. Her sisters gave acknowledging nods if we passed them, but no one spoke. There was this quiet acceptance between them and me. Which was good, because there was no way I could explain my behavior, or why, when there were no more living to heal, that tug went away.

I stuck with Kirby until the end of their task. The Valkyries flew away when they had enough souls. Even Kirby had to leave. The gods stayed. Freyja fussed over me and the men stuck close, as if expecting someone to try and snatch me right from under them.

No one outwardly asked me about my behavior, but there were many questioning looks. Maybe they'd ask later, and maybe by then I could explain myself, but for now, I wanted to focus on bringing the fallen home for their final burial rites. It was the last thing I could do for them as thanks.

The spoon clanked against the jar before sinking into the honey contents. I scooped the thick liquid into the waiting cauldron of hot water. Frida's thrall, Theo, used a stirring stick to mix the honey and water. Mother moved about behind us with grace and precision, picking the best berries for the next step.

"How are you doing, Astrid?" she asked. "Ready for these?"

"Almost." I finished adding the honey and searched for the starter we created last week. "Where's the mead jar?"

Theo rushed off to another part of the house and returned a moment later with a cloth-covered jar. Both were working at a quicker pace than I felt was needed. Well, I knew Theo would match Mother's speed, as she was in charge of him right now, but that didn't explain my mother's rush.

Leif and Frida had all the mead they'd need on their hony moone. This new batch would hardly be ready for their needs during the next month; it was supposed to be a means of replenishing our stock. And it was a means to keep Mother and me occupied instead of staring at the door with worry.

Theo set the jar down and continued his stirring until the honey was well mixed. He then scooped the warm honey water into a waiting jar. Mother gathered the dried juniper berries and added them to the vessel. I removed the cloth from the jar holding the foamy water while Theo tested the heat of the water. It was still a little too hot, so I used my magic to cool the water before I added the frothing water.

We covered the jar and set it aside to fill another. I was covering the last one when someone knocked on the door. Mother instructed Theo to store the mead while she opened the front door.

When she gasped and the dark aura of her magic coalesced around her hands, all muscles in my body tensed and my magic built up, ready to be used.

Then Mother relaxed, placing her hand on her chest and letting out a sigh. "You startled me, Týr. I didn't expect you of all people to knock, especially since you've returned home with my husband still alive—and in one piece, from the looks of it."

My back straightened, and a tingling sensation fell over my fingers. *Týr and Father are back?*

"I apologize," Týr's familiar voice rumbled from the other side of the door. "I had no intention of experiencing the strength of your magic."

Mother chuckled and stepped back, beckoning him into the house. "No, I suspect that is reserved for a different völva."

My brow furrowed. What did Mother mean? Did Týr know other völvur? And what was with Mother's teasing tone? My gut clenched. Could this völva have caught his attention? I wouldn't be surprised if that was the case. *I'm sure she's perfect.*

"Astrid," Týr's voice penetrated my thoughts.

I blinked when he called my name a second time, and jerked my head up. His intense blue eyes met mine, and I jumped back, startled by his closeness. Then I noticed the blood.

My eyes widened. "Are you hurt?"

I took his arm and frantically searched.

"Astrid."

My search continued, but was interrupted when Týr grabbed my hands and repeated my name. I looked up at him, brow furrowed. It wasn't until I heard Father's booming laughter did realization dawn on me.

Heat rose to my cheeks, and I pulled away. "Right. Gods heal fast. Of course you're not gravely wounded."

Týr smiled. "I appreciate your concern."

He was saying that to be kind. I was sure he didn't need a mortal fussing over nothing with him. I knew gods healed quickly; it was foolish of me to forget. And really, if he'd been gravely wounded, I was certain he would have sought a far more experienced healer right away.

I darted around Týr to reach Father, acutely aware of Týr's strong gaze following me, and interrupted Father's attempts to remove his blood-stained armor by throwing my arms around him. "I'm so glad you've returned in one piece. Do you need any healing?"

He smiled and patted my back. "I could use some, yes."

He sat in a chair and I checked him over. Father's wounds weren't terrible, thankfully. I'd been worried sick ever since he'd departed yesterday with the other seasoned warriors. I'd wanted to go with them, help fight, but Rune wanted Mother and me to stay behind. He'd also kept a number of skilled warriors behind.

According to the jarl, it was a precaution in case the enemy tried to do something to Runavík while the main warrior party had been engaged in battle. At much sense as that made, a part of me had been displeased. I knew I wasn't as battle ready as Mother, but after what had happened the other day, I had wanted to be there for the revenge.

Father was the perfect patient as always, and made sure to speak up when I'd done something to cause discomfort or pain. Mother flew around the house, back up to the pace she had been at before the interruption, Theo trying to keep up.

Father and Týr watched her with great amusement, and Týr even offered his assistance, but she wouldn't have it. She wasn't doing much in the way of chores, more giving Theo instructions of things he needed to do. I really wished I knew what had gotten into her today.

"There, you're done," I said to Father, the golden light of my magic fading.

Theo came in from outside. "The bath is ready for them."

Father patted my hand and stood. "Then, Týr, we should wash up before we're late."

I blinked. *Late? Late for what?*

"I just need to speak with Astrid for a moment," Týr said.

Mother, the confident woman she was, pushed him toward the door leading to our bath behind the house. "You can do so after you wash up. You're both filthy."

Týr was clearly surprised she could force him to move, but he couldn't see the magic assisting her feet in order to do so. "Randi, please."

"I will make sure we're both ready as well," she said, not stopping. "Now go."

He sighed and relented, but not before passing me a glance I wasn't able to decipher—possibly on account of my increased confusion.

"Mother, what's going on?" I asked when she shut the door.

"No time, let's get you ready."

"Ready for what?"

She didn't answer and pushed me into the adjacent bedroom. Theo brought me a bowl of warm water to wash my hands and face.

In the same flurry I'd seen from her all day, Mother pulled out a different dress for me to slide into, as well as various pieces of jewelry. She even left the room to fetch some, returning with pieces I'd never seen before.

She put more time in my hair than usual, and I was suddenly struck with the concern I'd been married off without my knowledge. But who would I be wed to? And what did that have to do with Týr?

I froze. It couldn't be… *Him?* My pulse quickened. No, I had to be wrong about that. Wouldn't Father tell me beforehand? Wouldn't there be more planning involved if that were the case? Why would there be a wedding so soon after a battle? *Týr wouldn't agree to something like that, either.*

"Sunshine, are you all right?" Mother asked.

I forced myself to breathe and then relaxed. "Yes, I'm fine."

She pursed her lips, but before she could question me further, someone walked into the room. I smiled. "Freyja, you've also returned. Welcome back."

She smiled pleasantly. "Are you two ready?"

"No," Mother said for me. "I still need to get her makeup done, and then I'll work on myself."

Freyja flicked her hands and shooed Mother away. "Then go do that. I'll take care of Astrid."

Mother didn't fight the goddess, and rushed out without another word. Freyja chuckled. "She's excited."

A perfect eyebrow lifted when she looked at me. "You seem… confused."

"I am. No one has told me what's going on. Hel, no one has even stopped to tell me how everything went."

Her brow furrowed. "Týr told us he'd inform you."

"He wanted to talk to me, but Mother sent him to bathe. And she wouldn't tell me what was going on when I asked."

Freyja pursed her lips, then snatched up some makeup. "Well, then if you don't mind, I'll let Týr tell you. He was so eager to do it, I don't want to ruin anything."

Why did that not make me feel any better? I nodded my agreement anyway.

Freyja applied the makeup, and when she was done, the reflection gazing back at me in the enchanted mirror surprised even me. I'd never looked this good in my life. I felt so exceptionally beautiful. Almost on the same level as Freyja. *Almost.*

The goddess pulled me into a hug. "You are stunning. Eyes will turn toward you all night."

"Is that… good?" Given I didn't know what was going on, I couldn't be sure.

She chuckled, a glint in her eye, and pulled me toward the door. "I'll let you decide based on Týr's reaction."

"My reaction to what?" he asked as we walked out of the bedroom. His back was to us. He wore a new tunic of a deep blue, and his hair was freshly braided and decorated.

Týr turned around to face us, and stilled, his eyes pinned to me. The longer he stared, the more an urge to fidget tugged me.

"Well?" Freyja prompted.

He opened his mouth, but nothing came out. Freyja hummed triumphantly and headed for the front door. "I see our work is appreciated. I'll leave you two to talk. Try not to get ahead of yourself, Týr. You have all evening to lose all control and have your way with her."

My eyes popped wide, and I stared at her. Týr didn't seem to hear her; she laughed and left the house.

He continued to stare, and I fidgeted with my dress sleeve, feeling self-conscious under the scrutiny of his gaze. "How do I look?"

"You… pretty… uh, beautiful… stunning."

He clamped his mouth shut. I hid a giggle behind my hand. I couldn't recall the last time my appearance had ever turned a man stupid before. A long time, that was for sure. I loved a confident man as much as any woman, but a part of me liked seeing him so speechless.

Týr ran a hand through his hair. "You've struck me dumb. I was unprepared. Perfect. You look perfect for the celebration."

"Celebration?" I gazed up at him. "What's going on, Týr? Is whatever this all is related to the battle? How did that go?"

"Ah, so no one told you. I guess I should be thankful, since I wanted to tell you myself." He grinned. "We won."

I blinked slowly. "Well, I suppose I might have assumed that in some capacity, since none of you came back looking like wounded dogs."

Týr laughed. "Yes, well, as strong as Kronus was, he hadn't expected the force we brought. Even Kirby and the other Valkyries engaged in battle."

My lips parted. How spectacular the winged women must have looked. I had always thought Valkyries only soul ferries for heroic warriors, but my time with Kirby had shown me how little I actually knew about such stunning women.

"Nor had he properly calculated the strength of us gods," Týr said. "Or the other south gods who aided us."

I cocked my head. "More gods from another place?"

He nodded. "It appears this titan was imprisoned in a place called Tartarus. The god, Zeus, and several of his siblings had sealed him and a few other titans there for crimes they wouldn't disclose to us. They were unaware that Kronus had managed to escape, and they were more than eager to capture him again."

"Did we learn what Kronus wanted?"

"We're still not entirely sure on those details. It appears he believed Odinn stole something important from him. He also accused Zeus of this as well. However, we never learned what he thought they stole. Half of the things he said sounded more like mad ramblings than anything sane."

"I see." I chewed my lower lip. "So… everything is going to be back to normal?"

Týr approached and his fingers grazed my cheek. The contact sent a surge of heat through my face. "No god will ever touch you without your permission again. You are safe."

That was good. I hadn't been allowed to leave without Mother or a god present since my abduction. Everyone seemed worried I'd be targeted again, especially after the gods came to my rescue just as Kronus had predicted. I didn't blame them for their caution. It made sense. I still didn't have to like it.

"So, does the victory have anything to do with how strange everyone is acting?" I asked.

Týr grinned. The look created a twist in my gut. *Here it comes.*

"We're holding a celebration. All the warriors who fought with us are invited to join. They're also allowed to bring their lovers to celebrate with them."

That sounded amazing. And now that I knew what this was all about, some of the tension my wild imagination had caused eased up. *Wait, he said lovers were allowed to join…* "Then, why is everyone making a fuss about my appearance? I'm no one's lover, so I'm not going anywhere."

Týr took my hand in his. His intense gaze sent my heart skittering. A tingling sensation crawled along my skin. *He's… not going to… There's no way…*

"You may not have participated in this battle, but you were as involved as anyone who was. You were remarkable, and showed all the qualities of the strong woman you are while Kronus held you captive. As such, I'd like to extend a personal invitation for you and ask you to come as my guest."

Air returned to my lungs in a rush. The pleasant feeling growing inside me dropped. *Guest. Of course.* Why else would he ask me to go except as a guest?

I smiled. "I'd be honored to go with you."

"Excellent." His face brightened in a way I'd never seen before. It made my stupid heart skip, as if it thought his expression meant something, when we very much knew it didn't by the type of attendee I was.

The front door flew open and Freyja barged in. "Have you asked her yet?"

I nodded. "I'm more than happy to attend this celebration as his guest."

"Guest?" Her eyebrow rose and then she shot Týr a pointed look. "She's your *guest?*"

Týr's eyes narrowed. He opened his mouth to speak, however, Mother sighing loudly from up in the loft interrupted him. She glided down the stairs, Father following her. "Yes, he did in fact ask her to attend as a guest."

Freyja let out an annoyed breath and pressed her palm to her forehead while shaking her head. "Unbelievable."

I glanced between the two, confused. *Was he not supposed to?*

"Did I hear she's free for the taking?" Fenrir asked, sauntering into the house.

I rolled my eyes, and he laughed. Týr, on the other hand, had a dark look and stalked toward Fenrir. He pointed at the wolf god. "Out."

Fenrir held up his hands and backed up, grinning. "Maybe you should mark your territory better."

Mark… his territory? My mind swam. I had no idea what was going on anymore. Fenrir's behavior with me was normal. I'd become used to it over these past weeks, and honestly found his antics amusing. But some days, Týr reacted strangely to Fenrir's actions.

Freyja looped my arm into hers. "We should leave before they actually go at it and break the house."

"I would prefer to not have to rebuild," Father said.

Freyja collected those of us who remained after she ferried most of our warriors out earlier, though Týr and Fenrir were being difficult.

I held out my hand. "Týr, Fen, we should be off."

Fenrir grinned and slipped away from Týr, then wrapped an arm around my waist and stood right behind me. Týr predictably stalked toward us, until my outstretched hand pressed against his broad chest. His superior strength didn't allow me to keep him from nearly stepping on my toes, but at least it made him aware enough to not outright squish me between the two men.

Freyja rolled her eyes, and a moment later we were no longer in Runavík. An open field sprawled before us, cut almost too cleanly from the dense surrounding forest and towering mountains in the distance. Grass swayed gently in the glow of the low sun, much of it now packed down in the buzz of bodies.

A massive bonfire crackled at the center of the gathering, its warmth welcoming against the cool air. Tables were piled high with feasts of food, some of which I'd never seen before, and the delicious scent of roasting meat and spiced mead filled the air.

I slipped out of Fenrir's grip to get away from him and Týr. It was a bit much, and I didn't like the attention the behavior was drawing.

I gazed around, taking in all the decorations—and the people. Mortals, gods, fae, and other immortals all mingled and celebrated, drinking, telling stories, and some were dancing. I'd never seen such an eclectic gathering before.

I squeaked when masculine hands grabbed me and lifted me off the ground. Midgard spun. I laughed when I realized it was Baldr.

He set me back on my feet after a moment and smiled down at me. "I'm honored to be in the presence of such stunning beauty. There is none fairer in Midgard."

Heat warmed my face. *These gods and their compliments.* Coming from his lips though, it sent extra powerful feelings flooding through me. "Careful, Baldr, your words might go to my head. Especially when it is you who outshines even gold."

He'd cleaned himself up nicely. His tunic was of a deep red material embellished with gold embroidery and fit his strong body perfectly. His hair was decorated with rings and beads, and he'd adorned himself with arm rings and a necklace.

Baldr grinned. "That means more coming from you than from anyone else here."

Then he turned. "And you, Randi, have somehow made yourself look even fiercer. If I wasn't an honorable god, I'd steal you from your husband."

Mother laughed and patted his shoulder. "Bold of you to say so."

He was right. I hadn't gotten a chance to take in her appearance with the oddness that happened at the house, but somehow, the dangerous aura Mother had every day had been enhanced, and mingled with her beauty to turn her into something beyond any mortal man's dreams. *Father is a lucky man.*

Baldr grinned. "Courage is something I am in no shortage of."

I cocked my head when I noticed something different about Baldr's eyes. "Your eyes are glowing."

The vivid blue was like nothing I'd ever seen before.

"A result of all the prayers during battle," Baldr said.

That made sense. Freyja told me once that prayer affected each god differently. I could see how it could have a visual effect for some. And if this battle was as intense as Týr said, Baldr must have received all manner of prayers for courage to face the enemy.

A large presence loomed over me, and I tipped my head up to smile at Týr. He had a strange look on his face again as he focused on Baldr, but it went away when he shifted his gaze to me. "I'm going to have to keep a close eye on you, or someone will abscond with you."

"Well, she is only your guest," Mother muttered before walking off to join Father.

Baldr's brow rose. "Guest? What, did her beauty turn you dumb when you laid eyes on her?"

Týr glowered at his friend. I wasn't sure what to do. This topic continued to come up and I didn't understand why me being a guest was such an issue. *We're not lovers, so what else would I be other than a guest?*

I blinked when I spotted an enormous wolf grab a cask. "Um, is Fen going to try to drink that in one go? Because I think he'd be more likely to choke on something that large."

Baldr and Týr threw their heads back and roared in laughter. Freyja, who was apparently behind me, grabbed my arm. She, too, couldn't contain her laughter. "I'm so glad you're here. Tonight is going to be fun. Let's go inform him how little faith you have in him handling girthy casks."

I bit my lip, and that made her laugh even harder. "Please make that face in front of him, too."

Her eyes flicked to Týr, as did mine out of reflex. That look he had at the house had returned, and this time, the corner of his mouth turned up. Warmth rose in my cheeks and I looked away.

We joined the festivities, and I had the most fun I'd ever had at a celebration. The food, the drink, the company. I couldn't complain about any of it. While Kirby and the other Valkyries hadn't arrived yet, I was finally introduced to Kirby's lover, Starkad.

I could see why he'd caught her attention. Impressively tall, tattooed—including a wolf Berserker mark, and with corded muscle in all the right places, this Berserker could make any woman weak in the knees.

"It's a pleasure to finally meet you, Astrid," Starkad said. "Kirby speaks highly of you."

I smiled. "She does the same with you. And I can see why."

He gestured to the burly man with dark brown hair and beard next to him who I'd watched guzzle down a whole cask of ale in a drinking competition not too long ago and acted as though it weren't a difficult feat. "This is Davyn."

The bear tattoo peeking out from his tunic told me Davyn was a bear Berserker like Rune and Bjarke, as if his size hadn't been a dead giveaway. He was as massive as all the other bear Berserkers from Runavík. Even Hilda was a large woman.

Davyn held out a giant hand. "Good health, Völva Astrid. I've heard a great many tales of your feats. I was disappointed you weren't able to partake in the battle. Seeing your skills with my own eyes would have been a highlight."

Great, who is spreading exaggerated tales about me already? I smiled and clasped hands with him. His grip was about as impressively strong as I expected, and I could tell he was controlling that so as not to harm me. "I'm interested to know which stories you heard."

Someone called a challenge at Davyn and Starkad. The two men were not keen to back down, and promised to finish our conversation after. I was not stupid enough to stop them, and figured it'd be an entertaining watch.

The festivities continued. Týr stuck close by me, and acted oddly when any man paid extra attention to me—especially when an incredibly beautiful elven man asked me to dance with him and I accepted.

I wasn't a naïve woman. If he were any other man, I'd see his behavior as him having some sort of interest in me, and trying to keep me from being taken by another man. But with how he'd acted around me since I met him, I just didn't know how to interpret his behavior.

"They've finally arrived," Týr said, gazing up at the sky.

I tipped my head skyward. My breath caught. Women clad in armor swooped down, their stunning wings of varied colors propelling them forward. Women with black wings summoned weapons and shields before engaging in mock fights, their movements regaling the tale of the battle.

"Show-offs," Fenrir muttered before loudly tearing into a haunch of meat.

"Don't be jealous," Freyja teased. "Besides, some people are enjoying the display."

I was part of that group. I couldn't look away. *They're stunning.*

The elegance in their movements and ferocity in their strikes—it was like nothing I'd ever witnessed. A sudden yearning tugged my chest. *What would it be like to be a Valkyrie?*

To be immortal and viewed by everyone as someone so stunning and fierce. Maybe then, this feeling I experienced when I was around Týr wouldn't be so out of place. *Maybe I'd be worth more...*

A loud *bang* made me jump, and I crashed into Týr. My ale spilled on the two of us, and I swore. This was such a nice dress, too. And of course I'd soiled Týr's tunic and trousers.

We both glowered in the direction of a large man with long red hair and beard and a lean man with golden hair and beard, who raucously laughed. *Thor and Loki.* Lightning crackled around Mjölnir, the hammer he carried. I may have had a lot to drink by now, but I was still sober enough to know exactly what the god had done.

I'd been advised to stay away from a number of gods here by Týr, Baldr, Fenrir, Freyja, and even her twin brother, Freyr, whom I'd come to meet. I'd known Týr didn't get along with Odinn all that well, but my gods had opened my eyes more as to how often gods tended to be at odds. And Thor and Loki were not the gods my favored deities liked associating with.

I was starting to see why.

Thor held up his drinking horn, and a woman hurriedly filled it for him. He lifted the vessel to his lips. *He will not get away with his actions.*

Focusing on Thor's arm, I projected my magic to not come from me, but him. A tendril of gold grew out of Thor's arm, causing him to pause and stare with slight undisguised alarm. Like I'd been practicing, I controlled the tendril to wrap around the tip of his drinking horn and yanked.

His horn tipped in his hand, spilling mead all over him. Thor froze, and then turned livid eyes on me. I offered him a smug smile before sipping my own drink, while the gods around me laughed. Even Loki laughed at him. Fenrir mentioned once that his father's loyalties lay only with himself, so it made sense.

Thor rose to his feet, and Týr and Baldr mirrored him, no doubt to protect me, but before any of them could do anything, a Valkyrie with black wings swooped down and blocked Thor. It took me a moment to realize it was Kirby. *Is her hair shorter?*

"Move," Thor ordered, sparks flicking off him.

"You know the rules, Thor," Kirby said. "The völvur are off-limits. And seeing as you instigated things, she had a right to retaliate. I'd say her retaliation was also quite kind, compared to what she could have chosen for slighting her."

His lip curled. "You would protect this one."

She grinned. "Of course I would. But really, I don't need to. It's more for your pride than anything. She'd have you begging before you could touch her."

I did my best to keep my expression passive, while internally I screamed. What was she doing? She knew I was still training in my magic. And yes, while I'd made leaps of progress, that didn't mean I was on my mother's level. I couldn't take on a god.

A low rumble of laughter rolled through the gathering. If the altercation with Thor hadn't silenced all the merriment, this interchange certainly had. I turned my attention and everything inside me froze.

A tall, older man clad in armor, with an eye patch and white braided hair and beard with streaks of gray approached, a raven perched upon his shoulder. *Odinn.*

A pale man with gaunt features and dark hair walked with him. His golden eyes were unusual and unsettling.

Odinn's eye swept over us before settling on me. "You are the young völva my ravens have told me about, and the one Kronus thought he could use to lure me into a trap."

My gut churned. Why did his knowledge of me feel like a bad thing? "It's an honor to meet you, Allfather."

He lifted a hand covered in blood, where he carefully carried a raven. "I would ask you to heal—"

I gasped and was reaching for the bird before Odinn could finish speaking. "Muninn!"

How I could recognize him, when he otherwise looked identical to the one perched on Odinn's shoulder, I didn't know. But I knew I was right.

I cradled Muninn in my arms. He was a little larger than I was expecting. Blood slicked his beautiful feathers. "What happened to you?"

Odinn appeared a little displeased but he continued as if I hadn't been bold enough to interrupt him. "Our enemies made the mistake of harming him, and for some reason, he isn't healing as he should."

"Don't worry, Muninn, I'll figure out what's wrong."

The raven weakly croaked. *"Thank you."*

His eyes were half lidded, which was a strange look for a bird. But even still, that eerie intelligence I'd seen in him the first time we met was there, staring up at me.

I hovered my hand over his body. The golden threads of my magic slid through his feathers, searching for the wound that oozed blood. I did my best not to rush, while understanding I couldn't take my time. I wasn't sure how long he'd been injured, and a small body like his only had so much blood. I didn't know if Odinn's ravens could die from blood loss, but I wasn't going to take any chances.

My magic dipped into his body, finding the wound. I focused my efforts, channeling my magic into it. Muninn squirmed and snapped his beak. *"Ow!"*

I murmured calming words in an attempt to keep him from fussing, but it didn't help much. My brow furrowed when my magic snagged.

Muninn squawked. *"Ow! Don't do that."*

Something is blocking my magic. I tried to probe the obstruction; it had to be what was preventing Muninn from healing.

"What is it, Astrid?" Týr asked.

"There's… something embedded in his body," I said. "I'm not quite sure what just yet."

A small fae woman approached, her steps tentative. "Would you like me to try and pull it out? My fingers are slender."

I cocked my head as I continued to assess the object with my magic. My brow furrowed when a cold sensation washed over me. "No. No fae should come close. This is cold iron."

The fae woman scuttled back, and a chorus of hisses and contempt erupted from the gathered fae.

Kirby approached. "I'll assist. I have experience removing cold iron from fae."

I nodded, grateful for the offer, and laid Muninn on the table. Mother also came to assist. After showing Kirby where the wound was, Mother and I held the raven still while Kirby sank her fingers into the wound.

Muninn let out a muffled cry, his beak held shut by my hand as I didn't want him biting, and wiggled against our hold. I did my best to calm him and assure we'd be done soon, but his pain was too great for him to listen. He began shrieking in my head, begging me to stop. My heart squeezed at the sound, but I couldn't allow myself to give in.

Kirby withdrew her fingers finally, and with it, she pinched a lumpy ball of iron. I didn't take any time to gawk at the strange object, instead focusing on healing Muninn. I sat back and let out a relieved breath when the last of his wound stitched together.

Mother released the raven, and he lay there for a moment before rolling onto his feet.

"Better?" I asked him.

Muninn looked at me with those intelligent eyes and then jumped up onto my shoulder. He rubbed his beak against my cheek. *"Thank you, Sister."*

I tentatively reached up and stroked his sleek ebony feathers. "I'm glad I could help you like you helped me. You still have my thanks for that."

Muninn crooned. I grabbed a strip of meat off the table and offered it to him. He'd need to regain his strength. The raven eagerly snatched it before flying back to Odinn.

The god smoothed his beard. "Quite the talent you have, Völva."

Kirby handed him the ball of iron. "I've never seen anything like this."

His eyes narrowed. "Nor I. We will look into this, but after the celebration. You have my thanks, Völva. I will be watching your progress."

A feeling of unease fell over me. I didn't think that was a good thing.

Odinn left to sit on a throne set up for him. The man with him watched me a moment longer before following. He made me even more uneasy.

Kirby pulled me into a hug, drawing my attention away. "I'm glad you came, Astrid."

I smiled and hugged her back, careful with my bloody hands. "Happy to be here. I almost didn't recognize you with the short hair."

She tugged on the golden locks. "Battle casualty after my hasty braid came undone."

"And here I thought your Berserker got a little too rough trying to get those braids out," I teased.

Laughter erupted around me. Starkad tried to deny he'd be that careless, but the heckling Fenrir and Freyr gave him made it difficult for anyone to believe him.

I encouraged Kirby to sit while I washed my hands. Her wings pulled tight against her back and then disappeared, revealing the cutouts in her armor that exposed her now-bare back. She'd told me once that all Valkyries were capable folding away their wings. I found this ability to do so fascinating.

I took locks of her silky hair and braided a thick section toward the back of her head. While I worked, I noticed the man with Odinn was watching me.

"So, you've noticed, too," Kirby murmured.

"Who is he?" I asked.

"That's Garmr. He's a wolf shifter, and Odinn's most loyal enforcer. He does anything Odinn orders, without question, and it's usually the dirtiest work that needs to be done."

"Why is he watching me?"

"That is something I'm trying to figure out," she said. "I don't know why Odinn even asked you to heal Muninn, since all of us Valkyries have the ability to heal. Any one of us could have found that object if we attempted."

"He was testing her," Týr grumbled before tearing into a lamb leg.

I frowned. "Why?"

"Good question." Týr eyed Odinn with undisguised suspicion. "But I don't like it, especially now that he's told you he'll be watching."

Kirby's lips twisted. "I don't think it's anything nefarious."

Though, as the words left her lips, I spotted the conflict in her eyes. She had her loyalties to Odinn, but I wondered if the clashes between the gods had her questioning that.

Fenrir leaned closer. "Say the word, and I'll rip that pup apart. You're safe with me."

"She's already safe with me," Týr nearly snarled.

Fenrir chuckled. "A little testy for someone who is only your *guest*."

Kirby shot Týr a dubious glance. "He's not serious, is he?"

"Oh, he's quite serious," Freyja said in a taunting tone before popping a small fruit in her mouth.

Kirby rolled her eyes. I did my best to ignore the conversation. I really couldn't figure out why this was such a big deal. We weren't lovers, and if he wanted us to be, he would have made that clear by now. *Wouldn't he?*

Týr launched to his feet. "Back off."

Fenrir chuckled. "Let's see if you can force me."

I sighed and pointed away from us. "If you're going to fight, do so over there."

They paused and stared at me. I sensed other eyes on me, too. "I've gotten enough ale and blood on me for one day. The last thing I want is this entire gods-forsaken table on my lap."

Týr looked as though I'd told him his presence repulsed me. I didn't understand why. I just didn't want them brawling right here.

Mother's piercing laugh cut the silence. "You two heard her. Entertain us over there."

Cheers erupted. A good fight during a war celebration was something any warrior would enjoy watching or partaking in.

"Astrid, are you all right?" Kirby murmured.

"I'm fine."

She made a thoughtful sound. "All right then. We won't make mention of your status anymore."

That wasn't the issue. *Isn't it, though?* Maybe I was a little snippy because of that recurring conversation. But it didn't matter. If I wasn't worthy enough for most mortal men unless they knew of my magic capabilities, why would a god see me any differently? *As much as a part of me wishes that wasn't the case…*

"There, your hair is done," I said to Kirby.

She smiled and gave me a strong hug. Her Berserker swooped in and pulled her onto his lap, murmuring something in her ear that got her giggling. I chose not to eavesdrop. That would be rude, and I wanted no part of hearing some lovers' semi-private moments. Nor did I want to worry about me reacting poorly around lovers' interactions with each other when I sat here as one of the only *guests* in attendance.

Instead, I filled my cup with wine that I was told had been imported for the celebration, and settled in to observe the brawl. These two were always finding reasons to pummel each other, so it wasn't anything new for me to watch. Honestly, I did enjoy it. Mostly I enjoyed watching Týr untether this side of himself.

All that power he possesses and is able to control… He could use some of that on me, and I wouldn't complain one bit. Heat pooled in my belly and I gulped down more wine. That would never happen, so no point thinking about it. *Find happiness in what little you've been offered, Astrid. It's more than your damned curse allows otherwise.*

People cheered and hollered, drawn into watching the two gods brawling. Warriors especially looked ready to jump in and have their own fun. The excitement only heightened when Fenrir shifted into his wolf form. The Berserkers were most excited; even Starkad struggled to stay seated.

On occasion, a man would come and sit next to me, trying to engage in conversation or gain some sort of interaction from me. I didn't understand why. Maybe it was the alcohol. Whatever the reason, I was polite, but didn't have much interest in engaging with them. Once I didn't do whatever they were hoping I'd do, they'd slink off. Freyja eventually sat next to me, with Baldr beside her, which seemed to dissuade anyone else from interrupting my enjoyment.

My mind fuzzy from all the drinks, my sense of restraint waned, and a funny idea came to me. Freyja seemed to notice the face I was making and shot me a quizzical look. I winked before I focused on Fenrir and imagined my magic tendrils taking the shape of a ribbon. I thought about it snaking around his legs and then wrapping around his muzzle.

Not a moment later, Fenrir tripped and he struggled against a tight, golden ribbon restraining him. Týr froze, staring at his fallen friend. Silence blanketed the gathering, until Freyja's peal of laughter shattered it.

All eyes fell on her. I did my best to hide my amusement as Fenrir struggled against my magical bindings, the corners of my lips twitching. I never planned for the spell to be useful against a god, even if I did practice it on Baldr, but that was the fun of magic—it sometimes held the best kinds of surprises.

Týr shook his head and went to help his friend, but he hadn't noticed the ribbon I'd wrapped around his ankles. He crashed to the ground, and this time I couldn't hold back my laughter. Many others joined in as Týr stared at me, bewildered by my actions.

Of course, someone decided to try and ruin my fun by shouting out several unkind words at me for "ruining" the brawl. My amusement was cut short, and magic built up in me again. Blades manifested around the man, who froze and swallowed as he stared down the threatening display.

Baldr mumbled something about my facial expression again, while adjusting how he sat. Freyja snickered and teased him. He and Týr always had this unusual reaction when I used my magic this way. I didn't even know what look they meant.

Rune laughed. "Tread lightly, boy. Our völvur are not as soft-hearted as they seem. They'll carve a lesson into you, and you'll count yourself lucky if it's only your words they silence."

Maybe Mother, but not me. I was still training, and hadn't established the same reputation as my mother. And I doubted I would, since most still only saw me for my healing magic. But if our jarl wanted to make me seem more fearsome, I wasn't going to say anything. Especially while I held blades aloft threateningly.

"Do not involve yourself in matters you don't understand," Týr said, his words hard.

My gaze slid to him. I watched him snap the ribbon around his ankle while glaring at the offending warrior. *At least he's not mad at me... I think.* Fenrir broke free of his bindings as well, and soon after, my magic failed, ribbons and weapons disappearing.

Fenrir stalked toward me, still in his wolf form. Most would have been intimidated, but he didn't scare me when I was sober, and he certainly was less threatening after everything I'd drank.

His hot breath wafted into my nose, and I made a disgusted face. "Your breath stinks, Fluffy."

He grunted while laughter rolled through the gathering. *"You've drunk too much."*

His voice penetrating my mind felt incredibly weird, with the fuzziness already blanketing it. I poked his nose with a finger. "Never enough."

His nose twitched. *"Apologize, Astrid."*

"No."

Fenrir shifted and bent close to my face. "Apologize."

I poked him in the nose again, causing Freyja, Baldr, and Kirby to laugh. "No."

He let out a long sigh and turned to Týr, who now approached. "She's your problem. You deal with her."

His brow rose. "Problem? I don't see a problem."

"Yeah, I'm not a problem." I stuck my tongue out at him. "I'm trouble."

Týr laughed and Fenrir rolled his eyes. I smirked and created the ribbon again, wrapping it around his arm and bending it behind his back.

Fenrir gave me a long look. "Astrid."

"What?" I gave him my most innocent look. "I'm just sitting here, drinking and enjoying this celebration."

Týr came up to me and grabbed me. I let out a startled squeak, breaking my concentration on my magic, thus freeing Fenrir, and found myself suddenly on Týr's lap.

Týr didn't say anything to explain his actions, and even though it was a little embarrassing to be sitting on a man's lap who wasn't a lover of mine, I didn't hate it, either. *Accept it, Astrid. You'll never get this chance again.* "Do you need any healing assistance?"

Týr scrutinized me. "I don't think you're in any position to be healing."

I waved my hand. "It'll be fine. You're gods. What could go wrong?"

He chuckled and handed me bread. "Eat."

I took the food, not really understanding why, and tore into it anyway. *This is good.* All the food here was delicious. Immortals knew how to celebrate. "We need another entertaining fight."

Cheers of agreement erupted and the fights continued. There was no order to how warriors challenged each other. Fae faced mortals, berserkers turned things into a free-for-all. Bjarke even challenged the rude warrior in my honor. He nearly tore the man's arms off. It made for the best entertainment.

I blinked when Týr took my cup and drank from it. Heat surged into my face. That couldn't mean what it did with mortals… *Right?*

Týr made a disgusted face. I giggled and took my wine back. "Well, I like it."

He shook his head and grabbed his ornately decorated drinking horn from his belt. A woman rushed over to fill it with ale for him.

The flash of black feathers distracted me. Valkyries joined in the brawls. But as I watched, I noticed it was only Valkyries with black wings, much like the aerial mock battles.

"Kirby," I said.

She glanced up from her drink. "Yes?"

"Why is it that I'm only seeing Valkyries with black wings fight?"

"Oh, that's because of our specialized training. Only those of us with black wings have had a taste for battle."

I made a thoughtful sound, my eyes sweeping over the other Valkyries who still had their wings out. I spotted silver and gold, and a few shades of reds. There had been others, I thought, but I was too intoxicated at this point to think that far back. *I wonder what the other colors mean?*

"Tell me, Astrid, what are you going to call that spell you used on Fenrir?" Freyja asked, interrupting my musing.

I tapped a finger against my lips. "Gleipnir."

Fenrir snorted. "It doesn't need a name, because it'll never be used again."

Freyr nudged him. "I wouldn't be so sure."

Fenrir shot me a sideways glance. "Don't you dare."

I grinned and sloppily held out my hand, spilling my drink a bit. "You can't stop me, Fluffy. And maybe, just for you, I'll teach it to someone else."

Týr and the others laughed. Fenrir shook his head. I had a feeling I'd be in a lot of trouble if I did teach someone that ribbon trick, but I didn't care. It'd be too fun not to. *It just has to be the right person.*

The rest of the celebration passed in a blur. The brawls continued until it was only the immortals with their fast-healing abilities still carrying on as entertainment. Several blood sacrifices were made to the gods. Týr and I danced—a lot. And I danced with Baldr. I enjoyed the dancing more than the fights.

I might have also pulled some tricks on a few people, with no regards to their status. Those had gained Loki's attention, and may have been influenced by him a few times. He wasn't as bad as Týr and the others made it seem, and I chose to forgive him for encouraging Thor's mischief.

Now we stood back in Runavík, and I wasn't quite sure how we got here. Týr also stood next to me. I wasn't sure why he'd come with us, but I didn't mind. *He can stay forever if he wants.*

Father pulled Mother close, and attempted to murmur in her ear, but was too drunk to be quiet. *Everyone* heard what he wanted to do with her upon returning home.

"I'm going to take the long way home," I murmured, staggering in a direction other than toward the house. I did not want to hear any of that if I could help it. It was going to be difficult enough when Leif and Frida were back from their hony moone, given they'd only partitioned off their side of the bedroom we shared.

One of the men drunkenly stumbled after me. "Come with me tonight. I'll even share the good furs—"

Someone shoved him away from me. I gazed up at Týr. "That wasn't nice."

"I'll be accompanying you so you don't get into trouble."

"Me? You're the one pushing people."

He smirked and tucked my arms around his. "Then you can accompany me to keep me out of trouble."

I grinned. I couldn't stop him from doing anything, especially not with my mind feeling like this from all the drinking. But I liked the idea of walking with him. It meant he wasn't leaving quite yet.

"You seem happy," Týr said after a moment of us being alone.

I leaned my head against his arm. "I'm with you."

"So, you're not mad at me?"

I gazed up at him and blinked slowly. "Why would I be mad at you?"

"I just…" He shook his head. "Never mind."

I would have questioned him more, had my feet not decided to forget how to move mid-movement, tripping me. I yelped, and Týr grabbed me by the waist, chuckling. "I think you've had too much to drink."

I shook my head, only to regret it when my head swam and also pounded. "No, I haven't had enough to drink."

"Why do you say that?"

"Because I can still think." There went my drunken mouth. This was not something I needed to be sharing with him. He'd think me foolish.

His brow furrowed. "You don't want to think?"

"I don't want these silly thoughts in my head."

"What silly thoughts?"

"Doesn't matter." They were idiotic and not something to bother him with.

I squeaked when he slid an arm under my legs and lifted me. "You're going to hurt yourself at this rate."

"My hero!" I wrapped my arms around his neck. A little dramatic? Perhaps. But I felt too good to care.

He chuckled. "Are you going to tell your hero your silly thoughts so he can maybe help you?"

"He cannot help. They're silly mortal thoughts. He's got better things to worry about." I rested my head on his shoulder, his strong masculine scent invading my nose. "You smell nice."

"Astrid, do you not remember what I told you?" Týr asked, ignoring my comment about his scent.

"You've offered many sweet words to please me."

"They weren't only to please you, Astrid. I was sincere."

"Maybe." I didn't believe him, but I didn't want to fight. It wasn't worth it. *I'm not worth it.*

Týr sighed. "What can I say that will convince you?"

"What is there to convince? You'll forget me. You can say you won't, but you will." I leaned up and kissed his cheek. "And that's fine. We can't all be immortal."

Týr frowned. Like the first time I'd tested the waters, I shouldn't have kissed him. He didn't appreciate that boldness from a pathetic mess of a mortal. *Good thing no one is around to see.* "There is so much I wish to say right now, but I can't. Not when you're intoxicated."

"You wouldn't tell me even if I wasn't."

His eyes narrowed. "I would."

"No, you wouldn't." If he planned to say something important, he would have by now. If I'd truly captured the interest of him or of Baldr, they'd have made their intentions clear. I accepted this. I wasn't special. I wasn't lucky like Starkad, who'd captured a Valkyrie's affections.

I rested my head at the crook of his neck. My eyes hooded, heaviness pulling at my mind. "And it's fine. You being here makes me happy. I'm content with that."

Týr's fingers grazed my cheek. "I will prove it."

My eyes closed. *I want to believe you. I just... can't.*

THIRTEEN

ASTRID

Waves splashed and the boat rocked. The wind tugged the ship's sails, and salt stained the air and clung to my face. I'd never been on the ocean before. Anywhere we traveled was easily reached by foot or horseback. But King Geir had summoned Jarl Rune, as well as me. It seemed word had continued to travel about my magic capabilities. No one was really surprised.

Our family had a reputation because of the long line of völvur we produced—and each one had made a name for herself. It was only a matter of time before I made mine, considering everything that'd happened since my magic manifested.

Mother's fingers glided through my hair. She selected locks she wanted and braided them together, adding jewelry where she saw fit. "How are you feeling? Not too much strain on you?"

Along with this being my first voyage, I was charged with using my magic to create the wind for our sails. This was usually Mother's job when she went out on the ships, but she wanted me to do it this time.

"I'm fine," I said, feeling little strain from the magic coursing through me. "I'm more worried about being distracted and my magic failing."

Mother hummed thoughtfully. "Worried about your brother, or something else?"

"I'm worried about Frida more than Leif," I said. "You know how he's been lately, with her and her pregnancy. He was terrible all winter, fretting and fretting, and now with her due soon, he's gotten worse. And she's stuck at home with him, without us to steer him into other things."

My mother chuckled. "Don't fret. Frida can handle herself. Your father was like that, too, when I first became pregnant with you. It gets easier for them. Besides, we're not going to be around forever, so they're going to need to figure out how to make it all work when they don't have us to rely on."

She had a point, but it didn't make me feel any better.

"You're doing an excellent job with the wind, Astrid," Rune called out.

"I think this is the smoothest sailing we've had in a long time," Father said, a wide grin on his face.

Mother let out an indignant snort. "At least I get us there quickly."

"Quickly, but I have to pray to every god I'll see our destination, let alone return to my family," another man said.

Laughter rolled through the boat. I pressed my lips together so I wouldn't join in. Mother wasn't known for her restraint with her magic.

"You'll miss my way of sailing when I'm gone," Mother said.

My stomach churned. She'd been talking like this a lot the past few months. It made me uneasy, as if she expected to die soon.

"We're here!" someone shouted.

On the horizon, the sprawling city of Bergthorshöfn came into view. The harbor was full of docked ships and crowded with people. Rising up beyond that on the sloped landscape, were more buildings than I'd ever seen in my life. I stood to get a better view. *It's amazing!*

Mother guided me to lessen my magic once we reached the middle of the harbor, and the men took over with the oars. We docked our knarr and disembarked once it was tethered. Mother showed me how she wove a ward around the ship to ensure nothing happen to it while we were away.

Our tradesmen went about their jobs while I followed my parents, Rune, and several others into the city.

There was so much going on everywhere that I held hands with Mother so I wouldn't get separated in the chaos of the city. People crowded popular buildings and market stalls, others strode by with purpose, whether on horseback or on carts. The sheer number of children running around playing and causing mischief was astounding. We didn't have nearly this many children in Runavík.

"We'll part here," Father said, turning to us when we'd made it hallway through the city. "Enjoy your time in the market, just don't go overboard."

His eyes flicked to Mother briefly. She liked to shop. "We'll call for you when the king is ready to speak with you."

I nodded, not knowing what else to say. This was all new to me.

We strolled through the market. Mother wanted to look at everything, from textiles and jewelry to tools and a few thralls for sale. Even things she wouldn't be caught dead with, she looked at for the sake of looking. I had a feeling she did it on purpose, because it would get back to Father in some way or another.

Mother smiled the whole time, enjoying herself. I did as well. This was fun. And we did find a few things we needed. There were several items I wanted, but were too expensive. We were a well-off family, but I knew better than to spend everything we had.

We stopped when someone caught Mother's eyes. It was a young woman, maybe a winter or two younger than me, with flowing rust-colored hair. She noticed us watching her.

"A völva…" she said in breathy awe. "Two völvur. The two everyone is talking about visiting the king today."

How did this woman know we were völvur? We looked no different than other wealthy individuals walking these streets.

"You, I've seen you before." Mother squinted at the woman. "A great destiny awaits you."

The woman blinked and pointed at herself. "Me?"

"A destiny like none have ever seen." Mother's face grew grave and her eyes unfocused.

A Valkyrie made not like any have ever seen
Not one to a single god she prays
Not to Odinn like those this day
But behold, a great tragedy will befall you first
A curse of the gods, to wander and live but to forget and live anew
Half an eternity the sun shall rise and fall before they free that
which binds you

Mother's eyes refocused. Then her head slumped. I grabbed her by the arm, afraid she'd fall, but she remained motionless.

I stared at my mother, in awe and terror. I'd never witnessed her having a vision, but Father had warned me what it was like. However, no matter what he told me, I doubted he would have been able to prepare me for this.

And the poor woman. She remained rooted in place, petrified. Those around her gazed at us, either in sympathy for the woman's poor future or in reverence of being in the presence of a völva.

Mother came out of her stupor and walked on, as if nothing had happened and the woman no longer existed. I gave her one last glance before following my mother.

"Randi. Astrid," someone called out.

We turned to see several people from Runavík approaching.

"King Geir requests your presence."

We followed them to the King's hall. My pulse picked up the closer we got, and by the time we arrived at the imposing structure, it was racing. I glanced at the building built from dark wood and carved with stories of the gods and heroes of legend. Colorful paint accented important elements of the murals, and magical runes were strategically woven in, emitting a slight glow.

There were more people here than I expected, and their eyes all turned to us when we entered through the red painted doors. Torches illuminated the building, along with a central hearth that stretched the length of a hall, its warm fire inviting, as if it tried to banish the unease in me—or lure me into a false sense of security.

Father and Rune stood at the far end of the room near a raised dais where a tall, broad-shouldered man in his late thirties to early forties with scarred, sun-darkened skin and golden hair sat in a fur-lined throne. He sat in a relaxed, lounging posture, and even though his eyes lit up upon seeing us, he didn't adjust himself.

"Völva Randi, it's good to see you again," the man said in a low, rolling voice. His pale eyes shifted to me. "And this must be Völva Astrid that I've heard a great deal about."

Mother and I both bowed respectfully. It was then I noticed how tense Mother was. She'd never had anything bad to say about the king when she'd been around him in the past, and she hadn't warned me to be careful, beyond being on my best behavior.

Something didn't feel right.

"I am told you have the power to heal anything," the king said.

"I'm afraid I can't confirm everything is in my power to heal, King Geir. I only just came into my abilities last summer. I am still learning what I can do, and thus far, I've only been capable of healing certain injuries."

His piercing gaze watched me. "How old have the injuries been, that you've been able to heal?"

"I have not been capable of healing scars, but old bone injuries that did not heal properly have mended under my power in some circumstances." My lips pressed into a thin line. "I can't say it would be a pleasant experience, either. Many of those for whom I fixed old bone injuries experienced a great deal of pain."

King Geir gestured to his left. Others parted, revealing a woman around my age with dark brown hair, lying awkwardly on a bench. Her leg was propped up and... didn't look right.

"My daughter, Estrid. As a child, her leg was damaged and didn't heal right. I want you to fix it."

I swallowed hard. That was a large request, especially for the King's daughter. *And if I fail...*

Mother subtly nodded. She knew my limits and trusted me to handle this. Even if that meant admitting when I couldn't perform this task. I would play it safe, but I couldn't outright refuse to try.

Taking a quiet breath, I padded over to the woman. She smiled pleasantly, and I introduced myself before sitting down with her. I didn't check her leg immediately. I needed to understand her overall health first to determine if I could risk trying.

She had a minor problem in her hand, which was an easy fix and a good test to see how she'd handle the pain for her leg. Estrid didn't utter a single complaint and was more in awe when she flexed her healed hand. I never tired of that look. It brought warmth to my chest.

When I was ready to attempt the leg healing, I had her moved to the floor, where she'd be more comfortable. My mother also came over to assist, along with a few others I'd need to hold Estrid down when she started thrashing, because I knew the pain would cause that.

Her damaged leg was like nothing I'd seen in a person from a wealthy family. A farmer, yes, I'd seen a number of nasty injuries from their livestock that reminded me of this, but I would have never guessed the king's daughter would obtain such an injury. I would have expected they'd have gotten her a healer with the ability to set this far better, long before it healed.

Once Estrid had a strip of leather in her mouth, and was as relaxed as possible despite anticipating what came next, I gave her a quick warning we were about to begin, and then hovered my hand over the woman's leg. Magic built up in my chest before the tingling sensation spread through me and into my hands.

Estrid twitched almost immediately, and those holding her down braced for the inevitable. The healing worked slowly, seeping into her skin and then her bones. She whimpered when the pressure of the magic penetrated fully.

This was the tricky part. I would have to ignore her agony to focus. If I pushed too quickly, I'd harm her, but if I didn't push enough, she'd suffer longer than needed, and it might result in her passing out, or worse, the healing to fail.

Her screaming came soon into the healing, and it took everyone involved to hold Estrid still. I sensed even the King rose to his feet. I blocked it all out.

There was a moment I thought to stop, when it seemed the pain was too much for her, but I sensed we were almost done, and pushed on. She'd have to be strong and fight this.

And Estrid did. No matter how agonizing the pain was, she fought to remain awake and see the end of this.

I let out a tired breath and my magic slipped away. "It is done."

Collective sighs filled the room. Estrid panted, and her eyes threatened to roll into the back of her head. Sweat trickled along and pooled on her skin and hair. Most of those who helped me stepped away. Mother remained, cleaning the woman with a cloth. Estrid's brother also stayed by her side to monitor her.

I assisted Mother and gave Estrid instructions. "You mustn't walk on this leg until tomorrow. When tomorrow comes, do not put your full weight on it. Your body hasn't walked properly in so long it will need time to adjust. Take it slow over the next few days. If you push too quickly, you'll re-injure yourself."

Estrid lazily nodded her head, but I suspected she didn't hear most of what I said. Her brother had, though, and assured me my instructions would be followed.

When she was carried off to rest, Mother and I faced the king. He now sat in his throne again, but he had a more attentive posture. His eyes gleamed, and for some reason, this made me even more uneasy than when I first arrived.

"The rumors don't serve your abilities justice, Völva Astrid. That settles it." The king leaned forward, resting his arm on his leg in a posture that was both predatory and imposing. "You will be my new wife."

Silence.

Not a single person even breathed. The only sound I heard was of my own racing heart. *Did he just—*

Mother broke the quiet with strained words. "I'm sorry, King Geir, I'm not sure I heard your declaration clearly enough."

My blood ran colder than it already was from the king's words. Her strain wasn't from suppressed joy, but fury.

King Geir grinned. "I was quite clear, but I will repeat myself out of respect for you, Völva Randi. I will marry your daughter, and we will form an alliance like no other. Two powerful families that will bring us glory against our enemies."

One pounding heartbeat.

Then another.

Then the words that came out of my mouth were the most surprising ones to be uttered today.

"I refuse."

FOURTEEN

TÝR

Bergthorshöfn bustled with people and horse-drawn carts. Merchants shouted their wares, happy children ran by, laughing and weaving through the crowds, and the sharp *tang* of hammers on anvils mixed with the chatter of the market.

People moved out of my way as usual. It was nice being in a home territory where the mortals knew me. Any time I had to travel to a foreign land, the people moved about as if I were just like them. It helped in some situations, but overall, I preferred how the people here worshiped and respected me, even outside of battle.

The only exceptions were Astrid and her family. I craved the casual air about our interactions. Especially Astrid. Thoughts of her filled my mind all the time. I couldn't let her go, and I needed to figure out the best way to make my intentions clearer.

I could tell her father to give her to me as debt repayment, but that was too hollow. I needed Astrid to want me, not feel obligated to me.

I paused at a stall where a merchant sold fine jewelry. Astrid deserved such things. *But what should I get her?* This was the most difficult part of providing her gifts. She tended to dodge any questions that would help identify what I could spoil her with.

A tiny mew cried from the cage I carried on my back. Hopefully, she'd at least like this gift.

Something caught my senses, sending me on alert. My back straightened, and I looked around, not being subtle at all. *Who is watching me?* I looked up and narrowed my eyes.

A raven perched atop a nearby building—beady black eyes fixed on me. *Huginn.* Of course Odinn would send one of his favorite spies to check on me.

Having been spotted, the bird croaked and then flew off.

I glanced down at the stall wares again before moving on, unable to choose anything specific, and continued my search. My pace slowed when I heard something unusual murmured through the mingling people—talk of two völvur visiting the king today.

One völva visiting was rare enough, but two at the same time? *Could they be Astrid and Randi?* I hadn't seen Astrid in a few weeks, having been kept away with other responsibilities. But I was aware of her name spreading, particularly regarding her power. If the king found out about her—and I'd be surprised if he hadn't by now—it wouldn't be a surprise she was summoned.

Then, when someone mentioned both völvur having red hair, I knew it was them. I abandoned my search in favor of a new one—the King's hall.

The building came into view. People crowded around the entrance, unable to go inside, but hoping to catch a glimpse of the goings-on within. They murmured amongst themselves about a völva who was healing the king's crippled daughter. That confirmed this had to be Astrid and Randi.

Since knowing Astrid last summer, I'd searched for more witches with true magic affinity to understand the spread of magic within the mortals. Among the confirmed witches I found, none had the ability to heal on the scale Astrid was capable of. Their abilities only extended to superficial wounds or organ damage.

I'd witnessed Astrid heal a nobleman who had an old arm injury from his younger days, and Baldr told me of the mangled leg she fixed that a wolf Berserker had. *She's the most amazing woman alive.*

The crowd gasped and murmured. I couldn't help but smirk. She'd proven her ability, increasing her notoriety. Everyone would know her name soon. *And then they'd know she was mine.*

I pushed through the throng of people. Why, I wasn't sure. I could wait until Astrid was finished with her audience with the king and then see her after, but something in the back of my mind flashed in warning. Maybe it was the murmuring from the crowd still. Or maybe it was the snippet of a memory where I overheard two people discussing when they thought the king would remarry after his wife's death last winter.

Astrid isn't married.

"The rumors don't serve your abilities justice, Völva Astrid. That settles it." The king's voice rang out clear to me over the crowd when I drew closer. "You will be my new wife."

My feet stopped. I stared at the closed door, everything inside me coiling and growing cold. He had not just said that. He was not trying to lay claim on *my* Astrid.

"I'm sorry, King Geir, I'm not sure I heard your declaration clearly enough," Randi said.

"I was quite clear, but I will repeat myself out of respect for you, Völva Randi," the king said. "I will marry your daughter, and we will form an alliance like no other. Two powerful families that will bring us glory against our enemies."

My teeth ground together and I barely had the presence of mind to gently set down the animal cage in a safe place against the building wall.

I placed my hand on the door, and paused when Astrid's voice rang out.

"I refuse."

Gasps and murmurs came from both inside and outside the building.

She… refuses… Astrid, the woman I craved, refused a king. Where any woman would feel honored for such a proposal to become a queen, Astrid hadn't hesitated to refuse.

The king laughed. "Refuse? You act like you have a choice."

My lip curled. *How dare he.*

"She does have a choice," Bjǫrn said. "I listen to what she wants. I will not approve of this alliance or marriage."

More gasps and murmurs, but they barely penetrated the fog in my mind and blood pounding in my ears. My nails bit into the skin of my palms. My vision focused on the door, and I shoved it open.

"Bjǫrn, you can't possibly—" the king's words cut off and more gasps and murmurs spread through the onlooking crowd.

"Týr," Astrid murmured.

My focus was so tunneled to the man sitting on his throne, I almost missed her presence. But I could never ignore it. She stood with Randi, who had a familiar dark aura around her. I'd seen her in battle, and even I found her a terrifying woman. She was ready to kill anyone who defied her.

The king leaned back and rested his cheek on his fist and had an amused expression. "I'd heard rumors a red-haired völva had bewitched the mighty Týr. And here you are. I wonder if these tales are true, or if this is mere coincidence."

I struggled to keep my breathing even and calm while an inferno raged inside me. "No one controls me. Nor do they control Astrid. She and Bjǫrn have given you an answer."

The king laughed. "Do you know who I am? Only a fool would refuse an alliance with me. I am a king, and I take only the finest at my side. A strong völva, young and full of power, will bear me sons and daughters worthy of my name—that is what I deserve, and what I will have."

I snarled. *How dare he think he can demand what isn't his to take?* "You cannot have her."

"I can, and I will."

My pulse pounded in my ears. Everything around me muted, and I took a tense step forward. I would crush him—scatter his entrails for Odinn's ravens to feast upon, and lay his head upon a spike.

A soft hand slid over my arm, and then *her* voice, soft and calming, broke through the haze of my rage. "Týr, stop."

The room melted back into existence. Men who were brave enough brandished weapons. I, too, carried my axe.

Astrid pressed against me, her snaring eyes gazing up. "Týr, put the weapon away. Everyone should put their weapons away. There's no need for violence."

That's where she was wrong. I would cut down anyone who thought they could take her from me.

"Týr," she said again. The sound of my name on her tongue wrapped around my very being and seeped deeper than my bones. My body relaxed, the need to fight this battle lessening, and yet it was still there, simmering just below the surface. But she was here with me and no one else.

"He who controls the völva controls the god," the king murmured.

"Father," a man hissed. "Stop antagonizing the gods."

My muscles tightened, but before I could spit out a retort, Astrid spoke up. "I do not control him, King Geir. No one controls the gods."

That wasn't true. She absolutely held the keys to my undoing. I'd do anything she requested if it made her happy. But I would not allow this king to think he could control my Astrid.

"Bjǫrn, take Astrid and Randi outside," I commanded.

He'd gone to his wife to keep her calm. An inky blackness seeped into her eyes. She was as ready to kill everyone as me, consequences be damned.

Astrid's grip on my arm tightened. "I'm not leaving until you put your weapon away and promise me you won't kill anyone unless they attack you first."

My gaze flicked to the warriors who readied to protect their king. They couldn't hurt me, so a weapon wouldn't be needed. I dismissed my axe. "As you wish, Valkyrie. You have my word I will not kill unless it is necessary."

She smiled, and her touch slipped away. The simmering rage rose again, but I managed to keep my head clear enough to adhere to my promise.

Astrid and her family left, along with Rune, the door closing behind them.

I stalked toward the king. My pulse beat in rhythm of my steps, like pounding drums of war. His men stood their ground for maybe a moment, then their knees wobbled and they backed away. Geir's cocky smirk faded as he watched no one stand up to protect him.

He opened his mouth to speak, but my hand clamped around his throat. I squeezed tight and lifted him off his pathetic throne. The pitiful man scrabbled at my hands, his nails doing nothing to save him.

I pulled him close to my face, our noses almost touching. His fear-stricken eyes reflected the crazed rage of my own expression. "You ever try to touch *my* Astrid, and you and your line, and even your ancestors before you, will feel the extent of my wrath."

I shoved him back into his throne, nearly toppling it with the force, and spun on my heels without another word.

No one attempted to stop me. They weren't foolish enough to go against one of their gods. But I knew this king would be. And he'd rue the day he crossed me.

I threw the doors open, immediately looking for Astrid. She and her family were nearby. Astrid crouched by the animal cage, playing with the fluffy kitten inside. The remnants of my anger dissipated, replaced by warmth. "Do you like her?"

Astrid glanced up. "She's cute."

I lifted the cage, and she stood. I unlocked it and scooped the kitten out with one hand, offering her to Astrid. "She's yours."

She gasped, her eyes going wide. "Really?"

I continued to hold the squirming kitten out to her. She snatched the feline and snuggled her against her chest. I'd never felt more jealous of a cat than in this moment.

"Thank you for your assistance, Týr," Bjǫrn said. "I'm sorry my family has troubled you again."

I shook my head. "The only one who caused me trouble was a pompous king."

"How did you know we were here?" Astrid asked.

"I didn't. I was here for my own needs and heard of the two völvur visiting the king. I gathered from there it was you two and thought to drop by."

She smiled. "I'm glad you did."

So was I. "What are your plans for the rest of the day?"

She looked to her parents and Rune.

"Supply run, and then we ship back out for home," Rune said. "I don't believe it's wise for us to remain here longer than we need to."

"I will accompany you," I said.

All four mortals seemed surprised by this.

"You needn't trouble yourself," Bjǫrn said.

I shook my head. "I've made my decision." I then shifted my attention back to Astrid. "What do you need?"

She stared up at me as if I'd grown an extra head. *Why is it that my insistence to be around baffles her?*

"There were a few nice pieces of jewelry she was eyeing earlier," Randi said casually.

Astrid set hard, livid eyes on her. "Mother."

I smirked. "Where was this merchant, Astrid?"

She shook her head. "No. No. No. No."

I grasped her chin and tipped her head toward me. Her cheeks flushed an alluring shade of crimson. "Tell me where."

Astrid let out a resigning sigh. "All right, I'll show you."

I smirked. *I believe I've finally found your weak spot, my Valkyrie.*

FIFTEEN

ASTRID

Leif paced back and forth behind me. I plucked another spiky leaf from a sprig and dropped it in my mortar. Normally I'd pick faster, but this was the only thing keeping me calm as my brother continued on about his worries with Frida's condition. She was in her last month and, as I anticipated, Leif had grown more unbearable.

"Are you even listening to me?" Leif asked.

"Nope," I admitted. "You're repeating yourself for the fifth time. If I listened anymore after the second, I'd have thrown you out of this house."

"You can't throw me out," he snarled.

"Watch me."

He groaned and paced some more. "Please, Astrid."

I whirled on him. "What do you want me to do, Leif? I'm making her a tonic to help ease her discomfort, but that's all I can do. She is with child. She's not going to be comfortable. This is what happens to all pregnant women right before the baby comes."

I may not have come into my magic until last summer, but that didn't mean I hadn't been learning anything. I had always found myself drawn to healing, and dedicated my time learning herbs and medicine. Mother had also taught me all there was to know about midwifery, and I'd assisted several women through their pregnancies and deliveries. Frida's wouldn't be any different.

The woman in question waddled into the room. "Leif, I told you to stop pestering her."

"Why are you up?" He rushed over to his wife and fussed. "You should be lying down and resting."

She rolled her eyes. "If I lay in bed any longer, I'll get bed sores. Besides, I need something to do."

Leif wouldn't let this go, and my patience reached its limits. I couldn't put up with his behavior a moment longer after all these months of suffering.

"Leif, shut up and sit down!"

The two of them stared at me.

"I'm sick of dealing with this. Your fussing is only making things worse, and you're being absolutely ridiculous. Enough already!"

To my surprise, Leif dropped down on a chair with a heavy sigh. "I'm sorry I'm worried."

"Yes, you've made that abundantly clear for the last *eight* months." He flinched.

I hated yelling at him. Leif and I rarely fought, even when we were little. But sometimes we just pushed each other a little too far.

I focused on the tonic so I wouldn't say anything more. When I finished, I ensured Frida drank it all and sent her to rest more so Leif would stay off our backs and to for the tonic to take effect. I wanted her to go out for a walk after. It would be good for her.

"What's this?" Leif asked.

My cleanup paused, and I took a deep breath to handle my brother. It wasn't about Frida's condition, so I couldn't yell at him. I turned around to face him and my stomach dropped. *No...*

My brother had pulled out a basket I'd stored by his chair. Inside was a piece of clothing I'd been working on.

"It's nothing." I tried to sound as casual as I could.

"Doesn't look like nothing to me."

He pulled the tunic out of the basket, and I groaned internally. *Why can't he leave well enough alone?* "It's nothing, as in nothing special. Just a new tunic I'm working through."

"Looks nice." Leif looked it over more. "Too big for Father or me."

My gut clenched. I'd hoped he didn't notice that. "I messed it up. I have to fix it."

Liar, liar, Loki for hire.

My brother's gaze flicked up to me, and he smirked. "You really think I'd believe that?"

My jaw clenched.

"Your face is growing red."

"Because you're looking at something I didn't want anyone to see. I don't like people looking at my failures." Gods, I wasn't even believing myself.

My brother rolled his eyes. "You can admit it's for Týr, Astrid."

"It's not."

His brow spiked. "He'd like it. It's nice. I'd love a tunic this nice."

"I heard that," Frida muttered from the other room.

My stomach churned and knotted. I didn't like this conversation, least of all with my brother. "Why would I make Týr a tunic?"

Leif sighed and dropped the tunic back in the basket. "Astrid, I know you think you're cursed, but you're not."

Except I was. Three failed almost-marriages, and now my heart yearned for a god I couldn't have. If that wasn't a curse, what was? "I'm nothing special."

"The hel you're not. A king wanted you to marry him. And you've got at least one god following you around like a well-trained hound. How do you not see that?"

I worked my jaw. Týr was around a lot, and he insisted on giving me a number of gifts. My favorite two so far hung around my neck and slept on my bed, curled up and purring louder than Thor's thunder.

But I honestly didn't understand why. Why would I be anything special to him? I wanted to be. Gods, did I want to be. And yet, when I was with him, I felt that distance between us—that barrier I, the puny little mortal, wasn't allowed to cross.

"Father is waiting for him to request your hand," Leif said.

I blinked. "What?"

He gave a half-laugh. "Did you really not suspect it, Astrid? All the rejected proposals? Not just from random families, but also a jarl for his son and even the king himself? The king, Astrid!"

My gaze fell away. Father told me why he rejected Rune's request. The logic was sound. It fit the same reason he would agree to refuse the king, since I publicly declared my rejection.

And yet, I couldn't help but wonder how far Father would wait on that promise. There wouldn't have been a better alliance opportunity than with the king himself, even if he only wanted me because of my magic. It would be foolish to think that wasn't my best option in life. *Unless you were certain your daughter had the only alliance worth even more than that.*

My chest constricted. And my curse struck again—cursed to die alone. "The tunic is not for Týr. He… has no intentions."

"Astrid…" my brother said softly.

I grabbed my herb basket. "I'm going to forage. Once Frida's tonic takes effect, she needs to talk around."

"Astrid, wait," he called.

I opened the front door and breeze past Mother. "Astrid? Astrid, what's wrong? Leif, what happened?"

I quickened my pace. I didn't want to hear Leif retell her our conversation. I didn't want to hear him repeat the words that had come from my lips.

I needed to be alone.

The gloomy sky above corresponded perfectly with the raging emotions within me. In the past, I would have prayed for help to ease them. But these days, I didn't pray much. It felt… it was too strange now that I'd become so connected to them. And it wasn't like any of them could help me. *Or even want to help me with this.* What did they care about some mortal's insignificant issues?

Runavík disappeared behind me, and I found the patch of herbs I needed. I picked and dug, soft earth coating my hands. This usually calmed me, but not today. My emotions still twisted and tormented me.

He was kind to me. He listened to me. He went out of his way to make me smile and laugh, and make me a part of things no other mortal could dream of experiencing. And yet, I couldn't be convinced it meant anything. *If he had intentions… if I meant something to him… he would have told me by now.*

Warmth trickled down my cheek. I gasped and furiously rubbed away the tears. *Stop it, Astrid! Stop it!* It wasn't worth it. I just needed to let it go and accept how things were. I'd angered the Norns as a child, and this was my punishment.

Water splashed on my arm. I ignored it.

Another splatter. Still, I ignored it.

A light pitter-patter echoed through the forest. I realized a little too late that I shouldn't have ignored my surroundings.

Rain splashed down from the canopy above. I gasped and snatched my basket, jumping to my feet. The water fell harder, and I dashed for the safety of a tree.

I pressed my back against the trunk and held my basket close to my chest. Dampness surrounded me as the rain fell harder, seeping quickly into my clothes and clinging to my skin. The tree protected me from most of the water falling from the sky, but not all of it. I'd be soaked by the time this stopped, if it did any time soon. I suspected it wouldn't, and it'd have to run through it to get back home. But for now, I'd remain here with my thoughts—my pain.

A calloused finger brushed my cheek, breaking the streak my tears created. I gasped and jumped back, my basket clattering to the ground and my collected herbs dumping out onto the wet soil. Instinctively, my hand flew up, magic tendrils coming to my defense, while my other hand went to my axe, except it wasn't there since I'd stormed out of the house in a snit.

Týr took a startled step back. I relaxed. "Don't scare me like that."

"I'm sorry. I…" He frowned. "Why are you crying?"

I bent to clean up my mess and rubbed my face to rid the evidence of the tears. No one ever saw me like this. I was usually more careful. "I got into a fight with Leif. Don't worry about it."

And now I was lying to him. But really, he didn't need my problems. Especially with the unusual look he had about him.

Normally, when Týr came for a visit, he had a smile on his face for me. But today… He didn't quite frown, but he definitely wasn't happy. It was like something was weighing on him. And if that were the case, he didn't need to deal with my insignificant mortal problems. *Especially since it has to do with my dumb heart's feelings toward him.*

"Do you want to talk about it?" Týr asked.

"No." The lie tasted foul, but I couldn't tell him. "Why are you here?"

"I was looking for you."

"Why?" The word was out of my mouth before I could stop it.

"Why was I looking for you? Should I not have been?"

My jaw clenched. That wasn't an answer. It was a dodge. "Never mind. Forget I said anything."

What did I expect him to say? He was looking for me because he cared? Because every time he left, he couldn't wait to return?

"Astrid, do you want me to leave?"

"No." Again the words came quickly, and this time quiet. I didn't want him to leave. Ever again.

A bright flash lit up the sky, and then a booming crack. I shrieked and jumped back, right into Týr's hard body. He wrapped an arm around me, and instantly I felt safe and warm.

"Let's get out of this before the storm gets worse," Týr said.

I didn't want to go home, where my family would be to say something I didn't want them to. This place was better—even with the storm, it was far more peaceful. I could forget reality existed for a little longer here. "I'm staying a bit longer. But you can leave if you wish."

It hurt to say those words. It cracked the little fantasy I was in, but I had to say them.

Týr's grip tightened, and he pulled us back into the tree more. "No, I will stay with you."

Warmth bloomed in my chest. Those were words I liked hearing.

We sat between the roots of the tree. The rain continued to come down, and soon the tree struggled to protect us. Týr threw his cloak over my head to shield me. His thoughtfulness made me smile. And it brought a thought to mind. *Can I protect us from this?*

Mother had taught me all sorts of spells. They didn't have incantations, or require special items. It was a thought in my mind's eye. I had to picture what I wanted and tap into my magic to make it reality. That made things difficult when I didn't see something like she did. But could I make something that kept the rain at bay?

I pictured how the rain rolled off rooves and imagined it doing that with my magic, but not in a way that I could see with my eyes, so as not to ruin the beautiful scenery.

My magic built inside me and then expanded out. A brief shimmer caught my eyes and then, the rain stopped falling on us.

I leaned forward to take a peek. High above, just as I'd pictured, the water rolled to either side of us, creating a watery curtain against the invisible force. A broad smile tugged at my cheeks and excitement burst through me. "I did it!"

Týr held out his hand, searching for water. "This is impressive."

My joy and pride doubled.

A bright flash and an even louder crack of thunder. I shrieked again and ducked back against the tree trunk. "Thor must be angry today."

"He is," Týr said. His eyes scanned the sky. "No doubt furious he can't find me or Baldr."

I was hesitant to inquire, but did anyway. "Did something happen?"

He made a thoughtful sound. "Yeah."

"Do you… want to talk about it?" I doubted he would, but I made the offer nonetheless.

Not surprisingly, he remained quiet. A deeper piece of me wilted under the rejection, and I wished it hadn't. I didn't belong in the lives of gods. It was why I did my best not to inconvenience him with my insignificant mortal problems as much as possible.

"I don't know how to put it into words just yet," Týr said quietly, surprising me he wanted to talk about it at all. "Why are you angry with your brother?"

I pulled my knees up to my chest and shrugged. "We had a small argument. Tension has been high lately, so it was bound to happen."

"Because of the baby coming?" Týr guessed.

"Leif has been annoying through the whole thing. He means well. He's just worried. But because we're in the last month of Frida's pregnancy, he's gotten a bit worse." I shook my head. "Mother said it's normal for first-time fathers to do this, but honestly I think he's being a little too dramatic."

Týr let out a laughing snort. "Is this all that's caused the tension, or is there something else?"

I chewed my lip. There was something else, something that had me out of sorts that Leif didn't know about. "No, there's something that's been bothering me…"

It didn't feel right to bother Týr with this, but by the way he watched me, I knew he expected an answer. "I overheard my parents talking to Rune. The king is furious with my behavior. They're worried he might do something to retaliate."

My grip on my legs tightened. "I shouldn't have refused him. None of this would have happened if I hadn't."

"No." Týr's voice was hard. "You did the right thing."

Did I, even when it caused my family problems? When that was the best realistic marriage prospect I had?

I couldn't voice that to Týr. I couldn't voice it to anyone. It bubbled and roiled deep in my chest, turning to frustration that I couldn't do anything about. I had no lover, no family of my own, no one who could relate to what I was going through to talk these feelings and issues through.

I was utterly alone.

And it was suffocating.

Silence fell over us. It wasn't quite comfortable, but it wasn't uncomfortable, either.

Lightning flashed and splintered overhead, thunder following. The rain picked up, and yet I still didn't want to leave.

I let out a startled squeak when Týr suddenly rested his forehead where my shoulder and neck met. "Týr?"

He didn't say anything, just breathed hard. Even through such little contact, I felt the tension roiling through him. Whatever was bothering him today, it really was hard for him to put into words.

With slight hesitation, I reached up and wrapped my arms around his head. My fingers tangled in his hair and I pulled him tight against me. I didn't care if this was appropriate or not. He needed me now. "I'm here."

Týr responded by wrapping his arms around my waist and crushing me to him. His powerful, masculine scent enveloped me and my heart thundered in my chest. I was sure he could hear it, and I didn't care.

This was something I'd wanted from him. Maybe not in the exact way I'd longed, but I'd take a dose of reality with my fantasy if it meant I could have a small slice.

"She's gone…" he murmured in such a pained quiet voice, I almost didn't hear him. "She's gone… Odinn… Odinn killed her."

I ran my fingers through his hair. "Who?"

"Kirby."

I froze. "W—what?"

Kirby, the beautiful Valkyrie. Kirby, the Valkyrie who was grace and power. Kirby, the warrior who taught me how to better fight with a weapon should my magic fail. Kirby, the woman who was fun to be around, who I could call a friend and not feel strange doing so. She was…

"Why?"

Týr pressed his face harder into my chest, as if he could hide from reality. "She disobeyed. Her lover, Starkad, died in battle and she brought him back to life instead of sending him to Valhǫll. She… manipulated his life force to make him immortal."

My skin tingled and the cold sensation numbing my insides spread throughout my body. *She made him… immortal?* "Is that… even possible?"

"Yes," Týr said. "Some mortals have the potential to become immortal, either on their own or through some outside assistance. Most Berserkers, due to their unique souls, will become immortal in time if they survive all the war they see. But the way she did it… it was unnatural for Berserkers. And the ability to do what she did has never been seen in Valkyries before. We're not sure what kind of effect this will have."

"And Odinn killed her for this?"

Týr's grip tightened. "He didn't just kill her. He cursed her soul.

Claimed she would live a thousand lifetimes until she understands what it means to be a Valkyrie."

What it means to be a Valkyrie? What would Odinn know about what it meant to be one compared to a Valkyrie herself?

"I tried to stop him," Týr said. There was so much pain in his voice, it made my chest ache. "I told him it wasn't right and that I wouldn't stand by and allow it. Even Baldr sided against his father. That only infuriated Odinn, to see his favorite son side with me. And Kirby… she still died. I failed her, and the gods are now at odds…"

I ran my fingers through his hair some more and stroked his back. Soft hushing sounds came from my lips as I tried to calm and console him. "You didn't fail her. Wherever her soul is now, she'll know you tried. She'll never fault you for that. I know I wouldn't if I were her."

We didn't say anything more. I continued to hold him until he calmed.

"Thank you, Valkyrie," he murmured.

There was that name again. He'd said it when we were in the King's hall. Why was he calling me that?

I banished those questions. This wasn't the time. "You don't have to thank me. I may not be a god or immortal, but I am strong enough to hold you up if you need me."

Týr pulled me tighter into him. My body molded to his. Such a perfect fit, but—I refocused my attention on the jewelry in my hair to keep me from going down that rabbit hole again. My mother gave me a number of metal beads to represent the gods, and I now had some I didn't want anymore.

I tugged on Odinn's bead. It would be the first to go.

Týr released me and watched. "What are you doing?"

"Odinn doesn't deserve to have a bead." I wouldn't forgive him for what he did.

Týr reached out and wrapped his fingers around the metal accessory. With startling strength, he snapped it with a quick twist. The pieces dropped to the ground.

I reached for Thor's. He sided with Odinn, and I wouldn't treat him with any kindness either. Týr helped me with that one as well, and then took a few more out. I didn't mind his initiative. I didn't want to associate with any god who was Týr's enemy.

"That should do it," he said. I didn't count how many he destroyed. I didn't care. I still had the important ones.

I blinked and stared up at him when he brushed the back of his hand against my cheek. I couldn't look away, ensnared by those blue depths. From the bridge of my nose down, his thumb traced the sensitive scar marring my face. No one had ever touched me there, especially not so tenderly. Most tried to avoid looking at the ugly thing.

I opened my mouth to speak, and his gaze flicked down to my lips. Warmth spread over my face when thoughts of him kissing me flashed through my mind. *What was I going to say to him again?*

A loud crack and boom overhead. I shrieked and practically jumped into Týr's arms. He threw his head back in raucous laughter. "I think it might be best we head for true cover."

I nodded, trying to calm my racing heart. It was a miracle my magic hadn't failed us yet, though I could sense there were some holes now.

I gasped when Týr lifted me into his arms. My pulse picked up, being so close to him like this. This was the first time he'd carried me like this when I was sober. "What are you doing?"

He smirked. "No sense in us both running. Think you can protect us from the rain?"

I squinted at the angry sky. "I'm not sure."

He lifted his cloak over my head to shield me. "Just in case."

I leaned into him, his warmth and strength inviting and calming to my racing heart. "Just in case."

Týr took off from under the cover of our tree, and I concentrated hard on moving our protective magic barrier with us.

SIXTEEN

ASTRID

Water splashed under Týr's boots. The dark sky flashed with bolts of lightning, and thunder cracked and rolled right behind it. I gripped Týr tightly around the neck, surprised by the speed he could run while carrying me.

The magic above us cracked, letting more rain in. Weariness flickered across the back of my mind. This wasn't easy to keep up, especially with us moving. I'd never done this before.

The house came into view, and not a moment too soon. My magic fizzled out, and the rain pelted down on us. I squealed and tucked us further under Týr's cloak. Týr laughed, and we ducked under the awning of the house. His laughter was contagious, and we both fell into a fit. Dripping wet and chilled, we laughed without a care. The sky rumbled in protest of our amusement.

Týr set me down. I opened the door, calling out as I did. "I'm home! And we have a guest."

I blinked and looked around. A fire roared in the hearth, but otherwise no one was around.

"Mother? Leif?" I ventured a little farther in. "Frida? Um, Theo?"

No one answered me—at least, no human. My kitten poked her head up from behind a chair and mewed. The poor thing had her fur all fluffed out, terrified of the raging storm outside.

I set my herb basket down and wrung out my skirts. "I wonder where everyone is. They started a fire."

"Maybe they're at another home after being caught out in the storm?" Týr suggested.

"Maybe…" I wasn't entirely convinced. Something screamed this was a planned absence, and a possibly recent disappearance. "Warm up by the fire. I'll see if we have anything that'll fit you to change into. I'm not sure we do."

I tried not to shiver and walk over to the fire myself. I could get warm once I was wearing dry clothes.

My kitten scampered over to me and I picked her up to snuggle for a moment. She was a little too squirmy to cuddle with for long. When she had enough, I grabbed a fluff of wool she enjoyed playing with, and tossed it for her to chase after.

Týr watched her for a moment before playing with her. I should have gone to find clothes, but observing him was far more fascinating. For such a large man, he was so gentle with the kitten, even when she thought she was bigger and more ferocious than she was. I couldn't stop myself from wondering if this would be how he'd act around children.

He glanced up, catching me staring. "What?"

I smiled and entered the adjacent bedroom to search for clothes instead of answering. There was no point trying to justify myself. I'd just look like a bigger fool than I already felt.

Lightning cracked and lit up the sky, thunder rumbling so deep I felt it in my bones. Rain crashed onto the roof. I glanced out the window to see water flooding in front of it in a thick curtain. *The storm is picking up out there.*

It was a good thing we decided to come home. This storm wasn't getting any better any time soon.

I left the bedroom with some trousers for Týr. I wasn't sure they'd fit, but we could try. The tunics we had were out of the question.

I stopped short in the threshold of the central room. My heart seized at the sight of Týr holding the unfinished tunic. Even from here, it was clear that would fit him, and there was no hiding who it was for.

Týr looked up when he realized I'd returned. "I thought you said you weren't sure you had something that would fit me."

"That's not—what I mean is—" My tongue wouldn't work as my brain panicked. I couldn't tell him it was for him. "It's not finished."

His brow spiked. Then he looked at the tunic again. "Looks finished."

Whatever magic kept me rooted in place released its hold and I rushed over to him, trying to grab it. "Týr, no!"

He held it out of my reach, grinning like a mischievous cat. "And why not? Is there something you're not telling me? Is this for someone else?"

"No!" I nearly choked after that confession. "That's not—I mean—"

Týr chuckled. "Trickster god stolen your tongue, Valkyrie?"

My heart thumped. There was that name again. Why did I like it so much when he called me that? "It's not good enough."

That was a truth I could allow. He was a god. He deserved the best. And that tunic wasn't the best. *Neither am I...*

Týr rubbed the fabric between his fingers. "I think the quality is superb. I'm going to try this on, unless you have any legitimate objections."

Heat seared my cheeks. "None that'd you take..."

Gods, why hadn't I hidden that instead of running off in a huff? Now this was just going to be one embarrassing moment when he rejected—

Týr loosened his belt and pulled his soaked tunic over his head. The hard muscles of his abdomen and arms flexed and pulled taut with the movement. Every thought in my mind left me.

My eyes lingered as he stood before me, half-naked and unashamed to display so much masculine temptation in front of me. My mouth dried and liquid heat pooled between my legs. My chest heaved as I struggled to keep my breathing even and my hands from reaching out and gliding along those planes of muscle.

Týr grinned, as if satisfied to see what his current state of dress did to me. I wouldn't be surprised if I looked as much of a mess as I felt right now. He pulled the new tunic on.

The garment slid over his body, fitting like a glove. I'd managed to make it perfectly for him.

Týr tested the fit and felt the fabric again. "I've never had such a fine tunic before."

Heat of the same intensity pooling between my legs seared my face. "I highly doubt—"

He pressed his thumb against my lips. "I meant what I said."

I held his gaze. That was a mistake. My knees wobbled, threatening to bend under the intensity of his stare. "You like it?"

"It's for me, right?"

I bit my lower lip and nodded.

He grinned. "Good. I wouldn't allow you to give this to someone else."

My heart thumped hard against my ribcage.

Týr hung his wet tunic up by the fire to dry along with the boots he'd kicked off, and plopped down in a chair. He looked about to get comfortable.

"Týr, you can't wear it yet," I said. "It's not finished. I wasn't lying about that."

He pulled at the material and looked at it. "Looks finished to me."

I dropped the trousers in my hands and stepped closer, grabbing his tunic. "Please take it off. I need to finish it."

I gasped when he grabbed my arms and yanked me onto his lap. My body molded against his powerful form, and I was acutely aware of the large, hard object pressing against my legs that was distinctly not a sword.

Týr chuckled low against my ear. "And what are you going to do about it, Valkyrie? Do you think you can make me remove it?"

A pleasant shiver ran down my spine and between my legs. I swallowed, my pulse thumping in my ears. "I didn't realize you would be the most difficult man to disrobe."

It was such a risky thing for me to say. But I couldn't stop it. I couldn't contain my want. I'd held onto this secret too long. I needed to know if he desired me as much as I did him.

Týr's nose dragged across my cheek and down to my neck. His hands slid down my back, sending tingles through me. "Hmm, maybe it's because I'm more concerned about helping you out of this wet dress?"

My lungs ceased to operate.

I'd let him rip this dress off me if he so desired. But I had enough presence of mind here to desire one thing more before I gave into his seducing touch. I wanted an answer, to know where I stood.

"Recite me poetry," I murmured.

Týr stilled. I couldn't stop the frown and sudden suffocating disappointment.

It was fine. He didn't see me that way. His poetry was meant for someone else, and that was how it was. I was to pay a debt my family owed. A night with a god was still more than most would ever experience.

"I don't want to embarrass you," Týr murmured.

My disappointed thoughts froze.

"I am one god who can't recite poetry. It's… well, Freyja would say it's comical, where I'd say it's painful. I… don't want to subject you to that."

That was his reason? This whole time, he hadn't tried to seduce me with words because he didn't think he was any good?

"I want to hear one." I didn't care if it was terrible. I wanted to know if I truly meant something to him.

Týr took a slow, deep breath.

> Behold, you are beautiful!
> Your eyes are like rocks by the river, green with moss
> Your hair is like molten metal when they skim the dross
> Your skin is like Sleipnir's mane, or a flock of shorn ewes
> Your mouth is lovely and your lips are red hues
> Your neck is like a tower built with rows of stone
> Decorated with a thousand shields from warriors grown
> Your two breasts are like two of the stags at the branches
> of Yggdrasill
> I compare you to Freyr's horse that passes through flames
> and darkness chill

I bit my lip. I… didn't know what to say.

Týr gave me an awkward, sheepish smile. "I tried to warn you."

I struggled to keep a straight face, and a giggle escaped. "I just have to know, is that really how you compare me?"

His eyes went wide. "No! No, it's so much better than that. I just… when I try to put it to words… When I look at you, the words I'd like to say seem… unworthy, and I'm left searching for my breath and my tongue."

I could accept that answer. He tried. It was absolutely the worst poem I'd ever heard, but he tried. And I could forgive him because of it. I understood now why he had never made attempts before. All his other actions made so much more sense now. He did his best to make up for his lack of poetry in other ways.

I leaned close, my lips brushing against his ear. "Then, we'll just have to make some poetry together."

Týr's grip on my dress tightened, and I swore I heard something rip. "You're a tease, Valkyrie."

I slid my fingers through his beard along his jaw and lightly kissed his cheek. "I can be more than a mere tease."

He turned to gaze into my eyes. His hand slid into my hair. I gasped when he grabbed a fistful and a surprisingly pleasant sensation rushed through me. "When I'm done with you, it'll only ever be my name you scream, and you will be the most worshiped and pleased woman in existence."

My heart beat hard in my chest, and my breathing hitched. Týr leaned in and captured my lips with his. Firm and demanding, but with a hint of gentleness. The kiss stoked the heat pooling in my belly until it spread like a raging wildfire through my entire body.

I tangled my hands in his hair, my pulse pounding in my ears. Everything he was enveloped me, enticed me, made me crave more.

A hungry, possessive growl rumbled through his chest. Fabric tore, and I gasped when air cooler than my skin hit my back. Týr took advantage and plunged his tongue into my open mouth, devouring me.

His strong hands roamed my bare skin, yanking and tugging at any fabric that dared impede his exploration until I was naked from the waist up, and my skirts were torn and only in place because of the way I sat on his lap.

I didn't care about the dress. I desperately wanted it gone, along with his clothes. I didn't want to ruin the tunic I'd made him, but hel if it and his trousers weren't in the way right now.

Týr broke the kiss, and I panted for air. My veins simmered and my body tingled with more need than I thought I could handle. He held my gaze as his hands continued to roam my body.

I groaned when his calloused hands dragged along my heaving breasts. I kissed him again with fevered demand and tugged on his tunic. "Týr…"

He grinned against my mouth. "I've hardly started making love to you and you're already a mess. I'm going to enjoy watching you writhe under me."

Love? Týr kissed me again, stealing my thoughts. His fingers dragged along my breasts and flicked my aching nipples. I moaned, wanting more of that. He obliged, teasing, flicking, and pinching the sensitive peaks.

I needed more. Using his shoulders for balance, I pulled myself farther onto his lap. My dress scraps fell away as I swung my leg over him, seating myself comfortably in his lap, facing him.

His hard cock strained against his trousers and pressed against my needy pussy. It felt so huge. It couldn't possibly be in reality. No man, not even a god, could be that large. My mind was merely drowning in too much desire.

Týr's hands roamed my naked body, stoking my overwhelming need. I rocked my hips, grinding into his hardness, desperate to alleviate some of my overwhelming desire.

Týr groaned in response and tried to still me. "Patience, Valkyrie."

I scrabbled at his belt. "No."

His belt clattered to the floor. I tugged on his tunic next. It needed to go. All his clothes needed to disappear.

I bit and sucked on Týr's lower lip. He growled, the sensation reverberating through me in an intoxicating way.

Týr's hands slid over my ass and gripped me tight. I gasped when he stood and wrapped my legs around his waist. Without his belt, his trousers dropped and he stepped out of them, heading for the bedroom.

I kissed him desperately, until he spoke against my lips. "Which bed is yours, Valkyrie?"

I vaguely gestured to where my bed would be. It was the only exposed one, as Leif had partitioned his after the wedding, and Mother and Father had their own room in the loft. I didn't care if we made it to my bed or not. He could take me anywhere he wanted, I just needed him—on top of me—inside me.

My back pressed into soft furs, and my hair pooled around me. Týr pulled away and gazed down, hungrily drinking in every visual piece of my naked flesh, save for the necklace around my neck and other jewelry I still wore. "You're stunning, Valkyrie."

Under his intense, gleaming eyes, I felt like the most beautiful woman in existence.

Týr pulled his tunic up and over his head, tossing it away without a care. I didn't either. Pulse pounding in my ears, I raked my gaze over his perfect, masculine body. A craving desire to touch him and feel every godly part of him gripped me. My eyes continued to dip lower until it froze at the size of his massive, throbbing cock.

My breath hitched, the desire pooling between my legs turning into an aching need. *Gods, he's a damned stallion.* I'd never wondered if a man could fit, but now…

Týr leaned in, bracing his hands on either side of my head. "Better?"

He wanted confirmation that I approved of him more than what I'd seen of Fenrir. I licked my lips. "I'd rather ride a stallion than a wolf."

He captured my mouth with his again, as hungry as I felt. My thoughts disappeared, and I fell into my desires.

I ran my hands along his muscular chest, feeling each dip, peak, and valley of hard muscles and scars. A groan rumbled through him and Týr grabbed a fistful of my hair again. I gasped, enjoying the pleasant thrill that came with it.

His mouth left mine, trailing hot kisses down my neck and over my collarbone. My chest heaved with effort; my mind fuzzed with heady desire.

Týr's tongue swathed over my skin, tasting every part of me he desired. He followed paths of freckles, exploring and teasing until he returned to my chest. His tongue trailed along the side of my breast. He nipped and kissed the sensitive skin and my body arched, aching for more attention. My body knew what it wanted, and I craved it, too.

I gasped when his hot, wet tongue flicked my hard, aching nipple. He grinned, his teeth scraping my skin, and he continued, licking and teasing until he wrapped his lips around the aching peak and sucked. Hard.

My head rolled back as a pleasured moan rumbled through me. My limbs tingled and my back arched again, desperate for more attention like this.

Týr continued to suck and lick, switching between both my breasts, ensuring neither was neglected. But it wasn't enough. I needed more of him.

My hands pawed at him, desperate to touch and feel. I let out a frustrated whimper when he snatched my wrists and pinned them above my head with one of his massive hands.

His other hand roamed over me, and I squirmed. My whole body was on fire. When his fingers slid along my inner thigh, I whimpered more. The sparks of sensation felt so good.

Týr released my nipple with a *pop*, and he grinned against my sensitive skin. "What do you want, Valkyrie?"

I swallowed; my mouth dry. "I want…"

My breathing hitched when his fingers slid up my inner thigh and teased the sensitive flesh between my legs. My hips tilted into his touch, as if begging. "That… I want more of that."

My words sounded more like a plea than anything.

Týr slid his fingers along the slit between my legs, slowly working his way between my folds. I moaned when he hit a deliciously perfect spot. The pleasure it sent through me was the right amount of delectable satisfaction I'd craved.

It'd been so long since I'd enjoyed a man. Those times with my almost-future husbands had been enjoyable, especially my last one. I never thought I'd find a better lover than him. But this… this was already so much more amazing than I could have ever imagined, and this god was only so far pleasuring me with his hands and mouth.

The fire inside me stoked to a wildfire of pleasure. My hips rocked, intensifying everything. My breathing hitched and tension coiled deep in my center. My toes curled, and I knew I was so close to the one thing I wanted.

"Týr…" I moaned.

He gazed deep into my eyes, the stare intense and soul-stealing. "You want more of this, Valkyrie?"

"Yes," I said, my voice pleading and breathy. "More."

He slid a finger inside me, and then another. I gasped, embracing the sensation of him sliding his fingers in and out. It undid me.

The tension building inside me exploded, bringing with it a rush of euphoria. My head flew back, his name screaming out, and my hips bucked, an orgasm taking over.

Týr's intense eyes glowed and his grip around my wrists tightened, as if something about this affected him more deeply.

I came down from what I could only assume was Valholl, my breath heavy, and chest heaving. Týr didn't cease his attention. My sensitive body squirmed, protesting and desiring.

He bent over me, his lips brushing my ear. "I'm not done with you, Astrid. I'm not even close to done. Pray to me like that again."

My heart leapt into my throat. *Pray? Is that what happened?* Was this now our own unique prayer exchange?

I closed my eyes when another wave of pleasure coursed through me. I wanted more and happily took what he offered. The tides of orgasm crashed over me again, quicker and more intense than the first.

When I was a panting, twitching mess, Týr finally relented. I sucked in deep breaths; my body more weightless than I'd ever felt before.

But my reprieve was short-lived. Týr slid a hand along my thighs and spread my legs. He leaned over me again, fisting his cock and sliding it teasingly along my quivering folds.

He murmured into my ear again, his hot breath and words sending tingles down my spine. "If I am too rough, tell me, Astrid. I will only hurt you if you beg me to."

My response was a deep, gasping breath, and my back arching as he slid his hard cock inside me. Thumb length by thumb length, he stretched me. I bit my lip, pain mixing with pleasure. *Creation, this hurts, but feels so good.*

"Are you all right?" he asked with a strained voice, his gaze intent on me. "Am I too much?"

I shook my head, and breathed in deeply as my body greedily took him all. "Keep going. Please. It feels good. *You* feel so good."

Týr continued until he was fully sheathed inside me. We gazed at each other for a long moment, enjoying the feel of this complete sensation building between us. This felt so right, like he and I were meant to be like this forever.

My back arched when he pulled almost all the way out and then thrust into me, faster than before. I gasped and then moaned. *This feels so incredible.* I needed more.

"Creation, you're perfect, Valkyrie," Týr said before devouring my breath with his mouth and thrust even harder into me.

The force jarred through me as a mix of pain and pleasure. My mind fuzzed. I moaned into him, wanting more. His thrusts picked up. I fought against his restraining hand, craving to touch and feel him.

He grinned, and I gasped when he pulled out and flipped me over on my belly. Týr lifted my hips, and without warning, plunged deep inside me. I moaned deep in my chest, my hands fisting the fur pelts beneath us.

Skin slapped skin as he picked up his pace. His hand fisted and yanked my hair again, making me gasp. "Týr…"

"That's it, Valkyrie, pray to me. Beg me to give you what you crave."

I did. I begged and I prayed for more. Týr reached around my front and found that perfect, sensitive spot between my legs. A heated inferno sparked through me once against and I fell into desire, rocking into his hard thrusts, increasing the pleasure until I ached to my very core.

He slammed into me harder, mixing more pain into my pleasure, and I craved it. Never had a man been so rough with me and I wanted it—desired it.

The familiar sensation of building orgasm coiled in me, and then exploded. I screamed, overtaken by pleasure.

Týr braced himself on either side of me and nearly roared as he, too, orgasmed, spilling his hot seed inside me. We collapsed in a tangled, sensitive heap.

My body quivered and shook. Týr rolled me into him, and I pressed into his hard form, pulling my arms around him and embracing the warmth and protection he offered.

We lay in each other's arms, listening to each other's mingling heartbeats.

"Did that please you, Valkyrie?" Týr murmured after a moment.

I made a thoughtful sound as I looked up at him. "Why do you call me that?"

Maybe I should have accepted the new name and left it at that, but I was curious.

He brushed a damp tousle of hair away from my face. "Because that is what you are to me. You ease the rage within me, pacifying it like no other can. You coax and ignite a fiery passion none can take credit for. You hold the keys to my soul, my fight for battle, and all that I am, and have the power to stave or encourage it all. You are my Valkyrie, forever and always."

My heart beat heavy in my chest, my face growing hot. That felt so close to a confession of—I blinked when he traced my face scar. I pulled away from the touch this time. "What are you doing?"

"I've wanted to know since I met you, how did you get this?" There was no disgust in his eyes. Only affection and curiosity.

"Ah, well, um…" I chewed my lower lip. That story I swore to Leif I'd never reveal to another soul. "That's a secret."

His eyebrow spiked, and he tucked a finger under my chin to tip my head up. "A secret? And what must I do to earn the knowledge of this secret? Who must I kill for daring to harm you?"

My pulse quickened. The look in his eyes told me my promise was doomed at this rate.

The front door clacked open and all the heat in me drained until I was ice cold. Someone had returned home, and we'd left a noticeable mess in the other room.

Týr cocked his head. "What is wrong?"

"Uh… Oh, um… I…" What was I supposed to say?

"Who do you think is here? Your father?"

I shook my head. "Father is out on a hunting trip. But…"

It didn't matter who saw. Father would find out regardless.

"Then what's the matter?"

"If anyone finds out… they'll tell him… and…"

Týr leaned close. "And what, Valkyrie?"

My gaze flicked up to him, my heart stopping. He was not worried in the least. Hel, he even seemed quite smug to be found out what he'd done to me, as if that was something he wanted.

"And my father might…" I swallowed the lump forming in my throat. "He'll think… that you wish to marry me."

"Hmm," Týr traced a line down my cheek. "Not a terrible assumption."

I blinked and shook my head, unable to believe what he might be implying. "You don't want to marry me."

He tipped my head back and gazed deeply into my eyes. "Don't I?"

My heart thumped hard in my chest. "There are so many more worthy women out there for you, Týr."

He adjusted himself to lean over me. "There is no other woman in existence more perfect and worthy to bring me to my knees than you."

I swallowed hard, my heart hammering against the cage of my ribs. "I'm mortal."

"I'd rather battle with you by my side for a mortal's lifetime, than go through an eternity of glory never having met you." Týr leaned in, his lips brushing mine. "I love you, Astrid. You are, and forever will be, my Valkyrie. Marry me."

My heart stalled. *He… he loves me?*

A woman cleared her throat. I shrieked. Týr caught me when I unceremoniously half-jumped into him. We both snapped our attention to the fair-haired woman now standing in the room.

I relaxed when I realized the intruder was Freyja. *Wait, why is she here?*

Týr exhaled and mirrored my thoughts out loud. "Freyja, what are you doing here?"

"I'm sorry to interrupt this," she said, vaguely gesturing to our current states. "But I wouldn't unless it was important. You're needed, Týr. Thor and Odinn are still out of control, and Loki is adding fuel to the fire, per usual."

My pulse slowed. This didn't sound good.

Týr scowled. "And why do I need to handle it?"

Freyja crossed her arms. "Because like the moron Fenrir is, he tried to deal with it alone and got his arm ripped off."

My hands flew up to my face as I gasped.

Freyja passed me a reassuring look. "Don't worry, Astrid, you won't need to patch him up. He'll be fine. He can regrow it. It'll just take a few hours, and it's incredibly painful. It'll be a good lesson for him."

Týr's mouth twisted in displeasure. "They have to ruin everything. I'm sorry, Astrid."

I rested my hand on his chest. "It's okay. This is important."

"You'll need these if you're going anywhere."

We turned to find my mother standing in the doorway. In one hand, she carried Týr's previously wet tunic, trousers, and boots. In the other hand—my heart stopped—she carried what scraps remained of my dress.

Freyja choked on a laugh, my face inflamed, and Týr wasn't apologetic in the slightest.

"These are expensive," Mother said.

"I will replace it," Týr vowed. "And gift her a few more in the likely event it happens again."

I choked, and Freyja finally laughed. Mother did, too, while holding up his clothes a little higher. "Come get these so you can go pummel a god, or whatever it is you plan to do in such a hurry."

Týr climbed out of the bed and walked toward her with all the confidence of a god. Mother didn't flinch at his nakedness, not that I expected a confident and comfortable woman like her to. I got a nice view of Týr's backside, and Freyja winked at me.

Týr dressed and then returned to my side. Mother made an impressed face to me with his back now turned, making Freyja smirk. Týr bent over and planted a kiss on my forehead. He murmured against my skin.

"I'll return in four days to speak to your father. If you don't want this, I expect you to speak up. But I will also give you time to think it over."

Heat prickled my cheeks, and my heart thumped slow but hard in my chest. Týr pulled away, and pivoted toward Freyja. His armor manifested; Freyja placed her hand on his shoulder and they disappeared.

Mother tossed my ruined dress aside to be disposed of later and came over to me. "Let's get you cleaned up. I've already got a bath drawn."

I nodded and followed her through the house, out to the covered stone bath outside. The storm still raged, but it was safe under here. I stepped into the steaming water, piped in from a nearby hot spring. I hissed when the warm water soaked sore and sensitive areas but I soon relished the soothing warmth.

Mother helped me with my hair. "How do you feel, Sunshine?"

"Pleased," I murmured, lulled by the bath.

She hummed. "Good. I'd be concerned if he couldn't perform well enough."

I ran a hand through my damp hair. "When will Father be home from his hunting trip?"

"I expect the next few days." She leaned forward. "Any particular reason why?"

I chewed my lower lip and played with a lock of hair. My pulse picked up as reality settled in. Týr was giving me a few days to think this over, but I didn't need to. I already knew what I wanted. "Týr desires for us to wed. I… also wish this."

The largest smile I'd ever seen on my mother spread over her face. "For a god, he sure likes to take his time. But I'm also not surprised."

I blinked. What did she mean by that?

"Do you know why I suggested your name to your father to consider?"

I cocked my head. "Because you hoped I would be beautiful?"

She smiled. "I didn't hope, I knew. During your birth, I had a vision. I knew then that you would be beloved by the gods in more ways than a mortal could ever dream imaginable."

She took a comb to my hair. "Your father will be pleased he'll be able to watch your path with the gods with so much pride."

The way she worded that didn't sit well with me. "You will be too, right?"

"You have always been the light in my life. Never doubt how much you mean to me."

That was a dodge. Why was she dodging my question?

"You'll be the most beautiful bride."

I scrubbed my arm. "You'll help me through all this, right?"

Her tending to my hair paused for a split moment, and she didn't answer me. I turned to face her, and the bittersweet look on her face hit me like a raging Berserker.

"Mother…" I took a steadying breath. "What aren't you telling me?"

She kissed me on the head. "You are my blood, my heart, and my greatest gift. I will always stand between you and harm, no matter the cost. I would give everything for you without hesitation. Carry this with you always, my daughter, my love and protection will never waver."

My skin prickled, and everything she'd said over the last few months swarmed the back of my mind. Something bad was going to happen, and I needed to protect her.

SEVENTEEN

TÝR

Chaos swirled around me. The deafening clash of steel on steel, and cracks of splintering shields mixed with war cries and pained screams filled my ears. Sweat and blood mixed with burning wood and churned soil. The tides of battle swelled deep within me, spurring me on and filling me with greater strength.

I swung my engraved onyx sword, slicing through one man, and then pivoted to block another attacker with my shield. Usually, I didn't need to worry about mortals harming me, but a surprisingly powerful völva strengthened them.

I don't have time for this. My true quarry, King Geir, fought amongst these mortals, hiding from those more powerful than him. *Coward.* He brought this fight upon us, demanding reparations for Astrid's insulting behavior when word got to him about Astrid's and my betrothal. I refused to allow his ego to bring harm to her, her family, or her people. *He will die for his insolence.*

Fenrir howled and snarled nearby, tearing warriors and shield-maidens apart with relative ease. Baldr fought with reckless abandon to my other side. Blood streaked his skin and a wildness crazed his eyes. Freyja fought somewhere around here as well, all three coming to my aid to protect my Valkyrie.

She, along with her mother, were safe at the back side of the battle, using their magic to aid our warriors. Our numbers weren't as large as the king's, but with two völvur to bolster them, and four gods, the king's army did not hold as strong as one would have expected.

It helped we had warriors from allied villages and towns willing to defy the king. Even two of Geir's own sons and their loyal warriors fought with us. They disagreed with their father's actions, calling him mad. His behavior was out of character for any king. He may be possessed. Or he may merely have too large of an ego.

My senses picked up the presence of Valkyries, watching the battle for souls they would deem worthy of Valhǫll after this fight ended. I blocked them out. I didn't care what they did.

A familiar battle cry came behind me, and a sword sliced into a warrior whose attack I had blocked. Leif, covered in the blood of our enemies, swung his sword again and cut down the warrior. A concussive blast pushed back even more of them. My breath hitched at the sight of Astrid this far into the battle.

Before I could yell at her, Leif turned to me. "Have you seen our mother?"

Muscles in my back tightened. "No. Why is she not with you and Astrid?"

"King Geir had a force of warriors that pushed harder than expected. It separated Mother and Father from us. We think some other warriors are with them, but we can't be sure."

Rune and Bjarke, their bodies transformed into their bear forms, entered the fray around us, keeping the warriors from reaching Astrid. Her magic filled the air, empowering all her allies, but I could see the weariness on her face. She wouldn't last much longer at this rate.

"Go find her," Rune snarled out. *"We can hold them off. I don't know if Geir meant for Randi to be the one singled out, but I don't trust he wouldn't take advantage of it."*

I turned to Fenrir. "Fen, can you smell Randi?"

The wolf-god shook his head. *"Too much blood and death in the air."*

Creation, that wasn't good. "You and Baldr protect us from behind with Rune and the others. We're going after her."

Baldr tossed one warrior into another in response.

Leif, Astrid and I ran off in the direction they last knew their mother and father had been pushed. My pulse pumped hard. Something didn't feel right. That force shouldn't have gotten past us gods. And if Geir was the reason for it, he should have been after the force protecting Astrid. *Unless…*

I pushed harder. Astrid wasn't his target. She may have said no, but in his eyes, she had no power to do so. It was her father who had the ultimate say. Bjǫrn sided with her, and ultimately gave her to me instead upon her request.

And everyone knew how devoted he was to Randi.

Leif and Astrid both struggled to keep up, weary from the battle, but they managed, their desires to protect their mother driving them forward.

Arrows rained down on us, and in perfect unison, we pivoted and ducked in with other warriors, shielding together. Astrid bolstered our defenses with a thin magical barrier.

I'd trained with these men and women through these past few days of preparation. Leif and I even found good synergy. It was a shame he, too, was mortal. I would be happy to have another warrior like him alongside me for all battles.

I grabbed Astrid's elbow when she listed to one side. "Are you all right?"

"Fine. We need to find Mother." There was unconcealed panic in her voice.

"We will," I assure her.

Astrid's breath came quicker. "We need to. I think… she saw her death in a vision. I can't… I can't allow…"

Her panic overwhelmed her ability to speak. My blood ran cold. Astrid had been acting all out of sorts lately around her mother. I assumed it was because Frida was due to give birth any day now. But now… Now I understood.

We pushed harder, fighting our way through when needed.

And then we found her—along with King Geir.

He and Bjǫrn exchanged blows, neither giving the other an opening. Randi used her magic to bolster her husband as well as fight off warriors that other allies weren't engaged with.

Leif charged ahead, renewed with vigor through the lust of battle and the desire to protect his family. Astrid used her magic to shield as many warriors as she could. I rushed for Geir. I would crush him with my bare hands if it were necessary.

Bjǫrn stumbled back from a hard blow by Geir. And the king did what I feared. Instead of attacking Bjǫrn again, he charged Randi. The witch blocked him with her shield, but she wasn't strong enough to withstand the strike and stumbled back.

Midgard slowed as Geir thrust his sword and pierced Randi. She stumbled back, eyes wide, and choked. Blood gushed out of her wound, and soon it dripped out of her mouth.

Astrid screamed, and a concussive force sent a host of enemy warriors flying. But not Geir. His form shimmered with the protection of that gods-forsaken völva under his command.

Bjǫrn roared and attacked the king with more burning rage than the enemy expected. Geir cried out when Bjǫrn's sword sliced into his shield arm, nearly severing it.

I rushed in, rage burning and roiling. *He'll pay for that!*

Geir did not expect me, nor for my hands to wrap around his pathetic head. He cried out in pure agony and scrabbled at my fingers in vain as I squeezed. His skull cracked and blood spurted out of every orifice until his head exploded under my pressure. Blood, brain matter, and everything else that was his head splattered over my hands and the ground.

With fury-infused ragged breaths, I dropped Geir's lifeless, mangled body and turned. Bjǫrn held his wife in his arms, while Astrid knelt in front of her, trying desperately to heal her. Her hands shook and her breaths came heavy with the effort.

Leif hovered, shield and sword ready to defend them, along with the remaining warriors.

"No… no… no, no, no, don't fail me now!" Astrid shrieked, her voice quaking as fear set in and her magic faded.

She was too exhausted, too inexperienced to handle the strain of battle and now this.

Randi gently grasped her daughter's hands and weakly smiled, blood trickling out of the corner of her mouth. "You, my perfect daughter, are destined for greatness. Never forget that."

The woman's eyes glazed, though not from death.

The god's favor you will have
A life forever none can understand
The balance of justice and war you will be, a healer of souls to complete
But be wary of the snarling wolf
Cloaked in shadow he'll prowl close
Snapping teeth and drawing blood, he'll follow the fallen Valkyrie to her other life

Randi's focus returned, and she smiled at her daughter one last time before she turned to Leif, smiled and told him she was proud of him as well and that he and his line would bring honor to the family for a long time to come.

She turned her attention to Bjǫrn as he held her. He whispered sweet words to her, and with her last breath, she did the same.

Her eyes dulled and her hand fell. Her chest stilled.

Randi was gone.

"Mother…" Astrid said. "No… Mother…"

I wrapped my arms around Astrid and held her against my chest in a tight embrace, desperate to ease any of her pain that I could.

A screaming sob tore through her. The ground quaked and shifted. Earth and rock jutted out and briar grew and snarled until the battlefield was nothing more than a tormented landscape, a reflection of the grief and agony my Valkyrie felt in this moment of loss.

Whatever battles had continued after the king's demise now ceased. All sounds died to nothing, allowing Astrid's sobs to carry through the bloody and body-littered battlefield.

Fenrir and Baldr bowed their heads.

Valkyries swooped in, one angling for us. However, Freyja appeared out of nothing and stood in the Valkyrie's path.

"This soul is mine," she said solemnly.

The Valkyrie looked taken aback, as was I, but not because of Freyja's claim.

"You can't claim souls, Freyja," the Valkyrie said.

The war goddess set hard eyes on the winged woman. "All those who died honorably protecting Astrid and Randi have earned the highest honor of entering Fólkvangr. Those souls belong to me."

Freyja had been collecting souls for her own for some time, but had always done so in secret. How she did this with Valkyries around collecting their own Valhǫll souls, I never knew. But this was the first time she'd revealed what place of rest she'd created for the most honorable warriors.

With our issues with Odinn, and the prophesized events of Ragnarök by the dragons so long ago, it was wise for us to prepare our own warrior souls separate from Valhǫll.

Without waiting for the Valkyrie to respond, Freyja reached for Randi. Astrid watched, tears streaking down her cheeks and ruining her war makeup. Freyja caressed Randi's cold face, murmuring a prayer of claiming, and it was done.

The war goddess touched Astrid's head with a gentle hand and then moved to the next worthy warrior to ascend with Randi. Astrid calmed to the occasional sniffle. Leif shook, struggling to hold himself together, and Bjǫrn gazed longingly at his lost wife. He would mourn in private, as a seasoned warrior did.

With the battle done, those who had fought with the king surrendered. Geir's eldest son took over seeing the warriors home, including the fallen. Geir was retrieved as well. We also gathered our dead.

The ground rumbled under the thunder of horse hooves. I jerked my attention toward the direction of Runavík to see the approaching rider. Rune abandoned his current duty. "Ilka?"

His eldest daughter pulled on her horse's reins, drawing the beast up short. She wore half-armor and had a shield, but no weapon. She wasn't supposed to be here. She was no shield-maiden. However, she knew how to organize, so Rune had tasked her with handling the protections back in Runavík, should the king manage to break through our lines and try and destroy it.

"Leif," she called out. "Frida has gone into labor."

Leif bolted over to her, his eyes wild. "Now?"

"I wouldn't have risked coming here if she wasn't."

"You shouldn't have come at all," Rune said.

She ignored her father and kept her focus on Leif. "You need to leave with me now."

Astrid rushed past me and grabbed her brother and Ilka. "I'm faster."

The three of them disappeared before everyone's very eyes, leaving behind a now-riderless horse. Not surprisingly, that earned a mixed reaction from those who witnessed. Astrid hadn't used the ability in front of anyone yet. She wanted to be sure she had it down before revealing it.

As worried as I was about Astrid using it now, I couldn't deny my pride, either. Even after using so much magic, she had the confidence in herself and the time to recover from battle, to safely transport her brother back to his wife so the two could help her bring new life into Midgard.

My gaze shifted to Bjǫrn. He hadn't moved, still cradling his wife. I grabbed the abandoned horse and led it to the grieving man.

As a god, I didn't pray. The only thing above us was the dragons, and they didn't hear prayer. But this time, I did send a private thanks to Creation for this piece of light in the dark for Astrid and her family.

EIGHTEEN

TYR

A soft breeze blew, bringing with it the scent of flowers and the early Haustmánuður chill. Drums and other instruments played, my heart beating a rhythm of anticipation. Mortals, gods, and other allied immortals gathered around me at the river, waiting for the one boat I longed to see. My hand gripped the hilt of my sword strapped to my hip. We'd spent two winters planning this event, and now that the day was upon us, it hardly felt real.

Fenrir and Baldr took turns nudging and taunting me while Freyr watched them bemusedly.

My back straightened when the dragonhead of the boat appeared around the bend. Leif and Bjørn stood on either end of the boat, rowing with the current.

My fingers tingled, and my insides coiled. My red-haired Valkyrie sat atop a flower throne, Freyja standing with her. She was stunning in her embroidered cerulean-colored dress and fur shawl. An ornate crown made of gold and bronze and decorated with red and amber gems and flowers adorned her head, and her gorgeous red hair had been tamed back into an intricate pattern of braids.

A little girl with pale hair sat on Astrid's lap—Leif and Frida's daughter, Randi, named in honor of her grandmother.

Including the toddler wasn't traditional, but nothing about our wedding would be. Traditionally, mortals included Thor in their rituals. But with my continued poor relationship with the god, Astrid and I both agreed we would remove him from the celebration.

Baby Randi took the place of one of the traditional rituals, where a replica of Thor's hammer would have been placed on Astrid's lap on this boat ride, mixed with Freyja's presence as both fertility goddess and a stand-in for Astrid's mother. This change still had the same feel the mortals were after, but respected our decision.

The boat floated closer, and when it came within the shallows, I couldn't hold myself back any longer. I rushed out into the water.

Raucous laughter erupted from the shore, and even Bjǫrn and Freyja didn't hide their amusement. Astrid smiled widely at me and I tucked my arms around her, hauling her and baby Randi off the throne.

Astrid laughed, holding tightly to her niece as Randi giggled away. "Someone was impatient."

I leaned in and kissed her passionately. "For you, always."

I carried her and Randi to the shore. Astrid squirmed in my arms so she could hand Randi off to Frida, but I wasn't letting her go. Astrid rolled her eyes and the others around us laughed. Frida came up and took her daughter, allowing me to carry Astrid down the decorated path to the gothi waiting at the end.

It was only when I reached him that I allowed Astrid to stand on her own two feet.

Everyone gathered round, Freyja taking up a position near Astrid, acting in place of where her mother would have stood. Fenrir and Baldr took my side, the two barely able to keep themselves controlled.

The gothi began, though I hardly listened, unable to keep my eyes off Astrid. She smiled up at me with those soul-searing eyes, seeing everything I was.

The holy man finished his first ritual speech and went to the blót. An animal each was sacrificed for Freyja, Freyr, and then me, in place of Thor. Power welled up inside me when the blood was spilled in my name. Even Freyja and Freyr were visibly affected.

Fenrir shifted his weight, as if hungry for a sacrifice as well. Baldr nudged him. "Get married and you can have one, too."

Laughter rumbled through everyone, and Fenrir shoved our friend.

The holy man collected the blood into a decorative bowl from each animal and dipped a sprig into the bowl. He sprinkled blood on both of us, reciting more ritual verse.

And then it was time for the exchange of vows.

I drew my sword and held it with the dark blade facing the earth. Freyja handed Astrid a blade that had been crafted for this very moment. Instead of exchanging weapons for symbolic means, which would then be stored for our children, these blades would be exchanged for each other to wield and use as a symbol of our fierce love and devotion. Our children would earn their own blades for battle.

The gothi gestured to Astrid, and she spoke, beaming that irresistible smile. "There shall be one end for us both, one bond after our vows; nor shall our first love aimlessly perish."

He then gestured to me, and I said my vow, my pulse quickening. "Happy am I to have won the joy of such a consort; I shall not go down basely in loneliness to Hel. So let the encircling bonds grip my throat in the midst; the final anguish shall bring with it pleasure only, since the certain hope remains of renewed love, and death shall prove to have its own delights."

The two of us exchanged swords and spoke in unison. "Each world holds joy, and in the roots of Yggdrasill shall the repose of our united souls win fame, our equal faithfulness in love."

"The rings," the holy man said.

I removed the gold ring attached to a bracelet on my wrist, and placed it upon the pommel of my new sword. Astrid also procured a ring, but it was attached to the vambraces on her arms. The piece of armor would have seemed out of place for a wedding, but they had once belonged to her mother—a gift from her father to ensure she remained a little safer when she journeyed to the battlefield with me.

The gothi placed a hand on my shoulder. "Týr, by the honor as a god, and these fellow gods as witness, do you swear you want to marry this woman?"

I held Astrid's gaze, my heart hammering. "I swear."

The gothi placed his other hand on Astrid's shoulder. "Astrid, by the honor as a völva, and these gods as witness, do you swear you want to marry this man?"

She could hardly contain her smile. "I swear."

We tipped the pommels of our swords toward each other and took the ring the other offered. Then we took the rings and slipped them on each other's hands.

The gothi pulled out two ropes, red and green, and a single gold and blue silk ribbon. "Týr, Astrid, please grasp hands."

We shifted our swords to one hand and grasped each other. The gothi held up the first rope and Bjǫrn stepped up to take it. He murmured a well-wish in Astrid's ear, making her smile and her eyes sparkle, before he draped the green rope over our hands.

Leif was next; he, too, gave Astrid a well-wish before doing the same as his father with the red rope handed to him by the gothi. The remaining silk ribbon went to Freyja. She stood between us, in the place of Randi as acting völva for this ceremony.

Freyja didn't offer a well-wish, but instead, entangled magic with the ribbon she wound around us with the other two ropes.

When the loose knot rested on top of our hands, she stepped back and the gothi spoke. "As your hands are now bound together, so your lives are joined in a union of love and trust. The eternity knot of this binding symbolizes the vows you have made. Like the stars, your love should be a constant source of light, and like the earth, a fine foundation from which to grow. May this knot of love remain forever tied, and may these hands be blessed. May they always be held by one another. May they have the strength to hold on tightly during the storms of life. May they remain tender and gentle as they nurture each other."

I sucked in a deep, anticipating breath. Astrid smiled at me, and we spoke our final vow in unison once more. "By destiny we are aligned, our love eternal and true. We will face challenges together, and find strength in our union. By the sun, moon, and stars, our love is blessed. May we always be as happy as we are today."

We pulled on the long ties, slipping our hands away from each other, and knotted the ropes and silk together.

The gothi threw out his arms. "You are married!"

Cheers and roars erupted. I pulled Astrid into my arms and kissed her with every emotion that had built up inside me through the whole ceremony.

My Valkyrie. My wife. Mine for all eternity.

When our lips parted, Astrid gazed up at me with sparkling eyes. Her perfect lips then twisted in a grin, and she disappeared. My chest constricted as panic rushed through me, only for it to be cut when her father started laughing.

I snapped my head in the direction of the mead hall, where I spotted Astrid, gathered skirts in her arms, already halfway there. *Shit.* I took off in a full sprint after her, leaving the boisterous laughter and slower-to-move wedding guests behind me. *Cheating Valkyrie.*

She knew she couldn't outrun me for this part, so of course she'd give herself some leverage. She was still fair, choosing not to immediately appear in the hall, but that didn't change anything.

Astrid's laughter carried back to me. She glanced over her shoulder several times to gauge how quickly I closed the distance. And I was fast. In moments, I was hot on her heels, the thrill of this chase pushing me harder.

The hall closed in, but she wouldn't win.

Astrid squealed when I grabbed her and lifted her into my arms. I pivoted and ran backward into the open entryway. Warmth of a roaring hearth fire and the smells of cooking meat and other food from the banquet greeted us. Fenrir and Baldr, not ones to ignore a challenge, were close behind.

"No fair!" she said through laughs.

I chuckled and pressed my lips against her ear. "I don't think you have a right to talk about what's fair."

The insanely tempting woman in my arms tipped her chin down and gazed up at me with wide fake-innocent eyes, and puckered out her bottom lip. "You can't be upset. I'm not a god. I needed a way to realistically compete."

Creation, what is this look, and why does it make me feel guilty and want to give her everything she requests?

Bjǫrn's laughter drew my attention away. He walked past me and patted my shoulder. "She mastered that from Randi. Good luck, it's your problem now."

The guilt morphed into concern. *Why do I feel like a dead god walking now?*

Astrid giggled and kissed my cheek. "I'll be nice today since it's our wedding day."

That didn't make me feel any better. "Break out the ale!"

Fenrir and Baldr cheered and punched a hole into the casks they had commandeered for themselves. This kickstarted the energy for the rest of the day.

We feasted, danced, and played competitive games. Astrid danced and mingled with gods, immortals, and mortals. She smiled and laughed. And when I needed her close, I had her sit in my lap where we shared from the same drinking horn and we whispered sweet words or pulse-racing promises.

Fenrir, Baldr, and I fell a little too hard in our friendly banter when Astrid danced with them both a little longer than I wanted, resulting in a bit of a brawl breaking out. Astrid drank and watched us with Freyja as if we were the entertainment for the night. They heckled and cheered, and somehow struck up a betting pool. I wasn't sure if this was typical at a wedding, since I'd never been to one as gods rarely married, but no one seemed to take issue as they picked sides.

I came out the winner, and not because my two friends went easy on me on my wedding day. No, I was sure they went harder on me, Baldr especially with his inability to feel pain, and Fenrir once again taunted me about taking Astrid. Of course, Astrid was so used to his antics, she joined in. It certainly confused many if they weren't aware of the relationship she had with us gods.

Astrid kissed me and then healed a few damaged bones before handing me back my tunic. She'd insisted I not ruin it if I was going to fight.

The rest of the festivities continued until the sun hung low in the sky. Most of the immortals overindulged in the alcohol—we gods and immortals couldn't get drunk, which did mean we consumed even more than the mortals. Another reason this wedding planning had taken so long—we needed to be sure there was enough food and drink for the rest of the week of festivities.

Now, I helped Astrid into the boat she'd come in on. The flower throne had been removed, and it'd be only the two of us heading downstream. Freyja whispered something in her ear, and the face Astrid made, and her subsequent need for further private clarification, piqued my interest.

I grabbed the dragon head of the boat and pushed the watercraft away from the shore and hopped inside with my wife. Taking an oar, I turned the boat into the current, and we drifted downstream.

Astrid smiled at me as her home town slowly disappeared upstream. This wouldn't be the last we'd see of it. We'd return tomorrow for the next day of festivities, but tonight, she'd finally enter the home we'd share together.

I'd brought her close to it already. I wanted her to see where it was, since it was so far from her home and we'd use her magic to get us there, but she refused to go too close. She reasoned it was only "proper" as we weren't married yet. And to be fair, if she had entered that home, I was sure I wouldn't have allowed her to leave.

Runavík disappeared around the bend, and I pulled the oar into the boat. While we were ultimately teleporting to our home, leaving by boat was ceremonial, so Astrid and I agreed we'd follow the tradition until we could no longer the town.

Astrid slid her hand over my arm and gripped the side of the boat with her other. Taking a deep breath, she concentrated on the destination lake, and in a blink the boat rocked on still water.

A new forest surrounded the lake we floated on. In the middle of the lake sat an island with a single angular home, made of ancient timber and long sloping rooves. Our home.

I paddled our boat to the island. Astrid took in the structure. It must have been the smallest house she'd seen before. Since it had been just me and one other living here, I had no reason to build a large home. Now with Astrid moving in, and eventually children running around, I'd have to look into expanding.

When we reached the small dock jutting out from the island, I tied the boat and climbed out. I then offered my hand to Astrid, helping her onto the solid planks of wood.

Astrid continued to gaze around. "Týr, this place is so much more beautiful up close."

"Ùna will be happy to hear that. She's worked extra hard to make sure the grounds were to your liking. She even went out of her way to make sure the garden had what you'd need for any tonics and potions you create."

Astrid blinked up at me. "Who is Ùna?"

Ah, whoops. Seemed I'd forgotten to tell her. "She's a fae who chose to serve me as a life debt payment. She keeps the house clean, and I gave her full control over the plants outside. She knows that you'll have more of a say in what we have going forward, but I think the two of you will be able to come to an easy solution where both of you are happy."

My wife smiled up at me. "I look forward to meeting her."

"She's a bit shy, and will make herself scarce for the next few weeks while we spend time together, but you two will meet eventually." I was looking forward to our hony moone. No one would interrupt us for the next four weeks after the wedding festivities were over. I wouldn't even leave for any issues with the gods. They'd have to keep their shit together for a full moon cycle.

My body hummed at the reminder of having Astrid all to myself. We were alone on this island, and I'd erected wards in the forest to establish my domain and deter uninvited mortals and immortals alike from straying too close to the lake. *I could take her right here on the dock.*

My gaze traveled down her body. I swallowed. I could take her out here later. I needed to get her inside the house this time.

Astrid giggled when I collected her in my arms and carried her to the front door. She gazed up at the ridges of both rooves and marveled at the dragon head carvings I'd commissioned. The carpenter had long since passed, but he had been a man of talent, just as Astrid's own father was.

The door swung open on its own. Ùna's magic. She hated it when I returned and got bloody handprints on it. Claimed it disrespected and tainted the old wood this house was made from. That hadn't been a battle I was willing to fight, so I let her do her magic.

I set Astrid on her feet and kicked off my boots while she gazed around the small lounging room. Weapons, tapestries, and shelves hung on the walls. A bench rested against the partitioned wall separating this part of the house from the rest.

A few more weapons were scattered around in various states of cleanliness. I collected weapons from forgotten battlefields. They hummed with the songs of glorious battle before their abandonment.

Her cat came scampering around the partition, meowing loudly. Astrid gave her the attention she craved before she bolted out the open door.

Astrid removed her shoes and wandered further into the house. The hearth in the center roared with warmth, courtesy of Ùna before she disappeared. Her eyes swept to the right, over to the exceptionally crafted table Bjǫrn created for me that I used for both eating and holding council. More tapestries and weapons hung on the walls, along with a few animal skulls.

The pantry was tucked in the corner, behind the stairs to our left that led to the loft, where she'd become acquainted with our bed quite quickly. I'd strategically built a dormer window to be able to gaze out at the scenery from the comfort of the bed, which I knew she'd love come tomorrow.

I drew up behind her, running my hands along her hips to her stomach. Astrid leaned into me.

"If there's anything you need this house to have, tell me. I'll make it happen."

Astrid hummed thoughtfully. "I'll keep that in mind. I think it'll take me a while to adjust to all this before I can even think about what I need."

I understood. Even though she could visit her family whenever she wished, this was her home now after twenty winters living elsewhere. This was a big transition for her and I'd give her whatever time she needed.

I nuzzled her neck. "I have a gift for you."

She chuckled. "Yes, I can feel it."

I smirked. My cock was ready to burst out of my trousers, but that wasn't what I meant this time. "No, that's a different gift. The gift I mean is right there on the table."

Astrid shifted her attention to the table, where something long wrapped in hide sat on top of the hard surface. She pulled away from me and approached the table.

She ran her hand along the leather, trailing the hide up and out where it flared on one end. "What is it?"

"You have to open it to find out."

She cocked her head, and her hesitation to open the gift confused me. *Can she sense what is inside?*

With slow, deliberate tugs, Astrid undid the ties holding it together and then unwrapped her gift. The leather fell away, revealing the axe within. Astrid gasped and ran her fingers along the long haft, runes carved along its length. She traced more of them on the obsidian axe head.

"There's magic in this," she murmured.

That confirmed my suspicions. "I know I gave you my sword, but I want to be sure you have everything you need to protect yourself in battle. A backup weapon is important to carry."

Her head tilted in my direction, showing she was listening, but her focus remained on the tool.

"The haft is made from your mother's staff."

Astrid jerked her attention to me, her eyes wide. "What?"

I rubbed the back of my neck. "Your father and I came up with this together. He wanted to give something special to you, that you could pass down in the family, since we were changing the sword tradition. And because the staff was so large, he thought it would be good to make a sister axe for Leif to pass down. I had no issues having both enchanted."

Tears pricked her eyes, and my gut twisted. *Did I mess up? Should I have not done this?*

Astrid lifted the axe and held it close to her chest. "Thank you… Thank you…"

I walked up behind her, and pulled her into me by the hips, my chest pressing against her head. I reached up and wrapped my hand around her throat. Astrid sucked in a sharp inhale and instinctively tipped her chin up. Our gazes locked and heat ignited in my veins.

"You will have everything you could ever desire and more, Valkyrie. I'll lay Midgard at your feet if you demand it."

I leaned down and captured her lips with mine, drinking in all that she was. Astrid groaned, and the axe clattered to the table. She turned in my arms, her arms snaking around my neck. Her kisses turned fevered and demanding, matching the need breaking through my careful control.

My hands ran along the curve of her sides and hips. My fingers dug into the fabric of her dress and it tore, though not in the way it had in the past. The seams separated more easily than a typical dress, courtesy of a design Freyja helped come up with for Astrid.

Astrid had gotten tired of me ruining her dresses all the time. The final straw had been when I shredded her favorite dress after expressing she didn't want anything happening to it. I wasn't allowed to touch her in any way for weeks after that, even after I'd profusely apologized for losing control and bought her a host of new dresses, including a near-exact replica of the one I ruined.

Freyja allowed me to flounder for a while before revealing the new dress design and explaining to my thick head that it wasn't just the damaged dress that was the issue. It was my lack of respect for her clear request.

I hadn't meant to disrespect Astrid. It was just so damned hard to control myself around her. I craved her like nothing else in Creation's existence. And it didn't help that she was so fragile. I had to be extremely careful not to hurt her. And I was fairly rough with her during sex as it was. So if her clothes were the only thing I ruined, I was happy with that.

I accepted I'd made a mistake, and worked together with Astrid to fix it and grow stronger together.

My hands gripped Astrid's ass and lifted her onto the table. She giggled against my lips and tugged at my tunic. Our mouths parted as I complied with her request. My belt dropped to the floor and Astrid tugged down my trousers while I pulled my tunic over my head.

I dropped the clothing without care and gazed down at Astrid. She ran her fingers over my chest, feeling my scars and muscles. Her touch simmered my building desire.

I leaned in and captured her lips with mine. I slid my hand up her belly to her chest and lightly pushed. "Lie back, Astrid."

She hummed thoughtfully, her hands teasing my skin and her breasts bumping against me, kicking up my desire to touch her more. "No, I don't think I will."

A low growl rumbled in my chest. A new desire hiked deep within me, pushing to fight against her.

Freyja said love and sex were their own battles. I'd never experienced that until Astrid. Some days she embraced the throes of our passion with reckless abandon. Others, she pushed back, turning it into a strength of wills. When she did, it stirred something within me as a god of war, and the explosion of passion from the drawn-out shared satisfaction was something more powerful than I thought I'd ever experience with someone. It also carried an extra effect that no mortal man could ever have.

I pushed her harder, biting her bottom lip. "Lie back, Astrid. Freyr gave me a bit of advice I want to try out."

She chuckled and didn't comply. Instead, she tried to glide her hands lower, toward my hips. "And what if I want to try some advice Freyja gave me?"

I snatched her hands and pinned them to the table, my mouth slanting and trailing kisses along her jaw, then down her neck. "Then you'll have to fight me for that."

Astrid bit her lips, suppressing the groan I knew she wanted to release. Her body betrayed her by arching—begging to be ravished in the one way I knew she enjoyed. "I can resist you."

I chuckled against her skin and continued kissing her lower, my mouth brushing her collarbone. "No, I don't think you can."

Neither of us could fight each other for long, but we sure as hel tried during these moments.

I licked swaths of her delicious skin. Astrid continued to fight against the promised pleasure and her body's craving to give in. Her stifled moans were like battle cries to my inner fighter. It drove me on, craving her surrender.

Astrid's tipping point came when I ravished her breasts. Licking and sucking her taut, delicious nipples, I drove her to the edge of her control until she whimpered and strained against my restraining hands.

I released her with a *pop*. "Lie back, Valkyrie."

Her body arched into me, and she groaned in surrender as she did as I ordered. I grinned in satisfaction. The roar of a battle won heated a consuming fire in my veins and demanded I take my prize. I kissed her between her breasts and then migrated.

Lower and lower I kissed and licked, claiming all of her as mine. My hands roamed her naked body. I could have her forever and never tire of feeling her softness under my rough touch or her taste on my tongue.

My lips brushed her navel and then a little lower and Astrid sucked in a surprised breath. "Týr?"

I grinned and continued my path south, my hands sliding along her thighs and nudging them apart. I teased her inner thighs with my thumbs. She squirmed and her breathing hitched with her anticipation.

I slid my fingers past her red curls and along her sensitive flesh. Astrid bit her lips and stifled a groan. All my teasing had her slick and ready for anything I gave her, and I had a lot more to offer.

Kissing her inner thigh granted me a sharp inhale from Astrid. "Týr, what is this?"

I chuckled and murmured against her skin. "Something I'm told you're guaranteed to enjoy."

I kissed higher up her thigh and spread her soft lips with my fingers, teasingly sliding them against her slick flesh. I kissed her again before dragging my tongue along her slit and flicking her sensitive bud. Astrid's back arched and she gasped.

I licked her again. Then kissed. And licked and sucked, searing her taste into my mind. Astrid moaned and writhed under this new attention. Her fingers slid into my hair and gripped me tightly as I continued.

"More," she begged. "More."

Her hips lifted, and she placed as much pressure as she could with her hands to push me farther between her quivering legs. I didn't let up my attention, her begging simmering heat throughout my entire body, and reheating the flames of battle.

While she begged, I sensed her resistance to fall completely into the pleasure I offered her. She knew how much I craved to see her come undone by my touch, and she'd prolong it just to rile me up.

I would win.

I slid my hands along her thighs, and then along her heated flesh, never ceasing my attention with my mouth. Astrid bit down on her lip, attempting to fight back her anticipated groan.

She failed and cried out when I slid two fingers inside her, pumping in rhythm with my tongue. Her grip on my hair tightened, and she rocked her hips into me, her hold on her control slipping with impending surrender.

"That's it, Valkyrie, enjoy this," I murmured between kisses and licks. "Surrender to me."

Astrid tried to hold back, but her body craved harder than she could control. She rubbed her pussy into my face, begging for more. I curved my fingers, and with one final twitch, my Valkyrie came undone.

Her body convulsed and she screamed in erotic release. The sound was the most intoxicating battle cry.

I didn't let up until she was panting and her body twitched away from my attention. I leaned over her, slowly wiping away her lingering taste from my lips. She breathed heavily, her body languid and flushed with the most tantalizing color.

I lowered myself and kissed her neck. She groaned in response and her legs slid up along my hips, as if begging me to continue. It took every ounce of control I had to not plunge into her immediately. I would savor this first night together with no barriers between us.

As a god, I could control the aspects of potential pregnancy from my side. And as much as I'd craved over these last two winters to see her holding my child in her arms, I'd held back for this moment.

I ran my hands along her hips, my hard cock teasingly resting atop the apex of her thighs. I didn't have to hold back anymore.

One more kiss on the neck and I gripped her hips, lifting them up to meet me as I plunged into her. Astrid gasped, and I sucked in a tight breath as I buried deep inside her pussy. I pulled out and then drove into her again. And again. Skin slapping against skin.

Astrid moaned, clamping her legs tighter around me, as if that'd pull me deeper inside her with each thrust. Our mouths locked in desperate hunger for each other, our breaths gasping and strained. Desire inflamed my veins and my pulse pounded in my ears. Her intoxicating scent surrounded me and her taste consumed me.

Her nails dug into my skin, the action not harming my harder god skin, but doing everything for her as she threw her head back and the tides of orgasm crashed over her again. "Týr!"

My body tightened, her tight and convulsing pussy milking me to the edge. I roared as I crested over the peak of my own release and exploded inside her. I may have slammed my hand on the table, cracking it, but the haze of orgasm muddled my senses.

The two of us lay in a crumpled heap. The only sounds in the house were the crackling fire and our mingling heavy breaths. My hard cock remained inside her, the result of our battle. A feat no mortal man could ever dream to give her.

When I regained feeling in my limbs, I kissed her on the lips and lifted her off the table. Astrid slipped her arms around my neck and locked her legs around my waist. I groaned, feeling myself slide deeper into her, and Astrid sucked in a tight breath.

"Another moment," she murmured.

I nibbled her ear. "I can't hold this for much longer without stimulation."

She chuckled. "You seem impatient for something. It's not like you won't be ready for more in a little bit. I know you."

She did. I'd taken her wherever I desired and she allowed. Sometimes multiple times a day.

I nipped at her neck and slowly slid her up and down my cock. Astrid moaned at the slow tease of her overworked pussy. "I am impatient."

She bit her lower lip. "For what?"

"To see you heavy with my child." I lifted her up and slammed her down on my cock. She cried out in pleasure. "I'm not letting you leave until you are."

Astrid gasped. "We are expected to return to the festivities tomorrow."

I chuckled. "And?"

Her nails dug into my neck, and her breathing hitched. "That's not possible."

I increased my thrusts, fucking her harder. "Don't underestimate what your god can do, wife."

NINETEEN

ASTRID

My hands twisted together. Pain constricted my stomach, and I didn't like the look on Freyja's face. I didn't want that to mean my fears were real. I didn't want her to confirm what all the other healers we'd consulted said. She was my last hope.

I should have gone to her first, but I was worried about what she'd say. As a fertility goddess, she'd know the truth.

"Well?" I finally asked her.

Freyja pulled her hands away and frowned. I noted the slump in her shoulders, and the knot in my stomach tightened. *No…*

"I'm sorry, Astrid," she murmured.

No…

"The reason your three pregnancies… didn't come to term… is because… your body isn't capable of handling a full-term pregnancy."

Numbness crept through my limbs. *She was supposed to tell me the others were wrong, not confirm their claims…*

Týr's hands gripped my shoulders. "Freyja, is there anything that can be done?"

"I just tried a few things; I'm afraid they didn't work. There's nothing more that can be done."

I barely heard her.

"Come, Valkyrie, let's go home," Týr said, placing pressure on my shoulders in encouragement to stand.

I complied, barely aware of doing so. The numbness set in so deep, I wasn't aware of much around me. Týr may have tried to talk to me, but I couldn't respond.

We arrived at our home island, though I wasn't sure how. I didn't do it. I also wasn't sure I cared.

"Valkyrie?" Týr murmured.

I didn't acknowledge him; my feet moved on their own for the house. A quiet voice squeaked out my name, but I ignored that, too. I walked up the stairs, still ignoring Týr's calls to me, and curled up on the bed, my arms wrapped around my midsection. *I'm a cursed woman after all...*

We'd been trying for a family for several years, with the same agonizing result. Deep down, I had always known the truth, but I didn't want to acknowledge it. I'd been foolish to believe that just by Týr choosing me, my poor luck with marriage prospects had simply been because he hadn't come along yet—that my curse was made up.

The numbness cracked, despair leaking out. Tears trickled down my cheeks and I curled tighter into myself, pain raking over me.

I was a disgrace. I'd failed at my one sacred duty as a wife. If I couldn't honor Týr with children, what purpose did I have?

He deserves better than me...

"Astrid," Týr's quiet voice came again. He was close to me, but seemed so far away. "Astrid, please talk to me."

I couldn't. What would I say? Why was he even talking to me? Why would he want to be near such a worthless, broken woman?

His presence grew and his arms wrapped around me, pulling me into his firm chest. "I'm here for you, Astrid."

"You shouldn't be," I managed through my sobs.

His embrace tightened. "Yes, I should. I love you, Astrid. No matter what."

He shouldn't... I don't deserve it.

A fresh wave of grief hit me. I sobbed until I was too exhausted to remain awake. And yet, waking wouldn't relieve me from this nightmare. I existed in a fog that was only broken by the waves of grief and physical pain it brought with it.

I found no joy in the day. So I lay down early, hoping I'd wake from the nightmare.

Day after day, I did this. I lacked all purpose—all love for things I once did. What was the point? I failed as a wife, and failed at the one thing I wanted most. There would be no small hands to hold, no giggles, and no laughs. No one to teach to be strong warriors and powerful völva. *I'm a disgrace to all völva who came before me.*

Týr's deep voice came from behind me. "Astrid."

I didn't respond verbally; I turned just enough to show I heard him. I wouldn't even look at him. I couldn't.

"Please talk to me," he begged.

It hurt to hear his pain. I was the cause of it. My existence hurt him. I turned away.

Týr grabbed my hand. "Please don't shut me out. Let me help however I can."

My lower lip trembled and I pulled out of his grasp. "You can't."

I didn't know where I went after that. I knew at some point I cried myself to sleep again and woke feeling worse than before.

I shouldn't be here. I had no right. If I left, he could find someone more worthy.

"Astrid, what are you doing?" Týr asked.

I paused and looked at my hands. I held a bag with some clothes and had been in the process of stashing my dowry in it as well. "I don't belong here."

"The hel are you talking about?" He drew closer. "Of course you belong here."

I finished my packing. "I'm not worthy of being here, with you."

He grabbed my shoulders. "You are the most worthy woman for me to dedicate my life to."

I tried to pull away. "You should be telling me to leave. I am worthless to you. Cursed."

Týr held fast and crouched before me. "Astrid, look at me."

I couldn't.

"Look at me."

I tried to pull further away instead.

Týr framed my face with his hands, gently, as if he thought I'd break, and made me look at him for the first time in I don't know how long had passed. "You belong here, with me. I swore to eternity to love you until my last breath, and Creation help me, I will."

His blue eyes snared me, and his words made my chest ache. "I do not need sons and daughters to be happy. I need you. You are my heart, Valkyrie. My reason to live. And nothing will ever get in the way of that."

Fresh, hot tears flowed down my cheeks. I didn't know how I still had any left, but I did.

Týr kissed my forehead and lifted me into his arms, cradling me as if I were the most precious thing in existence. A part of me desperately wished I was—I wanted to be close to him. But the broken, desperate-to-flee part held strong.

Týr carried me to our bed and laid us down, holding me close. He murmured loving words that sent an ebb and flow of emotions through me. One moment, I felt loved and appreciated, despite my flaws, and in another I felt so unworthy to be this close to him.

He never left, not even after I fell asleep. I awoke with him still holding tight, like he was afraid of me disappearing. I wasn't sure I deserved such devotion.

TWENTY

ASTRID

The fog wasn't so heavy today, yet the pain remained. I did something. Not much, though more than I had in a while. Then I sat at the edge of the lake, staring out into the forest. I didn't know why; normally I sat inside, staring at nothing.

Týr and Una hovered nearby; they always did. The lessened fog made me aware of how often I hadn't been alone through this whole ordeal. I heard Freyja's voice, too. I was sure she had come by a lot lately. Fenrir and Baldr had been by at some point; I'd heard their voices, though I didn't know when.

A large presence approached from behind. I assumed it was Týr coming to check on me. But to my surprise, it wasn't him who sat down next to me. I gazed up at Baldr, confused as to what he might want.

He didn't look at me, though, just stared out at the scenery like I had been. I returned my gaze to the forest, a comfortable silence falling over us for a long moment.

"I've walked this path, and I know the ache that comes with it," he finally said. "It's not easy to hear, and it's not something you should carry alone."

My heart lurched.

"It does get easier, even if right now that doesn't seem possible."

I stared at him, my lungs seizing. "You… know what it's like?"

He nodded slowly and stared out for a moment longer before turning his gaze down to his hands as they hung over his bent knees. "I never thought something like that would affect me so much. When I was young, I couldn't give less of a shit if I fathered children. But then a point came where those thoughts changed."

His lips pressed into a thin line. "And then I found out I couldn't. Me—a god—infertile? It was such a ridiculous notion, I refused to believe it at first."

My gut knotted. He was like me. I'd refused to believe it. I didn't even want to believe Freyja.

"The denial eventually gave way to desperation. I had to find a way to fix it. I had a reputation. I was Odinn's perfect son. I couldn't have that tarnished. I couldn't have the choice of parenthood taken away from me like that."

My breath caught. *He understands…*

Baldr shook his head. "I went through all this alone. I didn't talk to anyone. It made it harder to get to the point where I finally came to terms with my position. And yes, every now and then, I feel forlorn about something I'll never have, but those times become fewer and farther between, the longer I accept things as they are."

He reached out and wrapped his large hand around my smaller one. His callouses bit into my skin, but not in an uncomfortable way.

I stared at his hands. Baldr's closeness usually caused me to feel conflicted. His presence and how he treated me, even after I married Týr, made me feel things I knew I shouldn't. But this touch… it wasn't like that. This was different.

He and I understood each other on a much deeper level as of this moment. He'd just exposed himself—showed his vulnerability, to help me. The least I could do was offer the same.

I squeezed his hand. "I feel like… my purpose is gone."

"You're strong, even if you don't feel it now. There are many ways to leave a mark." His thumb caressed my hand. "How can we help you see that? How can we help show you you're not cursed?"

My lower lips quivered. "I… don't know yet."

He nodded. "That's okay. We stand by you through this. Whatever you need, we're here."

Someone walked up behind me and sat. I didn't need to look at Týr to know it was him this time. With my senses more awake, it was easier to see how I'd made the mistaken identity with Baldr.

Týr wrapped his arms around me and pulled me into his lap. He didn't force Baldr to release my hand, though I was a bit surprised he didn't. It wasn't like I minded; his calm and strong aura helped me right now. But why wasn't he concerned Týr might be upset? Why wasn't Týr upset?

Instead, he patted Baldr on the shoulder in the way he always did to affirm something with his friend. Týr then kissed my head. "I love you."

I leaned against him. I wanted to say it back, but couldn't right now. I'd be able to again one day.

And day by day, things got better for me. I found myself crying less and feeling positive more often. I'd slip backward a few times, but Týr and the others were there for me.

Baldr was there to talk to when it was too difficult to tell anyone else what I was feeling. He listened and affirmed in the ways I needed, allowing me to accept and overcome. Our bond strengthened in new ways from this—in ways I didn't quite understand yet.

TWENTY-ONE

ASTRID

I gazed out the dormer window next to the bed. No pain constricted my chest. The dark thoughts didn't swim in my mind, and I didn't feel like a failure. It'd been some time since I'd felt this well.

I slipped out of bed and brushed my hair before walking quietly down the stairs from the loft. The grinding of metal welcomed my steps. I knew Týr was sharpening something. I hated it when he sharpened his tools in the house, but he rarely went far from me these days.

When I reached the bottom step, Úna's adorable face was the first to greet me, her large multi-colored eyes gazing up. I smiled at her. The small fae's face lit up and she skipped away, her ethereal tail lashing about, and broken gossamer wings trying to flutter in her excitement.

I had worried her so much. I felt bad. I didn't mean to make others fret. I'd just been so consumed by my grief, I'd made rash decisions that hurt more than just me. *I'll make it up to her.*

Týr stood at the table, his back to me. He focused on his axe, careful with his sharpening technique. I leaned against the wall to quietly observe. As much as I hated him performing this task in the house, I did enjoy watching him work.

"I know you're there, Valkyrie," Týr said.

"I'm not hiding," I said.

He paused. "Then what are you doing?"

"Watching you."

He set the axe down and braced his hands on the table. "Is that all you wish to do?"

My eyes flicked down his body, enjoying the view. I chewed my lip. It'd been so long since I'd allowed us to be close. I hadn't felt worthy enough. Those thoughts weren't there anymore.

One step at a time I closed the distance. I wrapped my arms around his waist, and pressed my face into his back, inhaling his masculine scent.

Týr tensed and then relaxed, grasping my arms with his massive hands. "How are you feeling?"

"Better than I have in a while."

He turned in my grip, and wrapped his arms around me, pulling me in a tight embrace. I buried my face into his chest, my hands fisting his tunic. I mumbled something.

Týr chuckled, his chest rumbling in the most soothing way. "I don't understand what you said, Valkyrie."

I tipped my head back. "I said, I'm sorry."

He brushed a strand of hair out of my face, his fingers grazing cheeks. "No, don't be. I should be the one apologizing. I wanted to do more, but I didn't know what to do."

I placed my hands over his heart. It beat strong, like him. "You did help. You stayed. You refused to let me leave. You never gave up on me."

My chest swelled and my lower lip trembled as emotions rose up within me. Tears brimmed my eyes. "You were my ship when the waves tried to drag me to hel, even if I didn't realize it at the time."

Týr cupped my face, the pad of his thumb caressing my cheek, wiping away the tear that broke free. "I will always fight for you, Astrid. I love you. You have my heart for all eternity."

I arched into him, emotion overwhelming me. "And eternity we'll have."

Eternity wasn't available to me as a mortal, but my soul yearned so hard for him that should I be blessed with another life, I'd choose him all over again.

Týr leaned down. Overcome with the need to show him how much he meant to me, I popped up on my toes to meet him halfway. But in my haste, I overshot and our mouths collided. I yipped and he grunted when our teeth clattered and pain split through my mouth. Another unfamiliar sensation crawled through me, under my skin, settling in my chest around my heart, but the metallic taste of blood slathering my tongue distracted me.

I jerked back and touched my mouth, feeling the slice in my lip. "I'm sorry. I… I let my eagerness get the better of me."

"Eager is an understatement, Valkyrie." Týr chuckled. "You drew blood."

"Yes, I can feel my cut." I pushed a little healing into my finger to seal the wound.

He shook his head and wiped the blood from his mouth. "No, you drew my blood."

I blinked. How was that possible? I'd never been able to draw his blood. Not even during our more intense nights together when I dug my nails into his skin.

He smirked. "Well, I can't say that was an unpleasant surprise."

My brow pinched together. "You want me to hurt you?"

Týr tipped my chin up. "I want you to unleash your passion. I want to feel the strength of your adoration."

He dipped his head and brushed his lips against mine. When he spoke again, his words came out in a strained rasp and crawled along my skin like temptation manifested. "It drives me mad with a desire only you can sate."

His lips captured mine, making my heart leap. When it came down, it brought with it a warm heat that pooled in my core and quickly spread through me. I tangled my fingers in his hair and kissed him back, the lingering desperation and despair within me pushing aside for my surging need for him.

Our tongues wrestled and explored and my body arched into him, desperate to be closer. I needed him to touch me—love me—heal me in the way only he could.

Týr lifted me in his arms without breaking our contact and carried me up to the loft. I didn't see a need for the move; he liked to take me wherever we were at that moment when the mood struck us. But, even in my desperate haze, I noticed how carefully he held me. I realized how gentle his kisses were, compared to my more forceful need.

He laid me down, my hair fanning out around me, and broke our kiss as he pulled away to gaze down at me. I blinked slowly, trying to understand. I was so used to him being rough, this tender approach… it was as if he thought I was so fragile I'd break with the slightest pressure.

Maybe he was right. Maybe I was a little more fragile than before. And that was okay. We'd fill in each little crack together, one day at a time.

I beckoned him with a finger. Instead of complying, Týr loosened his belt and pulled his tunic over his head. My eyes took in every scarred inch of him, my pulse and breathing kicking up in tandem with my building need to have us close again.

I sat up and reached for him. Týr grabbed my hands and tried to gently push me back. "Lie down, Astrid."

Heat pulsed in my chest, and I swallowed. I liked it when he called me Valkyrie. It made me feel powerful and strong. But when he called by my actual name—the way the word rolled off his tongue as if he put every ounce of adoration he could—it affected me far more in these situations.

"No." I pushed his hands away and ran mine along his sculpted chest. Leaning in, I kissed his skin and glided my hands along his hard body, feeling every peak and valley and scar of his perfect form.

"Valkyrie…" Týr groaned when I licked the large scar on his ribs.

I kissed him a little lower… and then lower. My hands trailed down to his trousers and loosened them. They dropped to the floor and his hard cock sprang free. Tempting as it was, I didn't offer him any relief as my hands slid along his muscular legs.

Týr hissed when I nipped his taut stomach and then licked a deep scar that cut down to his hip. I kissed a line toward his navel, and then slowly lower—painstakingly so.

"Astrid," he rumbled, the sound igniting my veins and kicking up my pulse.

My hands slid back up to his hips, and then along his massive shaft, the touches feather-light and teasing. He groaned and his cock jerked. I grinned against his skin before nipping the sensitive flesh below his navel. Týr hissed in anticipation.

I flicked my gaze up to him, snaring his powerful, unwavering attention, and dragged my tongue along his throbbing cock, my tongue bumping over the slight ridges of his veins.

Týr tangled his fingers in my hair and groaned. "Valkyrie."

Heat thrummed under my skin, my heart pounding hard in my chest. I had total power over this god, and all I wanted was to shower him with my adoration and worship.

I teasingly licked around and under the sensitive and velvety head of his cock while wrapping my hands firmly around his girth and stroking him. He groaned again, his grip tightening in my hair. My breath hitched, pleasant tingles rushing down my spine. *There's a sliver of the rough war god I love.*

Pressing my lips against the head of his cock, I teasingly swirled my tongue around it before easing my lips around his impossibly large girth. Týr's breath caught.

Slowly, agonizingly so, I took him into my mouth. Týr's head rolled back as he groaned. His grip tightened and he attempted to coax my pace with pressure to my head, but I planted a hand on his hip to show him I'd fight his request. I set the pace of my worship, not him.

"Valkyrie," he hissed out through clenched teeth.

I chuckled in response, eliciting another frustrated hiss, and slid him as far as I could take him. I set the same slow pace sliding him out. My pace picked up when I pulled him back in. And then again. My tongue slid along his shaft in tandem, feeling the sensation of his throbbing, and taking in bursts of his taste.

I pushed the threads of Týr's control, never increasing my pace quite enough for him.

"Hel, Valkyrie," he groaned before threading his other hand into my hair, framing my face. He'd reached his limit, and I was all too willing to finally give him what he wanted.

Gripping his hips, I slid his cock in and out of my mouth at a rapid pace. Týr rocked his hips, forcing him deeper. We never broke eye contact, the connection intense and consuming.

He swelled and throbbed harder the longer I sucked him. And when I thought he'd tip the edge and release his seed into my mouth, he withdrew.

I panted, my mouth remaining partially open. His hands still firmly grasping my hair, Týr bent over and pressed his forehead against mine. "Dammit, Valkyrie. You know how to shred every ounce of control I have."

"You didn't have to stop," I mumbled.

"I did not win that battle, and that wasn't how I wanted to take you today."

A flash of triumph burst deep within me. I'd won our little battle of wills. It wasn't often I did, but when it happened, I relished the victory.

I hummed, one of my hands teasing his still-hard cock, the other sliding up his naked chest. "Then, tell me, what does my godly husband want?"

His chest rumbled. "You."

Týr claimed my mouth, forceful and demanding. I groaned, my pulse leaping. But then, he pulled away.

"Lie back, Astrid," he said.

I waited for him to physically encourage me, but it never came. My brows knitted together. Something wasn't right. When we fell into our passion, he rarely showed such control. If he asked something of me, it was more a command that I chose to listen to or rebel against. "Who are you, and what have you done with my husband?"

He chuckled. "What do you mean?"

"This is not how you usually make love to me."

"No, but does that mean I can't do something different?"

I frowned. "I'm not fragile, Týr."

He kissed me, long and deep, stealing my breath. "No, you're certainly not, Valkyrie."

His words flowed over me like a teasing caress. It made me feel strong and loved at the same time. But still, I couldn't shake his behavior.

"Then what is the reason? The true reason?" I asked.

I searched his eyes when he hesitated with his response. "Týr, what is it?"

He sighed and cupped my face. "While you went through this, I feared I'd been the cause. I'm so rough with you, I thought…"

His shoulders sagged and he sighed again, closing his eyes. My heart sank. "Freyja assured me I wasn't the cause, but I've still been struggling."

My chest clenched. I'd been so consumed, I never once thought about how this could be affecting him. I grasped his arms and pulled him closer until our foreheads touched. "I'm sorry."

"Valkyrie, please don't. This was difficult on us both. We are healing. Together."

He was right. Being hard on ourselves for this wouldn't help.

I took his face in my hands and kissed him gently. "Make love to me."

I pulled away, dragging my fingers along his jaw and through his beard before lying back, my arms resting lazily around my head. I would not pressure him and would be pleased with however he chose to go about this. I just wanted us to reaffirm our love after so much struggle.

Týr gazed down at me, heat simmering in his eyes. "You have too many layers hiding your beauty from me."

I still wore my sleeping gown. My lower lip caught in my teeth and I twirled a lock of hair. "And what are you going to do about it, mighty Týr?"

He smirked and leaned over, pressing his lips gently against my forehead. I closed my eyes and sighed, enjoying the tenderness. His lips trailed down my cheek to my jaw, and then my neck. His hand caressed the other side of my face, down my neck, and along my collarbone.

I rolled my head back, falling into the tender touches, each one sparking an ember along my skin. I moaned when he kissed and then licked my collarbone.

Týr grinned against my skin. Fabric tore, and cool air hit my chest. My eyes popped open wide and I gasped.

Stuck in his teeth was some of my dress. His fist claimed another portion. And between, my breasts lay exposed, nipples pebbling.

My lip caught in my teeth again. I didn't like my dresses turning into scraps. It was why Freyja helped me obtain new dresses designed to come apart in ways so that I didn't have to completely replace them. But there was something incredibly appealing about Týr tearing my clothes.

His need to remove all barriers between us so quickly, but with enough control not to harm me when it'd be so easy for him to break me, was enough to arouse me by the thought alone.

Týr released the ripped ends of my dress and kissed between my breasts. "Mmm, better."

His words were more growl than syllables, which vibrated against my skin and through my entire body. The embers of desire he started fanned hotter, urging me to arch into him and beg for more.

I closed my eyes and resisted asking for too much too quickly. I wanted to experience this new way of loving him without dictating just yet how it went. My desire hadn't quite grown strong enough to take over those controlled thoughts. But with the way he kissed my skin, I knew it was only a matter of time.

Týr set a leisurely pace along my body. Following paths of freckles, he explored and teased, pulling my dress off slowly, until I was fully on display for him. He didn't stop to stare and appreciate as I expected, however. Instead, he continued to kiss me—claim me.

Each area he chose, it felt like he was leaving an invisible mark. When he was done, I would glow with his aura, showing all of Midgard I was his. And that drove me crazy.

Heat seared my veins. Thoughts of what I wanted him to do to me consumed my mind. I fisted the furs beneath me, trying my hardest to not give into the temptation.

"Something the matter, Valkyrie?" Týr asked before kissing my hip.

"Is this revenge for earlier? Because it's starting to feel like it."

"Revenge?" He chuckled and kissed my thigh. "Now what would give you that impression?"

I sucked in a tight breath when he kissed the sensitive area between my navel and the apex of my thighs. Yes, he certainly was drawing this out as an act of revenge.

His tongue ran along my inner thigh; his calloused fingers rubbed circles on my other inner thigh. He teased in a way that I never thought I could be until I squirmed, unable to take it anymore. This satisfied him, and he finally gave me what I craved.

His fingers slid between the apex of my thighs and slid along my slick folds. I gasped and then arched my back when his fingers found my most sensitive and pleasurable spot.

My blood heated and burned hotter the longer his skilled fingers pleasured me. When he grinned against my thigh, my breath caught in my throat. Týr kissed my skin again, then glided his tongue along my slick need.

I threw my head back, threading my fingers into his hair and tipping my hips, pushing my pussy farther into his mouth. Týr licked runes around my pleasure spot, finishing each with a hard suck. I moaned and panted with each stroke of his focused attention.

Tension coiled in my core. One last rune, a claim defining me as his, and I came undone. I screamed his name, grinding and writhing as ultimate pleasure coursed through me.

Týr didn't ease up, instead sliding his fingers inside me, pushing me higher just as I came down from Valhǫll, sending me back almost immediately.

When my soul returned to my body a second time, he eased his attention. I lay on the bed panting, my body languid and numb with the best type of pleasure. I brushed a damp curl of hair out of my eyes and mumbled, "It's not fair."

Týr hummed and kissed my belly, making my sensitive body twitch. "What's not fair, Valkyrie?"

I closed my eyes and swallowed as he trailed a path up. "That I can't do the same for you without having to lose a battle to you."

He licked my nipple and I groaned. "Yes, that is a bit disappointing, but, unlike those quick replenishing immortals, my breaks allow me to go all day if I wish. Like today."

I swallowed and arched when he pulled my taut bud into his mouth and sucked. "I want that."

I wanted to make love to him as long as my body would allow it. I needed to make it up to him.

Týr lavished my breasts until he couldn't hold off his needs any longer. He gripped my hips, and teased me with his hard cock before slowly entering me. My mouth fell open, and a deep, guttural moan came from my throat. How I missed this sensation—of his thick member stretching and filling me with everything he was.

He didn't stop his amazing yet agonizingly slow pace until he was fully inside me. Then he withdrew just as slowly.

"You like that, Valkyrie?"

"Yes," I breathed out.

It was so different from what I was used to with him. And I wanted more. I wanted his control—his power—his love.

He entered me again, at the same pace. And then again. But by the fourth time, I noticed the tightness in his grip on my hips. It wasn't easy for him to maintain this control he sought. And I wasn't always the kindest wife.

I rocked my hips as he entered me again. The sensation it sent flooding through me made me gasp.

"Valkyrie," Týr groaned in warning.

I bit my lower lip and did it again, driving him deeper and harder into me.

He licked his lips and tried to maintain his slow control, but failed when I lifted my hips again.

"Have it your way, Valkyrie," he growled.

Týr slammed into me and I let out a gasping moan. His gentleness disappeared; the rough war god I knew intimately now unleashed anew. I fell into the pleasure he brought as he roughly fucked me.

His thumb slid between my thighs, rubbing more pleasure into me. Already sensitive from before, I didn't last, and neither did he.

We crested the edge together. I screamed his name, clenching around him, and the warmth of his hot seed filled my pussy.

Coming down, we were a tangle of breaths and pleased bodies. Týr held me close, pulling out of me and rolling onto his back. I laid against his chest, listening to his powerful heartbeat. I missed this—missed him. Even when I felt unworthy of him, I wanted him. It had hurt to push him away, just as much as it'd hurt to be so close.

But that pain wasn't there. I didn't feel happy with myself, but I was at least happy with him. I could find that other happiness in time.

I propped myself up and ran my fingers through his beard. He smiled and played with a lock of my hair.

"I love you," he said.

I kissed him. "I love you, too."

"Promise me you won't leave me again."

I kissed him again. "You are my god, my shield, and my husband. That I vow, forever and for always."

He sucked in a breath, as if my words caressed him like a prayer. He brushed my cheek with his fingers. "You are my Valkyrie, my völva, my wife, forever into eternity."

As we gazed into each other's eyes, a powerful sensation churned in my chest. We meant these words, and nothing would tear us apart. Not even death.

TWENTY-TWO

ASTRID

The market bustled around me. Stalls of weathered wood and colored fabrics lined the square, their merchants selling strange and fascinating goods. A fae tried to snag my attention, to lure me to his store and convince me to buy something I didn't need. A quick glance told me I couldn't find what I needed with him.

A woman with glimmering wings and brilliant silver hair that shimmered in the sunlight stood behind a stall selling vials of sparkling white liquid. She smiled at me with pointed teeth, her eyes twinkling with a hint of mischief. *Don't go to her stall, either.*

The scents of spices, rare herbs, and blooming flowers thickened the air from a nearby stall I did wish to patron. Not for the reason I originally came, but if I found something I could use in potions or enchanting, I wanted to obtain it. Of course, it all depended on the price. Because in the magical community, the cost wasn't always coin.

A large centaur with a coat as dark as night tended this stall. He watched me with intense interest.

Baldr shifted behind me. He bent over to whisper in my ear. "This stall? Are you sure?"

His hot breath on my skin sent a shiver down my spine. I did my best to suppress it. "It's possible there's something of interest here. I won't know until I check."

He made a thoughtful sound and allowed me to browse, while keeping a close eye on the centaur. I understood his unease. There were many stories of how wild and unpredictable centaurs could be. And some even said a woman like me would never be safe in the presence of one. But that didn't mean they were all like that. And this one was rather calm and collected.

"Anything of interest to you?" the centaur rumbled in a deep, resonant tone.

My eyes slid over several herbs that were hard to come by. Mostly because they could only be obtained from the fae domain, a place someone like me could not go. They couldn't grow here in Midgard, making it impossible to steal them. You had to know the right fae to get a plentiful supply, or hope to find them in special markets, like this one.

"How do you treat?" It was best to know the type of currency exchange he had in mind before I set my heart on anything.

He gazed at me a moment, his eyes drifting down my body and feeling like a physical weight I wasn't a fan of. "Healing."

I blinked slowly, not sure I heard him right. "Healing?"

"I know your power, Týr's wife. And I will trade my goods for healing."

His knowledge wasn't surprising. My name was known by many across Midgard. I had a reputation, some good, some bad, it all depended on who told the story, and what agenda they had. Though one thing remained—I was Týr's wife, and a powerful witch you needed to think twice about crossing.

Some even dared to call me a new Valkyrie, one not tied to Odinn. Of course, I knew that one was because of the name Týr called me, not because I actually was blessed to be a Valkyrie.

"What type of healing are you after?" The interpretation for healing was rather vast, and I was far more experienced now than I was when I first came into my power.

"It won't be for me, but for one of my wives."

One of?

"She's with child, but I believe something is wrong. I want you to look at her, and heal her if I am right."

"And if she does not require healing?" I needed to know if he expected an open-ended favor. Those were never good to make.

"Your side of the transaction will be fulfilled."

Seemed easy enough. Too easy? Possibly. But I did catch the traces of worry lines on his face. "I will show you what I want of your goods, and we'll decide if that trade is of equal value."

He agreed and I collected the various items I wanted. I ended up creating two amounts, one if I only looked at her, and another if I had to heal her. We agreed it was a fair deal and he left his stall to fetch his wife.

Not long after he returned, two centaurides following him. I was surprised, though, to see a human woman sitting atop one of their backs. And she was the one heavy with child.

The centaur helped his wife off his centauride, and I instructed her where to sit. Baldr gave us space, but watched intently as all three centaurs shifted nervously, their hooves clacking on the cobblestone with every step. I was putting myself in a dangerous position, but I could protect myself if needed. Plus, Baldr would do anything to keep me safe.

I talked with the woman a bit to understand what might be going on. She was the soft-spoken type and did her best to be an easy patient, answering honestly. It seemed she'd noticed something felt wrong for a few weeks now, but couldn't place what.

This was her first child, and her centaur husband's first as well, so she admitted it could be them being nervous. Sometimes that was the case, and a healing check would do wonders to ease their worries, but I wouldn't discount something being wrong, either. Intuition was important to pay attention to.

My magic slid along her body. I checked her all over, to be safe. Nothing seemed wrong there, which was a good sign. Having gone through those emotions myself, a woman hearing that her body was the issue in her pregnancy didn't usually go well.

This left me to focus on her unborn child. At first, nothing seemed amiss, and false hope bloomed in me. It died soon after.

"Something is wrong, isn't it?" the woman said, noticing my increased concentration.

I didn't answer right away. I needed to double-check this feeling. "Yes, there is something wrong with your child."

The centaur stomped a hoof hard on the ground. Baldr took a warning step forward.

"However, I think there is something I can do," I continued. "Please give me a moment longer to be sure."

Healing what I could see was easy. Healing the unknown was much more complicated. But, this child was in luck, as it wasn't the only unborn I'd been asked to heal before.

"I need to ask you not to move, as much as possible," I told the woman. "No matter how much your child moves around inside you, or if you feel alarmed by the sensations. I assure you, everything will be fine."

She sucked in a calming breath and then nodded.

My golden magic spread over her belly and sank into her skin. It traveled deep within her and wrapped around the growing form of her child. It wasn't the shape I was used to. This was clearly a centaur offspring, and for a moment I worried for her having a safe delivery, but that was not something to focus on right now. Nor was it my place to worry unless she expressed any fear around it.

The child moved a little when my magic touched it, but the reaction was less than it should have been. *This child is dying.* If I hadn't been here to help, it wouldn't have survived for much longer.

My brow creased with concentration as I pushed my healing into this unborn child. The moments ticked by, and I feared I was too late. Then, the child squirmed. A lot.

The woman gasped, her hands flying to her belly and her eyes widening. "He's moving again."

"Please be still," I said. I understood she was excited, as she should be, but if she moved, it could make things worse.

More moments passed, with the woman and the centaurs becoming increasingly restless as I worked.

Then I was done.

I sat back on my heels, letting out a slow, relieved breath. "You child will now be fine."

Brightness and unshed tears shone in her eyes. The centaur lifted his wife in his arms and held her close, tender but strong. It was a lovely sight. He clearly cared about her. And from the relief and excitement the centaurides showed, they, too, wished for this outcome. It made me bit curious about this situation he had. I'd heard centaurs and kelpies had harems, but I'd never seen it myself.

"You have our gratitude, witch of Týr's," the centaur said. "You may take what we agreed."

I nodded and did just that. There was no need to be attached to the situation any more than I had been. This was transactional. It was why no names were exchanged.

Baldr and I left the stall to continue on my quest.

Some of the remaining market stalls seemed interesting, but none had what I needed. I was beginning to worry this market also wouldn't have anything. It was the third one we visited today. *Am I being too picky?*

I blinked when Baldr stopped at a stall. "Did something catch your interest?"

He made a thoughtful sound in his throat. "Maybe."

I stepped up next to him and peered at the available wares. My eyes widened at the mesmerizing collection of jewelry. Each delicate piece, more intricate than the next, were unique in almost every way. Some had color-changing crystals, while others held tiny living flowers in perfect bloom. Another one, a necklace, shimmered like stardust. The only element that was the same about them was their metal base—elven silver.

I squinted at Baldr. "I don't think these fit your style."

He gasped and held a necklace up to his neck. "You mean this doesn't match my eyes?"

The piece of jewelry was possibly the most delicate thing I'd ever seen made of spun silver. At the center, a teardrop-shaped crystal hung. It glowed with a faint light that, when the light caught it just right, cast tiny rainbows.

I pursed my lips. "Far too elegant. Something sturdier is a better fit for you."

Baldr placed his hand on his chest, as if he were offended, and then set the necklace back down. The fae woman who owned the stall laughed, the sound a tinkle like ringing bells.

She was stunning, standing tall and slender, with an effortless elegance to her. Her soft luminous skin faintly shimmered with an iridescent sheen. When the light caught her just right, her skin reflected colors of pale gold, silver, and lavender.

Her hair flowed like liquid silver, and cascaded down her back in soft waves. She had large, oval-shaped eyes with irises that shifted in colors of blue.

"I can recommend these pieces here," she said in a melodic voice. She pointed to the far side of her display. "While I can guarantee all of my jewelry could hold up against anything, if you are looking for something to show that it can as well, these are my recommendations."

I lifted a silver cuff with intricately engraved knotwork patterns and a sapphire stone inlay. The moment I touched it, I felt the hidden magical enchantment. "This looks more your style."

Baldr glanced at it for a brief moment, then focused back on the same pieces from before. "That is nice. But I'm not looking for myself."

I cocked my head. "Who are you shopping for?"

He didn't respond, focusing on the jewelry. He was acting… strangely. Had he found someone he was interested in pursuing long-term? An uncomfortable twisting sensation tugged in my belly. I had to take a calming, chastising breath. *I don't have a right to act that way.*

Baldr lifted a pair of spun-silver earrings with several gemstones that looked like rain and then held them up to the sides of my face. I blinked stupidly, my mind not quite cluing in to what he was doing.

He shook his head and set the earrings down, selecting another pair to hold up to me. His lips twisted and then he shook his head again and returned the jewelry.

"Baldr, what are you doing?" I asked, a tiny laugh in my voice.

The responding grin he gave caused a fluttery feeling in my belly. "Isn't it obvious?"

I pursed my lips and watched him peruse the selection and this time pick up a beautiful silver cuff with gold inlay that curled into a sun design. An orange gemstone was embedded into the sun's center, and the silver seemed to shimmer, like it was coated in stardust.

Baldr took my hand and slipped the cuff onto my wrist. Magic pulsed from the jewelry. Realization dawned on me as he smiled and said, "Perfect."

I was already shaking my head. "Baldr, we're shopping for Týr, not me."

"Correction, *you* are shopping for Týr. I can shop for whomever I want. And I'm shopping for you." He turned to the shopkeeper to negotiate.

I stared at the cuff on my wrist, heat slowly rising in my cheeks. It was a lovely piece of jewelry, and it wasn't like gifts were an oddity with me and my gods. They just… felt different with Baldr.

There was always this attraction I had for him that I buried deep. I knew it was wrong. I married Týr, while Baldr was and had always been a good friend.

But even still, there was always something there between us that felt like more than friends. And no matter how much I told myself I'd promised eternity to Týr and such feelings were not appropriate, and with how much time had passed for me to get it together, my heart continued to be greedy and yearn for more.

Baldr turned toward me after agreeing to some sort of payment I wasn't paying attention to—likely a favor. He had a big smile on his face. I smiled back, fighting the warmth spreading through me. This was my problem, not his, and I wouldn't cause a scene trying to deny a simple gift. It would only make things worse, and probably hurt him more than it hurt me to pretend there was nothing amiss. *I must ignore it. I must not betray Týr.*

Baldr placed his hand on my lower back and ushered me away from the market stall. I was acutely aware of the heat from his touch seeping into my skin. His touch was always tender and protective.

"Do you like it?" he asked. "I should have verified that before I paid, but I know you, and I didn't want you thinking you could tell me not to buy it."

I huffed while I looked at the cuff. He knew me all too well. "Yes, I do like it. It's pretty. And it reminds me of you."

He continued to smile. "Good. If you didn't like it, I could go back and exchange it."

"But not return."

"Never."

I rolled my eyes to hide the rising heat in me, making him laugh.

"It does have a protection enchantment," he said. "The fae woman said it had limitations, but most would never reach them."

Considering the battles I was involved in with the gods, I had some doubts I wouldn't find that limit. Only time would tell.

"You know, now this means I have to gift you something."

He smirked. "Ah, yes, well, you did say this trip was only intended for you to buy for Týr."

I grinned. "I never said I was going to buy you something right away."

"Hmm, that's a dangerous proposal, Sunshine." The grin on his unfairly handsome face made my stomach swoop. "I could find more gifts for you by the time you get around to getting me one."

My eyes narrowed. "You wouldn't dare."

His grin turned downright diabolical. I puffed out my cheeks and returned to searching. Baldr chuckled.

We reached the last of the stalls at this market and still I'd found nothing. At this point I was getting frustrated. This was supposed to be a fun trip where I'd get a little distracted but would find the right gift without much trouble otherwise. Yet that was far from the case. *Is there truly nothing perfect enough for this occasion?*

After a quick moment of private moping, I teleported us to the next known market. It was busier here, and there were more stalls being manned. At first I dared be hopeful, but after passing the first few stalls and it felt everything was the same as the last markets, I struggled not to lose hope with this place, too.

"How are you feeling?" Baldr asked. "Be honest."

I stopped in front of another stall and glanced quickly at the goods for sale. I blew out a breath and then moved on. "I don't feel like I'm going to find anything. I'm being too picky. It's only an anniversary gift, and Týr has so much already."

"No. There's nothing wrong with your decision making." He tucked his finger under my chin and lifted my gaze to his. "One hundred years deserves this level of perfection."

One century. A thrill still ran down my spine every time I thought about it. I never expected more than a few decades with Týr. Never could I have imagined being blessed with immortality, and spending eternity with him.

I wasn't even really sure what caused it. I just knew it happened around the time I came to terms with my infertility.

Baldr continued as if I wasn't somewhere else in my head. "Especially when you factor it's so uncommon for us immortals."

I blinked slowly, my brow knitting. "What do you mean, uncommon? Immortality would mean your marriages last for eternity."

He gazed at me with matching confusion. Was I not understanding marriage for immortals? Thinking about it, I wasn't sure how many immortals I'd met that admitted to having a wife or a husband, or any sort of permanent lover. *That centaur might be the first in a long time, and he had three wives... is that even possible?*

"I thought you already knew." He paused to think. "Though, I suppose with you being so new to immortality, you haven't been around us immortals long compared to how long we've lived, so you may not have realized this."

"Explain it to me?"

"It's quite simple, really. Because of our long lives, it's not common for immortals to take permanent lovers. If we do, it's rare there's any official marriage ceremony. Hel, if we take on a permanent lover, they're usually not the only one."

"I see." If that was the case, why did Týr marry me? He could have asked me to be his lover instead of wife, and I would have happily done so.

My mind finally caught up with what Baldr said at the end. "Wait, what do you mean, more than one? Týr never mentioned anything like that to me."

Was that why the centaur had three wives? *Have I been denying these harbored feelings for Baldr for no reason?* I couldn't recall a mortal ever taking more than one spouse, but maybe they did and I'd never met them?

Baldr thought for a moment. "I can't speak for Týr, but I can say from observation, I've never known him to have more than one lover at a time. Well, actually, you're the first long-term partner I've ever seen him take. He could have had one before I was born, but no one has ever talked about it."

Týr never mentioned previous wives or long-term lovers with me either. I never once questioned it, though maybe I should have?

"There have been others like him that I've met," Baldr said, "but they're anomalies amongst immortals. We don't see a reason to limit the desires of our hearts. We live too long to deny such pleasures in life."

I crossed my arms over my stomach. So did that mean my hidden feelings weren't wrong, but not something I could act on? If Týr hadn't brought up the possibility of us seeking partners outside our marriage, then that wasn't what he wanted for us, right?

Even if he was okay with it, how would that affect us? Would I love him less? Did my heart yearning for another already mean my love for him wasn't strong? Was that why Týr chose to handle our marriage this way?

"Sunshine, are you well?" Baldr asked.

I smiled to reassure him. "Yes, I'm processing what you've said. The concept is so new to me."

"If it helps you, mortals also do this," he said. "Maybe not the same way as us immortals, but multiple partners, harems, and the like do exist in various cultures, or smaller communities within a culture."

It did reassure me in an odd way. That meant I just hadn't been exposed to this, and my feelings, which had begun when I was mortal, hadn't been unusual. But I wasn't sure it changed anything for me.

Týr didn't want anyone but me. That meant, no matter what my heart may tell me, I would honor my vow and make him the sole focus of my heart's affections. I could be happy with that.

I jumped when weight landed on my shoulder. Ebony feathers flashed in my peripheral. I pressed my hand against my chest. "Muninn, don't startle me like that."

He cackled and then played with a strand of my hair. *"Don't be jumpy, Sister."*

I rolled my eyes and gave him an affectionate pet. I couldn't remember when he started calling me "sister," but I liked it. I enjoyed the relationship that had blossomed between us since we first met. His brother, Huginn, wasn't too fond of me, but I wasn't really sure what I could do about that.

As far as Baldr understood, Huginn's hostility stemmed from his loyalty to Odinn, and relations between the Allfather and Týr had not improved over the last century.

Why Muninn didn't take issue with me, I wasn't sure, and he was never forthcoming with that answer. I always got the simple answer of "because I like you." The answer didn't matter to me, honestly. I was glad to have him around. He was wonderful to talk to, and had his own fascinating shares to offer.

"I found something," Muninn said.

My brow lifted. "Huh?"

Baldr smirked. "I had asked him to go out and search for possible gifts."

I blinked slowly. "When did you do that?"

We hadn't seen Muninn for hours, and I didn't recall Baldr saying anything specific to the raven before he left us.

Baldr shrugged. "When you were healing that woman."

I stared at him for a good long moment. *This man.* "Well, thank you both. Neither of you had to go out of your way to help."

Baldr chuckled. "That's why we do it. Now, Muninn, what did you find?"

"Follow."

He flew off into the market. Baldr and I wove through the crowd of people. Muninn landed on an empty wooden rack in a market stall made of sturdy wood and metal reinforcements. A dark blue awning shielded the merchant and his wares.

The stall merchant, a grizzled man with sun-darkened and slightly reddened skin and weathered features, squinted suspicious, piercing blue eyes at the raven.

Munnin ignored the man and tipped his head back and forth, surveying the weapons and armor on display. *"In here, Sister."*

The man turned his attention to Baldr and me. "Does he belong to one of you? I don't allow pets in here."

"He belongs to my father, Odinn," Baldr said. "And he's not a pet."

The man grunted, surprisingly unimpressed by the name drop. "Just make sure he doesn't cause trouble."

Friendly. I decided to ignore his attitude and focus on his wares. The moment I stepped into the stall, a sensation of magic rolled over me. *He's had this place enchanted.* I guessed it to be some sort of anti-theft magic, given the type of wares he had, though I could be wrong.

My eyes roamed the racks and stands of weapons, all meticulously arranged from swords to axes and maces. Bows and quivers hung on a nearby rack, and a range of armor were displayed in the back side of the stall.

It's so… obvious and trite… Giving a war god weapons and armor as a gift? I'd done that a few times already. It was why I'd ignored other smaller stalls like this. Was I really going to consider buying something here just to get something finally?

Baldr nudged me. "Some of these would make fine gifts."

"It's not all that original of a gift to give a war god."

He shrugged. "Doesn't have to be. That's not what makes the gift special."

Maybe… I perused the displays regardless. It couldn't hurt.

Magic suffused the air and wrapped around each weapon. Some were easy to understand: weapons with elemental enchantments, swords that cut better, and common enchantments like that. But there were other ones, some subtle and some powerful, that I wasn't familiar with from magical sensing alone. I'd have to ask about them if I was interested.

"What about this one, Sunshine?" Baldr said.

I turned to find him holding up the most absurd-looking helmet I'd ever laid eyes on.

"He would look great in this."

I blinked for a long moment, then laughed. I held my sides as it took me over. The image of Týr wearing that ridiculous thing was too much.

The merchant grunted. "No need to mock it. It's not that strange of a design."

I shook my head and wiped away tears. "It's not that. If you knew my husband, you'd understand how silly he'd look in that. I'm sure it's a perfect design for someone else."

"Hmm…" *He's as eloquent as Týr.*

My browsing continued. Baldr pointed out some more possible gifts. Some serious, some silly. Muninn tried to get me to choose some of the shiniest pieces, but I was fairly sure he wanted me to get them for him.

I even considered some of the armor. Týr wouldn't wear it, but he could display it somewhere. However, none felt right.

"What specifically are you after?" the merchant asked. "This is some sort of gift for your husband?"

I smiled. "Yes. We're celebrating one hundred years together. I'm not exactly sure what I want to get him, though. Nothing I've found today has the right feel."

"Hmm…" He approached me and held out his hand, palm facing up. "Give me your hand."

My eyebrow spiked. "Give you?"

He grunted. "I'm not a fae."

Muninn landed on my shoulder and studied the man with a beady black eye. Then he bobbed his head. *"He is safe."*

Still a bit cautious, I offered my hand. The merchant grasped it with his own. His hands had the feel of a hard-working man, strong and calloused. Yet, like I experienced with my gods, he was gentle.

With his opposite hand, he pressed a finger to my palm, then drew invisible symbols along my skin. I blinked when power pulsed with each finished mark. *What is he doing?*

Then suddenly the man released me. He turned and headed for a door at the back of the stall leading into a building. "I'll be right back."

I blinked again, then turned to Baldr when the man disappeared behind the door. "Um… that was odd?"

"And yet, we can say we've seen stranger at these markets."

I laughed. That was true. *Still, what was that magic trick with my hand?*

The merchant returned and he carried with him a round shield. He set it down and gestured for me to take a look. "You wouldn't have found anything on display because I hadn't put this out yet."

Curious, I approached him and gave the armor a hard inspection. The shield was made of a dark metal with a large band of silver around the curved edge. An intricate engraving of a flame made up of inter-locking runes decorated the shield face. Small red, yellow, and clear gemstones were embedded into the silver edge. More runes ran along the band of silver, connecting the gemstones.

I reached for the shield, and immediately felt the pulsing magic within. *This has a strong enchantment.* Lifting it, I found the shield surprisingly light for its size and material. Not that I expected Týr to have any issues with it either way. The only question was, what enchantment did it have?

Without me having to inquire with him, the merchant reached for the shield and then surprised me by slamming his fist to the top of it. The magic activated, producing a near-invisible magical barrier that spread out.

"That's how you activate it," the man said.

This was amazing. And it fit exactly something Týr would want to use in battle.

"Well?" the merchant prompted impatiently. "Your thoughts?"

"This is perfect." I looked up at him. "How did you know?"

"Your energy told me," he said. "I can tell what a person is after, even if they're not sure themselves. If I have it, I can place it in front of them. If not, I can offer to make something unique."

"Is that a normal service of yours?" Baldr asked.

The man shrugged. "Depends on my mood."

I watched him, a strange feeling in my chest tugging at me. *He's lying.* Or maybe, not telling the whole truth was more like it. I wasn't sure how I knew, but I could tell there was something more to it. Something that caused him great pain.

When I was mortal and thought of immortality, I thought it just meant undying. I hadn't expected that it could also mean seeing changes in yourself after achieving it. Yet, I'd noticed this in myself, and its first sign had started long before I'd even been immortal. The day Kronus had abducted me.

In more recent decades, that sensation had grown and developed. It helped me with my healing, which extended beyond the physical sometimes. And it aided me in war. It helped me direct the focus of my gods, kill or let live.

And here, this man, his pain felt like a physical weight that pressed against my very being.

"The one you lost was a fae, weren't they?" The insensitive words tumbled out of my mouth before I could think to stop them.

Baldr's brow lifted, and the merchant stared at me.

"There are fae runes etched into this shield and act as part of the enchantment. Yet, you told me you are not a fae." My fingers glided over the edge of the shield. "This is pure silver. Its use in its purest form is only known to the fae, unless they bestow that knowledge to you."

I gestured to a few nearby pieces. "Everything here is the same."

The man bowed his head and grunted. "I should throw you out."

"How long?" I asked, ignoring his empty threat.

He hesitated a moment. "Ninety-nine years. And now I must live this cursed life without him."

An invisible fist clenched around my heart. The pain of losing the ones you loved and cherished... I knew that feeling all too well. And to live forever with that pain...

"Being one of undying is a heavy burden," I murmured. "It is not a path for the weak."

I shook off the strange sensations crawling under my skin and gestured to the shield. "I am interested in the shield. How do you treat?"

The man stared at me a long moment, then grunted. "Coin. I'm not interested in barters or whatever fae like to play their games with."

Coin was an unusual ask in these markets, but not unheard of. Given the man's honesty so far, I didn't have reason to interrogate his answer to be sure.

We discussed a price, and after a little bartering, as well as a little pestering from Muninn, I had a new shield in my possession, and the raven had a small, shiny gift.

"I pray this husband of yours keeps you safe with that," the man said.

I reached toward him and pressed two fingers to his chest. My magic flared for a brief moment and spread through him. "Healing and strength for you, my friend."

I left the man blinking and patting his chest in confusion. "I'll return again when I'm in need of something else."

Baldr followed me out. "Are you happy with your purchase?"

I gazed at the shield one more time before using my magic to banish it somewhere safe. "Yes. I'm glad Muninn brought us here and that you convinced me to give the shop a chance. It was the perfect find."

The raven, firmly holding his shiny gift in his beak, cooed, and Baldr smiled.

"I don't need anything else. Do you?" I asked.

He shook his head. "Let's get you back so you don't miss out on all your plans for tonight."

TWENTY-THREE

ASTRID

I fussed with the table settings, knowing full well I didn't need to worry about it. It'd be the last thing Týr would care about, but I wanted everything to be perfect.

The delicious aroma of meat, fresh bread, and spices filled the house. I didn't know what half the food was on the table, as Freyja had been the one to help out there and went all over Midgard to find new exotic foods for us to dine on for the occasion. All of it looked interesting, and my stomach rumbled the longer the smells teased me.

Unlit candles near me suddenly ignited, bathing the room in warm light. I turned to Ùna. Her large gossamer wings hung limply behind her. They tried to flutter in her excitement, but the extensive damage they sustained from an old cold iron wound prevented much movement.

Her ethereal tail, one feature of hers that took me a while to get used to, swished back and forth.

"There, everything is done," she said in a soft voice lilted with an accent. She turned large multi-colored eyes onto me. "Now you must stop fidgeting, Astrid. Everything is perfect. He will enjoy this."

I glanced at all the preparations everyone had helped me with. Even Fenrir was pitching in by distracting Týr and keeping him away. But I couldn't help feeling like more needed to be done.

"Astrid." Ùna's voice, while still soft, cracked like a whip and I flinched.

She was one of the smallest fae I'd ever met, yet that didn't stop her from being a force to be reckoned with—at least with those she knew. And even though she served Týr, and by extension, me, she was no thrall. She had no qualms talking back to us and pushing her weight around. And today was a good day for her to do that.

"You're right. It's perfect."

Ùna smiled and then limped off, leaving me to wait alone for Týr to return. I fidgeted with my dress as I stood there. The blue material clung to my body like no other dress I owned, and the neckline plunged deep between my breasts putting much of them on display. Freyja had gotten it for me to wear for tonight's occasion. Not that anyone expected it to survive the end of the night. *I hope he likes it…*

I shook the doubting thoughts from my mind. He would.

The door suddenly opened and Týr's large frame entered. The light of the low-hanging sun illuminated him, bathing him in an intense orange and yellow light. He was alone.

The hard expression on his face softened immediately when he laid eyes on me. His gaze roamed my body, a pleased smile on his face, then he began to notice everything else.

Týr blew out a breath and ran his fingers through his hair. "Here you go, outdoing yourself and making me look as though I've done nothing at all."

I smiled. "I did all this because I wanted to."

He approached and dipped down, lifting my chin with a finger. Our lips brushed as he said, "That may be, but I spent all day getting something for you, and you managed a whole feast."

My eyes hooded, his strong masculine scent enveloping me. "I hired others to make a feast. And I had help getting everything else in order. I spent most of my day also getting you something."

Týr chuckled and kissed me. It wasn't a long or deep kiss, but it was enough to spark heat deep in my core. You'd think after a century together this passion would die down, but it was as strong as ever. "You still managed a whole plan. I will not diminish that."

He straightened. "You also didn't need to use Fen to keep me out of the house for this."

I crossed my arm. "He wasn't supposed to tell you."

"He tried to keep it a secret, but I pressed after I was suspicious about his behavior when he continued to stall my return home."

I huffed. "Well, stop that. It was supposed to be a surprise."

Týr laughed. "This was still a surprise. He never told me what you were up to. Just that you threatened to turn him into a rug if he allowed me to return home before sunset."

The corner of my lips twitched. Fenrir's fear of my maybe-real threat was a decent consolation prize, I supposed.

Týr kicked off his boots at the door and hung up his cloak, then swept me into his arms and carried me toward the table. "Let's eat, I'm starved."

"You should wash up first," I said as he sat down with me in his lap.

He rumbled a wordless thought in his throat then pressed his face into the top of my head. "But then I'd have to let you go, and that's not happening."

I leaned into him. "Very well. I'll let it slide this once."

"We'll take a bath together." He chuckled as his hand slid over my dress, along the curves of my body. "We'll need it."

My heart skipped a beat, my body eager for his promises. I swallowed it down and reached for one of the plates of food. *Dinner first.*

Týr and I ate from the same plate and drank from the same cup. We fed each other and laughed and talked about whatever we wanted. Without children, this wasn't much different than a normal day, minus Ùna not eating with us. But that didn't matter to me. This was a wonderful dinner.

The food Freyja had gotten was delicious—most of it. There was some Týr or I didn't like, but that didn't diminish our enjoyment.

The bountifully sourced alcohol was also good. It warmed my body but never got me close to being inebriated, no matter how much I drank. A trait of being immortal I didn't understand, but had learned to adapt to and accept. No more hiding my feelings behind drunken states. Not that I needed to.

I relaxed against Týr when I couldn't eat anymore. I was too full and there was still plenty of food. Unsurprisingly, Týr continued eating a bit longer. I didn't know where he put it all—where any of the god men I knew put it. Hel, even Bjarke easily ate a table's worth of food and would be hungry later.

Týr pushed the food away and took a swig of mead. My eyes watched his throat bob as he swallowed and then the way he wiped his mouth with his thumb. I licked my lips. I could have helped him with that.

I walked two fingers along his chest. "Satisfied?"

His chest rumbled and he grabbed my hand. His blue eyes stared into me, unyielding and intense. "Not yet."

Týr kissed my fingers, then paused to look at my bracelet. "When did you get this?"

"Oh, Baldr got it for me. It has some sort of protection enchantment on it. Isn't it beautiful?"

"It is," Týr agreed. Then he mumbled. "Would have been nice if he'd waited, though."

I pressed my lips together. *He's upset. I knew I shouldn't have allowed Baldr to get it on a day like today.* I wasn't faultless, either. I should have remembered to take it off before Týr got home. Not because I needed to hide it, but because this night was supposed to be about Týr and me.

Týr lifted me off his lap and onto the empty spot he'd cleared on the table. He went to the front door where a bag sat on a bench. I hadn't realized he'd brought that in. He reached into the bag and procured a wooden box made of beautiful red wood.

He handed it to me when he returned to the table. "This is for you. I hope you like it."

I took the box and looked it over. A carving of Yggdrasill filled the lid, with gemstones embedded into the wood around her roots, sym- bolizing the nine realms. Runes and smaller images complimented the tree and gems, adorning the box on all sides. The silver hinges on the box were sturdy, and the craftsman had even taken the time to detail those as well. "This is so well crafted."

Týr didn't say anything and watched me turn the box in my hand. Something *clunked* against the inside walls. I flicked the clasp and opened the lid. Nestled in the box was a bronze cuff. I took it out of the jewelry box to inspect.

The bronze metal was smooth to the touch despite the details of silver inlays. The jewelry prominently displayed Týr's *Tiwaz* rune. It was slightly raised, contrasting against bronze metal. Silver knotwork was engraved along the edges of the cuff and curled around two large red gemstones set on either side of Týr's rune.

Magic hummed against my fingers. It was slightly different from the magic on my other cuff, but I could already tell the magic did similar things.

"Týr, it's beautiful."

He took the cuff to slip it onto my wrist. "It also has a protection enchantment. I want to be sure you're safe, all the time."

I smiled. He wasn't upset that Baldr gave me jewelry. He was disgruntled they had the same idea on the same day. "And now, I'll be extra protected."

"He still could have waited a day," Týr muttered.

I giggled and tugged him closer by his beard. I gave him a quick kiss on the lips. "I love it and will always wear it. Thank you."

I kissed him again, this time deeper and slower. My unyielding god softened under my touch. His fingers slid up my thighs and curled around my hips. I pulled away before we were too caught up in our passion. Týr grumbled his displeasure and tried to bring our mouths together again.

I laughed and pressed my fingers against his lips. "I've got a gift for you, too."

"You're the only gift I need," he mumbled against my fingers. His eyes were lidded, as if already deep in a haze of desire.

"Please, my love."

He blew out a breath and sat back in his chair. His intense, hungry gaze heated my own rising desire. "Well, Valkyrie? What is this gift you have for me?"

I swallowed. His rumbling tones sent my thighs squeezing together. *Focus.* Holding out my hands, I used my magic to pull out his gift. A leather-wrapped object manifested in my hands. I held it out to him.

Týr sat forward and took the gift. It wasn't hard to guess what it might be, even if it was wrapped. Still, Týr unwrapped it with care.

He stared at the shield for a long, quiet moment, then he stood. I blinked when it disappeared from his hands, then gasped when he surged toward me, his lips crashing into mine.

I squeaked and wriggled against his crushing hold. "I guess you like it?"

"I do." He kissed me more. "Very much."

"It's got... an... enchantment," I managed through his very insistent mouth.

"Don't care right now."

I rolled my eyes and grabbed his face, forcing him away so I could breathe and get my words out. "I do care. And you will control yourself a moment longer."

Týr's eyes narrowed and a growl rumbled through his chest.

"It has a type of protection enchantment as well," I said.

His eyebrow spiked. "What are the odds?"

I laughed. "The enchantment, when activated, will project a shielding extension. I don't know its limits, but I've seen it in action."

Týr's interest was a little more piqued, but it didn't last long. "I'll test it out later, then. For now, I'm indulging in my perfect wife."

His mouth crushed mine. I squeaked in surprise, and he took advantage of my parted lips, slipping his tongue inside. His and mine wrestled for dominance, while Týr's hands roamed my body, pawing at my dress.

My mind fuzzed as desire for him stoked to a molten heat and took me over. It burnt long and hot under my skin until I was craving more.

Fabric tore. I chuckled against Týr's mouth. This dress lasted longer than I'd expected, at least. And two could play that game.

Magic sprang from my fingers and seeped into his tunic. I gave a firm tug and his tunic ripped open in the front.

Týr broke our heavy kiss and looked down at the damage. He grinned and resettled his burning gaze on me. My eyebrow lifted. *I think he likes it when I do that, too.*

His mouth was back to claiming mine, stealing any useless thoughts from my mind. Týr tore my dress more, until it was nothing but scraps and I lay bare beneath him. His hands roamed me as if rememorizing every part of me.

Týr's mouth slanted, trailing to my cheek, then down my neck. I tipped my chin up to give him better access, but it wasn't enough for him. His hand fisted my hair and yanked. I gasped with the pleasant tingles that rushed through me.

He lavished my skin, down to my collarbone. I reached for him and he grabbed my wrists, pinning my arms above my head. Týr chuckled and continued, nipping the skin between my breasts. I squirmed against his hold, pretending to fight him. He liked it when I did. *I liked it when I did.*

I arched my back as his tongue dragged along my aching nipples. He ravenously licked and sucked, driving me mad. My raging desire spread throughout my body and pooled between my legs.

"Mine," Týr rumbled as he released my breast and kissed between them. His teeth sank into my skin, not painfully, but enough to pull an anticipating breath from me. "All mine."

"Is that so?" I said, my voice breathy.

He lifted his heated gaze to meet mine. "You are *my* Valkyrie."

I wiggled. "I don't know… I think you need to make a stronger claim."

His grip in my hair tightened. I gasped and then grinned at him in challenge. "Maybe I should go ask another god to bring me to the heights of passion. Or maybe a fae? I hear centaurs are quite the experience. What say you, mighty Týr?"

Týr's eyes glittered. "I think you're playing a dangerous game, Valkyrie. Choose your next words wisely."

My lower lip caught in my teeth. "And if I don't?"

"You're going to have trouble sitting for a while."

My pulse spiked and I swallowed. I wasn't sure if behaving or misbehaving sounded more fun right now.

Týr's fingers slid from my hair. He caressed my cheek, then dragged his fingers down my neck to my belly, then my inner thigh. "Behave, and you'll be rewarded."

I tugged against his grip on my wrists. "Are you sure you want me to behave?"

His fingers slid between my thighs. I resisted the pleasurable gasp as he slid his thumb along that perfect sensitive part of me, while plunging his finger inside my aching pussy. It was what I wanted, but I refused to give in so easily.

"Behave for me today, wife," Týr commanded. His fingers slid in and out of me rhythmically. "Behave."

I bit my lip to stifle a moan and shook my head. Týr continued, his thumb circling and rubbing in time with his fingers. Each thrust of his finger, and slide of his thumb, it became more difficult to resist, but Týr's determination to make me surrender was too much of a challenge to meet. I wouldn't submit. Not yet.

"Valkyrie."

I breathed deep, waiting for the perfect moment to speak and not give away my difficulty resisting. "What's wrong, my husband? Are you struggling to handle me? Is there a reason you don't try to ensure my only thoughts are consumed with you?"

His grip on my wrists tightened. "Valkyrie, you do not understand the ramifications of this game you play."

I bit my lip. "I don't?"

Týr's fingers withdrew, leaving my body disappointed and craving for more. "Have it your way, Valkyrie."

He reached into a pocket and retrieved a leather tie that he tightly wound around my wrists, in place of his hands. He dropped down in a chair, momentarily confusing me, until he grabbed my hips and pulled me to the edge of the table.

My mouth fell open in a silent gasp when he delved between my thighs, his tongue greedily devouring me. I tried to resist in every way I knew how, but when his fingers returned to increase my pleasure both inside and outside, touching every part of me that was intoxicatingly sensitive, my control broke.

I writhed and moaned. My pulse pounded in my ears and tension coiled alongside the rising heat of desire spiraling out of control within me. Just when I thought I was about to burst, Týr pulled away again.

I whimpered and wiggled, desperate for the relief that was now turning to frustration.

Týr chuckled. "I told you not to play games, Valkyrie. Now you will reap what you sowed."

His large hands gripped my hips and I gasped when he flipped me over onto my belly. A resounding *crack* echoed through the room and I gasped again at the sting on my backside. Týr's hand came down again, slapping my ass with firm contact.

I bit my lips, and stifled a reaction. I wouldn't give him the satisfaction. I wouldn't give into this sensation of pleasure mixed with the pain.

Týr's hand fisted my hair and yanked my head back. His eyes locked with mine. The possession in his eyes stole my breath. His other hand came down again, and again, and again. Each time, it became more difficult to bite back my reaction. Each time, my control over myself lessened.

His hand came down again. This time I cried out, the sting too much to fight. He grinned. "That's right. You will learn whose Valkyrie you are."

My fingers curled into the hard wood of the table. Tears pricked the corners of my eyes. My cries of pain mingled with gasps and moans of pleasure as the lines blurred.

When the pain suddenly stopped, and Týr's hand affectionately rubbed my tender, fast-healing skin, it took me a moment to realize the punishment had ceased. He was no longer pulling my hair. Instead, his fingers caressed my cheeks, wiping away my falling tears. *When had I begun crying?*

"Have you learned your lesson, Valkyrie?" Týr rumbled. "Or does my wife need further punishment until she relinquishes the names of those whose heads must be removed from their shoulders for daring tempt you away from me?"

I swallowed, my pulse jumping. As much as I enjoyed the thought of pushing him a little more to see this possessive side of him a little longer, I no longer wished to continue this. I wanted to fall into this man I called my husband. "No, my Týr. I am all yours."

His fingers wrapped under my chin and around my neck. He bent over and pressed his lips against mine. The kiss was firm, yet gentle. It coaxed the heat in my chest to ignite. I needed this—needed him. Now.

"Týr, my husband," I murmured against his lips. "Please."

"I cannot deny my Valkyrie." His belt clattered on the floor and his large, thick cock slid along the curve of my ass. My core pulsed with need, craving to be stretched and filled with his massive size. "I will not deny my wife."

He nudged my thighs apart and teasingly rubbed his cock along my entrance. The anticipation was sheer torment.

Týr's hand around my throat twitched, the only signal to prepare me. I gasped, my back arching, when he surged inside me. My fingers dug into the table, and my mouth fell open as I accepted him.

A low, slow groan rumbled through Týr. "You're too perfect, Valkyrie. You take me so well."

He filled and stretched me beyond what I would have thought possible before meeting him. I was sure, despite my confounding situation with Baldr, Týr had ruined me for anyone else. How could I not be satisfied with such a stallion?

I moaned when he pulled out and thrust inside me again. His rhythm increased quickly, pounding into me harder and harder. My pulse thundered in my ears and my desire burning in my veins ignited into a consuming inferno.

"Týr…" I moaned.

Týr slammed into me harder and harder. "That's it, Valkyrie. Take my cock like the good wife you are."

"Yes… please… more." Fingers gripping into the table, I rocked back into him. I cried out as intense pleasure burst through me.

Týr's hand slid from my throat into my hair. He grabbed a fist full of my fiery locks and yanked my head back. I gazed up at him with parted, moaning lips. Everything inside me coiled and pulsed. I was so close. So close.

"Keep going, my husband. Please." My eyes closed and I moaned as a new wave of pleasure crashed through me.

The tension coiling in my core snapped and I screamed my god's name. My body convulsed as intense pleasure forced my soul out of my body and I lost myself to the euphoria.

Týr roared out his release, his thrusts becoming more punctured as he spilled inside me.

I came down, gasping and twitching. Týr braced his hands on either side of me, breathing deep into my hair.

When I'd finally caught my breath, I tossed a glance over my shoulder to gaze up at him. His eyes were closed and he hadn't pulled out of me, his readiness for more *very* apparent with the way he filled me. Yet, he didn't continue like I was used to. "Týr?"

His eyes slowly opened, and our gazes locked. "I love you, Astrid."

My heart thumped in my chest. Týr called me Valkyrie so often, Astrid felt more special when he uttered it off his lips. "I love you, too."

To my surprise, he untied my wrists and pulled out of me. I rolled over and sat on the edge of the table. "Are you well?"

He nodded. "Thoughts are swirling."

I tipped my head. "Did my teasing earlier bother you?"

He chuckled. "No, it's nothing you did or said."

Týr slid the back of his finger along my cheek. "I have had you in my life for one hundred years. I thought I would only be blessed to hold your love for a fraction of that."

I smiled and leaned into his touch. "I'm so happy Creation gave us this. I wouldn't ask for a different life."

He leaned in and softly kissed me. "I promised you forever. That will never change."

I hummed quietly and kissed him back. My hands slid along his chest, feeling his hard muscles and tracing old scars. I pushed what remained of his tunic off his shoulders, the material dropping to his feet, where his trousers still pooled at his ankles.

Týr's hands roamed my hips, desire reinvigorating in us both. My fingers dug into his sides and I urged him closer. I needed him.

We made love again, Týr choosing to sit this time while I rode him.

And even after we hit a second climax, he wasn't finished with me. He played with and enjoyed my body, choosing new positions every time, some we'd had yet to try before.

I lost count of how many orgasms I experienced. I stopped counting, choosing to fall into this love for each other. I had to finally call it quits when my body was far too overstimulated for more.

Týr gathered me in his arms and carried me to the bath. The steaming water felt so good. I relaxed in Týr's arms, thanking Creation once again for this wonderful life it had allowed us to have together. It may have been missing a few things I had once dreamed of having, but that didn't make it any less perfect. I would do anything to keep this.

I promised Týr forever, and I wouldn't go back on that.

TWENTY-FOUR

ASTRID

Brush bristles scraped around the corners of my closed eyes. Ùna hummed a soft tune as she worked on my face. I remained perfectly still for her. She didn't like it when I moved.

A large presence entered the space. "Am I taking too long, my husband?"

Týr chuckled. "I'm merely checking on you, Valkyrie. Take all the time you wish. Odinn can learn patience."

Ùna sniffed. "He should already be well versed in such matters with women."

"He is a selfish man."

"Man is a strong word for him," I muttered. Týr laughed.

When I was mortal, the very idea of insulting any god, even Loki, would have been blasphemous. Now, with all this time I'd spent with them, I had come to realize how ordinary such extraordinary beings were.

I respected many of them and their power, as well as what they did for mortals, but that didn't mean they were infallible beings. Far from it. And Odinn, despite having such a high throne, was no exception.

Though, to be fair, my opinion of him had tarnished the moment he killed and cursed Kirby. He was still unrepentant of his decision, and it boiled my blood.

"Dear, you're squinching your face," Ùna gently chastised.

I immediately relaxed. I couldn't let those feelings ruin my day. We were looking for her still. We hadn't been successful in finding her, and we feared there was a chance the curse was killing her over and over before we could, but we wouldn't give up. I'd get my friend back, and I'd break that damned curse myself if I had to. *I'd kill Odinn myself for all he has done to—*

I released a slow, calming breath. I needed to control these negative feelings and thoughts. I wasn't even sure why they continued to grow stronger over the decades. It was like something inside me was trying to tell me something about him, but I didn't understand the language it spoke.

"There, you're ready," Ùna said.

My eyes fluttered open and I peered into the mirror at my vanity. The makeup was bold but complimented my features, and it went well with the outfit she'd picked out. Ùna had put me in something she claimed was highly popular with the fae women right now. I could see why. The colorful dress shimmered with an iridescent sheen and fit my figure perfectly, following the curves of my hips and cut low around my breasts, showing off a generous amount of them.

Týr had approved of the alluring dress, outwardly musing how he might be able to convince me to let us ignore Odinn's call so he could have me to himself all day.

I smiled broadly. "Ùna, you've outdone yourself."

Her damaged wings shimmered in their attempt to flutter, and she skipped out of the room. "Have fun. Try not to cause too much chaos."

I snickered. "I can't make any promises. It's expected to be a rowdy party."

Ùna sighed. "Aren't they all?"

Týr and I laughed. Although she could enjoy a large party, Ùna very much appreciated serene and quiet environments over anything else. I understood why. She'd once told me her story of how she'd come to serve Týr and where her permanent injuries had come from. It was such a sad tale, one I wished my magic could help fade into a distant bad memory. But sadly, not even I could heal the damage that had been done.

A raven called and then a large ebony-feathered bird flew through the dormer window. I smiled when he landed on my shoulder. "Heill, Muninn. Come to tell us we're late?"

He made a chortling sound. *"Odinn is not pleased, but you are not the only one late. Freyja is not answering the call."*

My brow furrowed as I looked to Týr. "That's odd of her. Should we check on her before we go to Odinn's hall?"

Freyja was one of the most punctual gods I knew. If she wasn't already at the gathering, then it had to be serious. *Or she's enjoying someone's worship, on a carnal level.*

He nodded. I gave Muninn a kiss on the beak and promised we'd be along shortly. He crooned and then flew off to harass other tardy party guests.

I noticed Týr glaring after the bird. "Týr…"

He blew out a breath. "I'm sorry, Valkyrie. I just don't trust one of Odinn's spies."

I shook my head. This wasn't a conversation I wanted to have. It wouldn't go anywhere. He couldn't see that Muninn wasn't out to spy on us. Huginn, yes, unfortunately, but Muninn just wanted to spend time with me—and cause a little mischief every now and then.

After ensuring I had myself looking my best for this, Týr took my hand and I teleported us outside Freyja's home. The serene forest of our lake home was replaced with a bustling marketplace.

No one noticed our sudden appearance. That was the thing with magic that I'd learned. If a person couldn't explain a phenomenon caused by magic, their mind would make something up to justify and then they'd move on. With teleportation, most just assumed they hadn't noticed you until now.

Freyja's magnificent home was made of ancient reddish-gold wood and decorated with flowers and carvings of her stories and feats, and her cats. The front door was open, and one of Freyja's beautiful large fluffy cats sprawled in front of the entrance, enjoying the warm sun.

"Heill, Trjegul," I greeted when the cat opened her eyes.

Her eyes squinted and she purred, but didn't otherwise move. Clearly she was too comfortable.

"Is Frejya home? I was told she hadn't arrived yet to the party."

The cat swiveled her head to look inside and then curled onto her back to expose her belly. Chuckling, I gave her a gentle petting before entering the house.

"Freyja," I called. "Freyja."

Bygul came running to my call, but there was no sign of the goddess in question. Her second cat wove around my legs, purring, and then scurried off down the hall she'd popped out of. *Freyja must be that way.*

We followed our feline escort through the decorated home filled with war and phallic mementos alike. A sweet smell hung in the air. It filled my lungs and prickled my mind with enough pleasure that it lured sensations of arousal. Týr's hand on my waist tightened, showing he too was similarly affected.

The house always smelled this way. Freyja loved to entice her guests and was never disappointed when they didn't resist such temptation. Creation knew Týr and I had tried to resist and failed a number of time when we stayed here too long. A few couches may have even been broken in the induced eagerness.

The house was quiet, so I had to guess we weren't about to walk in on Freyja fucking a lover of hers.

I stopped to stare at a painting on the wall. "Huh… that's new."

Týr's brow rose. "I can't say Freyja doesn't have some strange tastes."

It was perverse but fascinating, and the subject was quite… bold. Not one I would have chosen, but Freyja had her reasons. Maybe.

Bygul called for me. She was not going to wait.

We were led into a grand library filled with more books, beyond what most mortals would ever see. In the middle of the room, Freyja sat on a plush couch, a large tome in her hands. The small table in front of her had many more stacked on it, some even open to specific pages.

Bygul jumped up onto the back of the couch and walked up behind Freyja. The cat pawed her shoulder.

"Not right now, Bygul," Freyja murmured, not looking up from her reading. "I don't have time."

"How about for us?" Týr said.

Her head snapped up and she looked at us with wide eyes. "Oh, Creation! I'm late, aren't I?"

I gave her a reassuring smile. "You're not the only one."

She dropped the tome onto the table and jumped up. "I'll be ready in a moment. I was caught up."

I glanced at the stack of books again. "What are you reading?"

She breezed past me. "It's some research."

That was an oddly vague answer from her, but if she didn't want to share, I wouldn't pry.

In only moments Freyja was ready and looked ravishing—or that she was planning to be ravished by the end of this party. Both, really.

She linked her arm in mine. "Ready to grace Odinn with our beautiful presence?"

I grinned. "Only after you explain the new painting."

She belted out a hearty laugh. "Do you like it? I couldn't stop myself from commissioning it."

"Having Odinn sucking a Berserker's cock on a battlefield while a Valkyrie fucks him in the ass was a bold choice."

She grinned. "It's perfection."

Týr laughed. I couldn't stop the grin. The ways she entertained herself were too amusing.

She teleported us to Odinn's hall. We arrived outside. The mountain wind buffered us and the surrounding dense forest. The building was made of old, dark wood and iron. Murals of battle, Odinn's deeds, and his ravens, decorated the outer walls.

The roof was adorned with a dragon's head and decorated in gold. Two raven statues flanked either side of the massive double doors leading into the hall.

Loud cheering and banter leaked through the doors. We were most definitely late.

Týr flung the doors open, blasting us with sound. Tables lined the hall, all filled with people and food and drink. Massive pillars decorated with weapons and shields and war-carving murals were strategically placed about, supporting the roof. Magic hummed in the room. Some of it was Odinn's as this was his domain. The rest were magical protections for the building structure for when the parties got a little extra rowdy.

The jubilant atmosphere called us inside, the doors closing behind us. We were greeted immediately by those who knew us, mortal and immortal alike. Muninn landed on my shoulder to greet me briefly before flying back to Odinn.

The Allfather sat atop his throne made of black wood and gold at the far side of the hall, watching us. We nodded respectfully to him, but did not shout a greeting or intend to prostrate ourselves before him. We were here because Odinn required gods to attend these celebrations. I came with them as Týr's wife, much to Odinn's annoyance when Týr first decided this.

I had serious doubts there could be anything amicable between Týr and Odinn. Odinn had some issue with my husband, one I didn't quite understand, as I had yet to find any evidence of where Týr had done anything wrong, beyond not blindly following Odinn. No one seemed to know.

I, of course, stood by my husband and the gods who aligned with him. Which, to Odinn's frustration, were many. The longer I was among the gods, the more I realized how little harmony there was.

The gods we nordmenn worshipped were split into three factions: those loyal to Odinn, those loyal to Týr, and those who wanted no part in the nonsense and felt they didn't need any leadership at all.

The first two groups were easy to spot in the hall. Odinn's most loyal sat as close to this throne as they could, while the others were as far as possible.

I squealed when strong arms wrapped around me and lifted me off the ground. Baldr laughed as he spun me around. When he put me down I punched him in the arm. He feigned pain, only to use it to wrap his arms around me for a crushing hug. I squealed. Freyja laughed. Týr smiled and shook his head.

"Careful where you sit," Baldr advised, when he released me. "Fen has already tipped over one table. Sól was not pleased she had to go change."

I projected my voice so Fenrir, wherever he was hiding, could hear. "Well, if he doesn't want me ripping off his balls and sending him on a treasure hunt across Midgard to find where I buried them, he'll be careful around me."

Týr and Baldr winced. A husky voice chuckled in my ear. "That's not very nice."

I shrieked and my magic burst out, slamming into Fenrir and sending him crashing into the wall. Those around us burst into laughter.

"Oh look, Astrid's here," Bjarke called out.

"Fuck you, Bjarke." I made a rude gesture to him where he was clustered with other Berserkers and he laughed, raising a drink to me.

Most didn't quite get my relationship with Bjarke any more than they understood my relationship with Fenrir. There was no hesitation around either of them, and no wayward pining thoughts.

It was one of many reasons I was thankful Bjarke was blessed with immortality like me. It made this journey easier, having someone you knew go through the same adjustments.

Fenrir groaned. "That was rude."

I stuck my tongue out at him and then grabbed a goblet of wine from a table. "That was justice. Serves you right."

"Astrid, when you're done scolding the puppy, come here." I turned to the person calling me.

He was a pale man with a strong jawline, and tall, somewhere between Týr's and Baldr's height, with a similar lean, yet still sturdy and muscled frame as Baldr. He had hair as black as night bound behind his head, and a well-groomed beard. Some loose strands of hair had broken free of their captive tie and fell in wild, unkempt waves. A dark fabric wrapped around his face, over his eyes as a blindfold.

I sat beside him, and placed a gentle hand on his cheek. His skin was frigid to the touch. "I am here, Höðr."

His gentle smile that made me think of Baldr graced his lips, and he rested his hand over mine. "You are warm as always, like a welcoming hearthfire on the coldest nights of winter."

"And a tongue so sharp one would think Sól crafted it for her out of a blade of sun," the man next to Höðr said before taking a swig of his drink.

He wasn't nearly as tall as Höðr, but he has a similar jawline and lean build. Though unlike Höðr's calmer demeanor, this man had a potent aura about him. He had a youthful face and his pale, reddish hair was wild and curly.

"Don't pretend you don't like my sharp tongue, Váli," I said.

His keen blue eyes flicked to me and he smirked before drinking more.

"Astrid, can you check my eye?" Höðr asked. "It's been irritating me for a few days, and I fear I rubbed it and made it worse."

He didn't allow many to look under his blindfold. Rarely did someone not become unsettled.

I wasn't one of them. "Of course."

He turned away from any eyes that may wish to steal a peek, facing me, and unbound his blindfold enough for the cloth to dip, but not to be removed completely. He held a hand up to block any view from the side.

Revealed to me were two eyes so pale, there was nearly no color present to see. If that didn't shake someone, one of his eyes, where the dark pupil should be, was a white spot void of any speck of darkness.

His unseeing eyes tracked me, as if he knew my every movement, even the smallest ones. He could not see, but he was not blind.

I took his face gently in my hands and peered close, unfazed by his unique eyes. I squinted when I noticed the redness of irritation. "You… you have a wood chip in your eye."

Váli choked on his drink. "He what?"

Baldr leaned over me to get a better look at Höðr's face. "How did you not manage to feel that enough to locate it, brother?"

Höðr shrugged. "I rubbed, but didn't find anything. Is it large?"

"Yes," Baldr and I said in unison. I was a bit horrified by this finding and struggled to understand how Höðr hadn't found it himself. Baldr couldn't feel pain, but he was the only one of his brothers with that ability. And this splinter of wood was in there deep.

I took a slow breath. "I'm going to remove it. It will likely hurt."

"I am ready." His face was so relaxed in my hand. He trusted me implicitly to heal him.

Baldur leaned closer to watch. He trusted me, but he was protective of his brother. Muninn landed on my shoulder to watch as well. I wasn't sure if it was because of Odinn or not, but I didn't care.

Magic tendrils seeped from my fingers and slid up Höðr's face. My magic shuddered in response to touching him. It always did this, though I wasn't entirely sure why. It never prevented me from healing him.

My magic crawled along his eyes, finding no issue with the seemingly uninjured one. This allowed me to focus on the injury, though I left my magic on the uninjured eye to make sure nothing changed.

I used my magic to pry his eye wide and then focused. I didn't trust my fingers to do this job, so I'd have to rely on precision with my magic.

A tendril split into two and gently touched his irritated tissue. Höðr chuckled quietly and he twitched. The corners of my lips turned up. We'd learned a long time ago that my magic tickled him when I checked the state of his eyes.

My magic wrapped around the protruding wood. "Ready?"

He let out a calming breath. "Yes."

Váli and Baldr both held their brother just in case. The last thing I needed was for him to start thrashing. Yes, I could heal any damage that was caused, but I didn't want him to experience any unnecessary injury.

I took my own bolstering breath and then began pulling the splinter out. Höðr gritted his teeth, his breath laboring the longer I took. Then, the wood popped out and my magic flooded in to heal him.

Höðr sighed and his whole body sagged with relief as the tissue healed over. "That feels much better."

I laughed. How could I not? He acted like it wasn't a big deal that he'd gotten such a large piece of wood in his eye. I placed the splinter in his palm so he could feel what exactly I'd pulled out of him.

His brows rose high, and I had to press my lips together hard so as not to laugh, because with my magic making his eyes glow, he looked a little silly. "Now I understand why you were shocked. How did I not find this?"

"Well, he's either good at acting innocent, or he really did miss that and didn't have some convoluted ploy to lure a pretty witch close," Váli said. He sat back on the bench and drank some more.

Höðr's eyes narrowed, though he didn't risk turning toward his brother in case someone saw his uncovered face. "I have no need for such tricks, brother. I'm not you."

Váli elbowed his brother in the back and aggressively ate some meat on his plate. I shook my head. It was always entertaining with these two around.

When I felt Höðr's eye was sufficiently healed, I allowed my magic to die away. His eyes twitched and constricted the moment my magic left. They focused on me with more keen intent than before my magic touched him, almost as if he could see me.

Maybe it was the smile on his lips that made me think such an odd thought. But when his eyes relaxed into their usual unseeing state and the smile remained, I shook the thought from my head. My magic couldn't help his condition. We'd tried a number of times.

Muninn hopped over to Höðr's shoulder to check his eye. He crooned with approval and then flew back to Odinn. Höðr tightened his blindfold again.

"I have something for you." He reached into a bag on his hip and pulled out something brown and shimmery.

I blinked and my mouth parted as I stared at the wooden carving of a horse he handed me. Parts of it weren't wood at all, but a clear hard material with sparkling magic within that looked like snow. "Wow… This is…"

"I worked hard to make sure every detail was correct."

Correct? He'd managed to make an exact replica of Einvala. Of all the horses I ever owned, she'd been my favorite. There was no other like her.

Höðr, without a doubt, had heard me talk about her the most, but because he genuinely wanted me to. He always asked the most fascinating questions that would get me thinking how to describe her without my eyes. He'd made this special from everything I'd told him.

I suddenly became suspicious. "You didn't get that eye sliver because of this, did you?"

The table erupted in laughter. Höðr gave me a reassuring smile. "No. I'm quite certain it was a project after this. Do you like it?"

I more than just liked it. But before I could answer, a large presence walked by. Thor sneered down at Höðr. "It is pathetic, brother, you would waste time on such a woman. And for what? A smile?"

Instead of shrinking under his brother's words, Höðr grinned. "At least I can make them smile, instead of running away from my chambers with tears staining their cheeks."

I snickered, along with several others. Thor scowled. "It isn't wise to speak lies in Father's hall."

A Valkyrie with long, braided reddish-brown hair, and light brown eyes cackled on the other side of the table. She lifted her drink to her lips and spoke with a voice that was so sultry, I might have even been tempted by her if she tried hard enough. "Lies? I saw it happen just yesterday, Thor. It'd be easier to read the list of satisfied women who have shared your bed than the disappointed ones who ran to your brothers' arms and found a much better night than even the women you somehow managed to *satisfy*."

"Watch your tongue," Thor threatened, lightning sparking off his shoulders and his aura growing intense.

She drank some more, unfazed by his threat. "My wings are older than your limp hammer, Thor. Go amuse yourself. It's the best action you ever get."

The table roared with laughter. Thor grew red in the face, matching his hair. More lightning sparked, and Týr tensed beside me while Baldr took a threatening step toward his brother. They were always ready to beat Thor within an inch of his life.

A deep resonating *clang* echoed through the hall, sharper than any metal I'd ever heard. Energy hummed through the air, as well as a powerful chill, and Thor's lightning immediately snuffed out. I glanced toward Odinn. He gripped Gungnir, the flat end of its shaft pressed against the floor.

Odinn didn't say anything, but he didn't have to. While he was fine with brawls in his hall, the one that had been about to transpire was not one he approved of. Though I doubted it had anything to do with Odinn not wanting to see his son attack any of us.

No, I was quite certain it was his way of reminding us how much power he held here. I wouldn't doubt he'd privately encouraged Thor to stir up trouble.

Thor sneered at us before going to join the table closest to his father. Thor was really the only child Odinn had who was explicitly loyal to him. Baldr openly stood by Týr, while Höðr and Váli tried to remain neutral in the whole conflict, though they did both favor Baldr's company over the others.

And then there was Vidar. I didn't even know where to begin with that god. But he didn't seem to be here, which was no surprise, and I was glad for it. I'd prefer to be even in Thor's company than that man's.

Thor took his place and didn't refrain from making a threatening gesture toward our table. I decided it was time for me to be a little petty, seeing as I couldn't slit his throat like I'd like. Höðr would get more than a smile from me.

I leaned up and pecked Höðr on the cheek where everyone could see. "Ignore your idiot brother. I love it. Thank you."

He smiled widely and touched where I'd kissed him. "I'm glad."

Týr took the figurine to admire it as well. When he had it too long, I tried to take it back and only found myself in his lap and with my cup refilled magically, as all drinks were here, and no horse statue. I huffed but didn't fight him. He'd return it when he was done.

Baldr made a move to sit between me and Höðr when a tall female-presenting individual with dark hair plopped down in that spot. They had striking, sharp features, with high cheekbones and an agile figure.

They groaned and rubbed their very-far-along pregnant belly. "This is your fault, Astrid."

My brow rose. "How is your condition my fault, Loki? My magic doesn't allow me to get myself or others pregnant, least of all with a unicorn child."

More laughter arose around the table. Accepting I was infertile had been difficult, but these days I could make jokes like this without it hurting.

"You're supposed to be the voice of reason. Where was it when that dare was made?"

I hummed thoughtfully. "Off gallivanting with yours and Freyja's, I believe."

Freyja cackled. No one that day of the dare had had any reason in their skulls. I'd have blamed the influence of alcohol, except immortals couldn't get drunk.

Someone had dared Loki to track down a unicorn shifter and bed them, unrestrained. A deadly endeavor for a mortal, a difficult and potentially fatal one for even a god. And this trickster god took the challenge.

Not only had he tracked one down, he decided to change his physical sex for the encounter. That choice was the least surprising one Loki had made, given his identity was rather fluid, and he regularly altered his appearance and physical sex.

And here he was, now stuck with child because Creation decided to get in the last laugh.

"Eighteen months," he moaned. "Eighteen months!"

I offered him some food. "I don't know what you want me to do about it. I can't tell that baby to evacuate any faster than a fertility deity can."

"Can't we just cut it out?"

I chuckled and popped a piece of fruit in my mouth. "No, it doesn't work like that."

"Then what can I do?"

I shrugged, unsure what I could say. The fact that pregnancies could last this long was a shocking revelation to me. Immortality and magic did not care about perceived natural rules.

"You're no help," he grumped. He angrily ripped into some meat. "Use your special völva magic and be useful."

I rolled my eyes. "I am useful. I just can't help you with the consequences of your particular actions. That's not a failing of mine."

He sagged against me. "I'm huge, I'm emotional, and he kicks my organs harder than a Berserker and thinks he's going to be the next honored skáld with the way he uses my ribs as an instrument."

I did my best not to laugh while others around us had no reservation. They delighted in Loki's predicament. While I was amused sometimes, I did have sympathy for him. "You're not huge."

Loki turned his gaze up to me, his pregnancy emotions unhidden on his face. "I look like a whale that fishmongers dragged ashore."

"You do not," I admonished with a gentle tone, unable to stop the slight laugh to warble my words. "Your radiant glow rivals the fire of the hearth."

"You don't mean that."

"Have I ever lied to you?"

He pouted. "No. I don't think so, at least. Quite foolish of you, really."

"As you've told me before, and yet I continue the way I do."

No one really understood my relationship with Loki, any more than they did with my interactions with his son. Though, I didn't really understand it myself. We weren't friends per se—Loki didn't have any of those, according to him—but we were friendly. I wasn't immune to any of his tricks, but none were overly harsh like some others experienced, and they were at times quite funny.

I didn't trust him, as his loyalties were only to himself, but I didn't see him in the same light as many of the other gods who would rather blame him for all their woes, even if it were impossible for him to be the cause. I just couldn't see him that way.

I didn't feel pity for him… it was… something else I didn't have words for. Regardless of that reason or feeling, it felt right to act this way with him. Especially because it angered Odinn the most. And Loki liked that as much as me.

I twirled my finger. "Turn around. Let me ease some of your discomfort."

He didn't have to be told twice. He faced away from me and I turned in Týr's lap. His hand remained around my hips, so I wasn't going anywhere. Luckily, I didn't need to for this.

I pressed my hands to Loki's back and let my magic move around freely. It crawled along his body and seeped into his skin. Loki's head rolled back and he moaned the loudest, most ridiculous sexual moan he could have possibly mustered.

Týr and Baldr choked on their drinks. Freyja, her twin brother Freyr, and I laughed. Fenrir shook his head while Hel and Jörmungandr looked equally embarrassed and wishing to murder their father.

"Careful, Astrid," Helblindi, one of Loki's brothers, called out. "He might have that child right here if you're not careful."

Býleistr, Loki's other brother, grunted and took a swig of his drink. "If it gets him to stop bemoaning about his condition, let's hope it does. I've never heard a pregnant woman complain as much as him."

"If you want to experience the miracle of growing your own child, dear brother, I'd be happy to help you achieve that," Loki said.

I rolled my eyes and ignored the brothers' bantering. This magical healing was different from my usual way, healing the body in a relaxing and soothing way rather than in a literal sense, and it required a lot of concentration.

Loki's head rolled back. His eyes were closed. "Týr, I'm stealing your wife. I need this every day, even when I'm not pregnant."

Týr eloquently grunted in response while he continued to drink. "Good luck convincing her of that."

"Don't worry, Astrid, you'll have a beautiful golden cage and I'll feed you once a day."

I feigned being impressed. "Oh, how generous of you, Loki."

One of his eyes opened and he grinned. "I am quite generous."

We stared at each other a moment, one of my eyebrows cocked, then fell into a fit of laughter.

It cut short when Muninn landed on my shoulder. He nuzzled my cheek. *"Odinn wishes to speak with you."*

More like he was summoning me, and it was non-negotiable. For what reason, though, that unknown was the worrying part.

Loki chuckled. "It seems we've had too much fun in front of the Allfather, and gotten into trouble."

My magic left Loki's body and he walked away, though not without a second glance toward me that said, "be careful." He didn't have to remind me.

Týr hesitated to let me go, but he knew it'd look bad if either of us refused. Tension at the table didn't make it easy to keep up a calm mask as I walked over to Odinn. Muninn played with my hair as if nothing was amiss. It was possible nothing was, but it was strange he'd want to talk to me of all people, least of all in this way. It was rare for him to speak to me, and if he did, it was in a group setting where my gods were around me.

I nodded respectfully to Odinn when I reached the dais. "Allfather. You wish to speak to me."

"Yes, come, sit," he invited, all too warmly.

I glanced around. There was nowhere to sit close enough to speak with him, except at his feet. *No way in hel.* "Unless a seat is procured for me, I will respectfully stand. There are few gods I would sit at the feet of."

His hand resting on his throne curled with his irritation. Others nearby paused to stare at me. But no one called me out on the insult. It wasn't enough to make a scene.

"Very well, if that is your wish," Odinn said, feigning indifference. "How are you enjoying yourself?"

Such a strange question. Why would he care? "It's been quite enjoyable, as always."

Despite these affairs being mandatory, they were fun, so it made them worth bearing.

"I noticed Loki giving you trouble. It concerns me that Týr allowed it."

I shook my head. "Loki and I are not on hostile terms. Quite the opposite—he was rather pleasant today."

Really, everyone saw how much better he'd behaved, compared to Thor. Like anyone would believe I'd been forced to deal with Loki against my will.

He scrutinized me with his one keen eye. "You should be more careful with those you trust."

I smiled, a forced one. "Don't worry, Allfather, my mother and father taught me well how to be an *excellent* judge of character. It's an important skill for a völva."

He twitched, feeling the slight, but it was too subtle for him to again call me out on it. "That is good. You never know when someone may try to use you for their own ends."

Exactly, Odinn. I made sure to bite my tongue and nod my agreement.

Muninn flew down to the table where Thor sat with others and snatched a cluster of grapes. He flew back up to me to offer me some. I smiled and thanked him, sharing the food with the raven.

Odinn made a rumbling sound and I refocused on him, confused by the sound. I couldn't decipher his expression either. "Something the matter, Allfather?"

He shook his head and then stroked Huginn, who perched on his shoulder. "I am pleased to see you get along so well with Muninn. He speaks fondly of you when he has returned from visits."

I smiled, this one genuine, and stroked Muninn's chest with the back of my finger. "I greatly enjoy his company. He's fun and an excellent conversationalist. And of course, very beautiful."

Muninn puffed up and crooned, then played with my hair.

Odinn made a thoughtful sound in his throat. "I do hope that you may extend that fondness to me someday as well. It has been unsettling to see this divide among the gods. And, while you are not one, you fit remarkably well here. I would like to see us be capable of more than terse conversation."

If I were someone else, I may have been flattered. But I was suspicious instead. I held his gaze as I took a sip of my drink. "We both know why that would be a long way off, if not impossible, Odinn."

He continued to hold my gaze, his hand curling tighter around the shaft of his spear. Then I saw something strange—a flicker of fear. *Why? Why did me bringing up Kirby, and his refusal to undo her curse and admit he'd gone too far for no reason, make him fearful?*

"I see," Odinn said, his voice strained.

An awkward silence slipped in. Muninn dipped his head, and then after a moment flew to Odinn's shoulder. I took that as my sign he didn't want me around at this point. "If that will be all, Allfather, I'll take my leave."

I turned my back on Odinn and headed for my gods. It was a good thing Garmr had died a long time ago. As Odinn's most loyal shifter enforcer, he would have gone after me for such a display, even if Odinn hadn't ordered it. But, as it stood, I arrived back at the table unaccosted.

Týr wrapped his arm around me the moment I came into reach and pulled me against his hard body. "Are you well?"

I smiled and kissed his forehead. "Of course. I wasn't being tortured."

He grunted and then offered me some of his mead. I settled in for more conversation when Bjarke came over.

He slammed a hand down on my shoulder and bent close to my ear. "We need you."

My brow rose. "For?"

"New Berserker needs a nice little attitude adjustment."

I pursed my lips. "Not immortal?"

"And he doesn't realize you are, either."

A wicked grin curled up my face. "Then let's introduce him to the wall of shame."

TWENTY-FIVE

TÝR

Water lapped at the shore. My head rested comfortably in Astrid's lap while she ran her fingers through my hair, gathering locks into a complex braid to match the one on the other side of my head she'd already made.

I gazed at her, marveling at her beauty. Ageless. Perfect. Immortal and mine forever. Every day I thanked Creation for such a gift.

I'd had to learn a great deal with her. My existence as a god had numbed me to much, but Astrid, she had to experience what it meant to be immortal for the first time.

Time passed, and her father and brother grew older, eventually dying in glorious battle. Randi grew up, learning her magic through Astrid, and raised children of her own, continuing with the honor of providing her first daughter with the name Randi as well. But even she succumbed to her mortality, and her daughters and their daughters continued to take up the family mantle. Astrid lived through it all, and still managed to not withdraw from it.

She still went to Runavik and spent time with her people and friends, both new and old who became immortal themselves. She still engaged with her family, helping raise and train the next generation in ways we couldn't together.

A part of me still ached for what we couldn't have together, at least, not by natural means. Maybe we would see ourselves raising a family through a different path, but even now, centuries later, we weren't quite ready for that. Remembering what we went through—watching the light of my Valkyrie dim and struggle to return, and hearing her utter words about her bullshit curse and how she was unworthy of me, and how she would cry herself to sleep at night—it haunted me.

But I had her, as long as I had that, everything was perfect.

Astrid ran her finger down my cheek. "What are you looking at?"

"The most beautiful creature in existence."

She glanced around. "I don't see Freyja anywhere."

I sat up and cupped her face. "Freyja could never compare to you, Valkyrie."

I pressed my lips to hers, soft and gentle at first, but as her taste teased my senses, I grew hungry. Astrid chuckled and wrapped her arms around my neck, pulling me closer. There was no battle of wills this time, and I was absolutely fine with that.

My hands fumbled and tugged at the buckles and ties for her dress—the design specifically created for lounging around our island, and yet would give me both a challenge of removing it from her and that sensation of tearing her clothes off, while not forcing Astrid to have to mend her clothes all the time. Spending centuries with her did not diminish my burning need for her.

Her clothes fell away, and I claimed every visible part of her. Her intoxicating tastes and smells; her tempting moans and begs; her mirrored caresses; she was everything I craved—everything I needed.

Astrid's hips bucked and she screamed my name. The sound and feeling of her clenching around me sent me over the edge and I came inside her with reckless abandon.

We lay together in a spent but blissful heap. Her head rested on my chest, where she listened to my still-erratic heart.

"I love you," I murmured, trailing my hand up her soft back.

She snuggled into me more. "I love you too."

I'd be happy to lay like this forever. But something always interrupted.

A strong, tugging sensation snagged my war senses. This wasn't like when mortals went to war. No, those happened all the time, and were weak. This one, though, this one was much different.

Astrid sat up first, her back straight, her focus going far beyond the borders of our home. *She feels it, too.* I wasn't sure how, but the best I could guess was her magic was evolving. With her becoming immortal, it presented new chances for her unique magic to blossom, and since she accompanied me into battle, it made sense she'd start to develop abilities that would help her. And yet, I found it strange how closely it mirrored those of Valkyries.

I jerked my head to focus behind us when two new arrivals appeared suddenly. Freyja and Baldr stood several paces away, ready for battle. Astrid noticed them a moment later.

A bright smile appeared on her face and she quickly dressed before jumping to her feet. She ran over to the two. Baldr wrapped her up in a spinning hug. The two laughed, and acted as though it'd been some time since they'd seen each other, rather than just yesterday. I dressed slowly, watching them.

Astrid and Baldr had grown closer over time. I had always had suspicions about his interest in Astrid, but he never pursued her. Astrid seemed to have continued to see him as a close friend, but that bond was shifting.

One would think I was worried, that I would become jealous or put a stop to it. But I had urge for neither.

It wasn't common for immortals to stick to one partner for all eternity. That wasn't to say they didn't have any permanent partners, just that they were open to more than one. That was why many found my marriage to Astrid odd.

However, she was mortal at the time. I expected to only have her for a fraction of the eternity I'd spend existing. It was why I was so determined to keep her for myself. Though, I still had no eyes for any other. My heart belonged solely to her.

But now... in the wake of her own awakened immortality, if she wanted Baldr as well, I had no issues sharing her. Especially with him. I knew he would cherish her heart and worship the earth she walked on.

Astrid glanced around when Baldr set her back down. "Where is Fen?"

Baldr made a displeased face. "He rushed in before he should have."

Her brows pulled together, but unlike her, I now understood the war sensation surging through me. "It's time, then?"

Freyja nodded. "Odinn dies today."

Things had gotten worse with the god and those who allied with him. We knew war was on the horizon, and today was judgment day.

Astrid's expression didn't improve. In fact, I realized her confusion was actually concern, and it'd gotten worse. "And Fen is already engaging?"

"He was impatient," Freyja said.

"More like he wouldn't see reason," Baldr muttered.

My gut churned. Fenrir was impulsive, always had been. However, I could always count on him not to do anything rash in important situations.

"That's not like him," Astrid said, mirroring my thoughts.

"He's always been impulsive," Freyja said.

Baldr shook his head. "She's right. This isn't normal for him."

Not only did I agree with him, but there was something else neither of them seemed to remember. "Astrid, you pointed this out before, too."

She nodded, her lips pressed tight together. "More than once. I had hoped I was seeing things. But I don't have a good feeling about his behavior."

I summoned my armor and sword. "Then we shouldn't stall."

Astrid used her magic to summon new, more mobile-friendly clothes and armor, as well as her shield, sword, and even her axe, which hung at her hip.

She played with some jewelry on her wrists—protection bracelets Baldr and I gifted her centuries ago. She promised to always wear them, and unless she was staying home, she kept to that promise. She may be immortal, but that didn't mean she couldn't die. There were always ways to kill even a god.

"Are you leaving?" a small, quiet voice inquired.

We turned to Ùna approaching, her gait a bit awkward.

Astrid smiled. "We are. We'll be back before you know it."

The female fae blinked, and I noticed her pulled-in posture. She knew Freyja and Baldr, and never got nervous around them. So, this was a bit different.

"Please come back," the fae said. "Please promise me you will."

My gut churned. Ùna never acted this way when we left, even for battle. She always had confidence in us, and was usually sassy about our departures.

Astrid knelt and pulled the fae into a strong embrace. "Of course I'll come back. I always do."

Ùna hugged her back, blinking into Astrid's shoulder.

After a moment of embracing, Astrid joined me at my side, and we all touched Freyja for her to teleport us to Fenrir's location.

The peaceful lake was replaced in an instant with the chaos of war. Instinct kicked in, and I swung my sword, cutting clean through the arm of a warrior. Baldr rushed in with his usual reckless abandon, and Freyja split off with him. Astrid remained by my side. She summoned her magic and opened up large swaths of the battlefield by throwing warriors back with invisible force.

I had no idea which warriors were immortal, and which were mortal, but it didn't matter. They were the enemy, and they wouldn't stand in our way.

A wolf snarled and then howled in the distance. My pulse kicked up at the sound of Fenrir's familiar battle cry. But I didn't know where he was.

"Go to him!" Astrid yelled to Freyja and Baldr. "We'll take care of these ones."

I slashed through a wolf Berserker with ease. "We'll catch up quickly."

Our friends nodded and took off in the direction of Fenrir's howl, Astrid clearing the way. We could go with them, but these warriors would follow, so it was best to be rid of the nuisances now.

Astrid and I fell into practiced step. I cut down two warriors, and she speared three with summoned weapons. I slammed down another and Astrid blasted a warrior with brilliant magic when she foolishly thought she could catch me from behind. We'd fought so many battles together, we could be blindfolded and still we'd fight in perfect rhythm.

Many warriors died at my hand, while others, Astrid told me to leave. I didn't question, just acted.

Slowly, the number of warriors thinned, and we made progress toward the fight with Odinn himself. Those loyal to Odinn who remained were mostly Berserkers or immortals. Some were even both, like the Berserker I faced down.

The bipedal bear-like man snapped and snarled, his eyes crazed with the lust of battle. I'd met him on several occasions, both in battle and outside of it. Arnlaug was one of Odinn's most renowned and loyal warriors. While I didn't have any personal hatred toward this man, he stood in my way, and therefore needed to be cut down.

Arnlaug chuckled, the sound rumbling low and deep. *"How I've longed for this day, Týr, where I could finally tear you apart. You and your wingless Valkyrie will suffer for siding against Odinn."*

Wingless Valkyrie. It wasn't the first time I'd heard that name for Astrid. My affectionate name for her had turned into more than that for others after she became immortal. So many thought I had created a Valkyrie, even if she couldn't sprout wings or touch warrior souls like a true Valkyrie. Even Fenrir and Baldr called her that in battle, or teased her outside of it.

Naturally, these speculations did nothing to aid my poor rapport with Odinn. He seemed especially furious about the prospect that another god could have made a Valkyrie.

Arnlaug bared his teeth. *"Will you fight me like a proud warrior, Týr? Or is it true that your Valkyrie cut off your balls and you need her protection?"*

Astrid vanished and reappeared behind a wolf Berserker. She slammed her axe into his back, and the warrior dropped to the ground, twitching several times before going still. She snapped her gaze to me. "I trust you can handle this, my love."

I readied my sword and shield and focused on the warrior before me. "I can't disappoint my Valkyrie, Arnlaug. You'll have to die."

The Berserker roared and charged. He slammed a hard fist into my shield and then followed up with a swipe of his claws, looking to take me by surprise. I was not a god of war by chance. I easily deflected both attacks and used his momentum to slice into his arm with my sword.

Arnlaug's reflexes were better than I'd planned, and he managed to evade the worst part of the strike. His bulky arm remained attached to his body, but bled profusely.

The Berserker didn't pay his wound any mind and came at me again. I dodged and thrust my shield at his face, aiming to damage something vital. Arnlaug snapped his razor-sharp teeth and clamped down on the shield, the wood cracking under the intense pressure of his jaw.

The bear-man wrenched my shield out of my hand and spat it away. But that was his mistake.

I took advantage of his undefended stance and sliced my sword across his chest. He roared, and I followed up with a sweeping slash to his legs. The bear Berserker collapsed, but wasn't ready to admit defeat like the warrior he was.

Arnlaug swiped claws at me but missed, leaving his arms open for another disabling attack. My sword almost sliced through flesh and bone both. His unbalanced state temporarily saved him from that fate when he fell back.

I raised my sword to strike the killing blow when a soft hand touched mine. I snapped my focused stare on Astrid. She gazed down at the bleeding-out Berserker with cold, battle-hardened eyes. The look was a more mature one from that first time in the meadow when she first met Freyja and Baldr. These years of battle had steeled her heart to the darkness of war, and yet, when the battle ended, she still maintained her goodness.

Both sides of my Valkyrie stirred me in primal ways. Even now, as she disregarded Arnlaug's life, she was the most alluring woman I had ever been privileged to meet.

"Leave him," she said, turning away with no further explanation. I found that peculiar. She usually gave a reason why she wanted a warrior to live. But I didn't question her, and followed instead.

Arnlaug roared. *"You finish what you started!"*

"Think long and hard about your loyalties, Berserker," Astrid said without looking back. "Do not waste your honor by being loyal to the wrong god."

We left Arnlaug to wallow in his wounds and continued our fight. We pushed through warrior after warrior, until there were no enemies left. They were all dead, too wounded to fight, or had fled.

My breath came heavy and my body ached with exhaustion, yet it also sang with the glory of war. Astrid didn't fare much better. She'd used most of her magic during that battle. It had been a lot to take on for the two of us, but we'd done it. And that meant the others weren't as hindered in their fight.

"We need to get to the others," I said. By now, they should have already engaged with Odinn. A part of me, a more deeply tired side, hoped the battle was already done, so we could finally be rid of this centuries-long problem. But the war side of me craved to see Odinn's head roll from his shoulders. *He needs to pay for every crime he has committed.*

Astrid nodded and opened to her mouth to speak, when a wolf's snarling interrupted her. We whirled around. A horse-sized wolf prowled close. Blood caked its black fur and it walked with an awkward gait, as if injured.

"Fen?" I said. "Where are the others? What happened with Odinn?"

Astrid gasped. "Fen, are you all right? Do you need healing?"

He didn't respond, and instead prowled closer, his lips pulling back. My senses twitched. Something wasn't right.

Astrid stepped forward, her hands out. "Fen, what's wrong? Are you in pain? I can help."

"Astrid," I warned.

She stopped and looked back at me, her brow creased.

"Don't get any closer to him. He's not in control of his wolf." I advanced, weapon at the ready. "Fen, you need to come out of that form. I need to talk to you, but not man to beast."

Fenrir snarled and then lunged. I tensed and readied to throw my friend off, when he unexpectedly pivoted. Astrid gasped and threw up her hands, but no magic came out. *No!*

Midgard moved in slow motion. My feet dug into the ground.

Astrid backpedaled and screamed. Fenrir snapped his teeth. *No! No!*

My pulse pounded in my ears. I slammed into Fenrir's body. Astrid dropped to the ground and Fenrir whirled on me. Blood dripped from his sharp maw. He snapped his teeth and pain tore up my arm.

The tension roiling through me numbed me to the pain. My breath rushed out in hard gasps. I swung my axe, the blade slamming into Fenrir's face. He howled and snarled in pain. I didn't care. He went after Astrid. I didn't know what'd gotten into him, but that was unforgivable.

Fenrir backed off, his face bleeding profusely. He then turned tail and ran off. I whirled around, not caring where the mongrel ran off to. I'd deal with him later. "Astrid—"

I froze. Astrid lay still on the ground, eyes wide and mouth gaping. Blood gushed from the gaping wound torn from her throat. "No…"

I rushed over to her, clamping my hand over her wound. "Hold on, Astrid. Hold on."

I tried to lift her into my arms. I needed to get her to a healer. But something made it difficult to grab her. My hand covering her wound shook. Breathing became difficult. This couldn't be happening.

Astrid's eyes glazed as she reached up to me. Her mouth moved, but the sounds of her choking on her blood was the only thing to come out.

"No… Astrid… You can't…"

Her lip quivered, and then her hand dropped. She gurgled out one more breath and then stilled.

"Astrid…" I shook her. "Astrid! No!"

I pulled her limp, lifeless body against my chest, cradling her as numbness creeped through me. *No… Creation, no… She can't be…* My Valkyrie couldn't be gone. She was immortal. I'd have her for all eternity. *No…*

I tipped my head back and wordlessly screamed into the empty air. *He'll pay for this. Fenrir will pay.*

"Týr!"

I jerked my attention toward Baldr's voice. My breath was ragged and my throat raw. He and Freyja, both covered in the blood of our enemies and their own, slowly approached.

Freyja shook her head. "No…"

Baldr sprinted to me, falling to his knees in front of Astrid's lifeless body. He held up a shaking hand. "She's not… Astrid can't be…"

"She prayed to me," Freyja murmured. "She said…"

The goddess struggled to speak. Her steps toward us were slow and jerky. "She said… to take care of Týr for her… It's why I rushed us here…"

"How could this happen?" Baldr asked. "She was protected. She had—"

He lifted her left hand, and where his gifted bracelet usually was, there was a bare wrist. My gifted bracelet remained, but barely, the metal broken, and the magic gone.

Freyja dropped to her knees next to Baldr. Her lower lip quivered, and she reached for Astrid, only to stop. Her eyes widened. "Týr, what happened to you?"

I looked down at myself, and for the first time, saw what Fenrir had done. My hand was gone. Bitten off at the wrist. My skin was in the process of knitting together over the exposed bone. My awareness brought physical agony raging through me.

Baldr snarled. "Who did this to Astrid?"

My jaw clenched. I struggled to control my breathing. With my fading numbness, rage mixed with my pain.

I grabbed Freyja by her cuirass. "Bring me to him."

She stared at me, eyes wide. "What?"

"You hear me, Freyja. Bring me to him now!" My rage spilled over. My pulse pounded in my ears. "I'll kill him. I'll kill him for taking Astrid from me. That mongrel will pay!"

Her brow knitted together. "Mongrel? Týr, I don't know who you mean. Please try to stay calm. I'll help, I just need you to—"

"Fenrir!" I shouted. "Fenrir did this!"

Freyja gaped at me. "W—what? No. That's not possible."

I gripped her armor tighter. "I know what I saw, Freyja."

"Týr, listen to yourself. Astrid was our family. Fenrir would never do that. You know this. Baldr, please help here."

Baldr didn't speak up immediately, and I didn't take my eyes off Freyja. She'd help me find him. I didn't care what it required of me to force her.

"I want to agree, Freyja, but…" Baldr faltered. "You saw him before the battle. He wasn't acting right. Astrid was worried about him, and has been for a while. And… you weren't with us when we fought Odinn."

Baldr shook his head. "Fenrir didn't fight like himself. It was like he lost control. And I told you, after the fight, he ran off. I want to believe he wouldn't do this. But I can't."

My muscles coiled. "Take me to him, now, Freyja."

Her eyes narrowed, and she gripped my wrist. "Release me, Týr."

"Not until you locate Fenrir and bring me to him."

She shook her head. "I need more proof."

I bared my teeth. "I saw him!"

"And you're distraught!" Her grip on my wrist tightened. "There are other wolf shifters in existence. Hel, I fought some in this very war and plenty looked just like him. Fenrir acting out of sorts and you claiming it was him while emotionally distraught isn't proof he did this. I will not condemn him to death until I have proof."

I yanked her close, our noses almost touching. "If you're protecting him, then you're working with him! And that makes you my enemy."

"Týr," Baldr warned in a low growl. "You're out of line."

"I am not your enemy," she said, unfazed by my threat. "I will help you, Týr, but not to kill Fenrir unless you have absolute proof."

"That is the only way to help! It's the only way to avenge her!"

Freyja's eyes softened. "Týr, remember, I have magic. I might be able to do something here."

I froze.

"Like what?" Baldr asked. "It's not like we can bring back the dead."

"Maybe we can."

My grip loosened. *Bring Astrid back?* "You can bring her back?"

"I touch warrior souls to send them to Fólkvangr. If I can do that, maybe I can do the same with her soul. It hasn't left her body yet, I can sense that."

Freyja placed a gentle hand on mine and held my gaze. "I can't promise anything, Týr, but I will try."

Baldr rested his hand on my shoulder in quiet solidarity with me.

I sucked in a deep breath. "You'll swear a vow."

Her shoulders drooped. "Týr—"

"You'll swear, you'll help me until I am reunited with her, or I avenge her memory."

"She was already going to help," Baldr said.

"Swear it to me, Freyja," I said, my tone more forceful.

The goddess took a long breath and nodded. I released her. She pulled a knife from its sheath at her side and held out her hand while I held out my remaining one.

"I, Freyja, swear to you, Týr, to do everything in my power to return Astrid to us." She cut her hand deep with the knife, dark blood pooling. She then cut my hand. We clasped them together and power rushed up our arms.

"I, Týr, swear to you, Freyja, should you fail to uphold your oath, I will kill you."

Freyja's lips pressed together, but there was nothing she could do, now that I'd uttered the vow. I cared not for the history we had. If she failed me, I'd treat her the same as I would Fenrir, should he ever cross my path again.

"It is done." She stood. "Gather Astrid, and we'll go back to my place. My magic is strongest in my home domain."

Holding Astrid was no easy task with my missing hand, but I had assistance from Baldr. My chest ached watching him cradle her as if she were the most precious thing in Midgard. While my grief came out in the form of my rage and desire for vengeance, he was quietly grieving her loss. *He cared just as much as me, except he never got to tell her.* I couldn't imagine that type of pain.

Freyja teleported us away from the battle, and we found ourselves outside her home.

"I'll have to do some research," she said. "But to start, I'll need an altar. That will help me channel the magic."

"I'll build it," Baldr said. I didn't refuse him. The look in his eyes told me it was best to allow him to help in this way.

Freyja nodded and turned to me. "Before I start, I want to look at your—"

"I'm fine," I said.

"Týr, your arm isn't healing properly. You should already be regrowing what you lost, but it's not doing that."

"And it won't. Not yet at least." Not until I had Astrid back. It was my punishment—my reminder of how I failed her.

Freyja stepped away, understanding she wouldn't win this. She entered her house while I stood there, cradling Astrid, and Baldr built the altar.

I wasn't sure how long I stood there, feeling her body growing colder and stiffer. I didn't know how many times I replayed that moment in my mind of her life fading from her eyes, over and over. I didn't count the number of times the tides of grief crashed against my crumbling walls.

However long it was, it took Baldr's touch on my shoulder to rouse me. He didn't say anything, only nodded, as if understanding.

Freyja stood by the altar Baldr built. Braziers lit the area all around us. The sun was long gone, and a chill clung to the air.

I took slow, stiff steps toward the waiting goddess. My heart ached and fear crept at the back of my mind. *What if this doesn't work? What if I lose my heart for good?*

I took a steadying breath and laid Astrid on the altar. "Are you sure you have the spell you need?"

"I'm confident it will ensure the vow is fulfilled." I didn't like how she worded that, and Freyja's expression gave nothing away of her feelings.

"Explain what that means."

She shook her head. "I can't. I don't know what this will do exactly. I just know it will have the end result we agreed to."

I would have to accept this. I didn't have magic. And no one else would even make any attempt like this, binding oath or no. I couldn't bring Astrid back without her.

Freyja had me step back, and she began her ritual. I didn't understand anything she did, from the herbs used, to the magical artifacts, and even drawing her own blood while chanting. Magic didn't typically need complex rituals. A user thought what they needed, and it happened. But on occasion, more was required.

Freyja cried out to Creation, and magic filled the air. The fire within the braziers grew and then all at once extinguished to embers, along with the magic.

I stood still, watching Astrid's unmoving body and listening to Freyja's heavy breathing. Nothing more happened. "Well?"

Baldr stepped up next to me. "Freyja, what happened?"

He sounded as tense as I felt. Something wasn't right.

Freyja hovered a hand over Astrid's body. She then frowned. "Her soul couldn't reenter this body."

My pulse elevated and I pushed forward, my shoulder tight. Baldr grabbed me and pulled me back. "Týr, stop. Let her finish."

"The ritual didn't fail, Týr," Freyja said. "She will come back to us. But not immediately." She took a long breath. "She'll be reincarnated."

Everything in me slowed. "Reincarnated. Like Kirby?"

Freyja nodded. "In a way, yes. But unlike Odinn's curse, Astrid will only be reborn once."

"She'll be mortal again, right?" Baldr said.

Freyja shrugged. "I suspect she will be, but she may be lucky and be born an immortal this next time. We all know, even us gods aren't guaranteed to have immortal children."

The tension in my shoulders dissipated. *Reincarnated.* "When?"

"I don't know," Freyja said. "It's impossible for me to tell. I do believe her soul may give off a magic signature resembling my magic, which should help me identify her if I cross paths with her. But otherwise, I don't know how else to track her down once her soul is born again."

My fist curled and then uncurled. I would have my Astrid back, just not in the initial way I wanted. It had been a gamble, I knew that. The fact that Freyja had been able to do even this was a miracle. I had made a rather outlandish demand of her in my grief. "I will find her."

Baldr slammed his hand down on my shoulder. "I will help you. Only death could stop me from searching until we find her."

Freyja held up a finger. "Týr, I want you to keep this in mind. Even if you find Astrid, she may not be the same person we knew. There's no guarantee she'll ever remember any of us, and what she had with us."

I didn't care. I'd find her, fall in love with her all over again, and woo her like I had in this life. I'd accept if she never remembered. I'd embrace the new woman she was, and we'd make new memories.

I tipped my head skyward.

I vow to find you, Valkyrie. No matter how long it takes. I will not rest until I do. And I vow, in the name of justice and retribution, I will spill Fenrir's blood for the atrocity he has committed.

TWENTY-SIX

ASTRID
CENTURIES LATER

Tall green trees flashed past the truck window. The sky above was blue with white puffy clouds. I'd normally look around and take in this new place as much as I could, but I didn't feel like it this time. My eyes were glued to my reflection, an ugly scar now running down from my eyebrow, over my nose, down to the opposite cheek.

A warm hand gently grasped my leg. I turned away from the window to look at Daddy. He was old. All adults were old, but my dad had black and white hair and beard, like you'd see on someone's grandpa. I heard one lady call him a silver fox, whatever that meant.

Daddy adjusted his glasses, and my eyes flicked to the tattoos on his arms. Some were colored and others weren't. He let me color those in with markers whenever I wanted. It was fun. But today I didn't feel like doing that. Today wasn't a fun day.

"What do you think of the area, Ace?" Daddy asked.

I shrugged and looked out the window again. He let out a quiet sigh. "I know this change is a big one, Astrid, but I promise you're going to love this new home."

New home… Pain tightened in my chest. I didn't want a new home. I wanted my home. Where my mom was. *Where she used to love me…*

My eyes focused on my scar again. *What did I do to make her mad? Why don't I deserve her love anymore?*

"You're going to love this place," Daddy repeated. "The air is fresh, a lot of room to run around, explore and play, and there are all kinds of wild animals you'll be able to see."

That got my attention. "Will there be bunnies?"

Daddy smiled. "I'm sure we'll see some eventually."

I liked bunnies. They were so cute with their wiggly noses. "Where are we?"

"Upstate New York, in the Adirondack Mountains."

My nose crunched as I tried to say that word. "Adder-dick?"

Daddy belted out a hearty laugh. "I think I like that pronunciation better."

I giggled, my mood improving.

The truck slowed, and Daddy took a left onto a dirt road. It was bumpy, and I bounced around a lot, but it was fun. Daddy even made fun noises, getting me to laugh.

By the time the trees opened up, I was all smiles. It wasn't so bad. I had Daddy. He loved me. He said I was a blessing from the gods to be cherished and he promised he would love me for all eternity. I believed him.

"Daddy, can you do a magic trick for me?" I asked.

He smiled. "Once we settle in, I'd be happy to. But look, we're here."

I peered out the window. The trees thinned out into a large clearing. A lawn sprawled through the entire clearing and the largest house I'd ever seen sat in the middle. The road we drove widened into a drive-way for this house.

My eyes popped. "Daddy, this is our new house?"

"It's not our house, but it'll be where we live," he said.

I didn't understand what that meant. *Daddy said we were going to our home.* Did he mean this was only temporary? Maybe it was.

Maybe we weren't allowed to stay here long. But if we couldn't stay here, where would we go?

Daddy pulled up to the big house and turned the truck off. As he did, the front door opened, and two people walked out onto the porch. Daddy unbuckled his seat belt and then helped me with my booster when I struggled with the buckle.

My nose scrunched. I could do it myself. I just needed more time.

He at least allowed me to hop out of the truck on my own. I knew how to do that. It was easy and fun to slide off the bench to the ground.

My feet landed hard on the ground and my knees gave out. My hands caught me from falling on my face. "Oof."

"You okay, Ace?" Daddy asked. He sounded worried.

I giggled and stood, rubbing my dirty hands on my pants. "Yep."

I shut my door and scurried over to where he stood in front of the truck. He placed his hand on my head and we walked up the porch steps to the two people waiting for us. I ducked behind Daddy when they were too close, and peered around his legs.

They were both old. Like grandpa-and-grandma-ancient-old. The man was tan, like he'd been out in the sun for a long, long time, and had snow-white hair. The lady was pale like me and had long, braided pale blonde hair. Her blue eyes were vibrant, and she had a fairly muscled body for someone who was old. She seemed younger than the man, but I wasn't sure how much.

The longer I looked at her, the more familiar she seemed to me, but I didn't know why. I was sure I'd never met this lady before.

"You made it, Darius," the man said. He then smiled at me. "And you must be Astrid."

Daddy rested his hand on my head. "Astrid, this is Pete and Randi. They own this retreat."

Randi? Why does that name sound so familiar?

"It's nice to finally meet you," Randi said. Her voice was soothing. I liked it. "Your dad has told us all about you. He also mentioned you just had your seventh birthday, is that right?"

I nodded.

She smiled. It was warm and inviting, like a friend greeting someone they hadn't seen in a long time. "Well, we baked you a special cake to celebrate."

My back straightened. *A cake?* "I like cake."

She clapped her hands together. "Wonderful. Why don't we—"

A truck engine rumbled, and we turned to see a large one like Daddy's roll up the driveway. This one was blue, unlike Daddy's black truck.

"Ah, Xavier and Diego have returned just in time," Pete said.

Randi smiled at me. "You'll like Diego."

I merely blinked. I didn't know who they were talking about, or why I'd like them.

The truck parked and a man with a little darker skin hopped out. He had short brown hair and some hair on his face. He gazed up at us with dark eyes. "Ah, new arrivals."

This man spoke with an accent.

His eyes flicked to me, and I ducked back around my dad's legs. He smirked. "*Mijo*, get out here. You have a new friend."

New friend? Does this man mean me?

The other truck door opened and someone dropped to the ground. It shut and a boy who looked a lot like the older man walked around the truck. He was my age.

The two of us stared at each other for a long moment before he smiled and ran up the steps. I ducked behind Daddy. I didn't do well around people, even kids my age. It made it hard to make friends.

"*Me llamo* Diego," he said. He had the same accent as the other man.

"English, *mijo*," Xavier said. "Not many know Spanish here."

Daddy pat me on the head. "She's got a few lessons in her from last year's class. You understood, right, Ace?"

I mutely nodded.

Xavier shook his head. "Still, he needs the practice."

Diego smiled at me and repeated himself in English. "I am Diego." He paused and looked as though he was thinking. "What is… your name?"

I continued to cling to Daddy. "Um… Astrid."

Diego smiled wider, revealing a missing tooth. It made him a little goofy-looking. His smile was contagious.

He held his hands out. "We are now best friends forever."

Best friends? I tentatively took his hand. His warmth seeped into my skin and my apprehension slipped away. I believed him.

"Best friends forever."

TWENTY-SEVEN

ASTRID
SEVENTEEN YEARS LATER

Vibrant and rhythmic music played through the one earbud in my ear. The partner earbud was stuck in my seatmate's ear. Diego danced in his seat and lip-synced to the lyrics without a care who might be watching in the train car, per usual, and I could hardly contain my amusement.

It was never a dull moment with my best friend, and he made sure the two-and-a-half-hour train ride wasn't boring. I swore he'd be pulling me down the aisle to dance if it wouldn't disrupt other passengers.

Not that his exotic good looks of a strong profile, dusky brown skin, tall and fit frame, and just the right amount of stubble, mixed with a carefully offered smile couldn't sweet talk him into most people's good graces to forgive him for such a disruption. I certainly couldn't get people to forgive me like that.

Diego's dancing stopped when his phone went off. He brushed a wayward curl of tousled dark brown hair out of his eyes and pulled out his phone. Curious, I tried to see who'd messaged him, but he angled his phone away.

I narrowed my eyes. "What are you hiding?"

"Nothing, *amiga*," he said in a smooth, warm voice.

"Uh-huh. Then why are you acting so suspicious?"

His warm brown eyes shifted to me, and the smile that curved up his face tried to do all kinds of warm things to my insides. I wasn't going to admit it. I wasn't going to admit it. The reaction didn't exist. I was the only person in the world who was totally, definitely unaffected by my hot best friend's panty-melting smile. "Why are you trying to snoop?"

I stuck out my bottom lip to hide my totally nonexistent reaction. "I'm not a snoop."

He laughed. "Ah yes, snoop might be too mean. You're… so enthusiastically inquisitive, you should apply to be Inspector Gadget's assistant."

I huffed. "I was just curious who was messaging you."

"Nobody you need to know."

"Fine, be that way." I turned to gaze out the window of the beautiful scenery flying past, and listen to the music. He was probably texting that chick he met at the Chinese place last week. Or maybe it was the guy he swapped numbers with on the last day of classes. Diego had seemed fairly interested in giving the dating market a shot again.

After his last relationship ended in disaster, plus the insanity of this past college semester, Diego had put that all on hold. Not that him being off the market hurt him any. He always seemed to have an endless line of prospects.

"Did you ever get that guy's number?" Diego asked.

I blinked and then looked at him. "Huh?"

"That guy you told me about last week. The one you met at the library," he clarified. "Did you ever get his number?"

Weird out-of-the-blue question. I shook my head. "Didn't see him again."

Not that I'd expected anything really to come of it even if I had exchanged numbers with him. My dating life was in the toilet. I'd managed one decent relationship for a little while before it fizzled out and we parted on good terms. Everything else was one-nights and disastrous first or second dates.

It was fine. Focusing on my studies was more important anyway. My goal was the dean's list every semester, and I'd achieved that so far. And I had friends. Sort of…

I had a feeling, once we graduated, I'd lose touch with most of the people I hung around with in my classes. It happened like that with my high school friends, so a repeating pattern made sense for me.

Unlike Mr. Popular next to me, I'd never been great at making friends. I had some, but… Diego and Aya were the closest friends I had. Oh, and Zeke. Though he was closer to Diego than me, and despite the fact his contact with us had been spotty these last few years, he still counted.

And he happened to be the reason we were returning to The City early on our break instead of staying the whole week back home. It'd be nice to see him, it'd been far too long.

Warm fingers slid over the back of my hand and curled around my fingers. "*Mi amor?*"

My love. Not in that way, though. It was in a friend way. I turned to look at Diego. He was, for some reason, gazing at me with concern. "Hmm?"

"Are you okay?"

My brow raised. "Yeah, of course, why?"

He shrugged. "I don't know. I just got a weird feeling from the way you were staring out the window."

I gave him a reassuring smile and twisted my hand in his grip and squeezed. "Just daydreaming. I'm good."

Diego threaded his fingers with mine and squeezed back. The feeling of his strong fingers tangled with mine felt good. I always felt safe with him around, and there was this quiet reassurance that no matter what, he had my back. And I could tell him anything.

Well, almost anything. There were things I didn't tell anyone. But that was very little compared to what I shared with Diego. He was my rock, and the best friend I could ever have. If I could find a guy even half as amazing as him who wanted to see me as more than just a friend, I'd be lucky.

I pulled my Gameboy Advanced out of my backpack—yeah, I

could play something newer, but I liked playing my older games—and quickly passed the last hour of the trip.

The train slowed to a stop when it finally arrived at Penn Station and we collected our things to disembark with the crowd of other commuters. I noticed Diego was paying attention to his phone a little more again. It annoyed me for some reason.

Maybe it was the way he smiled at his phone. Maybe it was because he eagerly joined the other commuters filing out of the train car, leaving me to carry both coolers. Maybe all the traveling was just making me slightly cranky.

I stepped out onto the platform and squeezed into the crowd, trying to keep up with Diego. He was absorbed again in texting on his phone as if he weren't worried about running into anyone.

"Should we call a cab, or do we want to walk?" I asked, as I caught up with him. It'd likely be faster to walk, given the hour we'd be dealing with traffic, but the idea of carrying all this stuff wasn't appealing.

He didn't respond. He pocketed his phone and his pace quickened. His longer stride had him pulling ahead of me. He had a focused, eager look on his face.

"Diego?" I said, trying to keep up and not get swallowed by the crowd.

He didn't hear me. Or didn't listen.

"Mi amor?" I said. Unlike him, I rarely used the phrase for him. I wasn't as comfortable using it in the same context he was. There was a bit of a cultural mish-mash there. Diego never took offense, and because it was so rare for me to use the phrase, it usually got his attention. Not this time.

In a blink, I found myself alone in a crowd. *What the hell?* What was so goddamned important he'd ditch me like that? Another person? He had been eagerly texting someone. *Must be the person he didn't want me seeing the message from.*

I didn't get it. If he wanted to go hang out with someone before Zeke got in tonight, he could have just said so. *He didn't have to ditch me without a word…*

More frustrated than ever, I just wanted to get home. I'd be alone, since Aya wouldn't be back from her trip to Chicago to see her brother, but I could entertain myself. Being an only child, I got good at that.

The large station doors opened. Cool, fresh air breezed inside, as did the roar of the city—car horns and the rumble of buses, people shouting, and gods knew what else. *Home sweet home…* I missed home already. I didn't particularly enjoy living in the city, but my degree was important, so I did what I had to.

I briefly glanced around for Diego, hoping the dickhead wasn't far, but I didn't spot him. Accepting this other person was more important, I headed for the curb to flag down a taxi.

"Astrid," Diego called out.

I ignored him and tried to get a taxi's attention. Unfortunately, it already had passengers, forcing me to wait for the next one.

"Astrid," Diego said again, this time closer.

I continued to ignore him and hailed another cab, but someone else caught the cabbie's attention. Ignoring him was childish, but I was angry and I was right to be. No one liked being turned invisible, least of all by your best friend.

I blew out a breath. That wasn't the proper way to handle this. I turned in Diego's direction. He was a few feet from me. The light confusion on his face twisted into deeper perplexion. No doubt, my frustration was written all over my face like a billboard in lower Manhattan.

"What's wrong?" he asked.

"I don't know, Diego, maybe being ditched in a train made me a little pissy." I'd meant to explain myself a little calmer, but apparently that was going to happen quite yet. It would be easy to blame my temper on my hair color, but I knew this stemmed from a deeper-seeded issue I struggled to fix.

He took a startled step back, his eyes widening. "I… amiga… *¡Mierda!*"

His words melted into Spanish as he muttered curses to himself while rubbing his face. "*Lo siento.* I am so sorry, Astrid, really. I was so excited for this surprise, I tunnel visioned. I should have said something."

I exhaled a calming breath. I wanted to stay mad, but I couldn't. The sincerity in his eyes was too much. And I knew better than anyone, Diego wasn't the type to ditch me, not intentionally.

"Man, you two are boring." A hand clamped down on Diego's shoulder. A guy our age with brown hair and was maybe an inch or two shorter than Diego's six-foot height appeared next to him.

His voice dipped deeper. "I'm sorry."

Then it jumped to a higher falsetto, as if he were mimicking me, even though I didn't have a high voice. "Me too."

He shot me a playful, exasperated look. "I was really hoping to see some drama."

I blinked. Blinked again. "Doomsday?"

He grinned. "Hey, Red."

The nickname he'd given me the day we'd met when we were teens punched through the shocked haze. "Zeke!"

The coolers in my hand clattered on the ground and I launched at him. Zeke took a startled step back. He wasn't fast enough to escape and I crashed into him, wrapping my arms around his waist for a strong hug.

He chuckled and hugged me back. "Damn, you're like a little bullet. It's good to see you, too."

I gave him another squeeze before letting go. "Have you lost weight?"

He blinked. "Uh, I don't know. Does it feel that way?"

I nodded as I tracked the way he hesitated on that answer, and took in his appearance. He'd been a lean kid when we'd first met around sixteen, but he'd gained a healthy amount of weight and muscle shortly after, turning him into a rugged hunk. Now, it seemed he'd lost a lot of that again with the way his leather jacket hung off him.

He looks a little disheveled, too. Not in the he'd-been-traveling-all-day way, but in the has-he-even-showered-in-the-last-five-days kind of worrying way.

Zeke preferred to be clean shaven, yet his facial hair was well past five o'clock shadow, though not quite beard territory. It also wasn't well kept and groomed, like Diego's stubble.

And his short hair was looking shaggy around his ears instead of cropped tighter against his head. I remembered when he'd cut his long hair. It was a big deal for him to have done that. I couldn't imagine why he'd be growing it out again.

Zeke shrugged. "Money has been a little tight, so maybe I'm not eating as much as I thought."

That made sense. We weren't strangers to tight budgets. But I still couldn't shake the feeling that something wasn't quite right.

Zeke bent down and picked up a cooler. "Should we get a taxi? I've been walking around for a few hours, and a cab ride in the city sounds like fun."

I smiled. This was Zeke's first time here. We were determined to make it an awesome trip for him. Dad even gave us some extra cash after we told him about the visit.

Diego flagged down a cab, far more successfully than me, and while explaining to Zeke how it worked. The yellow taxi pulled up to the curb and we all climbed in, making sure Zeke got a window. I gave the cabbie our destination and he pulled out into the busy traffic.

I nudged Zeke. "So, what's with your early arrival? We weren't expecting you until dinner."

He shrugged. "My ride got me here earlier than I anticipated."

I narrowed my eyes Diego's way. "And how long did you know?"

Diego gave me that award-winning smile of his when he wanted to placate my wrath. "Since I got that text you were nosey about."

I rolled my eyes. Of course, it all made sense. "And whose idea was it to keep this a secret from me?"

Zeke grinned. I shook my head. *These two.* I should smack them both.

"So, Doomsday, what do you think of the Big City so far?" I asked after letting him gaze out the window for a bit and take it all in.

He chuckled. Zeke always found my nickname for him amusing. Though, I noticed there wasn't as much energy in his reaction like he had in the past. "It's bigger than what I'm used to. Way bigger than Shamrock Lakes."

I nodded, understanding the feeling. Recently, he told us he'd found himself in a sleepy town in Indiana where he decided to stay. Why Indiana of all places, I wasn't sure, but I understood the small-town appeal.

"What have you been up to lately?" Diego asked.

He shrugged. "Stuff. Spending more time with my art."

"That's great to hear!" I said. And I meant it. For some reason, his mom, Lily, took issue with his creative outlets, so he had to hide that passion. The only reason he was open about it with Diego and me for so long, was due to a conversation we'd had about my carpentry hobby. That seemed to help him see us as a safe place to be himself. "Do you have anything on you?"

"In my bag. I'll show you later." He nudged the cooler by his feet. "Was the hunting good?"

Why was this conversation so stilted? Zeke had always been easy to converse with. But now, it felt as though he wasn't interested in talking. Or that he was avoiding something.

I nodded. "The four of us hit tag limit within the first two days."

His eyebrows rose high. "That's fast. Must be a good spring."

I shrugged. "It's always easier to get the horny birds."

Diego and he laughed. I wasn't wrong.

The taxi arrived at our destination and we paid the cabbie before climbing out. Zeke needed a minute to take in the towering building.

Diego nudged him. "It's even more amazing on the inside. C'mon."

It took Zeke a moment to speak after he followed us into the lobby. "Are you sure this is an apartment and not a hotel?"

I laughed. His reaction matched ours when we first started living here. To be fair, the upscale appearance, with its marble floor tiles, exquisite wall paintings, and beautiful potted plants, wasn't something you'd normally see in an apartment lobby. Hell, this place even had six elevators. "We'll show you around later. I want to get our stuff into the apartment."

"Yeah, sure, but how does security work here? I was expecting some sort of locked entrance. Is this normal?"

Diego and I passed an understanding look. This place wasn't your usual apartment.

"No, not normal," Diego said. "I'm pretty sure no other apartment is like this, unless it's owned by Nyx."

"Is that your landlord?" Zeke asked.

"Yeah, she's awesome," I said. "Friendly, and sometimes makes us food. But that's probably because she's a family friend. I don't think she does that for many other residents here."

The elevator arrived before Diego could press the call button, and a few people filed out. We greeted the ones we knew and then stepped into the car. I pulled my keycard out and tapped it on the bulky card reader next to the floor buttons. I then selected floor thirty. Diego pressed the recreation button. I shot him a quizzical look.

"Some of this turkey is for her, remember?" he said.

Oh, right. Plus, Xavier had just returned from Spain and brought back spices, and other cooking ingredients.

The door of the elevator car behind us slid open to a large furnished room. Diego exited and then the doors shut behind him.

Zeke was quiet the whole ride up. And even when we stepped out onto our floor, he quietly took things in.

I made a mental note and led us to a door with *699* hanging over the peep hole. I held my card to the reader on the door, and it blinked green before the door unlocked. "Welcome to your home away from home for the next few days."

The door opened to a short hallway with a laundry room on the right and then an open-concept kitchen with an island and dining room table tucked into a little nook.

The sizable living room was finished with a large couch, coffee table, and jumbo TV and entertainment stand. A sliding glass door led to a small balcony. A bedroom door was flush against a living room wall and another hallway led to my and Diego's separate bedrooms and a bathroom we shared.

Zeke took it all in with wide eyes. "Yeah, you can't convince me this isn't a hotel."

I laughed while I hung up my jacket, and then set my cooler on the island. "I assure you, there's no room service or continental breakfast."

I unpacked and stored anything perishable in the fridge or freezer. Zeke continued to take the place in without exploring. I kept an eye on him. He wasn't acting his usual self. Something was up, but I couldn't place what yet.

By the time I finished, he still hadn't said anything, and was acting as though he were still taking the place in. I leaned on the island and watched him. Like *really* watched him.

Zeke had been acting unusual these last few years, and we'd been worried about him. *Really* worried. That feeling had only intensified today.

"Hey, you okay?" I finally asked.

Zeke blinked and looked at me. "Yeah, why?"

I didn't respond, merely stared into his deep brown eyes. *There.* I saw it. A hollowness that had taken over the spark that used to be there. Well, there was still a spark, but it was like it had been turned down—or it had only recently been reignited.

He leaned back. "You know, you still freak me out when you stare like that."

It wasn't the first time someone had told me that. I'd been told on a number of occasions the way I looked at people sometimes, they felt as though I was looking into their soul. Or something like that.

I was just perceptive. I could watch people and get a feel for things about them. It was something that helped me with my choice to become a therapist. And the better I knew someone, the easier it was to tell when something was wrong. Like with Zeke.

"You know, if there's ever anything bothering you, you can talk to us. No matter how strange or stupid it might sound."

He hesitated. He wanted to deny something was wrong, but the lie wasn't easy for him to say. Not when I'd caught on. "You don't need to worry about me."

I walked around the island and grabbed his hand, giving a comfort squeeze. "You're our friend, Zeke, and that means you're family. We always look out for our family."

I then smirked. "And I promise we won't subject you to amateur therapizing hour or anything."

This got him to laugh, the tension in his shoulders easing. "I'll keep that in mind."

"I'll be right back. I'm just going to put my bag down. Make yourself at home."

"Hey, Astrid."

I paused in the hallway and looked back at him.

"I'm glad you're not hiding that scar anymore."

I smiled, despite it being difficult, and entered my room. I dropped my duffle on my bed and let out a quiet sigh. Despite choosing to no longer cover the hideous thing, I still struggled to look at myself in the mirror. Covering it wasn't helping me, but keeping it uncovered wasn't doing me any favors either.

My hand went to my neck, where I played with the wooden pendant with an intricate rune carved into the surface. It was a gift from Aya. She made it herself and said it had magical protection in it that would always keep me safe if I wore it. She was a practicing heathen—a Norse pagan—like my dad, so I understood and appreciated the sentiment behind it.

Dad always gave me the freedom to believe or not. He let me partake in rituals and even some of our holiday traditions fell more on the pagan side. But despite me dabbling since my childhood and liking much of it, I couldn't find myself embracing the practice fully.

Even still, regardless of me not being sure if I believed this amulet worked or if it was a trick of my mind, I always felt a little safer with it on when Aya wasn't around. It was really the only time I felt compelled to wear it.

I turned toward my window and paused when I spotted two large black birds hanging out on my windowsill. Not just any black birds, two ravens. *Strange.* While raven populations were increasing across the state, especially back home, it was rare to see one in any of the boroughs.

One of the ravens looked down at the street below, but the other stared right at me. My pulse slowed and a strange sense of familiarity washed over me. I smiled.

Some thought ravens to be bad omens, but Dad always taught me otherwise. This was a good omen. I knew it, deep down.

The raven not looking at me croaked and flew off. The other watched me a moment longer then cooed and took off after its friend. A prickle of disappointment pulsed in my chest.

Refocusing, I reminded myself Zeke would be waiting, and it might be a good idea to pull out some things for us to do.

Rummaging around in my closet, I found my storage container of magic cards. I also pulled out a few map tubes and a box of miniatures, dice, and map props. It'd been a while since we played D&D. It'd be fun, even if it was only the three of us.

"Hey, Astrid?"

I gasped and whirled around. Diego took a startled step back. I pressed my hand on my chest and panted on air. "Don't do that!"

He grimaced. "Sorry. I didn't think I was being quiet."

"You probably weren't," I admitted. "I was just lost in my searching. What's up?"

He rubbed the back of his neck. "I just wanted to apologize again, for earlier."

I shrugged. "I'm over it, it's fine."

"Yeah, but—"

"Diego, really, it's fine. It's not like this is some recurring toxic behavior. You were excited and took *surprise* to an extra level you didn't plan to. It happens."

His frown wouldn't go away. He really didn't need to beat himself up about this. I flippantly waved my hand. "Besides, it's not the first time I turned invisible because of Zeke being around. I expected it this week."

Diego's brow twisted. "What's that supposed to mean?"

I made a non-committal sound. "I know better than to get in the way of you and your boyfriend."

Diego rolled his eyes and Zeke laughed from in the living room.

"Stop eavesdropping, Doomsday."

"Stop flirting with your secret boy-toy, Red, and making me think I'm going to have to leave when you two can't help but jump each other's bones."

"Fuck you."

"Bro code."

There was a beat of silence and then the three of us were laughing. This was the Zeke I remembered and loved.

When Diego calmed himself, he opened his arms. "Hug?"

I smiled and set my things on the ground, then turned into him. I squeaked when he grabbed me and wrapped me into his hard body, smooshing my face into his chest. I inhaled his strong scent and melted into his embrace. A blanket of Diego-sized comfort wrapped around me.

I loved our hugs. They were the best.

"I don't ever want you to feel as though you're invisible and unimportant," Diego mumbled. "You are the most important person to me."

For now. There would eventually be someone more important, because we were only friends. And that wasn't me being stubborn or not being willing to acknowledge anything. Any time someone thought we were together, he, too, would quickly correct them. We were *just* friends.

He was my best friend whom I totally didn't ogle when he walked around shirtless and definitely, totally, absolutely didn't fantasize about pushing me down on a bed and ravaging me while making sweet promises with—*Stop!*

"You're the most important person to me, too." I pulled away and looked up at him. "That's why it hurts. But I know you wouldn't intentionally hurt me. It's why I can forgive you. Best friends forever, remember?"

He chuckled. "Yeah, I remember."

"Are you two done with the verbal foreplay, or what?" Zeke called out.

I rolled my eyes and then picked up the gaming equipment. Diego helped. We rejoined Zeke, who'd hung up his jacket finally and sat down on the couch to relax. There were several Tupperware containers on the island.

"What's with the food?" I asked.

"Nyx," Diego said simply. "She said she'll have dinner for us later. She was *very* thankful for everything we brought her."

I shook my head. She was such a nice person. I'd have to do something for her. Then again, this would become an infinite circle of us trying to do something nice to pay back the other for being nice. Our longest record was fifty-nine days straight. "Well, Zeke, you're in for a major treat. Nyx is an amazing cook, and if you've never had the pleasure of authentic Greek, now you will."

"Sounds great." Zeke smiled. It was more genuine than earlier today. "It's also great you two could do me the favor of not attempting to get a quickie in while I'm here twiddling my thumbs."

I scoffed and smacked him in the shoulder.

He smirked and looked at the fun I brought out. "Are you inviting me into your dungeon? I told you, bro code."

Diego laughed and I rolled my eyes. Yup. Zeke was definitely returning to us. "I thought we could stay in today, since we've all been traveling a lot. We've got D&D, where I could DM something for you both. We could play Magic, like old times. Or we can play console games. If none of that appeals to you, we can do some brainstorming."

Zeke looked over the stuff I'd dumped on the coffee table, then opened the box with the Magic cards. He pulled out a few loose cards to look at them, and then picked out my mono-white angel deck.

There was something about the way he looked at the cards that set off the alarm bells in my brain. I slid onto the couch next to him, and he hardly noticed me. Diego took up the couch on his other side.

"She hated this game," Zeke mumbled. Something in his voice, the hollowness that matched his eyes, twisted my stomach. "No devil games, she'd always say. Yet, you came in with this deck and managed to convince her you were fighting the devils with angels and that was the purpose of the game. Someone had to pretend to be the evil force so you could practice being the holy savior."

His finger slid over the face of a card. "She bought it. It was the first time I'd ever been allowed to have fun with a game like this."

I watched the way his shoulders hunched, and his body began to quiver. I pressed my hand gently against his shoulder. "Zeke?"

His grip on the cards tightened until his knuckles turned white. His head dropped and he hid his face with his other hand. The sharp, shaky intake of air had the floor dropping out from under me before any words left his lips. "She's gone…"

I was already reaching for him. My arms wrapped around his shoulders and head, and I pulled him into me. Zeke didn't fight. He accepted the comfort he'd needed but hadn't allowed from us. His arms slid around me and he buried his face into my chest. His body shook as he couldn't contain the sobs.

Diego pressed his hands against Zeke's back while I murmured gentle reassurances and encouraged him to let out all the pain. The lessened communication… the behavior change… the weight loss… it all made sense now.

Years ago, we found out about Lily's tragic and violent death. We'd tried to be there for Zeke the best we could, reaching out and we even attempted to make a trip out to see him, but he insisted he was okay and we didn't need to. *He was always insisting he was fine. Maybe insisting too much.*

I couldn't blame myself or Diego for not realizing. How could we have known he hid how bad it was? You couldn't help someone who didn't want it.

And knowing Zeke, he didn't want to trouble us when he knew how much Diego and I were going through for school.

It took Zeke a while to calm down, but eventually, he pulled away and tried to rub away the evidence of his emotions. "I'm sorry for losing it like that. I told myself I would hold it together when I saw you both."

Diego gripped his shoulder. "Don't apologize for being human. That's nothing to be ashamed of. You've gone through something difficult, amigo, and you've done it by yourself."

"I didn't know what to do…" Zeke admitted quietly. "It was always just the two of us against the world. Then… she was gone and…"

He slowly shook his head. "I know you two have been there with an offered hand, despite how often I pushed back… but I haven't been able to talk about it. I wasn't ready, and I let it eat at me for so long…"

I nudged his shoulder with mine. "We understand. And we're here for you. Always have, always will."

A small smile pulled at his lips. "Thanks. And thanks for the boob therapy."

I raucously laughed and gestured to my large chest. "Best therapy around."

He and Diego laughed. Zeke then took some time calming down and I went to the kitchen. Diego leaned in closer, placing a hand over Zeke's shoulders, and spoke quietly with him, trying to offer his help and comfort.

The two of us could sympathize hardcore with what Zeke was going through, but Diego more so. He knew that pain, even if he'd experienced it much earlier than Zeke had. I understood, but my mom… she…

I shook the thoughts of that evil woman from my head. I wouldn't think about her. I wouldn't let that get to me. No matter the permanent scars she left behind.

I rummaged through the fridge for something to drink. I used the noise to push beer bottles into the back where Zeke would be less likely to see them. He didn't have to say how bad things got for him. Depression and despair were a bitch. I could guess all the common destructive possibilities.

Selecting a pitcher of yellow liquid, I retrieved glasses from the cupboard. "How about some fresh squeezed lemonade?"

"Is that what that racket was?" Zeke said. "I was convinced you were making a mess in there."

I rolled my eyes. "I had to dig it out from the back. I'm pretty sure Aya was trying to hide it so we didn't drink it all on her."

Not my best lie, but Zeke wouldn't know. And Aya would do something like that.

"That's your roommate, right? Will I meet her?"

I sat down next to him again. "Depending on when you decide you want to leave, you might. She's supposed to be back Sunday, but she did warn me, she might stay with her family a little longer.

"She sounds cool from what you've both told me."

Aya hit it off with just about anyone I did, so I didn't doubt the two would get along fine.

Zeke tapped the box of Magic cards. "Can we play a game?"

I grinned. "Duh. And while we do, you can tell me about this renewed artistic passion of yours."

I wanted Zeke to enjoy his time here. I wanted to remind him of the friendship all three of us shared and that he wasn't alone. I meant it when I told him we were there for him whenever he needed us. No matter how crazy it might sound.

"And if you're interested, I can tell you about some of the new blacksmithing techniques I've picked up."

"Absolutely spill about that." That skill of his fascinated me to no end.

Zeke held up my white deck. "But only if I get to use your cheating deck."

My head flew back in my laughter. Diego had started it with that name, and after I creamed Zeke with it one too many times, he joined in. "Fine, but I'm going to prove just how wrong you are about that."

He smirked. "Bring it on, Red."

About the Author

Shannon Pemrick is a full-time USA Today bestselling author of slow-burn romantic fantasy, fuller-time geek, and dragon obsessed. She also has too many novelty mugs, not enough chocolate, and a forbidden love-affair with all things shiny. When she's not burning her fingers across a keyboard handing out adventures and HEAs, she's rolling dice and getting lost in RPGs or searching for brides for her dragon overlords.

You can learn more about Shannon by visiting her website at:

shannonpemrick.com